PRAISE FOR THE RISEN SUN TRILOGY

The Shadow's Heir

"[*The Shadow's Heir*] showcases the author's impressive ability to create a nicely developed world populated by complex characters . . . I look forward to seeing what new developments are birthed from this author's labyrinthine imagination!"
—*Night Owl Reviews*

"A compelling and exciting story . . . K. J. Taylor has the rare gift for a fantasy writer of knowing how to keep the story moving . . . I am eagerly looking forward to book two in the series."
—*SFFANZ*

"*The Shadow's Heir* forms a great basis for an epic new story, one that I am looking forward to following. I've said it once, but I'll say it again: K. J. Taylor is a talented author who continues to bring us spellbinding stories, and if you aren't already reading her books, then you should remedy that!"
—*Speculating on SpecFic*

PRAISE FOR THE FALLEN MOON TRILOGY

The Griffin's War

"Taylor brings the Fallen Moon trilogy to a satisfying conclusion with a chronicle of pitched battles and political intrigue . . . Strong, realistic characterizations and an intricately conceived milieu make it clear that Australian Taylor is a talent to watch."
Publishers Weekly

"A strong climax to a fabulous trilogy." —*Alternative Worlds*

Ace Books by K. J. Taylor

The Fallen Moon

THE DARK GRIFFIN
THE GRIFFIN'S FLIGHT
THE GRIFFIN'S WAR

The Risen Sun

THE SHADOW'S HEIR
THE SHADOWED THRONE
THE SHADOW'S HEART

The
Shadow's
Heart

THE RISEN SUN
BOOK THREE

K. J. TAYLOR

ACE BOOKS, NEW YORK

THE BERKLEY PUBLISHING GROUP
Published by the Penguin Group
Penguin Group (USA) LLC
375 Hudson Street, New York, New York 10014

USA • Canada • UK • Ireland • Australia • New Zealand • India • South Africa • China

penguin.com

A Penguin Random House Company

THE SHADOW'S HEART

An Ace Book / published by arrangement with the author

Ace Books are published by The Berkley Publishing Group.
ACE and the "A" design are trademarks of Penguin Group (USA) LLC.

For information, address: The Berkley Publishing Group,
a division of Penguin Group (USA) LLC,
375 Hudson Street, New York, New York 10014.

ISBN: 978-0-425-25825-5

PUBLISHING HISTORY
Ace mass-market edition / January 2015

PRINTED IN THE UNITED STATES OF AMERICA

10 9 8 7 6 5 4 3 2 1

Cover illustration by Steve Stone; sword © Vertyr/Shutterstock.
Cover design by Judith Lagerman.
Map by Allison Jones.

Dedicated to my mother and sister—
two women with steel in their bones

Author's Note

So this is it. The end.

Every time I finish a trilogy, I do it with some degree of fatalism, knowing that each trilogy could be the last one I'm able to publish. But if this book must be the last one in the series, then I wouldn't be too unhappy about it. I think *The Shadow's Heart* is one of the best books I've written, and as endings go, it has one of the very best. But, I must warn you, it also has one of the most tragic. As Arenadd might say, all's unfair in love and war.

I hope you've enjoyed this journey I've taken you on, and that the ending I've made will be one that gives you some kind of closure. Six books, and it's been a long road to get there. Thank you for staying with me—I hope you still want to stay when it's over.

Finally, the usual notes on pronunciation: The Northerners speak Welsh, and in that language "dd" is pronounced "th." Some of the odder-looking names are pronounced this way:

Arenadd: "Arren-ath"
Saeddryn: "Say-thrin"
Arddryn: "Arth-rin"
Taranisäii: "TAH-rah-nis-eye"
Laela: "Lay-la" (I include this one because I've heard some people say it "Leela.")
Akhane: "Ah-kah-nay" (This name is actually one I made up, and is meant to sound a bit like the word "arcane," which fits his interests very well.)

And finally, as always, griffish is pronounced phonetically. Griffins can't read or learn how to read, and don't want anything to do with anything that could be called grammar or linguistics. Leave the pointless analysis to the humans, thank you.

1

Scrawlings

In her personal chambers high in the towers that made up Malvern's Eyrie, Queen Laela Taranisäii was alone.

Her brother, Kullervo, was gone, and so was her advisor, Inva. Her friend and former tutor, Yorath, was gone, too, and Lord Iorwerth, the man who commanded Malvern's armies while his partner, Kaanee, led the humanless griffins called the Unpartnered, hadn't yet returned from his conquest of Warwick. And her father, Arenadd, the only friend she had had in the world once upon a time . . . Arenadd was gone, too.

Once she might have turned to her own griffin partner, Oeka, but Oeka was not there. Or not all there, anyway. Her body was locked away somewhere underneath the Eyric, mouldering in silence while her mind wandered who knew where.

Her only company now was a book: her father's diary. Oeka had embedded some of her power in its pages so that Laela could open them and hear her father's voice read the words, but by now the effect had worn off, and Laela couldn't read well enough to understand most of it. Nor did she trust anyone enough to have them read it to her. Not with Yorath's having vanished.

And so, with nothing else to do for the moment while she waited for Iorwerth and Kaanee to return, she sat down and opened a book of her own. The pages were blank, but she had a pot of ink and a reed-pen ready to change that.

Tongue sticking out with the effort, she started to write, forming each rune slowly and carefully:

This is the diry of Quen Laela Taranisäii, who is the
dorter of King Arenath Taranis-eye. I dont no how tu
rite meny words, but thort I should rite down wat I no so
one day peeple can reed it an no wat I did and thort also
I thort it would be use-ful for future ~~sk skol book people~~
historeens to reed wat I wrote, so hear gos.

She stopped to wipe the sweat off her forehead and took a
deep breath before continuing.

My muthers name was Flell she was a Suthern girl whom
my dad might of raped but he says not an I never met her
so I dunno wat happned. I ~~was rai grew u~~ *come from a*
place in South called Stirick, not sure how to rite it never
saw it rit down. My dad wat raised me was Bran, but he
wast my reel dad that was Arenath. I never noo who my
real dad was an Bran didnt rite so he never showd me
how so I had too lern wen I was a woman. When Bran
dyed I left an went North.
   Arenath found me but didnt no he wus my dad. He
looked after me an I lived with him an helped him an
he made me griffiner after I puled him out of the water.
He said your my advi advu helper an we went to Amoran
together with Skander who was his partner. I got mar-
ried too a princ called Akhane an brought slaves back
home to be free. Arenath died the Nite God killed him an
then I got made Queen, but Arenath's cusin Saythrin
said no I should be Queen, yu are a half-breed an not his
real dorter anyway. I burned her temple to teech her a
lessen but she ran off with her son an dorter. I killed her
husband, Torc when she wouldn come back.
   Then my brother comes, he is called Kullervo an he
found Sennek who was my uncle Erian's partner before
my dad killed him. They went to Warwick where Saeth-
ryn was an Kullervo got cort but I sent Iorwerth an Kaa-
nee with the Unpartnered an they smashed up the place.
Senneck killed Saethryn's dorter an her partner Aenae
who wus Skandar's son. She killed Saethryn, too, but the
Nite God has sent her back to kill us all espeshuli me cus
the Nite God hates half breds like wut I am. I have sent

Kullervo an Senneck to Amoran to get my husband to help us an when Iorwerth gets back I will send him to Skenfrith where Caedmon is, he is Saethryns son an leeds the enemys now. Saethryn came to get me yesterday, but Oeka drove her mad an got rid of her. Oeka is my partner an she is madder than a cut snake which is wat Bran used too say.

Laela sat back to look at her handiwork. Her writing had crowded together in some places, and she had kept running out of room at the edge of the page, but she reckoned it was the best writing she'd ever done.

That was enough for one day. She blew on the ink to make it dry faster, closed the book, and put it aside. Then she got up and walked out of the room to go and see if Iorwerth was back yet. He and Kaanee had been away far too long, and she was starting to get worried.

The other thing she had to worry about was Saeddryn. Once Saeddryn had been an ordinary woman—and not a young one, either. She was Arenadd's cousin, and she had been his second-in-command back in the days when he seized power in the North. By the time Laela had come along, Saeddryn had become Malvern's high priestess, and she and Arenadd weren't on the best of terms any more. Arenadd had disowned Saeddryn's son Caedmon, who had been Arenadd's apprentice and heir apparent—until Caedmon turned on Arenadd. By the time Laela arrived at Malvern, there was no officially chosen heir to the throne, and Caedmon had fled.

But his mother was the far worse danger. When Senneck killed her, the war should have been all but won, but Laela had not reckoned with the Night God. The Night God had been Arenadd's master, and she had given him the dark powers he used to conquer the North.

Now those powers belonged to Saeddryn, and if Laela couldn't find some way to do away with her, then Laela would die for her throne. And Kullervo, Arenadd's only other offspring, would have to die, too.

Saeddryn's attempt to kill Laela might have failed when Oeka drove her mad, but after she threw herself out the window, her body had not been found, and Laela knew she was still out there. The fact that she was now insane did not make Laela feel any safer. Frankly, it made her feel worse.

The guards were scouring the city right now, but so far they hadn't found anything, and Laela didn't believe for one moment they ever would.

She paused by a window to look out over the city and sighed a long, weary sigh. Ruling the North was far harder than she had ever thought it would be, and in ways she hadn't expected. She spent so much time worrying about other people and what they were doing, and without a griffin to protect her, she couldn't leave the city. She had been stuck in Malvern for nearly a year— ever since her father's death, in fact.

Laela rubbed her eyes and turned away miserably from the window in time to see a servant come hurrying toward her.

She straightened up instantly. "What's goin' on?"

The servant stopped and bowed. "My Lady, Lord Iorwerth is here. He's waiting for ye in the audience chamber."

"Huh. Nice timin'," Laela muttered, and walked back the way she had come.

Sure enough, when she entered the white-marble audience chamber where the platform for the ruler and her partner to sit on stood empty, she found Lord Iorwerth and Kaanee ready to receive her. When they saw her, Kaanee glanced at his human. Briefly, but Laela saw it.

"There yeh are," she said unceremoniously. Not bothering to sit down or ask them to do the same, she folded her arms. "All right, explain yerselves. Where've yeh been an' why?"

Iorwerth, a middle-aged, strong-looking man, clasped his hands together. "I'm sorry, my Lady, but—"

"Where is your partner?" Kaanee interrupted. He pushed forward, tawny brown wings slightly raised. "Where is Oeka?"

"She ain't here," said Laela, not bothering to use griffish.

Kaanee's eyes narrowed. "Where is she? Is she dead?"

May as well be, Laela nearly said, but stopped herself. "No, she's just not here. She's busy."

"Busy with what?" said Kaanee. "She has not been beside you in a long time. Is she not interested in ruling her territory?"

Laela shifted uncomfortably. "Yeh'd have to ask her about that. It ain't my place to say. Now tell me what's goin' on."

Iorwerth opened his mouth to reply, but once again Kaanee obliged.

"We have been in Warwick, as you commanded, and after that we went to Fruitsheart. We found no enemies there, and now we have come back."

"Good," said Laela. "Because now I want yeh to go to Skenfrith. *That's* where they are now, that's where Caedmon is. Go there. Take the Unpartnered. Kill them all. Now."

"We cannot do that," said Kaanee.

Laela growled. "You'll do it because I'm tellin' yeh. We killed Caedmon's mother an' his sister. There ain't no way he's ever gonna give up with that on his mind. If we're gonna keep the North together, then he's gotta die, an' that's all there is to it."

"We cannot," Kaanee repeated. "I would do as you say, and so would Iorwerth, but the Unpartnered will not."

"What?" said Laela, blankly.

"The Unpartnered are not with us," said Kaanee. "We are late because we have spent our time trying to make them come back to Malvern with us, but they refused. They will not obey me any more."

"What?" Laela said again, much louder. "Why not?"

"They see no benefit in it for themselves. And there is no griffin at Malvern powerful enough to dominate them and force them to fight. Your partner is not doing her duty."

"Oh no." Laela put a hand over her face. She looked up at Iorwerth. "What are we gonna do?"

"There's only one thing you can do," he said unhappily. "If we're going to get control back, then you and Oeka have to go to them, and Oeka will have to impress them." When Laela didn't reply and instead pulled a grim face, he tried to reassure her with a smile. "Don't worry, my Lady. I'm sure she can do it. We all know how powerful she is, and it's not just about size. They'll bow to strong magic as well."

Laela opened her mouth, then shut it again. She coughed. "Yeah . . . I'll go see her, then."

She trudged out of the room, mentally listing all the swearwords she knew.

Oeka was not going to come, and she was not going to bring the Unpartnered into line. Laela wasn't even going to waste time hoping for that. Unpartnered griffins would never normally fight as a group to begin with—they'd only done it in the first place because the Mighty Skandar, as they called him, had had the sheer power to dominate more than a hundred griffins at once. And there was no other griffin in the world who was like him. What was that word her father had used? "Unprecedented." Without the Unpartnered, it would come down to whatever the *humans* in this situation thought. And Laela knew exactly who had the popular support right now, and it wasn't her.

A word that her *other* father, Bran, had used now sprang to mind.

"Shit."

M eanwhile, down in the city, someone else was on the hunt. Heath, of no fixed name and no fixed abode, also wanted to find Saeddryn. He had been at it for several days. He knew perfectly well that the entire city guard was trying as well, but they didn't bother him—even if he knew they would hang him if they caught him. Possibly it would be hanging *and* dismembering, depending on whether the Eyrie decided to class him as a traitor or just as a spy.

That was an unpleasant thought, but Heath figured the guard were too busy just now. They were looking for Saeddryn, not him, and he'd given them no reason to be looking for him anyway. Or, at least, not just now. Finding the country's most wanted woman was probably more important than tracking down a fraudster who hadn't been seen in Malvern for years.

That aside, Heath had already been arrested once, and that hadn't turned out to be half as bad as he'd thought. It had been touch and go for a little while, but thankfully he'd been caught in Skenfrith, just after Lord Caedmon took control of the city. Caedmon had talked to him and decided to recruit the wily thief as a spy rather than kill him.

As far as Heath was concerned, things were looking up. Besides, this was *fun*.

He strolled briskly along the main street leading through the lower end of the city, where some of the better-off commoners lived. Nobody paid him any attention. Today, he was in

a particularly good mood. It had taken him longer than he'd
expected, but if he, Heath, was any judge, then today would be
the day that he would finally do what everyone else had failed
to do: find Saeddryn. The guards were numerous, and he was
on his own, but he had contacts they didn't. Nobody, he had
pointed out to Caedmon before he left, lived the life of a scumbag like him without meeting useful people. A friendly visit
here, a bit of social drinking there, a little eavesdropping and a
coin in the right pocket bought him all the information he
needed. And after a couple of false leads and a near miss or two,
he had finally found the people and the place that he was after.

Spotting the alley he had been told to look for, he sauntered
over to it without a glance in any direction. Sneaking and hiding were all very well, he knew, but in his experience nothing
was easier to overlook than someone just walking along as if he
knew exactly where he were going and had no reason to be fur-
tive about it.

In the alley, he found a trapdoor not very well hidden under
a stack of boxes. Checking to make sure nobody was watching,
he shifted them aside and tugged on the trapdoor's ring. It
lifted, and after another quick check and a shrug, Heath opened
the door and jumped down to the bottom of the ladder inside.
The trapdoor fell shut behind him, and he found himself in the
dark.

Almost. He waited sensibly until his eyes adjusted, and
when they did, he spotted a faint light up ahead.

Heath took a deep breath. *This* was something he hadn't
done before. His world was lying and manipulating and getting
everything he wanted out of life. Fighting and infiltrating and
creeping into places owned by people who might well slit his
throat on sight hadn't been much a part of it. Still, it was always
a good time to learn.

He checked that his dagger was in his belt. It was, but he left
it there and moved cautiously toward the light, where he saw
something that made him start in fright. Saeddryn Taranisäii
herself, crouching on the floor in a little dirt-lined cellar. A lantern hanging from the roof cast dim light on her face, filling the
ugly crevasse of her missing eye with shadow. Her long, grey-
ing black hair was tangled around her face. She didn't look up

when Heath came in but sat staring vacantly at the floor, mumbling to herself.

Forgetting himself for a moment, Heath took a step toward her. "My Lady—"

"Stop right there!"

Two people appeared from the shadows, putting themselves between Heath and Saeddryn. He stopped, quickly holding up his hands in surrender, but after his initial surprise, he soon relaxed. The two people—a man and a woman—had knives in their hands, but they held them uncertainly and kept their distance.

Heath offered up his brightest, friendliest, most reassuring smile. "Hello. Sorry if I startled you, but there's no need to worry. I'm a friend."

"So ye say!" the man said at once.

"I do," said Heath. He became stern. "But who are you, may I ask? Are you a friend to this poor woman, or are you holding her prisoner?"

"We're her followers, not her friends!" the woman snapped. "This is the rightful Queen of Tara!"

Very amateur, then, Heath decided. "Good," he said. "Then I've come to the right place. One of you should probably guard the entrance before I say anything else."

"Nice try, but we ain't fooled," said the man. "Get outta here!"

"What, so I can run off and tell the guard exactly where Lady Saeddryn is?" said Heath. "No, I think it would be better if you kept me here."

They glanced at each other.

"Who are ye?" the man finally said. "How did ye find us?"

"My name's Heath," said Heath. "And I found you by talking to some of your friends. They were looking for new people to join the resistance here in Malvern. I'm not against a little treason, so I decided to join. And here I am."

"Prove it," said the woman.

"I found you, didn't I?" said Heath. "I didn't bring the guard. I'm not *one* of the guard. I'm just one man. I know things only your people know. I know that one of you found Lady Saeddryn after she fell out of that window and that you smuggled her into the city. I know you've been keeping her here while she recovers. How else could I know all that? Oh, and I also know that when she first came here, she went around the city talking to people and formed the resistance in the first place. That's how you knew where she was going to be, so you could rescue her."

They glanced at each other again.

"Fine," the man said at last. "If ye know all that, then I believe ye."

"Excellent," said Heath. "Now, may I see Lady Saeddryn? I should ask how she is."

The woman stood aside. "Ye can, but she won't answer. She won't talk t'nobody."

"Feeling shy, is she?" said Heath, feeling he could afford a little flippancy.

Neither of them smiled.

"She's . . . not well," said the man, choosing his words with care.

"Is that so?" Heath approached Saeddryn. "Excuse me?" he said cautiously. "Lady Saeddryn? Hello?"

Once again, Saeddryn did not react to his presence in any way. She hadn't moved since he had come in but stayed exactly where she was, staring blankly at the floor.

Heath shivered, and reached out for her shoulder. "Hello? Saeddryn? Can you hear me?"

The instant he touched her, Saeddryn came to life. She jerked upright and backed away, waving a hand wildly. "Not now!" she snapped, in a perfectly normal, irritated voice. "What are ye doin' here, anyway? Get back to yer post!"

Heath managed to stop his heart from thumping, and took a step toward her. "Saeddryn," he said. "Saeddryn! Can you hear me?"

"I said, get back to yer post!" Saeddryn rapped out. "Are ye daft? The Southerners could be here any moment. Do ye want me to tell Arenadd yer slackin' off? Is that it?"

Heath glanced at the two rebels. The woman looked sadly at Saeddryn.

"See what I mean?" said the man. "She can't see ye or hear ye. She just babbles like that."

Saeddryn had stopped talking again. She shook her head slowly, dazedly. "Mother, I can't do this," she said, in a much softer voice than before. She took a step toward Heath, reaching out beseechingly. "Please, don't make me do this. Yer the only family I got left."

Heath took her hand in his and held it to try and comfort her. "Saeddryn . . ."

She wrenched her hand away. "What if I don't want to?" she yelled. "I ain't ye! I'm me. I don't wanna just do whatever ye did; I want my own life, don't ye understand? I don't care about the stupid griffiners. They ain't botherin' us up here; can't we just live in peace? I want a life, Mother. I wanna marry Rhodri, an' I want a family. A *real* family. I ain't a child no more! Let me *go*. Please, if ye love me, Mother . . ."

"It's like she doesn't know where she is any more," said Heath, watching her with morbid fascination. "Like she's forgotten where she is in her life."

"Yer right," said the woman. "She's been doin' that for days; talkin' to people who died years ago, fightin' enemies she must've killed when she was young. Even . . ."

"Yes?" Heath cocked his head.

The woman smiled sadly. "Yesterday she told someone she loved him, an' then cried for an age afterward."

"He must have said no," Heath murmured.

The man looked at him. "What are we going to do? She's been like this ever since we found her an', she ain't getting better. If we can't fix her, she might be like this forever!"

Heath rubbed his face. "Ugh . . . I don't know. Listen, do you have any food down here? I think better on a full stomach."

"'Course," said the woman, and hurried off. Her partner sat down on a handy chair and offered another one to Heath.

Heath sat and gratefully accepted some food when the woman returned. Apparently, he was one of the gang now.

While he ate, he watched Saeddryn as she continued to wander about the room, reliving some girlhood argument with her long-dead mother. She showed no sign of seeing anything else, or even noticing when she walked into a crate, and as Heath watched her, he grew steadily gloomier. He prided himself on being a jack of all trades, but he wasn't a healer and knew nothing about how to cure madness, which was what he was more than ready to call this. What was he going to do? He'd found Saeddryn, but how was he going to get her back to Skenfrith when she was like this? He could get out of Malvern easily enough on his own, but doing it with a raving, instantly recognisable woman was another matter altogether.

"It's no good," said the woman, interrupting his thoughts. "Only the Night God can help her now."

Heath raised his eyebrows. "The Night God . . . ?" he repeated slowly. "Hmm."

The man was watching Saeddryn and looking almost tearful. "What did they do to her? My gods, what did they do?"

"I don't think I want to know," said Heath, not really listening. He kept his eyes on Saeddryn and let his new thought grow without prodding it too much in case it disappeared. Saeddryn had lost her mind, and with any other person that would be more or less the end of it. She'd be locked up somewhere and forgotten about, or left to wander at random until she died.

But, he reminded himself, Saeddryn wasn't an ordinary person, or even completely human any more. She was the Shadow That Walked now, and the Night God had chosen and blessed her. Everyone knew the Night God's chosen one was sent with a particular purpose to carry out, and Saeddryn couldn't very well do that if she was mad.

Therefore, it wasn't unreasonable to assume that the Night God would want to help her get better. Heath wasn't even going to question whether she had the power to do that; you just didn't spend time speculating about whether a god who could bring people back from the dead could deal with a little dose of insanity. Anyone with the power to cure *death* could probably cure just about anything.

The only question now was how to get the Night God to do it.

Well, Heath thought, how does one usually get a god's attention?

"We should pray," he said, without quite meaning to say it aloud.

"Eh?" said the man.

"I said we should pray," Heath said more loudly. He stood up. "You're right. Only the Night God can help her now. We just have to ask her."

"We have," said the woman. "We've prayed for her every night since she came here."

"Then we'll just have to make a proper show of it," said Heath, after a moment's consideration. "You there . . . er . . . can you get some rocks?"

The man looked blank. "What for?"

Heath shook his head. "Actually, never mind. I reckon we could use anything we can get our hands on. It's the shape that really matters."

"What shape?" said the woman.

"We have to make a circle," said Heath. "A stone circle. Or . . . I don't know, a circle of bricks or chairs or bits of wood."

"I know where there are some bricks," said the man, instantly latching onto the idea. "I can go and get them, if ye like."

Heath nodded. "Do it. We should have it built by moonrise."

"How many should I get?"

"Er . . . thirteen, I think."

"I think we have that many." The man darted off to climb a staircase into the house above.

While he was gone, Heath went to the trapdoor and poked his head out. He could see the sky, and he looked at it thoughtfully for a few moments before reaching into his tunic and bringing out a small mirror. It was made from a polished silver plate and was just about the only possession he'd managed to hang on to all this time. When he angled it correctly, it reflected the fading sunlight down into the cellar.

Heath spent some time experimenting with this and eventually retreated to check on Saeddryn. She had settled down again in the corner and was mumbling to herself. Heath thought he had never seen anything so utterly sad.

"Now then," he told the woman, whose name he wasn't planning to ask, "here's the plan. We build our circle right about . . . here." He scuffed a mark on the floor with his boot. "Once the moon comes up, we make Her Ladyship stand in the middle of it, and I'll direct some moonlight onto her. That should put the Night God's eye right on her."

The woman nodded. "What should we do while ye're doin' that?"

"Pray," said Heath. "I don't think the words would matter that much."

"I will, then," said the woman. "Yer plan sounds good."

"My plans always do," Heath said gravely.

The man returned shortly after this, carrying an armload of bricks. He dumped them on the floor and went back upstairs to get the rest of them, and while he was gone, Heath and the woman set about building the circle. They did their best to make it as round as possible, standing the bricks on their ends and spacing them out as evenly as they could.

Once the bricks were in place, Heath, still unsatisfied, took out his knife and scratched some symbols into the ground—circles to represent full moons in front of each stone, and some stars and different phases placed in a pattern around the rest of the inside. The pattern didn't mean anything as far as Heath knew; since he had to improvise, he picked one that looked nice. The Night God was a woman, he reasoned, so she probably liked things to look pretty. His two helpers were impressed, at least.

"Did ye learn that in the Temple?" the woman asked.

"I did," Heath said immediately. "It will sanctify the circle."

The man smiled hopefully; the woman looked positively awestruck.

"Now then, let's see if the Night God is awake yet." Heath went to the trapdoor to check. Night had indeed come, but he couldn't see the moon yet. Better wait a while, then.

He hung around in the cellar and enjoyed another meal courtesy of his two hosts, who took it in turns to check the sky every so often. The moon, however, seemed reluctant.

"Don't worry," Heath advised. "It'll come when it's ready."

He had noticed a blanket and a pillow on the floor, and happily claimed them both without asking permission. Before long, the tiring and troublesome day he had had made itself felt, and he fell asleep with one leg resting on another, as if he didn't have a care in the world. And because he was Heath, he didn't.

2

Yet Another Role to Play

A hand shook Heath awake.

He opened one eye. "Hm?"

"Sir? Er . . . Heath? The moon . . ."

Heath sat up and rubbed his eyes. "Shown itself, has it?"

"Yes, sir." The man helped him up.

Heath looked over at Saeddryn—she hadn't moved. "Then let's get to work! Move her into the circle, and I'll get into position."

Together, the man and the woman coaxed Saeddryn into getting up. She did it without too much effort and walked blindly between them toward the circle, like someone with no mind of her own. She kicked over several of the bricks when she entered the circle, but once her helpers let go of her, she stood in the centre among Heath's symbols and didn't seem inclined to move again.

While the man and woman put the bricks back in place, Heath went to the trapdoor and peeked out. Sure enough, there was a pale sliver of moon visible in the sky above the alley. He reached for his mirror, but the first thing his fingers touched was his knife.

He stopped, frowning to himself, then nodded. "Of course. Nearly forgot there . . ."

Saeddryn looked through him as he approached the circle. Beside her, standing outside the circle, the man said, "What are ye doin'?"

"I forgot that we have to make an offering," said Heath. "Just wait a moment . . ."

He brought his knife out and pressed the blade against the palm of his hand. "Well, Saeddryn," he murmured. "I promised Caedmon my hand would be useful to him if he didn't have it cut off. Let's hope it is."

He sliced the blade across his hand and grimaced as blood dripped onto the circle. "May this offering of true Northern blood summon you!" he said quickly, hoping it sounded suitably ritualistic.

He hastily wrapped up his hand before it could bleed on his clothes and went to the trapdoor. "Now, pray!" he said, and thrust the mirror out into the open air.

The effect was much less noticeable than it had been during the day, but when Heath looked back, he saw faint, silvery light shining into the cellar. He moved the mirror around, angling and reangling it until the light touched Saeddryn's face. On either side of the circle, the others prayed in low, murmuring voices.

Heath, holding the mirror as still as he could, looked up at the moon. In all his adult life, he had never prayed. It was too . . . unconfident. Too uncertain.

So he didn't pray now. Instead, he talked to the Night God as if she were another person right in front of him.

"Hey. You there. I know you can hear me; you're famous for it. Now, I understand you sent this woman here, Saeddryn Taranisäii. I was pretty certain of it before, but now it's a fact in my mind. So she's here to do your bidding, which is all well and good, but from what I can see, she's not doing it that well right now. So go on. Do your thing. Help her. I'm helping her. You can, too! Go on," he said again. "It's easy, isn't it? We both know what you want, and . . . honestly, I want it, too. Everyone who really believes in you does. So help *them*, too. Help us all. Help her. She's earned it."

He kept on like this tirelessly, not letting the mirror move, even after his hand began to shake. His other hand, holding up the trapdoor, stung fiercely. He could feel the blood congealing on his arm, and realised he must have cut himself more deeply than he'd meant to. But that didn't matter. All that mattered was this.

A ferocious determination that he had not felt in years rose inside him. It was the same feeling that had made him leave his home all those years ago, that determination that had come after he decided that he would not be poor ever again but would have all those things the rich took for granted and revel in them. But that determination had been selfish, and this was a different kind: a determination to help someone other than himself. It was quite a novel sensation.

Eventually, the moon drifted out of sight, and Heath couldn't hold his arms up any longer. He put the mirror away and shut the trapdoor, finally turning around to see what the results of his night's work had been.

Saeddryn was still standing there, unmoving and expressionless. The man and woman on either side of her both looked exhausted and miserable.

Heath ignored them. "Saeddryn? Saeddryn, can you hear me?"

Yet again, Saeddryn did not respond to him at all.

Tiredness, nerves, and sheer frustration finally got to Heath. He strode forward straight into the circle, knocking the bricks aside, and seized Saeddryn by the front of her dress. "I said, *can you hear me?*" he shouted.

Saeddryn blinked once, slowly, and did nothing else.

Heath had had enough. He pulled his hand back and slapped her hard in the face.

The man and woman started forward with furious yells, but they didn't get the chance to do anything else.

Before anyone could say or do a thing, there was a shout, a thump, and a cry and there was Heath, flat on the floor, with Saeddryn on top of him, holding a dagger against his throat.

For a long moment, nobody moved. Heath's breath was cut with pain, and one eye twitched. The knife at his throat—his own knife—had new blood on it.

"Er," he said eventually. "I, er, I think she's feeling better . . ."

Saeddryn stayed where she was for a few heartbeats, then she took the knife away and stood up, blinking dazedly. "What . . . ?"

Heath scrabbled away from her with astonishing speed and pressed himself against the wall. He dabbed at his face with his bandaged hand. "Sorry about that, my Lady, but it worked. Thanks for the reward. It was my pleasure."

Saeddryn didn't seem to hear him. She lowered the knife and rubbed her face, then looked blankly around the room. "What is this . . . ? How did I . . . ?"

Heath, seeing that his two companions didn't look ready to take the initiative, took it for them. "You're safe," he said. "And sane again . . . in theory. My name's Heath. I think you already know these two."

Saeddryn peered at them. "What happened?"

"Well," said Heath. "I don't know the full story, but apparently you came here—to Malvern—to assassinate the, er, the Queen. Something went horribly wrong, we don't know what, but you fell out of a very, very high window and were lucky enough to be rescued by some of your supporters, who brought you here to this cozy cellar. Unfortunately, you were a little confused for a while, but luckily I came along and came up with a brilliant plan to make you feel better. Then you slashed me across the face. Does any of that sound familiar?"

Saeddryn shuddered. "Oh shadows . . . I remember . . . so confused . . . didn't know where I was, who was there . . . just seein' things that had already happened, didn't know if they were today or yesterday or now . . ."

"But you're all better now," said Heath, trying to sound jovial. "Can I have my knife back, please?"

Saeddryn's eye narrowed. "Who are ye? Where did ye come from?"

Heath glanced at the other two. "Me, I came from Skenfrith. From . . . well, maybe you should see for yourself." He reached into his tunic and offered her a piece of paper with a wax seal on it.

She took it and scanned its contents. Then she smiled, and handed it back. "I see. He did well, to send ye. Here." She gave back his knife. "I'm sorry I hurt ye. I didn't know if ye were a friend, or . . . what ye were."

"Don't worry about it," said Heath. "Honestly, a scar from the Shadow That Walks should be an honour for anyone."

"Aye, an' I'll honour the half-breed with a few more before I'm done," Saeddryn growled.

"Of course." Heath took a few deep breaths. He'd succeeded. Now he'd just have to hope the scar he was probably going to have would make him look heroic rather than just ugly.

"Now . . ." Saeddryn dusted herself down and looked at her two followers. "Thanks to both of ye. Ye've done yer duty as true Northerners, an' I promise ye both that when this is all over, ye may tell Caedmon who ye are an' have any reward ye care to name. As for me, when I next see the Night God, I'll tell her both yer names an' praise ye to her."

"Er, I don't suppose you could maybe mention me?" Heath said, from the background.

"It's still night outside, an' I should go now," said Saeddryn, ignoring him. "The longer I stay here, the more danger I bring ye. I'll take Heath with me, an' thank ye both."

"And thank you from me, too," said Heath. "I couldn't have done it without you."

He nodded politely to them and followed Saeddryn out of the cellar. To his alarm, she climbed straight up through the trapdoor without checking if the coast was clear and walked off without waiting for him.

He hurried after her. "Wait!"

Saeddryn stopped near the alley entrance, and peered out into the street beyond before turning to him. "We're leavin' the city tonight," she said.

"Are we going to meet up with you-know-who?" asked Heath.

"Yes."

"Understood," said Heath. "Now, as for getting out of the city, I have a few suggestions. Just between you and me, I have some experience—"

Saeddryn took him by the arm. "Shut up. Yer comin' with me, an' yer gonna do it without talkin' or I'm leavin' ye here."

"Fine, fine. Just as you say, milady. Can I just ask how we're going to do this?"

"Hold on to me," said Saeddryn. "Don't let go, no matter what happens. Got that?"

Heath gripped her arm. "I think so, but—*argh*!"

Saeddryn leapt forward, dragging him with her, out of the alley and into a black void.

Dark winds blew over the winter landscape of the North. They carried snow with them, and dead leaves and bad news. But no news could be worse, or darker, or cause more death than the griffin that flew high above.

Few griffins could or would fly at night, but this one had no fear.

He made a massive shadow against the stars, a moving blackness that would terrify anyone who saw it, man or griffin.

No griffin was mightier than the Mighty Skandar, and everyone knew it. He was the master of this territory and always would be unless another griffin won it from him. But that would never happen.

He had been away for a while, waiting for his human to get better. Arenadd always got better, no matter what. This time it seemed to be taking longer than usual, but that didn't matter. He had been content to stay where he was, at least until the mysterious white griffin came to him in his sleep again. Last time he had seen her, he had done as she said he should, and it had made him master of the North. So this time he had been quick to listen to her again. He had flown away to Warwick and used his power to bring Saeddryn back to life, just as he had once done for Arenadd.

But when he realised that the white griffin meant for him to make Saeddryn his human, instead of Arenadd, Skandar rebelled. Saeddryn belonged to his son, Aenae, and besides, Skandar did not like her. She argued with Arenadd, made him angry, tried to stop him doing what he wanted. It was not her place to do that, when he was dominant over her. Fighting with him meant that she wanted to challenge him for his position as dominant human, and Skandar would not allow that. Aenae had wanted to challenge as well, had wanted to fight his own father and take his place. But Skandar had defeated him easily.

No, Skandar wanted nothing to do with him, or with Saeddryn. He wanted Arenadd with him, but if Arenadd was too ill to do that, then Skandar would go without him until he was better. He had had enough of waiting. He was coming back to Malvern now, back home to resume his place as supreme griffin, and nobody would stop him. He even relished the possibility that someone might. Killing them would be the fastest way to display his might to anyone who had lost respect for him while he was away.

Malvern was close now. He recognised its shape just ahead, and flew eagerly toward it.

Before long, the outer walls passed beneath him, and he made for the tallest tower of the Eyrie. At the very top, an opening beckoned to him—an archway much bigger than any of the others that dotted the sides of the tower. Faint light showed through it and helped him come in to land on the floor of his old nest.

He was pleased to find it unoccupied, and with only the faintest, oldest scent of another griffin. The straw hadn't been changed in some time, and the water trough had gone dry. Good, that meant nobody else had been using it.

Skandar took a moment to groom and sauntered off through the curtain and into Arenadd's bedroom.

There was someone in it. A human, sitting by the fire. For an instant, the black, curly fur on its head made Skandar tense, but then the smell hit his nostrils and he huffed sharply and shook his head. Not Arenadd.

The human reacted with fear when it saw him, but it did not back down far. "Skandar!" it said. "It's you!"

Skandar took an aggressive step toward it, but then he finally recognised the scent and stopped. He knew this human; it was Arenadd's friend, and had always done what he told it to. Therefore, it was not a threat or a challenger but a useful inferior. It had even helped Skandar once, by finding Arenadd when he was lost.

Skandar gave a friendly flick of his tail. "You human," he said. "You wait for me here?"

"I didn't think you was gonna come back," said the human, in fractured and clumsy griffish not that different from his own.

"Have," said Skandar. "I come home to be Mighty Skandar again."

"That's good," said the human—Laela, that was her name. "Where've yeh been?"

"Have been with human," said Skandar. "But now come back. Human come back later."

"Skandar, Arenadd's not comin' back," said Laela. "He's dead."

Skandar snorted; humans were all so stupid. "Human come back," he said. "Come back soon. Human is magic. Human never die."

"But he's dead now, Skandar."

Skandar decided to ignore that. It didn't matter if she understood or not. "Am home now," he said. "And will not leave again." Then, remembering; "Where you griffin? Where Oeka?"

"She's . . . gone," said Laela.

Skandar chirped. "Oeka leave you?" He opened his beak

wide in his amusement. "You weak human, if she leave! What you do? You make Oeka angry?"

"No," said Laela.

Skandar wasn't listening. He watched the human, enjoying the sheer pathetic idea of this. It was rare for a griffin to actually abandon its human; the death of either human or griffin was one thing, but for a griffin to actually leave . . . well, that only happened if the human had done something truly stupid or weak. He wondered what this one had done to make the little runt Oeka fly away.

"Listen," said Laela. "Skandar. I got an idea."

Skandar cocked his head. "What idea?"

"You ain't got a partner now," said Laela. "Neither do I. You wanna rule Malvern again. I'm tryin' to keep on ruling. So why don't we work together? Yeh know, help each other?"

Skandar just stared at her.

"Make me yer human," said Laela.

Skandar hissed. "Have human already! Not need you!"

"Then let me help yeh!" said Laela. "I helped you an' Arenadd before, didn't I? Let me do it again. I can go with you an' help yeh the way Arenadd would while he's gone."

Skandar huffed softly; this idea sounded interesting.

"There's somethin' I should tell yeh," said Laela. "The Unpartnered—remember them? Well, they've left. They went to Warwick an' then Fruitsheart, t'fight my—Arenadd's enemies, an' now they won't come back. They won't fight any more."

Skandar hissed. "Why not fight?"

"They won't fight without a griffin t'lead them," said Laela. "You, Skandar. Only you can lead them."

Skandar hissed again, louder. "They not leave! Not sit and groom when there are enemies!"

"They need you to go to them," said Laela. "But they won't listen if yeh don't have a human. Take me with yeh."

"I go," Skandar growled. "I make them follow, and we fight again! You —you human come, too, you come to help."

"I will," said Laela.

"Good! You good human, to help. We fight enemy together!" Skandar paused. "What enemy?"

"Saeddryn," said Laela.

Skandar cocked his head. "Why fight Aenae's human?"

"She wants to take over," said Laela. "She wants all yer power, Skandar. To rule Malvern like Arenadd di—does."

Skandar screamed his rage. "Human not rule! Aenae not rule! *I* rule! Arenadd rule!"

"That's right!" Laela shouted over his din. "Saeddryn doesn't rule the North; you do! An' her son, Caedmon, an' his partner Shar—they're helpin' her."

"I kill," said Skandar. "I bring Unpartnered, and I kill. Kill anyone who challenge. Kill *you*." He thrust his massive black beak toward her, glaring straight into her tiny white face. "Kill *you* if you challenge. Human hear this?"

"Yes. I won't challenge, Skandar. Promise. Oeka won't either."

"If she challenge, she die too," Skandar warned.

"She won't."

"Is good, then," said Skandar, pulling away from her. "I go sleep now. Human bring food, water."

"I will," said Laela.

Skandar retreated into his nest.

Once the curtain had fallen back into place behind him, Laela punched the air and did a little jig. "Yes, yes, yes, yes, yes! Hahahahah!"

She flopped down on the bed and tried not to laugh like a lunatic.

Her journal was under the pillow. On impulse, she pulled it out and went to the desk. There she sat down, and scratched out another entry. It was very short.

> *Skander is back an were gonna wipe those basterds off the map. Caedmon is finnished.*

3

Scars Are Heroic

Heath's journey back to Skenfrith with Saeddryn was much shorter than the one that had taken him to Malvern. Much shorter. But then, he was travelling Saeddryn's way this time around.

He didn't enjoy it much. Again and again Saeddryn would drag him into the shadows, and there would be nothing but a horrible, stumbling rush through a darkness that seemed to suck all the warmth out of his body. In between times, they would stop and rest in the light, but Saeddryn seemed desperate to get back to Skenfrith as fast as possible, and she gave Heath almost no time to eat or even sleep. She herself didn't seem to need it at all. Heath was too intimidated by her to complain and did his best to put a brave face on it. After the first day or so, he stopped wanting to eat anyway, but he wanted to sleep more and more. Only sheer terror of the darkness stopped him from dozing off while Saeddryn pulled him through it, and the rest of the time she constantly woke him up before he had had the amount of sleep he needed.

Also, his face hurt. Before long, it began to itch as well, and the ache behind the itch got so bad that it kept him awake even when he got the chance to sleep.

And all the while there was the darkness.

Heath soon grew to hate it. He felt weak and sick every time he came out of it—unlike Saeddryn, who looked stronger and healthier with every trip. She was massively strong while they were in the darkness, too; there was no chance of her ever losing her grip on him, thank the gods. When Heath slept, he had recurring nightmares where she let go of him and left him to wander alone in the darkness until it sucked the life out of him forever.

By the time Saeddryn told him they were close to Skenfrith's walls, he barely cared any more.

"Can we just walk the rest of the way?" he mumbled. He hadn't used his trademark smile in some time.

"All right," said Saeddryn. "It's not far."

"Thank goodnesh," said Heath. His mouth felt clumsy.

"Here." Saeddryn offered him her arm. "Ye've done well all this way, an' when we get there, ye'll have a nice rest. I'm sure they can heal ye, too. Ye don't look so good."

"Don't feel so good," said Heath. His mind felt all tangled up.

He stumbled the rest of the way along the road, letting Saeddryn guide him until she made him stop. As if in a dream, he heard her talking to someone and caught a glimpse of the gates of Skenfrith. After that, he walked some more, along what he thought were streets, until there was a door and some stairs, and there was Caedmon, and his friend Myfina.

Saeddryn let go of Heath and embraced her son.

Heath turned, and saw Myfina looking at him in shock. "Heath? My gods, what happened to you? Heath?" Her voice sounded distorted.

Heath tried to grin, and groaned when pain lanced through his face. "I'm fine," he said. His voice sounded distorted, too.

Another voice. "Heath? Dear gods."

Caedmon. Heath took a step toward him. "Back and all . . . all finished . . . sir," he said. The words felt thick and clumsy in his mouth. "Found your mother, she's fine, but I think I need . . ."

Caedmon's hands grasped his shoulders. "Heath? Heath, are you all right?"

"Need to sit down," Heath managed.

"All right. It's all right. Come this way."

Heath saw the chair and managed to grab the backrest. "Thanks."

Caedmon let go of him. "You just sit down and rest, Heath. You've done brilliantly."

Heath sat, but the chair seemed to be moving underneath him. "Caedmon," he said, trying to catch him by the arm and missing. "The darkness . . . you've got to . . . darkness takes the ... takes the life ..." His voice faded away in his ears. "Takes the life away," it said, so faintly he could barely hear it, even though it was his own. "Stay away from ... dark ..."

Myfina cried out in horror as Heath fell off the chair and crumpled onto the floor. *"Oh no!"*

She and Caedmon ran to his side and tried to wake him up, but he didn't answer. He was unconscious, and his skin was burning hot. On his face, the wound stood out horribly, red with swelling that had spread outward and pushed one eye shut.

Saeddryn knelt by his head and put her cold hands on his forehead. "Oh no ..."

"That wound's infected," said Caedmon. "It's made him sick; he's burning up with fever."

Saeddryn looked up, and she sounded as cool and detached as she looked. "This man saved my life. He saved all our lives. Brought me back from madness. An' this is how I repaid him."

"We have to get him to a healer, now," said Caedmon, running for the door.

Myfina stayed by Heath's side as he was lifted onto a stretcher and followed him to the infirmary. Caedmon went, too, but stayed outside when Heath went in, catching Myfina by the elbow to stop her following.

"Stop," he said. "You'll only get in their way."

Myfina stood beside him, shaking her head gently "No," she murmured. "Please Night God, don't take him."

Caedmon, watching her, felt a cold stab in his heart. But all he said was, "I'm sure they can help him."

"They will," Myfina said fiercely. "He can't die. He's Heath."

"Yes." Caedmon smiled. "Heath of no fixed name and no fixed abode. One day, I'm going to make him tell me his real name."

"Me too," said Myfina. "But he'll always be Heath to me."

"There's nothin' ye can do for him now," said Saeddryn, from behind them. "An' we have things to talk about."

Caedmon turned to her. "You're right. Let's go to the council chamber, and you can tell us both what happened."

The three of them hurried off there and shut themselves in before Saeddryn told them her story.

"Got into Malvern, an' did some talking. Gathered followers, instructed 'em on what to do when we come back there. They told me some nasty things about what's been goin' on in the Eyric.

Said the half-breed's partner, Oeka, had been doin' something in there. Working some sort of magic that killed anyone who got too close. They also told me about what happened to yer father, Caedmon. An' I wouldn't tell ye, but it's important that ye know."

Caedmon's mouth tightened. "What is it?"

"The half-breed had set things up t'kill him the usual way, but that didn't happen. When they brought him out, Oeka did somethin'. Spoke into people's minds. Everybody there heard her, in their heads."

"She can do that?" Myfina interrupted.

"Aye," said Saeddryn. "It's a rare power, but she's got it. Power over the mind. An' it does worse than just talk. She used it. On yer father, Caedmon. Did it t'show everyone what she could do."

"What did she do?" asked Caedmon, very quietly.

"Broke his mind," said Saeddryn, grim but steady. "Crushed it so bad it killed him. Then she warned everyone that she'd do the same to them. When I was in the city, people warned me it'd happen to me next, but I got into the Eyrie fine. I found the half-breed, an' I was about to kill her, and then . . ."

"Then what?" said Caedmon.

Saeddryn spread her hands. "I don't know. I don't remember anything that happened after that. I just remember pain, in my head, an' after that I didn't know what was goin' on any more. People told me afterward I jumped out the window an' fell all the way down the tower. Luckily, one of my new friends found me and snuck me out into the city. They did their best t'look after me until yer friend came along. He cured me."

"How?"

"Thought on his feet," said Saeddryn. "He built a circle an' made a ritual to the Night God. Called her up an' prayed to her t'help me. She woke me up. After that, I got us both out of Malvern an' back here."

"How did he get hurt like that?" said Myfina. "What happened to his face?"

"I did it," said Saeddryn. "By accident. When I woke up, I got confused an' thought I was still fightin'. I cut his face without realising I'd done it."

"I hope he'll be all right," Myfina said sadly.

"Look," said Saeddryn. "What we need t'be thinkin' about

here is this. I did my best t'do what ye asked me, Caedmon, but I failed. An' as long as that griffin is there in Malvern, there's no way I can do it. It's only sheer luck I wasn't caught. The only way we're gonna kill the half-breed is if she goes somewhere away from her partner, but I don't think she's gonna do that. She ain't stupid; she knows about me now, an' she must know that griffin is her only protection from me. I'm sorry, Caedmon. But at least I got back here, an' now I'm ready. So tell me: What are yer orders? What do ye want me t'do next?"

Caedmon frowned. "This is going to be harder than I thought. And don't worry; I'm not going to send you back there. The half-breed can fester in Malvern while she waits for us to come to her. But things aren't as bad as they might seem to you. I've had some news from Fruitsheart. The Unpartnered are there; they went with Iorwerth to get us, but obviously we'd gone by then. After that, they might have come on to here, but they haven't. Instead, they're staying in Fruitsheart, and Iorwerth and Kaanee have gone back to Malvern without them."

Saeddryn's eye narrowed. "Why?"

"I'm not sure," said Caedmon. "But I've been told that they're not doing anything in Fruitsheart; just flying around and eating all the food. My guess is they've rebelled. It was incredible that they agreed to leave Malvern in the first place; by the looks of it, they've changed their minds now. Maybe this Oeka isn't as powerful as she seems."

"Obviously," Myfina put in. "Without the Unpartnered, Malvern has lost the advantage. We can march on there now, and the entire Council has agreed that if the Unpartnered aren't there to defend the city, we should be able to take it without much trouble."

"What about Oeka?" asked Saeddryn. "She's the only real threat left in that case."

"She can't kill all of us," said Caedmon. "Not an entire army of us. All it'll take is for one person or griffin to get close enough, and she's dead. No more threat."

"I say we do it, then," said Saeddryn. "Is everything ready?"

"Almost," said Caedmon. "We're recruiting as many as we can, and some reinforcements are coming over from Fruitsheart. We're also trying to find a griffin with the power to break open the gates at Malvern. There should be one somewhere; Shar's interrogating them now. We weren't going to march until we knew what had happened to you, but that's not a problem now."

"When can we leave, then?" said Saeddryn.

"In a couple of days if everything goes to plan."

"Good. That should be soon enough. If that's everything, I'm gonna go clean up."

Caedmon nodded. "You can go."

"I'm going to go and see how Heath is," said Myfina.

"I'll come with you," said Caedmon.

Laela and Skandar left Malvern the day after his arrival and, more than anything else, Laela gloried in simply being able to leave the city after such a long time cooped up. She had grown more frustrated than she realised, forced to stay in her Eyrie while things happened out of her reach. Once she had thought that she would be able to leave when Oeka grew big enough to carry her, but now she knew that would never happen.

But she gloried even more in having Skandar with her. She had flown on his back a few times in the past, but always with Arenadd there, and Skandar had only carried her under sufferance and because his human insisted. Now he was carrying just her, willingly, and Laela was as close to being partnered with him as she ever would be. Just knowing that was a thrill. And knowing what they would be able to do together was even more exciting.

Every time she thought of it, she wanted to laugh the same cold, bloody laugh her father had used the day she saw him slaughter an entire crew of Amorani pirates. He had not done that alone; he had done it with Skandar, and now it was Laela's turn to take her father's place by the giant griffin's side. Now *she* would be the one to strike terror into her enemies, and with Skandar there, even Saeddryn didn't scare her any more. She revelled in the prospect.

For now, though, there were the Unpartnered to deal with. Iorwerth and Kaanee had come, and a couple of fighting griffiners served as an escort—more for the look of the thing than for any other reason since Laela didn't believe that anyone would need an escort with Skandar present. Skandar *ate* his enemies, for gods' sakes.

Fruitsheart, predictably, was a mess. The Unpartnered had spread through the city, nesting on rooftops and claiming entire buildings for themselves, forcing the original occupants to put up with them or move. They were eating anything they found: stealing animals from the city and venturing into the farmlands around it in search of bigger prey. The griffiners living in the tower had made some attempts to bring them under control, but with only a small Hatchery and few other places made for griffins to live in, the Unpartnered were everywhere. And they were done with taking orders.

Laela, Skandar, and the others landed at the governor's tower, where they heard all this. Iorwerth, who had obviously heard it all before, looked grim, and Laela groaned.

Skandar, however, only blinked and shifted his massive bulk slightly.

Laela turned to him. "Skandar, what should we do?"

Skandar turned his head toward her, and for a moment it looked like he was going to do what he usually did: stand there looking uninterested and wait for the nearest human to think for him.

But then he spoke. "Easy to do. Unpartnered have stronger griffins among them, dominant griffins. I find them, make them bow heads to me. Then every griffin who bow to them, bow to me also."

Laela stared in surprise. "An' where would those griffins be?"

Skandar clicked his beak. "Tower is best place to nest. Higher is better. Strongest Unpartnered will be sleeping there. I go find them now."

He loped off. Laela shrugged and grinned at Iorwerth before following. She had to trot; Skandar was surprisingly fast for his size.

The giant griffin seemed to know his way around since he didn't hesitate or wander at all but went straight out and into the griffin nesting chamber on the top level, which was supposed to be home to the governor's partner. Now, though, just as Laela had been told, the proper owner had been driven out by one of the Unpartnered. When she entered, she caught a brief glimpse of a great, hulking creature dozing in a heap of straw before Skandar made his move.

Without even breaking stride, Skandar pounced on the other griffin.

Caught by surprise, it fell heavily onto its side. Skandar didn't give it any opportunity to recover, but hurled himself on top of it like a dark-feathered avalanche. The other griffin, who was still quite large though smaller than Skandar, pushed back, and for several tense moments the two huge beasts grappled with each other, hissing and snarling.

But Skandar was the stronger, and the fight did not last long before he had the other griffin cringing and bowing its head in submission.

"You, griffin!" he screeched. "What you do here? You not do what meant to!"

"I am meant to do nothing!" the other griffin retorted, apparently not completely cowed after all. "I have decided to live here, so I have taken this nest."

"You not have nest!" said Skandar. "You Unpartnered. Have no human. Griffin with no human not have nest. Not allowed! You nest in Malvern, or in tree. *Not* in tower."

"I can do as I please!" said the other griffin—Laela saw now that it was a female, but she had a hulking, thick-limbed build that made her look a bit like Skandar. "And besides that," the female went on, "Who are you to tell me what to do? I see no human with you!"

Skandar hit her in the head with his talons. "Am Mighty Skandar! Am master of this land, master of griffin. You do as I say, not what you want, or I tear off head!"

"You are not mighty any more," said the female. "You have lost your human."

This time, Skandar hit her hard enough to draw blood. "Have human! Human only not here now. Have brought this one instead."

"You cannot do that," the female persisted. "A griffin can only have one human. It is the law—"

Skandar's beak snapped shut on the joint of her wing. He pulled, and began to shake it violently, wrenching it in its socket. The female screamed in pain, but he kept going mercilessly.

"What say now?" he screeched. "You say what I do *now*? You argue with no wing? Argue now?"

"No!" She tried to free herself, and Skandar stopped shaking the wing though he didn't let go.

The female slumped, her flank trembling. "I will not argue any more. You are right. Please, do not hurt my wing . . . Mighty Skandar."

That seemed enough to satisfy him. He gave her wing one last, agonising wrench, then let her go. "You strong," he admitted. "But not strong enough to fight Mighty Skandar."

The female wisely stayed on her side. Her wing stayed outstretched, the joint wet with blood. "No," she said. "I am not strong enough, Father."

Skandar snorted. "Knew you come from Mighty Skandar egg. You big! But none of Skandar's chicks are bigger than him. Now, you come. You bow head to me. Other Unpartnered do same."

"Yes, Father," said the female. "None of them will dare to fight you. I am the strongest of them, and they know it. I fought many of them for this nest. When they see that you have beaten me, they will remember their respect for you."

"Is good!" said Skandar. "We leave before dark. Go fight enemy."

The female stood up and managed to loosely fold her wing. "Where shall we fight them?"

Skandar grunted and looked toward Laela.

"Skenfrith," she said quickly. "They're in Skenfrith."

The big female tossed her head. "You are the Mighty Skandar's new human?"

"Er . . . yeah," said Laela. "Yeah, I'm his human now." When Skandar didn't disagree with her, she felt her chest swell a little with pride.

"Then you are the lead human of the North?"

Laela nodded. "I'm the Queen. Laela's my name. What's yours?"

The female seemed bored already, but she paused long enough to reply. "I am Seeak."

Skandar had already begun to leave. Seeak followed—limping slightly—and Laela went, too. Iorwerth and Kaanee, who had waited back in the governor's audience chamber, joined them along the way. Skandar, ignoring them, went straight up the ramp to the roof.

There he went to stand at the very edge, overlooking the city. Kaanee stood beside him, a little farther back, and Seeak took up a place on the opposite side. Laela stayed away with Iorwerth, and the two humans stood and watched, both knowing that neither of them had a part to play. This was a griffin thing.

Skandar braced himself and sent out a call. It was a different sound from the usual griffin screech. It sounded like a mixture of eagle scream and lion roar, as with every griffin, but this was a territorial call, modulated to include words.

"Mighty Skandar! Mighty Skandar! Mighty Skandaaaar!"

He called again and again, announcing himself to the world and claiming Fruitsheart as his territory, where every other griffin must submit to him or prepare to fight. It was a challenge, then, but Laela didn't realise it until she saw several griffins flying toward the tower. At first she thought they were just coming to investigate, but as they landed she took one look at them and their demeanours and felt her heart begin to flutter. Big griffins. Rough, tough-looking griffins, mostly males, and all advancing aggressively toward Skandar. Beside him, Kaanee and Seeak quietly moved out of the way.

Kaanee went straight to his human. "Come," he said. "We should not be in the way."

"They're going to fight?" asked Iorwerth.

"Yes, and Skandar must defeat all of them to be master of the Unpartnered again. Laela, you should come with us."

Laela was more than happy to obey. Kaanee herded her and Iorwerth back into the opening they had first come through, and together the three of them took shelter and waited.

Laela couldn't see past Kaanee's wing, but she heard enough to make her cringe. Screeches and snapping beaks, and the thud and slap of massive bodies smacking into each other and the ground. Talons on stone—and once an ugly, wet tearing sound that could only be a serious wound opening. And, during a brief silence, she heard the worst sound of all: the low, wheezing, whimpering voice of a dying griffin.

But a moment later, the sounds of fighting resumed, and Laela breathed easy again.

After a long, tense wait, Kaanee decided it was safe to emerge. Laela ran out with him and found a nasty sight.

Skandar was there, his sides heaving as he stood and bled. The Unpartnered who had fought him were now only three; the rest must have flown away. Two lay on their bellies at Skandar's talons, and a third was on his back a short distance away, breathing slowly and painfully as his life flowed out through an appalling wound in his throat. Seeak was still there, at a safe distance, having apparently stayed away from the fight.

Skandar turned his head toward Laela. "Have fought well," he panted. "Have won. Am now leader of Unpartnered again. These here will tell them, and we leave today!"

Laela bowed to him, with complete sincerity. "Yer everything the stories say yeh are an' more, Skandar, an' now I've seen it for myself. When this is over, I'll make a statue of you, right in Malvern."

"We leave now," said Skandar, as if he hadn't heard her. "Come now, on Skandar's back."

"Are yeh sure?" said Laela. "Don't yeh need some healin' or somethin'?"

"No," Iorwerth interrupted. "Don't ask questions, my Lady. The Unpartnered will come now or never. Do as Skandar says."

"Right." Laela went straight to Skandar, and climbed onto his shoulders as he bent down to let her on. He straightened up at once, and she quickly wrapped her hands around the harness he wore and held on tight.

Skandar walked to the edge of the tower again. The two defeated griffins had already flown off, and he waited a short while to let them fly over the city and call their message. Then he added his own voice to theirs, making his territorial cry as he had done before. This time, nobody challenged him.

Laela watched, astonished, as griffins rose into the air. Everywhere, the city disgorged more of them—from the walls, the houses, the civic buildings, and even the lakeshore beyond the walls. Skandar continued to call them, and they came, adding themselves to a great flock now forming over the city.

When the flood of griffins had slowed, and most of the Unpartnered were on the wing, Skandar took off from the tower. Kaanee and Seeak followed close behind him, riding on his slipstream, and the Unpartnered left the city under the leadership of the only griffin in the country who could ever be powerful enough to be their master.

They flew straight for Skenfrith, and Laela flew with them. And now she finally did give in to the urge she had had, and laughed with the same savage glee her father would have done, seeing bloodshed ahead and delighting in it. All her frustration and anger had built up to this, and there would be no more waiting, no more negotiating, no more trying to be clever. She would show them she was a true Taranisäii.

In other words, she wouldn't spare a single one of them.

4

Unleashed

Heath was dangerously ill.

Just as Caedmon had guessed, the infected wound on his face had spread poison into his blood, and the doctors now taking care of him said there was a chance he might not survive. For once, Heath had nothing to say; he stayed in his sickbed, delirious with fever, his face bandaged after the doctors had reopened the wound to drain it.

Myfina was the very image of concern, and in between her duties, she spent a lot of time by his side, trying to comfort him when he became distressed and started to ramble in his half-conscious state. Caedmon visited, too, when he could, but he knew there was nothing to do, and despite all he had done for them, Heath was only one man. No matter how much Caedmon cared about him, he had too much else to do those days.

He was glad to have Saeddryn back at his side. She was a great help, inspiring his followers and using all her old fighting experience to help refine the plan for the assault on Malvern. Shar was another great ally, of course, and it was she who had found the griffin they needed: a deceptively slight male, one of the few unpartnered griffins living in Skenfrith, who had the power to break down Malvern's gates. She had made him give a demonstration for both her and Caedmon, and it had satisfied them both. They had promised him whatever reward he wanted in return. The griffin had replied that he wanted the best human partner available, and nobody was unhappy with that.

Now, Caedmon judged, the time had come. They were as ready as they would ever be, and Malvern was waiting.

Myfina looked slightly unhappy at the news. She said nothing, but Caedmon noticed.

"What is it?" he asked her. "Don't you want to go?"

She nodded. "Of course, but . . . oh, never mind. It's silly."

Caedmon moved closer to her. "Come on, you can tell me," he said warmly. "I won't laugh."

"Oh . . ." She shook her head. "I just had some silly idea that Heath might get better in time so he could come with us."

Caedmon blinked. "Why?"

"I don't know," Myfina said sadly. "It's just . . . it feels like that now it's the three of us. You know what I mean? You and me and him."

"I know what you mean," Caedmon admitted. "I like him, too, Myfina. He's a good friend, and we couldn't have done this without him. And I'm sure he would have come to Malvern with us if we'd asked him. By now we both know he wouldn't say no to something exciting!"

Myfina smiled. "I never thought he could do all those things he did."

"He surprised us both," said Caedmon. He smiled back. "But don't worry about him. He'll be safe here, and by the time he gets better, he can come and meet us in Malvern for the celebrations! He'll like that. Maybe we could even let him sit with us since he's a hero now."

Myfina nodded cheerfully. Many of Caedmon's followers were indeed calling Heath a hero. The dangerous wound collected in the line of duty helped add to that image.

Caedmon, watching her, felt his heart seem to grow bigger inside him. It almost hurt. He reached out for her hand. "Myfina," he said, "I—"

The door burst open. "My Lord!"

Caedmon turned, letting go of Myfina's hand. "What? What is it?" The words came out angry when they didn't need to be.

The man who'd opened the door bowed hastily. "My Lord, ye must come now. Lady Saeddryn is above waiting for ye."

"I'm coming." Caedmon waved at Myfina to follow him and ran out of the room.

They had been near the top of the tower, so it was a short dash to the roof. Saeddryn was indeed there, with Shar, and Myfina's partner, Garsh.

"Caedmon!" Shar bounded toward them. "Caedmon, the Unpartnered are coming! I have called a warning."

"What?" Caedmon looked quickly at his mother, as if hoping she would say something different. "How could this happen, for gods' sakes?"

"I don't know," Saeddryn said sharply, "And now ain't the time t'be askin' questions like that. Go with Shar. Get everyone ready! *Now.*"

Caedmon pulled himself together. "Myfina, you come with us," he said. "We have to get the defenders on the wall organised, and fast."

She had gone pale, but she snapped out of it and ran to get onto Garsh's back. Caedmon climbed onto Shar, and the two griffins flew off for the walls with all speed, leaving Saeddryn to organise those in the tower.

As Caedmon flew with Shar, he looked out at the horizon beyond the city and saw all the proof he needed that she was right. The sky northward was marred by a patch of moving blackness that couldn't be anything but a flock of griffins.

He felt sick. In his head, the question asked itself again and again: *How could this happen? How could this happen?*

Before Shar even reached the wall, Caedmon had realised the situation was worse than dire. There were plenty of his followers in Skenfrith, and giant bows on the walls ready to shoot down the attacking griffins, but with few griffins on their own side, the defenders had very little chance of even surviving, let alone keeping the city. The Unpartnered could decimate a city. They had done it in Warwick, and only a handful of the rebels there had escaped to tell the tale. And Skenfrith was smaller than Warwick. It did not have the same good defences, and it had fewer antigriffin bows on the walls.

Shar landed, and Caedmon jumped down and ran to give his orders to the commanders on the wall, but as he did it, he knew what he must do. Prepare the city to evacuate, and fast. Otherwise, none of them would make it out alive.

* * *

Laela saw the walls of Skenfrith and braced herself for the attack. Her heart had begun to pound sickeningly despite Skandar's reassuring bulk underneath her.

She hadn't made any plans for the assault at all other than thinking over how she was going to handle herself. Skandar was the master of the Unpartnered, and he was in charge of this battle. There was no way for Laela to make his followers do what she wanted, let alone make Skandar follow instructions. Griffins did not plan.

Neither, of course, did Skandar. He flew in straight over the walls, ignoring the defenders on top of it and striking out over the city toward the governor's tower. Behind and around him, the Unpartnered spread out to attack wherever they chose, but Kaanee stayed with him, and the two big males landed on the tower-top.

There, Skandar lifted one foreleg and unceremoniously tipped Laela off his back. "You fight human now," he told her as she lay sprawled on the bricks. "I go kill griffin. Come back here later if not dead."

He flew off.

Iorwerth had also dismounted, and he helped Laela up. "Stay with me, my Lady, and I'll keep you safe."

Laela watched Kaanee fly off with Skandar to attack the handful of enemy griffins in the sky. "Ain't they gonna stay an' help us? All right, I didn't think Skandar would stay for me, but Kaanee's yer partner, ain't he?"

Iorwerth already had his sickle ready in his hand. "Of course, but no griffin will fight in the air if they have a human on their back, and their enemies are all in the sky here. Other humans are for us to deal with. Let's go into the tower, but not too far in. We don't want to get trapped inside."

"Right." Laela drew her own sickle—the same one that had once belonged to her father. It had stars and a triple spiral engraved on the blade, and Arenadd had kept it beautifully sharp and polished.

The tower had been designed to be pretty similar to the one in Fruitsheart though smaller. Iorwerth headed down the ramp and into the building, with his sickle at the ready, and Laela stayed close behind him. Going inside with just the two of them would be dangerous, of course, but much less so than staying outside, where even a griffin from their own side could kill them both by accident. Besides that, most of the tower's occupants were too busy trying to deal with the Unpartnered assault to worry about a couple of humans. Most of them had never even seen Laela before, and she had sensibly avoided wearing the crown, opting instead for a leather breastplate and bracers on her arms and legs.

She had also armoured her throat, which hadn't quite healed yet from Saeddryn's attempt to kill her. She wasn't making *that* mistake again.

The first enemy they ran into was no challenge. He was caught by surprise, and Iorwerth killed him before Laela had the chance to do anything.

"Come this way," he told her before the corpse had even stopped moving. "If we go into the governor's chamber, we might find one of the people we're after."

"Got it." Laela pushed forward to stand beside him, sickle at the ready.

The governor's chamber was right at the very top of the tower, as expected—large and well furnished, with plenty of room for griffins to move about. There didn't seem to be anybody there.

Iorwerth made a quick check behind the furniture and looked out the window. He shook his head sadly as he came back to Laela. "It's chaos out there. The poor bastards don't stand a chance."

Laela looked as well and couldn't stop herself from going wide-eyed. The Unpartnered had covered the city like a swarm of locusts. Everywhere she looked, griffins were tearing at rooftops, rampaging through streets, or swooping to snatch up running humans and drop them to their deaths. Others were fighting the defending griffins, who were pitifully outnumbered but putting up a good fight. One or two fires had already started at different points.

"Holy gods, they're gonna rip the city to bits!" Laela exclaimed.

"It can't be helped," said Iorwerth. "Let's move on and see if we can end this any faster."

They left the chamber and made their way down the tower, room by room. In one or two of them they found human fighters who were using the tower as a shelter from which to send arrows at the rampaging Unpartnered. Iorwerth and Laela fought them together, but Iorwerth somehow managed to both fight and keep himself between Laela and the enemy, leaving her to do not much more than watch while he took care of them himself.

Laela quickly grew frustrated. She had had nothing to do at Malvern but practise with her sickle, and if this kept up, she wasn't going to get to use the damn thing in a real fight at all! Damn Iorwerth; she was the daughter of Arenadd Taranisäii and was going to prove it today no matter what.

On the next level, they found a closed door. Iorwerth reached for the handle, but Laela pushed him out of the way and kicked it open herself. Beyond, she found a room full of beds.

And a young woman, pointing a spear at her. "Get out!"

Laela took a moment to get the measure of this new challenger. The woman was about her age, and pretty, but she was dressed for battle, and her face was full of fury.

Right. Laela thrust out an arm to hold Iorwerth back. "I'll take care of this."

The woman jabbed the spear toward her. "I said get out," she snapped. "I'm not fighting here, so leave me alone."

"Who are yeh?" Laela growled.

The woman drew herself up proudly. "I am Lady Myfina of Caerleon . . . *half-breed*."

Laela sneered. "A griffiner, then, are yeh? Then why are yeh standin' around in the infirmary while everyone else does the work?"

Myfina smiled nastily. "Waiting for you."

Iorwerth nudged Laela in the back. "My Lady, just leave her! I know her, and she doesn't know how to use that spear. She's just trying to distract us. We have to move on, or Caedmon will escape."

"Good point." Laela took a step toward Myfina. "Where's Caedmon gone?"

"The King of Tara has gone to protect his friends," Myfina said. "And now I'm going to protect them . . . from *you*!" She lunged forward with the spear.

Laela dodged it without much trouble, but as she stepped aside ready to attack she tripped over something on the floor. Unable to rescue herself, she hit the ground hard. When she opened her eyes, she found herself face-to-face with Iorwerth.

His eyes were wide open and staring into hers, but his face was white and splattered with blood.

Laela rolled and got up, but a hard blow came from nowhere and sent her tottering sideways. She spun around, lashing out with the sickle, but there was nothing there to hit. Myfina was standing in the same place as before, holding her spear across her body to protect herself.

And a voice came from the air. *"I am the shadow that comes in the night . . ."*

Laela tried to pull Iorwerth to his feet. "Iorwerth, for gods' sakes, get up!"

"I am the fear that lurks in your heart . . ."

Iorwerth's head lolled, blood still leaking from the slash in his throat.

"I am the woman without a heart."

Laela dropped Iorwerth's body and backed away toward the wall. "Oh shit, oh shit, oh shit . . ."

"I am the Shadow That Walks."

Something unseen hit Laela hard in the face, and everything turned red. She got up, clawing at the blood that rained into her eyes, trying to defend herself against an enemy she couldn't see, an enemy as strong as death.

Myfina began to laugh. "Run, half-breed, run!"

Laela ran.

She didn't care where she was running to, or what might be ahead. Terror made her blind and stupid, and she ran as if death itself were on her heels . . . which it was.

But no matter how far or how fast she ran, Saeddryn was always just behind her—not seen, but heard, and felt. Her voice taunted from the darkness, never sounding strained or breathless, and when Laela slowed, a stab or a cut would send her running off again. Here and there ordinary enemies showed up in her way, but Laela's fear was too deep to include them as well. She kicked them out of the way and slashed with the sickle, not stopping to fight properly or finish any of them off. None of them seemed inclined to go after her.

Saeddryn chased her lower and lower in the tower, away from those places where there were openings through which a griffin could enter. Away from where she could call Skandar to help her.

And then, finally, a room with a door. Laela slammed it shut behind her, and ran for the window, ignoring the few startled defenders around her. She looked out the window. It was big enough to climb through, and didn't look that far off the ground . . .

Behind her, the door broke apart. And there was Saeddryn, at last, appearing out of the darkness with her sickle in her hand and a hideous smile on her face. "Don't ye understand, half-breed?" she said. "There is no escape. Not from me."

Laela said nothing. She grabbed hold of the window-frame and kicked out the glass, climbing through without even noticing the cuts that opened on her hands.

Then she fell.

She hit a rooftop and slid off it to land on the ground, winded and groaning.

But pain didn't matter. She got up with a strength that managed to surprise her, somewhere in the back of her mind, and ran off into the city.

Where Caedmon had been waiting for her, all this time. He stepped out of a doorway, armed and armoured, his black eyes glittering in a way that made him look horribly familiar even though Laela had never seen him before.

She stumbled to a halt. Blood gummed around her eyes, making her squint. "A . . . Arenadd?" she faltered.

Caedmon did not smile. "Not Arenadd," he said. "Just his successor."

But he looked so much like him, Laela thought dully. The same curly hair, the same neat beard, and she knew in that moment that this was Arenadd's real son. This was what his son should have been, not Kullervo. This was the child of Arenadd that the world had wanted and the heir it had wanted. Not her. History had twisted, and she had been the one to do the twisting, she and Kullervo. The man in front of her now was how things had been supposed to go. But they hadn't.

And now he was here to put everything right.

Laela glanced up and saw the Unpartnered swarming around the tower. They must have entered it as soon as they had finished fighting the other griffins in the sky, ready to wipe out the human defenders in there.

There was no sign of Saeddryn.

"Yeh planned this," said Laela. "She chased me here, so you

could put things right. Didn't she? You wanted t'fight me yerself. So it'd be your victory, not hers. Right?"

"Yes." Caedmon nodded. "I am the rightful ruler of Malvern. My mother knows that."

Laela tried not to let him see her wincing. "So now we fight, then, an' you get t'be the hero what killed the nasty ole halfbreed, right? 'Cause that's how it is in your story. I'm the villain here, an' villains die."

Caedmon smiled very slightly. "You're smarter than you look."

"Kill her, Caedmon."

Laela did not turn around when she heard Saeddryn's voice, but she did stiffen slightly.

Saeddryn appeared, slipping out of the shadows to stand by her son. "Don't try an' run any more, half-breed," she said. "It ends here."

Despite everything, Laela smirked. "Yeah, right, if I was a lot stupider than I look." She bent and picked up a piece of broken brick from the ground. "You're dead, Saeddryn."

"I know," said Saeddryn, grim-faced.

"An' I'm gonna make yeh wish you'd stayed in yer grave," said Laela. "That's a promise. Oh—Caedmon?"

He drew his sickle and went into a fighting stance. "Yes?"

"Catch." Laela hurled the piece of brick. It hit Caedmon square in the head, and an instant later she was on him, following it up with a punch to the jaw. Completely ignoring her sickle, she hit him again in the stomach, then kneed him in the groin, which had the extra effect of knocking him over. Before he could get up, she brought her boot down on his ribs and was rewarded with a nasty, cracking sound.

Caedmon yelled with a mixture of shock and pain, but he wasn't defeated yet. He shoved Laela away and managed to get up. His sickle had fallen out of his hand, so he attacked her with his fists, punching her in the face.

This was not how it was supposed to be. Caedmon had spent his whole life being trained to fight with weapons, but Laela was made to fight with whatever she could get her hands on, and she had no scruples whatsoever. She kicked Caedmon in the kneecap, and when he caught her by the arm, she headbutted him in the mouth hard enough to make him let go.

But Caedmon was not a weak opponent by any means, and Laela did not have the advantage for long. He pushed her away, and as he took an instant to pick his next move, Saeddryn appeared by his side, silently putting his sickle back into his hand.

Humiliated, and suffering from a severe ache in his ribs, Caedmon snarled and darted in close, sickle aiming for Laela's throat. It bounced off the thick leather, but he struck again quickly, cutting her across the inside of her elbow.

Laela still had her own sickle, and she fended his off as well as she could, but she was not a defensive fighter. She struck back, laying open the back of Caedmon's hand and dodging his attempt to hit her in the face.

Saeddryn took no part in the fight. She stayed out of the way, watching in silence. And, for a while, it looked as if Caedmon was going to live up to his vow. He had far more experience with the sickle than Laela, and after a brief, nasty struggle, he had her on the retreat. With the city crumbling around them, there was no time to draw things out any longer. He closed in, ready to kill.

A screech came from overhead, so loud it made Caedmon freeze and look up. A shadow fell across him and Laela, and the Mighty Skandar came with it.

Caedmon sensibly ran for it, and not a moment too soon. Skandar landed with an almighty thud, right over Laela, who wound up lying between his front talons.

Skandar glowered at Saeddryn and Caedmon. "You . . ."

Saeddryn's face burned with pure fury. *"Skandar!"* she screamed. "How dare ye?"

Skandar huffed menacingly. "You humans," he said. "You enemy. Enemy to my human. Enemy to me."

Caedmon was far too intelligent to stay and argue. He took shelter behind a wall and lingered there, watching cautiously.

Saeddryn, however, advanced on the big griffin. "Ye are *my* partner now! The Night God commanded it!"

"Nobody command Mighty Skandar," said Skandar, unmoved.

"This isn't how it was supposed to be!" Saeddryn shouted.

"Not care." Skandar jerked his head toward her and scooped Laela up in his talons. "I keep this human. You not hurt!" Hobbling on three legs, with Laela cradled against his chest, he advanced on Saeddryn and Caedmon. "You go! You not fight us. Unpartnered follow me. Malvern mine! You come near, and I kill you." A rumble started in his throat. "Now you go," he said. "Go now. Not let me see you again. My human is master, and this human serve him. Serve me! *Go!*"

Saeddryn could see that the day was lost. She backed away, gesturing at Caedmon to do the same. "Go," she muttered. "There's nothing we can do here. We have t'get the others away before it's too late."

Caedmon took one last look at the hissing Skandar and the hated woman in his grasp. "You'll pay for this," he promised, and ran.

5

A Prince

Laela's brother, Kullervo, arrived at the island nation of Maijan on a beautiful clear day, after months at sea. He and his companions had left a Northern winter behind, but in Maijan they found heat and bright blue skies, and a lovely seaside town to welcome them ashore.

Kullervo went down the gangplank behind Inva and Skarok. They were the official diplomats for this visit, so Kullervo and his partner, Senneck, as part of their escort, stood aside quietly while their superiors were greeted by a small deputation of griffiners, griffins, and others. Most of them were local Maijanis, dark-skinned and lightly clad, some of them guards holding ceremonial spears. However, the core of the group, and the most richly dressed, were Amoranis. They were lighter-skinned, though still dark, and wore their own national dress. Most of them had griffins with them, and it was obvious from where they were placed and the behaviour of those around them that they were the ones with the real power here.

Kullervo, of course, had spent plenty of his time on the ship letting Inva teach him everything he would need to know for this occasion. She was a Northerner by blood, but had spent most of her life as a high-class slave in Amoran, and she knew far more about their customs than those of her own native land. Maijan was a separate country from Amoran, with its own culture, but it was considered part of the Amorani Empire. So

Kullervo and the others might be in Maijan, but they would answer to the Amorani governor.

Kullervo ran through all this in his head while Inva and Skarok made the formal greetings. He was wearing his best clothes, which Laela had given him, but he wasn't required to do anything more than nod and smile when Inva indicated him and spoke in Amorani, introducing him to the handsome noble who seemed to be in charge.

The formalities over with, the visitors—which included Inva, Skarok, Kullervo, Senneck, and two other griffiners with their partners—were taken up into the little city in a procession.

Along the way, Kullervo admired the buildings. They were mud brick, and had flat roofs, unlike anything he had ever seen before. Many of them had been painted in cheerful colours, and bright cloth awnings only made them even more pleasant to look at. There were plenty of people about, too—mostly Maijanis, appearing at windows or in doorways, or standing in the street on either side to watch the foreigners pass. Most of them looked excited or curious, and Kullervo guessed that they probably hadn't seen many Cymrians before.

Up at the highest point of the city, a large building stood out. Unlike the rest of the buildings around it, it was built of stone rather than brick and featured several domed rooftops. It looked awkward and uncomfortable, unable to blend in properly with its surroundings.

Like me, Kullervo thought with a wry smile, but he guessed that this building must have been built by the Amoranis according to their own preferences, even if it didn't fit with the rest of the city.

As he was admitted inside through an impressive, arched doorway, Kullervo wondered why the Amoranis had made their palace this way. Was it to remind the islanders that this was their place? Or didn't they believe that the Maijani style was good enough to make a palace worthy of them? Or maybe they just didn't want to stop doing things their way just because they were in a foreign land.

Maybe mud brick just wasn't any good for making palaces.

Kullervo imagined other buildings like this one, standing in other places where they hadn't been meant to go, in all the

other countries the Amoranis had conquered. Little pieces of
Amoran, reminding everyone who had built them and why.

The palace might have been out of place, but it was certainly
beautiful. Kullervo allowed himself to be led off with Senneck
to his quarters, which were big and airy, and attended by a pair
of . . . slaves.

Kullervo had never seen a slave before. These looked
healthy and well-fed, and along with the metal collars that
marked them as slaves, they wore clothes that looked well-
made and clean. They said nothing but provided Kullervo and
Senneck with food and drink before quietly retreating.

Kullervo had been warned to be ready for this sort of thing,
but he was still shocked. The slaves had both been Amorani,
which surprised him. He had expected Northerners, since in
Cymria they were the only people ever to be kept as slaves.

"The Amorani are different," Senneck told him when he
remarked on it. "They will enslave any kind of human, including their own." She yawned, and lay down on the rough wool-
len pad provided for her.

"I wish I could free them," said Kullervo, looking in the
direction the slaves had gone.

"You cannot," said Senneck. "And it would be bad manners
to try. Besides, I do not think they need your help. They were
not sick or hurt."

"Yes, but they're *slaves*," said Kullervo. "It's not fair . . ."

"They have accepted their place in life," said Senneck. "As
we all should."

"I suppose." Kullervo flopped down on his own bed and
tried some of the fruit that had been laid out for him. His teeth
had been broken in captivity, but they had recovered as much as
they ever would. He could eat properly again, anyway.

The fruit was unfamiliar, and he didn't like it much until he
worked out not to eat the skin, and after that, it was delicious.
When he was finished, he put the mangled remains aside as
politely as possible and lay back to rest.

He had been on board ship for so long that the bed felt as if
it were rocking underneath him, but that only helped send him
to sleep faster. Inva would be doing the talking first, and for
now he could afford a nap.

* * *

He slept deeply, and dreamed of Laela and a shadow. The shadow was in the shape of a person—a man or a woman, Kullervo couldn't tell. It wrapped dark arms around Laela, but whether to embrace her or smother her, he didn't know.

He woke up shivering, and the dream faded slowly. Senneck was where she had been, apparently sleeping, and the shadows on the walls had moved.

Kullervo sat up and rubbed his face. He spotted a jug of water and helped himself to a cupful. While he was drinking it, someone coughed politely outside.

Senneck woke up instantly.

"Come in," said Kullervo.

Inva appeared. When she was a slave, her head had been shaved; her hair had grown back now, but she had kept it short. The sunlight from the window highlighted a touch of grey among the black.

"My Lord," she said, bowing. "Holy One." She bowed again, to Senneck.

Kullervo put his cup down and stood up. "How are things, Inva?"

"They are well," she said, in a formal Amorani accent. "Skarok and I have spoken with the Prince and with his partner, Zekh. I have given them the message from the Queen and described the situation in our country as far as I was allowed. Now they ask to see you and Senneck, as I have told them that you are more important than I or Skarok."

Kullervo smiled to himself. Inva's stiff, formal speech had become very familiar by now, and he had decided that he liked it about her. "Thank you. Does he want to see us right now?"

"Yes." Inva allowed herself a small smile in return. "His curiosity is piqued."

"We'll come straightaway, then," said Kullervo.

Senneck had been listening, and she stood up at once to show she was ready.

"We will show you the way," said Inva.

Outside, Skarok was waiting. He led the way with his partner beside him and haughtily avoided looking at the two misfits following him. Thankfully, though he must know that Kullervo had been the male griffin who had rivalled him for Senneck's affections, he hadn't said anything and had left Kullervo alone. Kullervo kept nervously back from him anyway.

The palace interior was pleasantly airy and well lit, with arched doorways that matched the glassless windows. The air smelt of cool stone and unfamiliar plants that grew in a courtyard they passed along the way; Kullervo, whose sense of smell had always been a little more sensitive than that of an ordinary human, inhaled it very happily.

Inva took them to a large chamber not too far away. It was much bigger than Kullervo's guest room and had a huge, vaulted ceiling. Kullervo guessed it must be underneath one of the domes he had seen from outside.

Inside, Prince Akhane and his partner were waiting. The griffin, Zekh, was a slim, dark brown griffin of the smaller Amorani breed. He sat grooming himself idly on a richly coloured carpet, while his partner sat cross-legged on a cushion.

Inva announced the two newcomers and retreated, leaving Kullervo to approach with Senneck.

The Prince had stood up to welcome his guests, and he smiled at them both in a friendly way. "Come, my Lord Kullervo," he said, in very good Cymrian. "Come and sit with me. And you, Holy One . . ."

Zekh had not stood up. He turned his head toward Senneck. "I greet you as one griffin to another," he said lazily. "Rest with me while our humans talk."

Senneck inclined her head politely. "I shall be honoured, Zekh."

Kullervo took the cushion offered to him, opposite the Prince, who resumed his own seat. "I'm honoured to meet you, Prince Akhane," he said, using griffish.

"And I am also honoured," said Akhane. He was the same handsome Amorani who had greeted them at the harbour, Kullervo noticed.

"If you prefer to speak in the holy language, I have no objections," the Prince added.

"I'd like that, thank you," said Kullervo, still using griffish. Senneck had advised him to do so. Amoranis were sun worshippers, like the Southerners in Cymria, and they, too, revered the winged man. Therefore, Senneck had pointed out, it would be more fitting if he spoke the griffish language that Amoranis believed was sacred.

"So tell me," said Akhane. "The Lady Inva thinks it is vital that I speak with you. Can I ask you why, Lord Kullervo?" He looked and sounded very relaxed, but his dark Amorani eyes stayed fixed on Kullervo, summing him up.

Kullervo decided to get straight to the point. "You know about the war in my homeland," he said. "Inva told you?"

"Yes," said Akhane. "She told me that King Arenadd is dead and that my bride has taken his place, but that his cousin objects and means to tell her so with force."

"Exactly," said Kullervo. "But there's more to this." He leaned forward. "Queen Laela sent Inva as her diplomat, but I'm the one she really sent. Not to talk to the Empire, but just to talk to you."

Akhane leaned forward in return, listening intently. "Yes? What message does my bride have for me?"

Kullervo took a deep breath. "She needs your help, in more ways than one. So far she's been ruling alone. She needs a consort. Needs heirs."

"Needs help to fight her enemies, you mean," said Akhane.

Kullervo smiled. "Any help is good help."

Akhane chuckled. "I am willing to go to your country, and more than willing to become Queen Laela's consort and father to her children. But you must understand, I am only a younger son. I do not have great wealth or an army of my own. My help in warfare would have very little worth—far less than would be worth the trouble of coming all the way to Maijan."

"She knows that," said Kullervo. "We both do. But it's not military help that we need."

"Oh?" Akhane cocked his head. "What can a minor Prince do for you, then?"

Flatter him, Senneck had said.

Tell him what he wants yeh to, Laela had advised.

"It's said that you're a clever man, Prince Akhane," said Kullervo, who was already willing to believe it. "It's also said that you're learned."

Akhane shrugged. "I know what is written in books."

"But you have a great interest in magic," said Kullervo. "And other mysterious things. Is that true as well?"

A frown. "It is true. I told my bride that I had always believed that it is not only griffins that can use magic, and that was the truth."

"You were right. And that's why we need you."

"Yes?"

"Queen Laela's cousin, Saeddryn," said Kullervo. "The one making the rebellion. She has magic. Or power, anyway."

Akhane looked skeptical. "What power is this?"

"The power of the Night God." Kullervo used a hushed voice without quite meaning to. "She's the walking dead. It's happened before, with other people. The Night God chooses people who are dying and uses a griffin to bring them back with magic. After that, they have to do whatever she wants; she appears to them in dreams and visions and gives them orders, and if they don't obey, she takes their power away, and they're dead forever. They can't be killed with ordinary weapons, and they heal very fast. They can disappear into the shadows, and they use that power to hunt people down—people the Night God wants dead. The Night God wants Laela dead, and if someone doesn't stop Saeddryn for good, she won't stand a chance. But nobody knows how. So we thought . . . maybe you might help us find a way."

He had wondered how Akhane would react to all this. With laughter, maybe, or anger that anyone would expect him to believe such a ridiculous story.

The Prince did neither. He sat very still for a good long while, his face unreadable.

Finally, he said, "You say this has happened before?"

"Yes," said Kullervo. "At least once that we know of."

"And what happened to this one, this . . . ?"

"He was called the Shadow That Walks," said Kullervo. "He died."

"How?"

"He disobeyed the Night God," said Kullervo.

Akhane rubbed his chin. "And what would make such a man defy his own maker?"

Kullervo shifted uncomfortably; he hadn't meant to go into this. "She ordered him to kill his own daughter. He refused, and she killed him for it."

"Ah." Akhane smiled very slightly. "Then we know now how Queen Laela found her throne."

"Wait, how did—I never said—" Kullervo stammered, panicking.

To his credit, Akhane didn't laugh. "We had often wondered how a man said to be forty years old looked as young as his own daughter. So now the gift has passed to his cousin, you say."

"Yes," said Kullervo. "And we need to kill her. For good, this time."

"May I ask why you are so certain that she is what you say?"

"I can answer for him," Senneck interrupted.

Akhane looked toward her. "Speak, Holy One."

Senneck extended her talons. They were grey and gleamed dully against the red weave of the carpet. "I killed Saeddryn Taranisäii with these very talons. I tore her so badly that her body nearly came apart. But the next day, she was whole again, and moving about, and she nearly killed me in return. I have seen her vanish into darkness with my own eyes."

"And so have I," said Kullervo. He indicated a scar on the side of his neck. "She gave me this."

"Hm." Akhane shook his head slowly, as if there were too much knowledge in there that he couldn't make fit with everything else he knew. He looked up. "How do I know that this is true?"

"What?" Kullervo stared blankly. "Why would we make something like that up?"

"You must understand me," the Prince said quickly, "I have spent half of my life studying the unexplained. I have chased after such stories again and again, in many different countries, and every time, I have found nothing but lies and superstition. How can I know that this is not the same?"

"We saw it ourselves!" said Kullervo, outraged. "This isn't just a *story*! I saw her, I *fought* her, I nearly died!"

"I am sorry," said Akhane. "But I have heard others make claims that they, too, were there, that they, too, saw something they insisted was magical."

"All right, then." Kullervo had been warned that something like this might happen, and now that it had, he would have to use his secret weapon. It was one of the main reasons Laela had sent him away—that and the fact that he would be safe from Saeddryn here. "I understand," he said. "I really do. This story sounds ridiculous, you're right. So you're just going to have to take my word for it. And my word is worth more than . . . than a human's."

Akhane looked bemused. "Human, you say?"

"Yes." Kullervo stood up. "I'm not human, Akhane. Let me show you, but . . . don't be afraid." He unfastened the front of his tunic and let it slide onto the floor.

His wings unfurled. He had spent the last few days encouraging them to grow feathers—something he wouldn't have been able to do before Senneck's intervention. By now, they were an impressive sight. Mottled black and grey pinions opened out like fingers, managing to hide the fact that Kullervo had to strain just to unfold the wings and could never have used them to fly in this shape.

At the sight of them, Akhane's cool exterior finally cracked. He stood upright with astonishing speed, while behind him Zekh hissed loudly in shock.

"It's all right," Kullervo said hastily. "I'm not dangerous."

Akhane took one, very careful step toward him. "This . . ." He abruptly broke off into Amorani, mumbling something Kullervo couldn't catch or understand. He held up his hands, palms together, and returned to griffish. "Winged man . . . griffin man . . . most high sacred one . . ."

Kullervo hated himself for what he did next, but he knew he had to do it. "The Shadow That Walks is an enemy to life," he said. "And an enemy to Xanathus. She must be destroyed. If you won't believe my word as a man, then believe my word as the winged man."

Akhane reverently averted his eyes. "I will, Sacred One. I will come with you at once, and bring every fighting man under my command. We can use my own ship, which is much faster than the one that brought you here."

"We'll do that," Kullervo nodded. "But please keep this a secret. Don't tell anyone what I am."

"I will not say a word," Akhane said at once.

"Good." Kullervo saw Senneck looking at him with great satisfaction and hid his own unhappiness. He hated this, hated doing this to other people. He was not a holy man, he was not a sacred messenger from Gryphus. He was an ugly mishmash of two species that had never been meant to mix, and he would never fully belong in any world. But he wanted the life he did have to be a true one, and this was not it. Pretending to be human was fine, but pretending to be *this* . . .

Only the thought of the good he would be doing stopped him from saying anything.

Akhane was watching him, and though he looked afraid, his eyes were shining. "Thank you, sacred messenger," he said.

Kullervo blinked. "For what?"

"With one visit, you have fulfilled my life's dream. You have shown me a man who is more than a man—yourself."

"Not quite," said Kullervo. "I'm not human." This was more or less true, at least.

"Even so," said Akhane. "You have proven to me that there are magical things in this world that are not griffin or made by griffins."

"Yes . . ." Kullervo smiled. "I suppose that's true. And you're right. There are other powers in this world that don't come from griffins. They're called the gods. They're more powerful than griffins . . . and much more dangerous."

"Agreed." Akhane nodded. "At least this Night God is dangerous. Now I must go with you, and we must work together, to find a way to defeat my bride's enemy. That is not a thing I will argue against." His eyes narrowed. "We in Amoran know that it is not meant for the dead to walk. It is against the laws of life, which are the laws of Xanathus, and this is why he has sent you to punish this offence."

No, thought Kullervo. *Laela is the one who was sent. She stopped our father, when no-one else could. But nobody would believe she's the one because she doesn't look special or act special. She didn't even kill Arenadd by fighting him. She killed him by making him love her.*

"The heart," he said aloud. "The heart is the weakness, I'm sure of it. Maybe in more ways than one . . ."

Akhane looked slightly puzzled. "What do you mean, Sacred One?"

Kullervo shook himself. "Never mind." He put his tunic back on, tucking his wings away underneath it with difficulty. "I'll leave you now. You'll need time to get ready."

"Indeed." Akhane glanced at a nearby bookshelf. "I am only sorry that I have not brought more of my books with me from Xanthium, but I will search through what I have here for clues and decide which to bring. I must also speak with my friends and see which of them will come."

"Take all the time you need," said Kullervo. "In the meantime, I wouldn't mind seeing more of this island. Since I'll probably never come back here . . ."

"Of course." Akhane stood up, and bowed. "It has been the great honour of my life to meet you, Lord Kullervo."

"And you," said Kullervo, and as he said it, he felt the beginnings of a great surge of gratitude and relief that would stay with him for the rest of that day.

6

Lost

Skenfrith was lost.

Myfina saw it for herself through the window of the infirmary. She had spent the battle there, even after the half-breed had come and gone. She was no fighter, and besides, what could she possibly do against griffins? Caedmon and her partner Garsh had both commanded her to stay away, and she had comforted herself by thinking of Heath. He needed her to watch over him.

He was still very ill; he had barely stirred during the confrontation with Laela. Now he lay on his back, face bandaged, sleeping through the destruction of Skenfrith.

What Myfina saw through that window made her feel just as ill and kept her just as still.

She saw griffins everywhere. Griffins diving and lunging at each other, griffins grappling with each other in the sky. Griffins tearing open buildings to get at the people inside them. Griffins rampaging through the streets, destroying everything in their paths. Houses burned or collapsed.

People died. Griffins died.

Skenfrith died.

Seeing all of that was more than enough to tell Myfina the awful truth. But she didn't know for certain that the war was lost until she saw the monstrous dark griffin rise up over the burning city. There was a human sitting on his back, and it wasn't Saeddryn.

The Mighty Skandar was back, and it was he who had brought the Unpartnered.

That was when Myfina knew everything was lost.

She wondered, dully, if Garsh was still alive and if he would come to find her. If not, then she had little chance of getting out of the city.

Either way, she knew it would be best to stay where she was. Garsh knew she was here, and so far the tower had stayed more or less untouched.

And she would not leave Heath.

She went back to check on him. Iorwerth's body lay on the bed next to his, where she had put it. Iorwerth had betrayed the North by allying with the half-breed, but he had been a great hero in the past, and Myfina hadn't had the heart to leave him lying on the floor where he'd fallen.

Heath's forehead was burning hot, but he stirred when Myfina touched him.

"Dark," he mumbled through his bandages. "Dark . . ."

Myfina wet a cloth and dabbed away the sweat. "It's all right," she told him. "I'm here."

She glanced toward the door. The only thing she had to be grateful for was that there weren't likely to be any hostile humans about. The Queen hadn't had the foresight to bring any human fighters with her; the Unpartnered were faster, but not exactly suited for entering buildings or taking prisoners. The half-breed didn't seem interested in prisoners anyway.

Myfina sat down by Heath's bed and wondered how long it would be before the Unpartnered decided to come into the tower and how long it would take for them to find her.

"Myfina."

She looked up sharply, and nearly fell backward off her chair when Saeddryn slid out of the shadows. "My Lady!" she exclaimed.

Saeddryn came straight to her side. "Come," she said. "I'm here to get ye out of this forsaken city. Just take my hand."

"What about Heath?" Myfina asked at once.

Saeddryn looked at him and shook her head. "I can't take him through the shadows. He'd die."

"But if we don't get him out of here—"

"He's probably gonna die anyway," Saeddryn said bitterly.

"Like everyone else. But if he comes this way, he'll die for certain. I made him this weak in the first place by draggin' him with me."

"I'm not going, then," said Myfina. "I'm staying with him."

"Don't be stupid," Saeddryn snapped. "Caedmon needs ye. Now come on. Heath can take his chances." She ignored Myfina's argument and took her by the arm. Myfina tried to break free, but Saeddryn's grip was like frozen steel.

An instant later, darkness took them both.

L aela and Skandar returned to Malvern together, along with most of the Unpartnered. Neither of them had seen Kaanee, and neither of them expected to. Iorwerth was dead, and without him, the former leader of the Unpartnered had lost all his status. There was nothing anybody could do for him now.

Laela had spent the flight thinking, ignoring her injuries and the terror lurking around the edges of her mind. The moment her feet hit the floor of Skandar's nest, she was out of the room and off into the Eyrie, tracking people down and giving commands.

During her time spent trapped in Malvern, she had not been idle. The slaves she had brought back from Amoran still lived in the city, and she had found uses for them. Some had been given jobs as builders and craftspeople, some in the Eyrie as scribes. All of them had useful skills. But not all of them were simple workers. In Amoran, it was the practice to train some slaves as fighters. Laela had briefly employed one as a bodyguard. He was dead now, but there were others like him left. Plenty of them. She had long since realised that she would need a human army, and they were it.

She sent for them now, under the leadership of the commanders they had had in Amoran. They would march on Skenfrith.

Laela ordered them to search the city and arrest any rebels they found left. But she also sent builders. The core of the rebel movement had been destroyed, or close to it, and Skenfrith would never be their base again. Her freed slaves would rebuild it, and occupy it, and when they had done that, there would be no more need for the Unpartnered.

Laela watched them march out through the city and smiled

with grim satisfaction. That was it, done and finished. She had
torn the heart out of the resistance, and she would see to it that
it never regrew. Once she had rested and healed, she would go
with Skandar and visit every major city in the North. Her personal army would soon have a presence in every single one of
them, and she would appoint new governors to keep everything
in line. Caedmon and his mother would not sneak back in and
spread their lies again, and if they couldn't do that, then they
would never be able to gather the support they needed to challenge her.

She scratched at her upper arm and lost her smile. It was not
done, of course. It would never end completely, not until Caedmon and Saeddryn were both dead. Caedmon would be easy
enough, but Saeddryn . . .

Her arm still itched. She scratched harder, grimacing. Saeddryn was the real danger, and Laela would never be safe until
she was dead . . . or whatever.

The itch persisted, until Laela scratched too hard and it
turned into pain. She groaned and rolled up her sleeve to see.
When she did, she groaned again.

The tattoos on her upper arm, the ones she had been given at
her womanhood ceremony, looked very wrong. By now they
should have healed, and she should be seeing blue spiral patterns from her elbow to her shoulder.

Instead, she saw vague blue lines, mostly hidden under
lumps of swollen red skin. Her scratching had made it bleed,
but the blood looked thin and sickly.

"Gods damn it! Stupid . . . I didn't even want the things!"

She started to head for the infirmary, but stopped herself
and spat a swear-word. The tattoos weren't just decoration; they
were the signs that she was a true Northern woman and therefore allowed to rule her people. But if they were infected, then
what did that say? Nothing good, that was certain.

She covered them up again and decided to make sure they
stayed that way. She could treat them herself, probably.

After a moment's thought, she made for the infirmary anyway. Better have her other wounds looked at.

The doctors fussed over her, as she'd expected, all false concern over the cut on her face. She growled at them to get to
work and sat impatiently while they cleaned and bandaged and

recited the proper blessings to make them heal properly. As if the Night God cared. The miserable hag was probably the one who'd made the tattoos turn bad.

Afterward, she headed off down the tower. Skandar was asleep, and she should be resting, too, but there was something else she wanted to do first, even if it felt hopeless.

She hadn't seen her real partner in far too long, and it was past time she at least tried to find out what was happening to her. Oeka could project her mind wherever she wanted to nowadays, but Laela knew where her body was, at least, and that should be a reasonable place to start. Assuming Oeka wasn't still attacking anyone who came too close.

She passed the door to the library on her way down. It was ajar, and when she came close to it, something made her stop. The back of her head tingled. She poked her head through the door, and the tingle increased.

Moving carefully, with her hand close to the sickle in her belt, she went in.

The library was dimly lit, but there was someone in there, sitting at a table in the corner and scribbling something in a book. At first glance he just looked like another scholar, and Laela was about to leave, until she spotted the thing that made her tingle turn into a shiver.

The vague, ghostlike shape of a small griffin. It had colour, but its form was irregular, warping and shifting like a reflection in moving water. Laela knew that it wasn't a real griffin. It was only the thought of one, an illusory image created by a mind whose powers had been magically enhanced beyond anything that was supposed to exist.

Oeka.

The imaginary picture of her drifted around the ceiling, turning and twisting lazily as if it were swimming in the air. Its wings opened sometimes, but of course it didn't need them to fly.

Laela watched it for a while, almost marvelling. She had never imagined anything like this before, and nor had anyone else. As far as she knew, this was the first time it had ever happened.

"Oeka?" she called eventually. "What are yeh doin'?"

No response.

"No words," the writer in the corner said unexpectedly.

"Huh?" Laela turned to look at him. "What was that?"

"No words," the writer said again, scrawling away feverishly in his book. "No words, no words."

Laela moved closer, frowning. "What are yeh on about? What are yeh doin' . . . ?"

The man's hair and beard were wild and ragged, his face pale and the eyes sunken and red-rimmed. He didn't seem to see her at all. His eyes stared at nothing while his hands worked away with a broken pen, scratching something onto the open pages of a torn book.

Laela found the name somewhere, but saying it was almost too much. *"Yorath?"*

Her former tutor didn't look at her. "All past," he said hoarsely. "All gone. But it must be known, must be, must remember, yes yes. Can't forget. Can't ever forget."

"Yorath," Laela said again. "What did she do to yeh? Oh Yorath . . . oh no . . ." Her throat thickened with tears, and she turned and shouted at the image of Oeka. "What did yeh do? *What did yeh do to him?*"

Oeka did not reply. In his corner, Yorath kept on writing away.

Laela's legs weakened, and she nearly stumbled onto her knees. She put her hands over her face and mouthed nonsense that turned into sobs, and tears wet her fingers. It was too much, all of it. Was this her world now? Death, and madness, and nothing else?

I'm cursed, she thought. *We're all cursed. Everyone's gone. Dead, or left, or insane.*

She wanted to scream, or cry, or break something. Only the recollection that she was Queen made her pull herself together. Everyone was gone except her, and it was up to her to stay strong. She had done the same before, when Arenadd was still there. She had to do it again now.

Feeling dull and exhausted, she went to Yorath's side and looked at what he was writing. Then she saw he wasn't writing at all, but drawing. He had made a crude ink sketch of thirteen weird elongated objects, arranged in a circle, and there were people there in the centre, a dark spot at their feet.

"The stones," Yorath said abruptly, as if he knew she was looking. "The stones of Taranis, the oldest stones. That's where he is, that's where he sleeps, under the stones, that's where the one with Arenadd's face put him, and the woman who was like a serpent, and the griffin who didn't talk watched them, and he laughed at them, and at night the eye watches from the sky but she can't find him, not any more, but she wants him, she wants him back, because she still loves him . . ." He laughed weakly.

"Yorath." Laela touched him on the shoulder. "Yorath, it's all right. Please stop."

He paused then, when she touched him. But only for a moment. His hands had gone all claw-like, and moved as if they didn't belong to him any more. They turned the page, and dipped the pen, and he scribbled on. Writing this time, which Laela wouldn't have been able to read much of even if it had been neater.

"And here, here the white griffin and the black griffin fought, and the city fell down when the sun went dark in the day, yes, everyone knows, but where was Sacddryn? And Nerth and Garnoc and Hafwen, what were they doing? I must see . . . must see them there . . ."

Laela left him to his ravings and looked up at Oeka again. "Oeka? Oeka, please . . ."

Still no reply, but Laela tried one more time. She closed her eyes, and thought.

Oeka, she shouted in her head, thinking the name as hard as she could. Oeka could sense thoughts. Maybe she could hear them better than words. *Oeka, it's me. It's Laela. Oeka!*

The reply came in her head, as Oeka's voice always did now. But now it sounded faint and distorted, mixed with other voices saying other things. *Laela, I cannot hear you. There are too many of you, they all speak at once. Too many thoughts, too many people . . . I cannot . . .*

The voice faded.

Oeka! Laela thought frantically. *Please, talk to me!*

Oeka's mental presence grew fainter. *I cannot . . . the past is too much, there is too much, I see it too clearly, and I am lost . . .* The other voices grew louder, distorting hers and drowning it out. Laela caught the last of her partner's voice as it vanished, the words coming in snatches. *The past . . . all I see . . . cannot see . . . present . . . lost . . . no . . . !*

The sounds faded away from Laela's mind. She opened her eyes and saw Oeka's image rippling outward, losing its shape.

Everywhere around her, other images flashed in and out of existence. People, griffins, even objects like tables and chairs. She
caught glimpses of people talking, griffins wandering in and
out, furniture moving, books being written. And she saw people
die, trampling those same books as they fought for their lives
and lost them. Blood pooled on the floor and splashed on the
walls, then disappeared. She saw all these snatches of the past
before they vanished, and Oeka's fading shape drifted upward
through the ceiling and was gone.

Only Yorath remained, writing away endlessly at his table.
But Laela knew she couldn't do anything for him.

She left the library silently, closing the door behind her, and
went back up the tower to her own rooms. Yorath was lost, and so
was Oeka. Senneck had been right. No griffin was meant to have
this kind of power. She had said that Oeka would be destroyed
by it, and she had.

But as long as she was still alive, Laela knew that Saeddryn
would never dare come back into the Eyrie. Not after what had
happened last time.

Laela went through her bedroom and peeked into Skandar's
nest. The giant griffin was fast asleep in his straw, exhausted by
a hard fight and a long flight. His muscular flanks moved
steadily in and out as he breathed, and his huge beak rested on
his talons.

The sight of him made Laela feel better. More confident, at
least. As long as she had Skandar and Oeka, she was safe. They
would protect her together, until Kullervo returned, then they
would work together to destroy Saeddryn once and for all. And
with the Mighty Skandar beside her, even Saeddryn was barely
a threat.

7

We Can Be Heroes

Heath heard Myfina leave, but he was too weak to move, or even call a goodbye. He had no idea how long he had been lying here, or what might be going on outside. Only the belief that he was under Caedmon's protection had made him feel safe enough not to struggle. He had done his duty, had proven his loyalty, and for now there was nothing more he needed to do. So he let himself slip away, surrendering to the sweating, blurry grip of fever.

He slept most of the time—or stayed awake and hallucinated. It was often hard to tell the difference. But he saw things either way. He dreamed about his father, who looked like a tall man with a shadow for a face. He saw the Mighty Skandar, but he was tiny, a kitten with wings. A snake slithered over his face and felt so convincingly cold and smooth that he tried to swat it away. But Myfina came to stop him, and her voice and touch woke him up from what he hadn't even realised was a dream.

Sometimes he heard a voice, mumbling a constant stream of gibberish.

Eventually, he realised it was his own.

In time—he never knew just how much time—the dreams became less real. The fever was receding. He began to sleep—proper, restful sleep that left him feeling stronger when he was awake. Once during that time he became vaguely aware that something was happening—he heard sounds coming from somewhere outside. But they seemed muted, and he dismissed them as another dream and slept again.

One day, he woke up yet again. But this time it was different. His head felt clear for the first time in . . . in . . . however long it had been. He blinked and moved his head; his mouth felt dry and sticky, and he couldn't see properly. He tried lifting his arms— they moved, but so weakly and slowly that for a while he thought they must have heavy sheets draped over them.

He lay there for a while, resting and trying to put his mind back together. He dozed briefly, but his body seemed to have had enough sleep at last. His mind must have grown bored with being cloudy, too, because it cleared even further, and let him look around. That was when he realised that he could only see out of one eye, but he felt too dopey and sleepy to be afraid.

He lifted a clumsy hand to his face instead. His fingers touched rough cloth. *Bandages,* he thought. The wound underneath ached savagely. Fear only made it worse. *What's happened to my face?*

Ultimately, that fear was enough to make him move. He dragged himself out of bed with a strength that surprised him and hastily patted himself down. Arms, legs, stomach—all still there, thank goodness. His stomach did feel sore and fallen in, though. Food would be the cure there. But his face . . .

Squinting awkwardly through one eye, he stumbled around the room in search of something reflective, or something edible. He found a stack of clothes left on a table—his own. Someone had put a nightshirt on him at some point.

He reclaimed his clothes and put them on with fumbling hands. An unpleasant whiff told him that they hadn't been cleaned, and he grimaced.

"Argh!"

He waited until the line of pain over his nose and cheek went away, and ate some stale bread that someone had left lying around, feeling rather miffed that nobody had been there when he woke up to pat him on the forehead and tell him to rest and so on. He was sure that someone *had* been there, though maybe he'd only been imagining it was Myfina. Surely she had better things to do. Then again, she'd left, so maybe she'd gone off to do whatever those better things were.

As it was, there was nobody about. Heath sat down for a while to rest and lace up his boots. Maybe he should go and look around, assuming he wasn't hideously deformed now and people wouldn't just run away. He should probably look at that first.

There were no mirrors around, of course—those were so expensive that only high-ranking griffiners usually owned them. But when Heath checked the inside pocket of his tunic, he found his own precious mirror still there.

Rather than hideous, he looked slightly ridiculous. The bandages made a white stripe right across his face, covering his eye, nose, and one corner of his mouth. They looked clean, at least. He supposed he should probably leave them on, but . . . the fear over what might be underneath was too much to resist.

Very carefully, hesitating when the pain threatened to flare up again, he peeled the bandages away.

The wound began on the bridge of his nose, dangerously close to the corner of his left eye, and ended on his cheek. It was swollen and red, crusted with yellowy scabs, but it was much smaller than he had expected. More importantly, it didn't itch and burn any more. He rubbed cautiously at it and winced as a scab broke away, and blood appeared. But it was *blood*, at least, clean blood. The wound would leave a scar, but the infection was gone. He should recover. And even if it would mean having a big scar on his face . . . well, it would come with a good story, at least. How many other people could say they had been scarred by the Shadow That Walked? Not many living people, definitely.

Feeling much better, he put the bandage aside and smoothed down his clothes. He should find some clean ones before he went to find Caedmon and find out what was going on.

His relieved feeling and simple plan stayed with him as he made for the door. But both of them were torn away when he trod in something sticky. He glanced down and saw a patch of something on the floor, something dark and reddish brown. It almost looked like . . .

. . . blood.

Heath's skin prickled. He turned quickly, and saw more of the stuff, making a trail past his bed. It led to the next bed along—which was empty now, but the sheets were rumpled and stained. But there was more than enough blood around for him to know that whoever had left it hadn't got off that bed under his own power. And nobody, he thought nervously, nobody had changed the sheets or cleaned the floor.

Heart fluttering, he made for the door and opened it.

There was a corpse in the hallway.

Heath's heart started to flutter. He didn't stop to look closer at the body; the smell was enough to tell him it wasn't about to get up again. There were more dead people farther on, lying on the floor or propped up against the walls. He turned a corner, and sunlight hit his face. But it wasn't coming from a window. Someone . . . *something*, had torn a hole in the wall. Icy wind stirred his hair as he skirted around the crumbling gap in the floor. From here, he had a magnificent view of the city. But it only took a glance to tell him what had happened.

Smoke rose into the air from several different places, breaking and drifting apart as the griffins flew through it. Dozens of griffins. He saw them everywhere, perching on rooftops, flying over the walls, walking through the streets. None of them had riders. Heath knew there were a handful of unpartnered griffins living in Skenfrith. But these . . .

"The Unpartnered," he mumbled aloud. "Oh no . . ."

The fear grew in him, dull and numbing. He moved on through the tower, hurrying now despite his spinning head. But everywhere he went, he saw the same things, more and more of them. Dead people, lying where they had fallen. Furniture shattered, floors torn up, walls and doors broken down. Blood everywhere. He even came across one or two dead griffins, and those were the worst. Those were the first corpses that he saw torn open and mutilated, with the rib cages stripped and poking out through the withered hide like teeth. Something had been eating them, and he knew exactly what.

"Oh gods . . ."

He stopped by every dead human he found, feeling sick to his stomach, and the fear grew and grew that sooner or later he would find one that he recognised. Caedmon, or Myfina, or even Lady Isolde, who hated him. And if Skenfrith was destroyed, then they must be here, somewhere, unless they had been eaten as well.

Horror, and the lingering traces of fever, nearly made him vomit. But he took several deep breaths and went on. He knew what he had to do. If there were people here left alive, then they might need his help. If not, then he had to escape the city. Staying where he was would mean death.

Searching the whole tower took a long time, especially since he had to stop and rest every so often, but he managed it eventually. He didn't find anyone. The only living thing he saw was a griffin. Thank the Night God, it was asleep and he managed to sneak away without waking it up.

That was all. No Caedmon, no Myfina, no Saeddryn. He did find some people he recognised—some he knew by name, some only by sight. Caedmon's followers, all of them, and some of his councillors, all torn apart by talons and beaks.

A terrible loneliness and despair came over him. Was he the only one? The only survivor, the only living human being in this ruined tower? The only one of Caedmon's friends left?

No, he told himself. Caedmon wasn't here, and that meant he could still be alive. Heath vowed silently that he would keep going until he found him.

He rested again and began to climb back down the tower. If there were other survivors, then maybe they had taken shelter *under* the tower, in the underground storage chambers. He'd been down there once, and he knew the entrances were too small for griffins to fit.

Going back down the tower felt even more laborious than coming up it. His legs were starting to feel wobbly, and his dizziness started to get so bad that he even considered finding a bed and snatching some sleep. He took a few more deep breaths instead.

There was another problem. The sleeping griffin was still there, and with no way around it, he had to try and sneak past again. And, at first, it looked as if he was going to succeed. As far as he could tell, he never put a foot wrong, and never made a sound.

The griffin's eyes opened and looked straight at him.

Heath froze.

The eyes focused, and a low rasp came from somewhere inside the creature's throat.

Heath was not a griffiner, or a noble of any sort. Despite his fine clothes and refined speech, he had been born a commoner. He knew almost nothing about griffins and how to behave around them.

Which was why, when the griffin started to lift its head, he did what someone like Caedmon never would, and ran away.

The griffin, seeing movement, did what any predator would and bounded after him.

All of a sudden, Heath's dizzy head and aching legs meant nothing. Dodging broken tables and dead people, he sprinted down the spiralling corridors faster than he had ever thought he could go. The thudding paws of the griffin were so loud that they always sounded as if they were right behind him. He could hear the thing's breathing and nearly convinced himself he could hear its heartbeat as well. But it was only his own heart, thumping sickeningly in his ears.

Panicked thoughts raced through his head. He had to find somewhere to hide, somewhere the griffin couldn't follow. The storage chambers, if he could only get there before . . .

Indoors, he should have been faster than something as big as a griffin. But he wasn't. The griffin couldn't dodge the way he could, but it didn't have to. It just ploughed through whatever got in its way, and when Heath managed to slam a door in its face, it broke it down with a blow of its beak. The only advantage being indoors gave him was that there wasn't enough room for the griffin to make a leap and land on top of him.

But Heath was weak, and the griffin was strong, and that was enough. In his terror, Heath took a wrong turn and in an instant the griffin was on him. It backed him into a corner, blocking him when he tried to get past it and finally knocking him down with an irritable huff.

Heath tried to drag himself away, but there was nowhere to go. Visions of broken bodies flashed across his mind, and he covered his face and braced himself for the end.

Flanks heaving like a bellows, the griffin shoved at him with its beak. He felt it touching him and cringed when its hot breath blew over his skin. The sharp tip of its beak nipped at him, and he groaned. But the death-blow didn't come. He risked a look and saw the beast looking down at him through a pair of huge orange eyes.

"Er . . ."

The griffin cocked its head. *"Hssch,"* it hissed.

Heath thought fast. It wasn't killing him. It seemed to be inspecting him for some reason—now it started sniffing at him again.

In his old life as a professional thief and liar, he had mingled with many different people. One or two of them had been griffiners. And, thank gods, he had taken the time to learn a thing or two from them.

"Er," he said again. "Er . . . oh shitting gods . . . er . . . *eeshesh?*" The griffish word felt wrong in his mouth and sounded even wronger, but he thought it meant "friend."

The griffin pulled its head back. *"Aaaak,"* it croaked.

"Eeshesh," Heath said again. "Er . . . *keek yaa kran ee."* "Do no harm." Or so he hoped.

The griffin huffed at him and sat back on its haunches. It made some sounds he couldn't even decipher, let alone understand.

Very carefully, Heath stood up. *"Eeshesh. Esh kee kraa."* He finished by clicking his teeth, and bowed, having just promised to do whatever the griffin wanted. In theory. The griffin eyed him. It was male, judging by the ear tufts, and very unusually coloured—in shades of yellow and brown, with striking spotted hindquarters. He had never seen a spotted griffin, or one with such an attractive coat.

The spotted griffin made more sounds that might have been speech and put its head on one side.

"I'm Heath," said Heath, who had exhausted the limit of his griffish by now and felt some comment was required. When the griffin just stared at him, he touched his own chest in the universal gesture for "me," and said "Heath."

"Heeth," said the griffin. It—he—touched himself on the chest with his beak, and made a sound.

Heath looked blank.

"Eck-hoo," said the griffin, more slowly. *"Eck-hoo!"*

"That's your name?" said Heath.

The griffin clicked his beak. *"Eckhoo,"* he said yet again.

Very cautiously, Heath allowed himself a smile. "Echo, is it? Your name's Echo?"

The griffin prodded him with his beak. *"Heeth,"* he said.

Heath tried not to flinch. "Pleased to meet you, Echo. And, er, thank you for not killing me. Can I go now?"

Echo didn't reply, of course, but he let Heath walk around him and move away. Then he started to follow.

Heath knew he was being followed—a griffin walking in your footsteps wasn't exactly easy to miss. But since this one seemed friendly enough, he decided to keep on going and hope he would lose interest.

Echo, however, had other ideas. He overtook Heath in a few steps, and began to crowd into him, herding him into the nearest room.

"What is it?" Heath asked nervously. "You want me to go with you? All right, I'm with you . . ."

He let Echo push him into the room, which turned out to be someone's living quarters. They were empty now, but the furnishings quickly told him it had been meant for a griffiner. Echo kept going on into the adjoining nest chamber. Heath spotted a short sword hanging on the wall and grabbed it before he followed. He'd never used a sword before, but having one in his belt made him feel better.

In the nest chamber, Echo took a drink from the trough before turning back toward the door, where Heath stood. He unhooked something from a peg and dropped it at Heath's feet.

It looked like a pair of belts connected by a pair of long leather straps with loops sewn into them. Heath had seen enough of these to know that it was a griffin harness.

Echo pushed it toward him, so he picked it up.

"You want me to put this on you?"

Echo offered up his neck.

Shrugging, Heath put the harness on—luckily, it was fairly straightforward. He took a lot of care not to buckle it on too tightly; this griffin might have decided not to attack him after all, but even partnered griffins were more than willing to bite their humans. Every griffiner had a few scars from it, which was probably why the griffiners had developed such good methods for treating infected wounds. Heath had a personal reason to be glad about that nowadays.

Echo kept still until the harness was on, and once it was, he lowered his head even farther and bent one foreleg, presenting his shoulders to Heath.

Heath frowned. "What is it? Did I put it on properly?"

Echo shuffled closer to him and gave him a none-too-gentle shove with his shoulder. Heath stumbled, and instinctively grabbed the harness to steady himself. Instantly, Echo jerked away— pulling Heath with him and effectively throwing him over his shoulders. Heath got off instantly, and for a moment he thought

Echo's angry shriek was because of the unwelcome contact, but before he could try and apologise, the griffin was coming at him, turning, bending, displaying his shoulder and back, and finally trying, by shoving, to make Heath fall onto him again.

Heath blanched. "You want me to *get on your back*?"

Echo shoved him again.

Heath felt light-headed. A griffin was trying to make him ride it. Which was impossible, but it was happening anyway, and he was pretty sure this wasn't another fever dream.

In the end, only the thought of what Echo might do if he offended him made Heath obey. He took hold of the harness and put a leg over the griffin's shoulders. Echo straightened up at once, making him fall into place just behind his neck and in front of his wings. Heath settled down there as well as he could and put his hands through the loops in the harness the way he had seen Caedmon and the others do.

Echo didn't wait around to make sure he was comfortable. He walked away, through the nest and out onto the balcony. His shoulder blades, rising and falling with every step, made Heath grimace, but he forgot his discomfort the instant he realised what the spotted griffin was going to do.

"Wait," he said. "Wait, no! I don't want to—*auuaaaaargh*!"

Echo leapt into the sky.

The survivors from Skenfrith took shelter somewhere between the Rivers Nive and Snow, by the eerie shape of a frozen waterfall. Before—long, long ago as it seemed now—Caedmon had told his followers that if disaster struck, this would be the place to regroup. But that had been long ago, when he still had followers, and a city to rule, and a hope of claiming his crown.

Now there was nothing but snow, and silence, and the waterfall trapped by ice before it could flow on toward the Northgate Mountains, and the South.

Caedmon stood beside it, staring expressionlessly at its shining white columns. Beside him, he sensed Shar, standing over him. The griffin's presence was large and warm, and the thought of her loosened the knot in his chest slightly. He still had her. He had lost everything else, but he still had her. He was not alone.

She said nothing, and he didn't try to speak either. What could he possibly say? He had failed her more than anyone else, and nothing anyone said could change that.

Moving slowly and stiffly, he sat down on a rock and did the only thing he could do: wait. His head ached, his ribs throbbed, and his hand was bleeding. He could hear the faint sounds of blood, dripping onto the snow to turn it red.

He didn't try and make it stop. *Let me bleed,* he thought.

Beside him, Shar huffed softly.

Caedmon had not expected anyone else to come, but they came. Little by little, in dribs and drabs, they came. Griffiners all of them. Most of them were wounded. But they came to find him, landing in the snow above and around the frozen waterfall. The humans came to him, murmuring his name. Griffins went to Shar, bowing their heads.

Caedmon stood up and did his best to welcome the survivors though his heart twisted even further when he saw how few there were. He recognised most of them, and found himself smiling when he saw one in particular. Lady Isolde, stern-faced as ever, and dignified even though she would never be governor of Skenfrith again.

"I'm so glad to see you," said Caedmon, meaning it.

"And you," Isolde said stiffly. "How long are we going to stay here?"

Caedmon looked away and shook his head. What else could he possibly do? He wasn't going to pretend that they had anywhere else to go.

He was about to go and start helping the wounded, when Shar looked up at the sound of another griffin's wings.

The newcomer came in to land, and in an instant his rider was off his back and running to Caedmon, throwing her arms around him.

The embrace was agony for his ribs, but he held her in return anyway even though his followers were watching. "Myfina."

She was crying. "Caedmon, thank gods you're alive."

Caedmon rested his head on her shoulder. "Myfina, I'm so glad, I . . ." He broke off and let go, feeling his expression hardening. "Did you see anyone else? Did Heath?"

Myfina's eyes were red. "I left him. I'm so sorry, Caedmon, I didn't want to, but she forced me . . ."

"Aye." Saeddryn appeared, gaunt and pale and grim as always. "I got her back t'her partner an' we flew out of there. It was a near thing, too. We had to leave yer friend behind. He was too weak."

Caedmon looked steadily at her. "We owe him a lot. *You* owe him."

"People die," said Saeddryn. "A lot of them did, today."

"But—" Myfina began.

"This is war," Saeddryn snapped at her. "War's a time for tough decisions. An' if ye want *anyone* to live, then ye have t'make them quickly."

The others were all there, moving in closer to listen. Everything being said now was being said publicly. Any weakness would be public as well.

But Caedmon didn't care any more. "Mother, what are we going to do?" he asked, and to his shame he heard his own voice turn thin and afraid, like a little boy's voice, turning to his mother for help.

There was no warmth left in Saeddryn's eye, or in her voice. "Ye are going to lead, Caedmon. Ye are the King here, not me."

"Yes, but—"

"These are yer followers," she said, waving a hand at the little band of lost and wounded griffins and griffiners. "Let them follow ye." She turned and began to walk away.

"Where are you going?" Caedmon called after her.

"To pray," she said briefly, and was gone.

8

Help

Saeddryn did not look back at her son and his friends. There was no point.

She walked through the snow without noticing the cold, her mouth a rigid line. She had let Caedmon lead his rebellion as he saw fit, and now he was facing the consequences. But she couldn't blame him for everything. How could anyone predict Skandar's treachery?

Curse him! He was supposed to be the partner to the Shadow That Walked; that was what he had been *made* for. But after he had brought Saeddryn back, he had had the gall to spurn her and ignore his maker's commands. He had never liked her, she knew. But to turn his back on the Night God, who had given him his massive size and astonishing powers . . . he was as bad as his old partner, with his whims and his weaknesses.

Saeddryn found a clearing out of earshot of the waterfall camp and laboriously searched under the snow for rocks. While she made them into a circle, she felt the hatred eating away at the place where her heart had once beaten. The half-breed had won today, but she would lose. Ultimately, she would lose. Caedmon had been defeated today, not Saeddryn, and if it came to it, Saeddryn was more than happy to forget about his honour and kill the repulsive half-breed brat herself.

When the circle was complete, she knelt in the centre and felt stronger there. She glanced skyward. It wasn't nighttime yet, but the sun was going down. No moonlight, but she would take a chance anyway.

She cut her hand and spilled her blood in the circle, reciting the ancient prayers. Reaching out with love, as the Night God had said she must.

Nothing happened, but Saeddryn did not give in. She stayed in the circle, and chanted and prayed. She sang the sacred songs and blessed each stone with the incantation of the full moon, forgetting everything but her master.

In time, the first stars appeared. After them came the moon. Darkness closed over Saeddryn's eye, and she silently fell forward onto the snow.

Saeddryn . . .

Saeddryn opened her eye and found herself in the dark place where the Night God waited. She knelt at once. "Master."

The Night God looked sad. *Northern blood was spilled today. Faithful blood.*

Saeddryn grimaced. "I know. The Unpartnered are still on *her* side. And . . . Skandar."

I know. The dark griffin has turned on us.

"He should die for this," said Saeddryn.

Skandar is simple-minded, said the Night God. *I cannot force him to understand. He will not let his first human go.*

"They were very close," Saeddryn admitted. "Closer than any partners I ever saw. It was like they were brothers."

It does not matter, said the Night God. *Skandar brought you back, and that is enough. As long as Caedmon survives, this blasphemer can still be defeated.*

"I know," said Saeddryn. "I believe ye." She looked down. "Caedmon made a mistake in Skenfrith, but he did his best. He's only a boy . . ."

A man, the Night God said softly. *You cannot be his mother any more, Saeddryn. He must find his own way.*

"I . . . I tried."

And you did well. But you are his greatest ally now, and you must help him.

"I will, but I need help," said Saeddryn. "From ye, Master. What should I do now? What should *we* do?"

The Night God smiled. *You do not need me. You can do this thing yourself. Use the power that I have given you, Saeddryn.*

"But Caedmon—what should he do?"

Command you.

"To do what?" Saeddryn persisted.

To kill.

"But kill who? Caedmon should kill the half-breed himself, to win his throne. And . . . and there's . . . something in Malvern, something . . . I couldn't . . . can't . . ." Saeddryn couldn't look at her master as she stumbled over her words, hating herself for her weakness.

I understand, said the Night God. *There is a power in Malvern. The half-breed's true partner has done something to herself to make this happen. Even you cannot resist her, as you know now.*

"Then what should I do?" asked Saeddryn. "I can't go into Malvern with that . . . that *thing* there."

Do not be afraid. This griffin has made herself more powerful than any griffin has a right to be, and she will not survive long. Too much magic drains the life from a griffin. She is already barely sane.

Saeddryn nodded. "So if I just bide my time . . ."

The griffin's protection will be gone soon enough. And if the half-breed leaves Malvern again, you may catch her then. But you will need to be stealthy.

"I can do that."

You can, but not in Malvern. You will need a way to watch her. A way to know what she is doing, where she is going.

"A spy?" Saeddryn suggested.

Yes.

Saeddryn found herself thinking of Heath. "It's a good idea, but if they were caught . . ."

The Night God smiled. *Do not be afraid. I have a spy for you, one who will never be caught. A faithful companion, to help you in any way you ask.*

Saeddryn looked up. "Who?"

My servant, said the Night God, standing aside. *I offer him to you.*

Saeddryn stood up. *"Arenadd?"*

Arenadd's shoulders were hunched, his eyes fixed on the ground. He said nothing.

Go with her, the Night God commanded. *Follow her into the world of the living, and obey her every wish without question.*

Arenadd glanced at her but stayed silent.

Saeddryn, however, did not. "Master, no," she said. "He can't be trusted. Not against his own daughter."

The Night God put a hand on his shoulder. *He can now. Tell her, Arenadd.*

Arenadd finally looked up. "Yes," he intoned. "I will help you, Saeddryn."

Saeddryn's eye narrowed. "What's wrong with ye?"

Arenadd did not look any different than he had when he was alive, but there was something worn and defeated in his face and stance. "I have seen reason." There was defeat in his voice, too. "I was wrong to stand against you. I was weak. Caedmon is the rightful ruler."

"An' Laela?" Saeddryn said sharply, unable to ignore the sick feeling in her stomach at the sight of him. "What about her?"

"She's not the rightful Queen," Arenadd said in a flat, dead voice. "She must be removed."

Despite herself, Saeddryn wanted to reach out to him. "What happened, Arenadd? When did ye change yer mind?"

Arenadd's hands clenched and unclenched. "My master taught me the right way. I watched what happened in Skenfrith. What Laela did was monstrous. She must be punished. I must help you."

You do not need to be afraid of him, said the Night God. *He understands now. Take him with you and make use of him.*

Saeddryn felt sicker every moment she saw Arenadd and heard his voice. It was as if something—or someone—had sucked out every scrap of the fire and passion he had had in life, and left him . . . broken.

This time, she really did reach out to him. "Come with me."

Arenadd looked her in the face at last, and she saw a gleam return to his eyes. "Back home?"

Go, Arenadd, said the Night God, sounding almost motherly. *Be with your true love at last, the way you were meant to be.*

Arenadd kept his eyes on Saeddryn. "Yes . . . let me come with you . . . beloved." He took her hand, pulled her to him, and kissed her on the mouth.

Before Saeddryn could pull away, or kiss him back, or say a word, she felt the darkness drain away, taking the Night God with it.

She opened her eye, and light returned. Memories came rushing back, and she nearly leapt to her feet, turning around frantically to look. But she saw nothing but trees and stones, dark shapes against the snow. No Night God, and no . . .

It's good to be back, said Arenadd's voice, by her ear. *Isn't it, beloved?*

Kullervo spent two pleasant days on Maijan before setting out for home. The first day he stayed close to the palace and enjoyed a tour of some of the more impressive rooms courtesy of Akhane himself. After that, he helped the Prince to search through his collection of books and decide which ones might be useful. Or, rather, Akhane did the searching while Kullervo looked at the pictures since he could barely read Cymrian and didn't know a word of Amorani.

Akhane didn't complain, of course. He had remained in awe of Kullervo and went out of his way to show him every courtesy, addressing him as "my Lord"—or "Sacred One" if no-one was listening—and making sure he had everything he asked for. Kullervo found it embarrassing, but he knew better than to refuse, and he soon came to appreciate the splendid food served to him. But before the day was out, he suddenly found himself the owner of several new sets of clothing—all tailored to hide his wings as flatteringly as possible—and much more. Jewellery, boots, a magnificent sword with a golden hilt and a pommel in the shape of a sunwheel, and a silk pillow stuffed with sweet-smelling herbs. Senneck, too, was showered with gifts, including a beautiful new harness with silver fastenings and blue stones set into it that matched her eyes, and a set of golden leg-rings.

"They are like the rings I wore when Erian was named Master of Farms," she said, with what sounded like genuine awe. "But so much finer."

Kullervo felt red-hot with shame, but he cheered up a little when he saw how pleased she was. He might have trouble with being shown too much respect, but Senneck was loving every moment of it.

Despite his own misgivings, he knew better than to even consider giving the gifts back and accepted them with stammered thanks. Still, once he forced himself to relax, he couldn't help but admire the sword. He'd never owned one before. Swords were expensive, and this one looked doubly so.

On the morning of the second day, he washed himself with more care than usual and dressed in his new clothes. They were light and cool, made just for the heat of Maijan, and fit him bewilderingly well, especially considering that he'd refused to take his tunic off when they had measured him.

He put the sword on, too, with the scabbard and belt that had accompanied it. It was very unlikely that he would need it, but he couldn't resist bringing it along anyway, just to show it off.

Senneck groomed herself and held out her forelegs so he could put on her new rings. "In Cymria, there would be a ceremony for this," she commented. "In front of all the great griffins of the Eyrie. The Eyrie ruler would have his human put the rings on me and announce my ascension for all to hear."

Most humans had trouble reading tone or emotion into a griffin's voice, but Kullervo could catch a hint of sadness in hers. "That happened for you once, didn't it? With Erian."

"Yes. The Mighty Kraal himself accepted me as a griffin of Malvern, and my human as a Lord. It was the greatest day of my life."

Kullervo rubbed her head between her eyes. "I'm not the Mighty Kraal, I know, but I suppose I'll have to do for now."

Senneck *haaked* and shoved her head under his chin. "You are a Prince of Malvern, Kullervo. Even the Mighty Kraal is nothing beside that."

Kullervo laughed and kissed her on the beak. "Thank you, Senneck. And don't worry; when we get home, I'll make sure there's a proper ceremony, I'll ask Laela to give you an official position. I'm sure she won't mind."

"It would be strange," said Senneck. "But amusing. To hear my name screeched again in the council chamber. There will be griffins there that remember me, and how surprised they would be to see me on that platform after so long! Now, where shall we go today?"

Kullervo had to stop himself from kissing her again. "Wherever you want to go."

"I would like to see the city," said Senneck. "I have seen it from the sky, but not from the ground, and there is always more on the ground."

"That's true," said Kullervo. His face lit up. "Let's go and see the Temple! There's one above the city. I always wanted to see an Amorani Sun Temple."

"They revere griffins here even more than in Cymria," said Senneck. "I would like to see how much."

Kullervo gave a broken-toothed grin. "I'd love to find out what they'd say if I showed them my wings. I won't, though. Let's go!"

They left the palace together, unable to avoid a group of three slaves who insisted on coming with them as an escort. Kullervo would have preferred to leave them behind, but he knew he would need them to translate and show him which way to go. Besides, Senneck wouldn't hear of going without them.

Two slaves walked beside Kullervo and Senneck, shading them, while the third went ahead to lead the way. People always moved aside for a griffin, sometimes if only because people who *didn't* move aside were liable to get bitten, but here they stood back with much more reverence than Kullervo had seen in Cymria, bowing and murmuring in their own language. Some even held up their hands toward Senneck, as if they were asking her for something. Naturally, she ignored them completely.

The slave led them through the winding streets, past the odd, flat-roofed houses, and through a marketplace, where Kullervo and Senneck were both happy to dawdle a while and see all the unfamiliar things that were for sale. Pots, clothes, food, spices, wood carvings . . . Kullervo bought one of those last and pocketed it to take home for Laela. When Senneck looked at him reproachfully, he bought a lump of roasted meat as well and tossed it into her waiting beak.

Up at the top of the hill that overlooked the city, they found the Sun Temple. It was a beautiful building, made in the Amorani style like the palace below it, with a great domed roof. But this roof was coated in gold and, combined with the white stone of the rest of the building, made the Temple almost glow in the early-morning sun.

The front entrance was huge and grand, with no gate or door in sight. On either side were a pair of humans carved into the stone in reverent postures, with their heads bowed. Two griffins stood on their backs, talons reaching upward to make the lintel, and above them was the face of a smiling man with big, almond-shaped eyes. The face had been coated in gold as well, and the eyes were yellow gemstones.

Senneck sat on her haunches to take all of this in. "Ah, the mighty power of humans makes such beautiful things," she said. "Have you seen anything like this before, Kullervo?"

Kullervo found his voice again. "Never. It's amazing! I wonder what it's like inside?"

"We will find out," said Senneck, getting up to go through. On either side, the slaves moved away. They didn't try to follow when Kullervo went inside.

The interior of the Temple was all white. The stone, the carvings, the tiles, everything. Only the red mats on the floor stood out. That, and the statue at the far end.

The walls of the Temple were lined with archways that had no doors, only yellow and blue cloth hangings that billowed gently in the wind. It meant that the Temple was full of sunlight, and all of it seemed to focus on the statue.

It was a man, larger than life-sized, and covered in pure gold. He held a bowl in his outstretched hands, with a fire burning inside it that threw more light on his blue gemstone eyes, making them flicker with something that looked eerily like awareness.

Senneck gave a long, soft hiss. "By my wings . . ."

Kullervo said nothing. He approached the statue cautiously, almost as if he expected it to come to life. When he came too close, he stumbled.

"Are you hurt?" Senneck asked at once.

Kullervo winced but shook his head.

When they reached the statue, Senneck stretched out her neck and nibbled it gently.

Kullervo kept well back. "Do you think it's all gold?" he asked, sounding a little strained.

"I do not know," said Senneck. She moved back to her partner's side. "This must be the human these ones worship."

"Xanathus," said Kullervo. "Gryphus. They're one and the same, Laela says."

Senneck looked at him. "Are you certain that you are not hurt? You do not look well."

Kullervo grimaced. "I don't feel that well."

"Do you need food? Rest?"

"I don't think so." Kullervo shifted. "I just feel . . . odd. Uncomfortable." He took a step back. "Scared."

"Of what? There is nothing here."

Kullervo shook himself. "You're right." He went toward the statue, reaching out to touch it. But when his fingers were about to brush its surface, he pulled away and darted back to Senneck. "I want to leave," he said in a rush.

Senneck turned around, raising her tail aggressively. "What is this? What is wrong with you?"

"I don't know," Kullervo said in a panicky voice. "I have to get out of here. I don't like it. It feels wrong."

"Do not be a coward."

"I'm trying not to be . . ." Kullervo edged away toward the entrance. Senneck stayed where she was, staring challengingly at him.

"I'm sorry," Kullervo said at last. "I can't."

He nearly ran out of the Temple.

Senneck followed at a more leisurely pace, and found him a little way down the hill, breathing raggedly while the slaves anxiously fanned him.

"What was that?" Senneck demanded. "What were you afraid of?"

Kullervo took a deep breath. "I don't know. I'm sorry, Senneck. I tried, but . . . I just couldn't stand being in there."

"This is foolish!" said Senneck, confusion making her irritable. "It is a human nest, nothing more."

"But I feel better now," said Kullervo. "I started feeling bad the moment I stepped through the door, and the moment I left, the feeling went away."

Senneck shook her head. "We should go back now."

"Yes." Kullervo touched her gently. "I'm sorry."

"Do not say that. It does not matter."

Senneck walked back down the hill with him, keeping close to his side. She said nothing and let him talk—about other things than the Temple and what had happened in it. Senneck walked slowly, still limping slightly from her old wounds, keeping her eyes on the path ahead. She looked as expressionless as only a griffin could, but behind those eyes she was thinking.

When they reached their rooms in the palace, Kullervo took his boots and belt off and lay down on his bed. Senneck settled down nearby and groomed. When she had smoothed down the last feather, she lay on her own pallet and rested her head on her talons.

After a short while, she lifted it again. "Kullervo, there is something I must tell you."

He sat up at once. "What is it?"

Her eyes were blue, and fierce. "I knew your father. You know this. I fought against him. I saw his powers for myself."

"I know," said Kullervo.

"You know," Senneck agreed. "I saw his powers, and I saw his weaknesses as well." She lifted a forepaw and slowly scratched her neck. "Long ago, just before the war began, your father was arrested. For his crimes, he was hanged. In Malvern, in front of the Eyrie where you and I live. I witnessed the execution, along with Erian and many others. We thought he had been dealt with that day. But he rose again. Only moments after the hanging, before he could be carted away, he rose again. He went after Erian. He tried to kill him, and I was not there to protect him. Erian would have died that day, but he found shelter. He hid in the one place that *Kraeai kran ae* could not follow."

"Where?" asked Kullervo.

"In the Sun Temple. Malvern's own Temple. It is not there now, *Kraeai kran ae* had it destroyed after the war. He hated it, and all the Sun Temples, and for good reason. I did not see it myself, but Erian told me. Your father—*Kraeai kran ae*—could not enter one, not without suffering terrible pain. If he went inside, he would lose his powers and be weakened. Until now, I have not been certain if this was true. Today, I have found a reason to be certain."

"What reason?"

"You, Kullervo." Senneck nibbled her talon nervously. "You are the son of *Kraeai kran ae*, conceived after he had been given his powers. Your sister was made before then, when he was only a mortal man, but you . . . you were the son of *Kraeai kran ae*, and you have inherited something from him. You have the dark power, Kullervo."

Kullervo's heart froze. "I don't! Don't say that, Senneck. I'm not like him."

Senneck did not look away. "You are, Kullervo. You have not seen it in yourself yet, but I have. You look like him. And you have his power, or a touch of it."

The room was warm, but Kullervo suddenly felt very cold. He hunched down, clutching his upper arms. "I don't. Stop it."

"You pulled Saeddryn out of the shadows when I could not see her," Senneck said impatiently. "You knew where she was, and you reached into her hiding place without effort. And like your father, you cannot bear to be inside a temple to the sun. The darkness in you makes it hurt. You are the son of *Kraeai kran ae*, whether you like it or not."

Kullervo hunched down even further, trying to hide within himself. A tear ran down his nose. "I'm sorry," he whispered. "I'm so sorry."

Senneck stood up. "You do not understand. Do not be afraid, Kullervo. This knowledge is a good thing."

He looked up. "How?" he shouted. "*How* is it a good thing if I'm a monster like he was? If I'm . . . dark too." The anger left his voice as quickly as it had come.

"It is a good thing," Senneck insisted. "You are our weapon, Kullervo. And our knowledge. You can drag our enemy out of the shadows, and you have shown us both the key to defeating her."

Kullervo stilled. "What key?"

Senneck turned her head, tilting it to soak up a shaft of light from the window. "The sun," she said softly.

9

Born Again

Saeddryn turned around again, searching in vain for any sign of another person.

"Arenadd? Where are ye?"

With you, said the voice by her ear. *Always, Saeddryn.*

Still unable to see anything, she stopped still. "Why can't I see ye?"

His laugh sounded hollow. *There's nothing to see. I don't have a body any more.*

Saeddryn's neck prickled. "Are ye a ghost, then?"

An evil spirit, probably. Here, let me try something . . .

Saeddryn's vision flickered briefly, and she took a step back when she saw something appear in front of her. It looked like a shadow at first, but as it grew as tall as her, it lost some of its shape and looked like a faint black mist. The shape that remained looked just barely like the outline of a man standing there.

Saeddryn reached out. "Arenadd . . . I see ye."

The shape vanished abruptly. *Don't tell anyone about me,* Arenadd's voice told her flatly. *They won't see me, or hear me. Only someone with our power can do that.*

"I understand." Saeddryn wanted to touch him now. She wished his hand were there to hold. "Arenadd, what do we do now? Together?"

The only thing our kind can do, he said. *Kill.*

There was no joy, or excitement, or any life in his voice at all. Saeddryn shivered. "Arenadd, are ye all right?" she asked tentatively.

I've never been better, he said, but she had never heard anyone sound so far from it.

"Are ye sure?" she persisted. "Ye don't sound . . . right."

It's all right, he told her. *I'm different now, that's all. I've learnt to love her.*

"The Night God?"

Yes. With all my heart.

"But . . ." Saeddryn trailed off, unable to find words for what she was thinking. It was good that Arenadd had learnt to love the god the way every true Northerner should, but . . . but this wasn't right, not at all, it was all wrong.

"Caedmon's here," she said at last, hoping to get a reaction out of him. "He looks so much like ye."

He's the true King, Arenadd said, in a voice like death.

"I know the two of ye fell out," Saeddryn persisted. "But I know how close ye were before. If things had worked out different, I know ye would have been friends again."

I was wrong, said Arenadd, without the slightest change in tone. *Caedmon was always my true heir, and you were my true Queen.*

"Arenadd—"

Go to him now and tell him so, said Arenadd. *You serve him now, and I serve you. He will give us a task.*

"Later," said Saeddryn, feeling ill. "He needs some time alone, to think."

Of course, said Arenadd.

He said nothing more after that, and Saeddryn sat down outside her makeshift stone circle and waited in silence while the last of the day dragged out toward night. She had the help she needed now, and she knew she should be feeling grateful toward her master—and glad on behalf of Arenadd, who had finally learnt to see sense.

But despite all her efforts, she felt neither. She had Arenadd back now, and he was hers, just as she had always wanted, but he was *not* Arenadd. Not the Arenadd she remembered. The man she remembered had been angry and passionate, and bitter. He hated with all his heart and loved in the same way. He had done his duty even while resenting it, and once he had made up his mind, nothing short of a dagger in the chest would change it—and even a dagger would only slow him down for a little while.

Those were the qualities she had known him for, hated him for, loved him for, and now they were gone. And without them, he was not Arenadd any more.

Despair welled in her chest.

She wished, again, that she could find something to say. But there was nothing she could think of that would change anything.

Come on now, Arenadd said unexpectedly, and with a hint of gentleness finally showing through the deadness in his voice. *It's time to go to work. There's nothing to be afraid of. Not for us.*

Saeddryn did not move. "Arenadd, what did she do to ye? I want to know."

I told you. She taught me the truth.

"That's not what I mean," Saeddryn said sharply. "What did she *do,* Arenadd?"

She . . . Arenadd faltered.

"Tell me." Her voice was a mother's voice, and a commander's.

She made me love her, Arenadd said at last, and now it was his voice, his *real* voice breaking free. *She made me love her in the void, the way I loved Skade.*

Saeddryn's stomach twisted. "She what?"

Arenadd laughed softly. *I've slept with worse. She wanted me to do it. She said it was for me, but it was for her. Do you want to know the truth, Saeddryn?*

"What truth?"

She's like us. She's got no heart. That's why she needs us. Needed me. She needs to be loved the way we do, to take away the feeling inside. Gods don't love. They can't. But she tried.

Saeddryn wanted to cry. "So she made ye do that."

Yes, said Arenadd. *When I saw it, I knew I had to love her. Because I was all she had.*

"And me?" asked Saeddryn.

And you. One human needs another. I need you, Saeddryn.

She realised that she really was crying now, silently. "Ye told me ye didn't love me. Ye turned me away, made me marry Torc instead. Ye had Skade instead."

I met her before you, and I didn't want to betray her. After she died, I knew you were the only one who could be my Queen, but how could I steal you from Torc? He loved you, and he was my friend. He was a better husband than I would have been.

"So ye made Caedmon yer heir," said Saeddryn. "Treated him like he was yer own son."

Yes. My whole life I wanted a son of my own. Caedmon was the closest I would ever come. I tried so hard for him, and you, but . . . I was weak.

"No ye weren't." Saeddryn stood up. "It's too late for us now, an' we'll just have to live with that. But it's not too late for Caedmon."

No. Caedmon is our heir. Your son, my apprentice. The only heir to my throne. Go to him, Saeddryn, and we can make amends at last.

Saeddryn wiped away her tears. "Together, Arenadd."

Together, sweet Saeddryn.

While Saeddryn was gone, Caedmon pulled himself together and set everyone to building a temporary camp. The frozen waterfall and the clearing around it weren't the best spot to stay, but he knew that for now, at least, they would have to. Most of them were wounded, and all were exhausted. A night's rest would help even if they would have to go without food.

Before long, some fires had been lit, and several crude shelters built out of branches. All those there were griffiners and would share their shelter with their partner, which should keep them warm despite the lack of bedding.

Once that was finished, and several of the fitter people had wandered off to forage for food, Caedmon went off a short distance to be alone. Even Shar stayed behind, nursing a slash left across her chest by an Unpartnered's beak.

But Caedmon was not left alone to think for long. As he stood by a tree and stared out at the snowy landscape, he sensed someone coming up behind him. He didn't turn around, but his heart beat faster when Myfina slipped an arm around his waist.

For a moment, the two of them stayed like that, close but not quite embracing, and Caedmon felt Myfina's warmth soak comfortingly into his aching back.

"We could go back and find Heath," he said eventually, once the closeness started making him uneasy.

"Don't be silly," said Myfina, but without sharpness. "You know that would be suicide."

Caedmon did know. "He'll be all right," he said, hoping to convince himself as much as her. "He's a survivor. They don't know who he is, anyway, and they wouldn't kill a sick man in his bed."

"Wouldn't they?" Myfina said bitterly. "You know what griffins are like."

"The infirmary is too small for them to get in," said Caedmon. "I'm sure we'll see him again some day."

"Some day." Myfina let go, and moved around to stand in front of him. "Lord Caedmon," she said formally. "It's time we made plans. Where do we go from here? We should decide quickly because we can't stay here forever, and the others need to have a plan to follow, or they'll lose purpose."

"Yes," Caedmon found himself saying. "You're right. What do you suggest?"

"Lady Saeddryn," Myfina said at once. "She's our greatest asset now. We don't have a stronghold or many followers, but she can't be killed, and she can go anywhere she likes."

"Yes," Caedmon muttered. "We lost today, but that was my mistake. We weren't ready to try to defend a stronghold like that. With the Unpartnered out of the way, we might have survived, but we can't do that now."

"We need more followers," Myfina agreed. "We should use Skenfrith to our advantage. You saw what happened there. What the half-breed did was unspeakable. An entire city, destroyed just because we dared to stand up to her. People will listen to that. They'll be angry. Think of all the people in other cities who lost relatives today."

"Yes." Caedmon's eyes narrowed. "The half-breed won, but she also stabbed herself in the foot. Without the support of the people, she can't rule forever. Not if they won't allow her to. And today, she showed them her true colours."

"So we should use it," said Myfina. "Spread the word. We shouldn't try to raise open rebellion just yet, though, not until we're strong enough."

"You're right." Caedmon nodded to himself as he thought. "We'll send people out. Staying together was our downfall in Skenfrith, so we'll break up. Go our separate ways. If we do that, we can be everywhere at once. The half-breed won't know where to look."

"And Saeddryn?"

"I'll send her out, too. But not just to talk." Caedmon gritted his teeth. "I'll send her out to kill. She can help me decide where to strike. We need that half-breed dead. She can't stay in Malvern forever. Sooner or later, she'll leave again, and when we catch her away from home, she's dead. I don't care who does it."

"I understand why you wanted to do it yourself, before," said Myfina. "It's your right."

"I was stupid," Caedmon snapped. "I lost us our chance to be rid of her. If I'd let Mo—Saeddryn kill her when she had the chance . . ."

Myfina took his hand in both of hers. "There's no point in agonising over what might have been," she said gently. "Skenfrith would still have been lost."

"Maybe. Maybe not. But you're right." Caedmon let go of her hands. "Let's go and talk to our Shadow That Walks."

Saeddryn returned to camp shortly after this, as if she had sensed she was needed. She listened while Caedmon outlined his new plan to the others, and afterward, when he took her aside and gave her her own mission.

When he had finished, she nodded briefly. "Fear tactics. I know what to do. Give me my first target, an' I'll leave immediately."

"You can choose your own," said Caedmon. "It doesn't matter so much who it is as long as it's done right. Make them prominent, make them public, make them sudden. I want to see loyal officials killed from behind locked doors, Queen-appointed governors falling in front of their offsiders. Even griffins, if you can manage it. I want them to be afraid. I want them to know that we're out there, and that while the half-breed sits on my throne, no-one is safe."

Saeddryn smiled grimly. "Understood. I'll go now. Don't tell the others exactly what I'm doin'. Just a hint is enough."

"I know." Caedmon gave her a quick hug. He nearly whispered something to her, nearly let slip some apology, but nothing came out. His mother had raised him to be a doer, not a talker or a weakling, and she would only be irritated if he did something like that.

Saeddryn returned the hug, but it wasn't a pleasant one. It was cold and bony. Not a mother's hug but a killer's. "Don't be afraid," she told him as she let go. "The Night God is with us. Nothing can stand in our way forever."

She walked away. Caedmon turned to watch her go, but he lost sight of her almost instantly as she melted away into the gathering darkness. A predator, slipping away to begin the hunt.

Out of earshot in the shadows, Saeddryn tilted her head and scented the breeze. Her sense of smell had become much stronger now, and now it painted pictures of ice and pine trees, and the faint tang of living creatures hiding from the fear her presence put into them. Time to stalk now. Time to kill.

"Arenadd," she said, in a voice so low it was barely a whisper.
Yes?
"Seek."

10

Twisted Love

Laela sat by the fire in her bedroom and stared at the flames, trying to ignore the bruised itching from her infected arm. She had kept the ruined tattoos hidden and done her best to drain and dress them herself. They probably wouldn't kill her, but for now they were a constant irritation.

But her mind wasn't really on that, or anything in the present moment. That afternoon, she had had a private meeting with a couple of her new council members. They had asked—very carefully—about Skenfrith and exactly what she had done there.

"Wiped out the enemy," Laela had snapped back.

The councillor who had spoken first had looked hesitant. "With respect, my Lady, the normal practice is to discuss important decisions like this more thoroughly with the council."

"I didn't have the time for that," Laela had said. "We had to take 'em by surprise. Anyway, it worked, so what's the complaining for?"

The councillor had looked even more uncomfortable and had left his friend to answer for him. "Understood, my Lady, but we both felt you should know that there is unrest in the city. Skenfrith was necessary, but the people are unhappy. Even those who don't support the rebels feel that you went too far. Plenty of ordinary people—not supporters of Caedmon—were caught up in the massacre."

For the first time in a long while, Laela didn't know what to say. "We had to do it," she said eventually. "Caedmon had to be stopped."

"But he escaped," said the first councillor.

"Well, next time he won't," Laela had snapped back. "Now get lost."

She'd dismissed the pair of them, but it had left her feeling uneasy. They were right; plenty of ordinary people had died in Skenfrith. It was hard enough getting griffins to fight as a group as it was—expecting them to know the difference between enemies and innocents was just plain stupid. But it had seemed so clear-cut at the time . . .

Laela brooded and scratched her sore arm. How had it come to this? How had she ever gone this far? She had come to Malvern as a nobody; she'd never hurt anyone in her life. She had condemned Arenadd for the massacres he'd committed, and the people he'd murdered. But now . . .

"What've I done?" she muttered aloud. "What've I turned into? Gods . . ."

A fierce longing gripped her by the heart. In that moment, all she wanted was to see Arenadd again. She wanted him to be there beside her so badly it hurt. Without him, there she had no-one to confide in, no-one to help her, no-one to tell her the truth. With Arenadd gone, she only had Kullervo left, once he returned, but she couldn't rely on Kullervo the same way she had on her father. Kullervo was too timid, too eager to please. But she could have talked to Arenadd, and he would have understood.

Tears wet Laela's face. She couldn't bear to stay here, in this room where she had first seen her father's face.

With a sudden motion, she stood up and walked out through Skandar's nest. It was empty—Skandar often went flying at night. Alone, she went onto the balcony and looked up at the stars. They glittered above her, seemingly endless, but the darkness around them was nothing but a void.

Even here, though, the sense that Arenadd was there stayed with her, and it made her want to cry properly—to let herself give in to the sobs locked away in her chest. But she controlled herself. She was a Queen. She was Arenadd's daughter, the scourge of Skenfrith.

Laela smiled weakly. "Funny, ain't it?" she whispered to the invisible presence of her father. "Not even a year ago, yeh told me I was like you. I wouldn't listen, but it was the truth, wasn't it? I can see it now. I really am yer daughter." She shivered, and wrapped her arms around herself. "I've done somethin' terrible, Arenadd. I won't ever tell them, but I can see it. I killed my own people in Skenfrith. Didn't even think about it; I just did it. Is that what you would've done? I dunno, but it's what I did. They must hate me now. But what else was I gonna do?" she added, appealing to the sky. "What else? Was I just gonna sit here and do nothin'? Wait for Caedmon an' Saeddryn to come here an' kill me? An' then what? Once he's on the throne, Caedmon'll go straight for the South. I know that's what yeh wanted me to do. Keep the South safe. But I'm startin' to wonder if it's even worth it. They'll never thank me for it." She heaved a sigh. "They hated me for being a half-breed. Now they'll hate me because I'm a tyrant, too. But it's so hard . . . I just wish yeh were here, Arenadd. I . . ."

She trailed off, feeling both terrible sadness and vague embarrassment. Was she so lonely now that she'd resorted to talking to herself?

But as she turned away, she couldn't stop herself from whispering one last thing—to herself, to the sky, to the feeling she had that someone or something was watching her. "Arenadd, I miss you so much."

She went back inside after that, angrily wiping her eyes on her sleeve, unable to hear the voice that replied, whispering out of the shadows, inaudible to mortal ears but still real, and full of sadness and regret.

I miss you, too . . .

In the end, Prince Akhane elected to bring a band of about twenty people with them. Some of them were fellow nobles and friends of his, and the rest consisted of servants—none of them slaves, since Akhane judged that would be offensive—guards, and other fighters, some of whom were native Maijani, and a pair of priests. Most of Akhane's friends were griffiners, so it was just as well that they would be making the return trip on the Prince's own ship, which had been specially built to accommodate griffins. The crew was a mix of Maijani and Amorani—the former, Akhane claimed, came from a race of born sailors.

Kullervo got on board with Senneck and Inva and the rest of their own escort, and took up residence in a cabin. It was a pokey little thing, but he was more than happy to spend most of his time up on deck, watching the crew at work and mingling with Akhane and his friends. It would be a long trip home, and new friends would make it pass faster.

Akhane, ever polite, was more than happy to help. "This is Rhaki, and his partner Kargh. They have been friends to me and Zekh since childhood. And this is Lady Yuha, a fellow scholar. And this is Lord Vander, and up there is his partner Ymazu."

The last man to be introduced was an Amorani in his fifties or sixties, whose hair and neat little moustache were both peppered with grey. His face was shrewd and bright-eyed as he bowed politely to Kullervo.

"It is my pleasure to meet you," he said in a measured way that felt slightly familiar, but while he spoke, those eyes were fixed on Kullervo's face, taking in every detail.

Kullervo had the uncomfortable feeling that he was being summed up. "Er, I'm pleased to meet you too, Lord Vander. Are you a scholar, too?"

"Perhaps, these days." Vander allowed himself a smile. "Ymazu and I were the Emperor's chief diplomats. We had retired to a quiet life on Maijan, but when Prince Akhane offered us the opportunity to see the great city of Malvern again, we decided that we would enjoy another visit. A diplomat never loses his taste for travel."

"Did you ever work as a diplomat with King Arenadd?" Kullervo ventured, remembering Laela's story about how she had helped make an alliance with Amoran.

"I did," said Vander. "And I was sad to hear that he had gone. But not surprised, I admit."

Kullervo cocked his head like a griffin. "Why not?"

"The King was very ill the last time I saw him." Vander smoothed his moustache. "I travelled back with him from Instabahn, as far as Maijan. He left Amoran unconscious and did not wake until we were well out to sea. Even after that, he was confined to his bunk. When I visited him to say farewell at Maijan, he looked like a man on his death-bed. I think Tara will be a different country without him."

"It is," said Kullervo. For the better, he hoped.

Vander gave another one of his quiet smiles and excused

himself. Kullervo, watching him go, decided that he liked the
reserved Amorani. Clearly, he knew a lot more than he would
admit to just anyone. Kullervo decided he would make a point
of getting to know him better during the voyage.

Another person he talked to was one of the priests. There were
two, but one was more talkative than the other, who merely introduced himself briefly before moving on. The first, however, was
more than happy to tell Kullervo more about the Amorani god.

"Xanathus," he said. "His body is the sun, but it is too bright
for us to see. He has many names—in your country, he is
Gryphus—but all those names and faces of the sun belong to
the one god. He is the light of life, which makes the plants grow
and the warmth come into our bodies. He is the maker, the Tai-
lor Who Stitched the World, some call him."

Kullervo listened patiently. "What does he want? What do
his followers do?"

"To love life is to serve him," said the priest. "To love other
living creatures and nourish them. To plant crops and to father
children and raise them well, that is the work of Xanathus."

"Don't most people do that anyway?" Kullervo asked.

"That is what he made us to do," said the priest. "But it must
be done with love, and faith in him, and there are prayers and
rituals . . ." There was plenty more where that came from, and
Kullervo kept listening well after he had lost interest. During
his upbringing in the South, he had spent plenty of time with
priests, and he had heard them say things not much different
from this. But there was one difference that he soon noticed.
The priests of Gryphus had no qualms about advocating war
and persecution of Northerners and other "heretics." This priest,
however, described a philosophy of preserving life and never
making war except in times of dire need.

It was an attractive notion, but Kullervo remembered what
he had learnt about the Amorani Empire and its endless con-
quests of neighbouring countries, which it universally plun-
dered for treasure and slaves. Talk was all very well, he
decided, but the nature of human beings never changed, not
deep down at the core where it really mattered.

Still, it was interesting to hear the priest describe the great
temples in the mountains of Amoran, and some of the customs
and rituals that went on in them. Kullervo paid close attention,

and learnt plenty, and before long he was regretting not having gone on to Amoran. But he could do that later. For now, he had more important things to do. When the war was over, he could go back and see those places for himself. Senneck might like that, too, especially once she knew how griffins were worshipped and pampered in most of those temples.

The voyage back to the North went by, and far more pleasantly than the one that had brought him to Maijan. He spent his time with Senneck, learning about magic, or with Akhane, or anyone else on board who was willing to talk.

Akhane was full of stories about all the distant lands he had visited and the people he had met. He had seen giant serpents in Erebus, he said, and monstrous lions in Eire, and he had seen rain dances performed by the last of the lost shamans beyond the Dry Mountains. Smiling ruefully, he also talked about some of the rumours and legends he had chased and the lunatics and liars they had led him to.

"I have filled entire books with them," he said. When Kullervo asked, he duly presented one, filled with handwriting that Kullervo thought looked beautifully neat even if he couldn't read a word of it.

Vander, too, became a friend, even if he wasn't as open about his life as Akhane. Kullervo kept trying, however, and Vander seemed to find his innocent curiosity amusing since his quiet little smile returned nearly every time Kullervo spoke to him. He did tell a few stories of his own, mostly about the wars and conflicts he had been involved in over the years, but he did so in a quiet and cautious kind of way, often talking more about the palaces and the wealthy nobles in them than what they had been fighting over or how he had resolved matters. It reminded Kullervo of Inva, and one day he went so far as to point that out.

Vander smiled. "A slave is trained from birth to see much and say nothing. And so is a diplomat, for much the same reasons."

"But you're not a diplomat any more," said Kullervo.

Vander touched his neck. "No more than I am a slave any more. But a man cannot put aside a lifetime's learning."

Kullervo nodded absently, then breathed in sharply when he grasped what Vander had just said. "Wait, did you say you were a slave?"

"In my boyhood," Vander said calmly. "The law in Amoran

says that any slave who is chosen by a griffin must be freed at once."

"Oh." Kullervo grinned. "That must be why Inva likes you."

For the first time, Vander looked genuinely taken aback. "What is this?"

"Oh, I'm sorry, I thought you knew," Kullervo said.

"I do not think that I did," said Vander, more restrained than ever.

"I've seen her looking at you," Kullervo went on guilelessly. "Sometimes she smiles, too. But she looks down if you look at her. I think she's too shy to say anything. But I heard Skarok say she's been grooming carefully and putting perfume in her hair. I think that means something."

There was no trace of Vander's little smile left. "I see," he said slowly.

"Maybe you could talk to her," said Kullervo. "She never says much, but I think she's a very lonely woman. She doesn't have any friends that I know about. You could talk about diplomacy, maybe." He grinned nervously.

For a few moments, Vander was unreadable. Kullervo quickly became uncomfortable and even started to try to find hostility in the diplomat's mask.

But then Vander smiled. "You are not a man who keeps secrets, are you, Lord Kullervo?"

Kullervo reddened. "Er . . . well, I've never really had to. But some things shouldn't be kept secret."

Vander raised an eyebrow. "What things do you think they are, my lord?"

"Love is one," said Kullervo. "And sadness. And suffering. If you keep those secret, they'll only hurt you. Sometimes, it's better to set them free."

For the merest instant, Vander looked a little sad himself. "You are wiser than you seem. But I hope for your country's sake that you are never entrusted with state secrets. They will fall out of your tongue like coins from an open purse."

Kullervo laughed. "You'd be surprised. I can be very stubborn when I want to be. If I weren't, I'd still have teeth."

"Ah. Then that was not a simple fight?"

"No." Kullervo picked at his broken teeth. "I'll tell you about it some other time."

He never mentioned Inva to Vander again after that, but a few days later he noticed that the two had begun to spend some time together. Neither of them gave anything away, of course, but one day they flew out on their griffins together to enjoy a leisurely flight over the sea. They didn't return until evening, when the first stars had begun to show, and Kullervo was the only one to see them steal away to the little balcony at the back of the ship.

Unable to resist, he went up onto the main deck where the wheel stood, and peeked over the railings. He saw the two diplomats standing together below him, looking out to sea. For a while it looked as if they were only talking, but then Kullervo noticed that they were holding hands. As the moon rose, Vander leaned over and kissed Inva's cheek.

Kullervo smiled to himself and snuck away.

As he headed back toward his cabin, he realised there was someone else there, looking over the railings just as he had. They had been standing so still that he had completely missed them.

"Hello," he said cautiously.

Prince Akhane turned his head, and smiled. "It is said that the messenger of Xanathus is sometimes sent with a message of love, to tell a man that he is meant to be with a woman. I have wondered if that was true."

"You're not sure if you believe it, are you?" said Kullervo.

Akhane's smile became cautious. "I am not a man to blindly believe, Sacred One."

Kullervo shook his head. "I'm just too ordinary, aren't I? I haven't taught you how to be a better person, or healed the sick or anything. You must be disappointed."

The smile disappeared. "Sorry. I am sorry . . . I would not suggest that you are not what you say you are. I am only curious, Sacred One."

Kullervo grinned, to put him at his ease. "It's all right. It's good to be curious." A sudden, wild impulse gripped him. "You want to see what I can do?"

Akhane's face lit up with interest, but he hid it quickly, saying, "No, it is written that Xanathus cannot be questioned . . ."

"Don't worry," said Kullervo. "I'm offering to show you. I know you like seeing new things. Besides, it's been too long, and I . . . it feels right for it, tonight."

Akhane's forced doubt disappeared instantly. "Very well. I would be eager to see your power if you are willing, Sacred One."

Kullervo glanced around. "Not here. Come with me."

He led the way down into the hold, which was deserted at this time of night. Akhane came, too, bringing a lantern from the passage outside.

Kullervo chose a secluded spot, surrounded by crates. "Here should do. Now . . ." He undid his shirt and hung it up neatly on a nail. "This won't be pleasant to watch, but don't be afraid. You won't be in any danger." He took off his boots, and his trousers as well, without embarrassment.

Akhane's eyes widened when he saw Kullervo's tail, but he quickly looked away again. "Why must you be naked?"

Kullervo coughed. "I'm sorry, it's just that these clothes were made just for me, and I don't want to ruin them. Now . . . watch."

He crouched with his hands resting on the deck in front of him, and concentrated.

For a griffin, using magic only needed concentration—and strength. But when he was human, Kullervo found it took more than that. He closed his eyes and focused not on his magic but on his past. He thought back, bringing up every bad memory he had, everything that had ever hurt or threatened him, everything that made him afraid. Everything that made him believe he needed to become stronger.

Sure enough, his body reacted. He heard Akhane gasp, as fur and feathers sprouted all over his skin. That part didn't hurt much. The rest of it did.

He stayed upright for as long as he could, but before long he had fallen onto his side, twitching and contorting as the changes took hold. Under his skin, bones broke and shifted, forming into new shapes. The skin on his forearms thickened and cracked, turning into rough scale. His teeth fused and thrust out of his mouth, becoming a beak. Flight muscles bulged out on his back. Nails became claws and talons.

The change was much faster now than it had been, but it would never stop being ugly and painful. Still, it was done, and Kullervo managed to stay awake.

He stood up, clumsy on four legs, and looked straight at Prince Akhane.

Akhane hadn't moved. He stood there frozen in a position of utter shock, one arm nervously raised.

Speaking in griffin form was very different. Kullervo hacked and rasped and coughed, before he managed to form the words. "I'm finished."

Akhane took a step forward. His dark Amorani eyes were bright with awe. "Sacred One . . ."

Kullervo raised a wing. "My other shape. Only two other people have ever seen me do that."

Akhane didn't seem to know what to say. Kullervo watched him peacefully, relaxing as the pain faded out of his body. As a griffin, he was no larger than he had been as a human—to a real, purebred griffin, he would be trapped as a scrawny adolescent forever—but he had the shape of an adult. His feathers were mottled grey, his hindquarters silvery like old slate, and his undersized, pale beak was chipped and jagged along its edge. Anyone who had seen him as a human but hadn't seen him change would never recognise him, but if they knew it was him, then they would have noticed his eyes. They had stayed the same as they always were: big, yellow, bright with innocence.

As some strength came back to him, Kullervo stretched like a cat, feeling his spine click into place. He yawned, unconcerned, while nearby the Prince finally found his voice again.

"Sacred One, I am . . . , I am humbled, I have never seen . . . in all my life, I have never seen a thing like what you have done." All of Akhane's scholarly calm had escaped him.

Kullervo tried to smile and remembered that he couldn't now. "It's only another kind of magic."

Akhane knelt, partly in reverence and partly to look Kullervo in the eye. "What is it like, my Lord? Can I ask you?"

"It hurts," Kullervo said matter-of-factly. "I can feel my bones and everything being wrenched around inside me. Once . . ." He stopped himself there. He had been going to say that, once upon a time, he had been unable to transform without putting himself into a coma, sometimes for an entire day, and that afterward, he needed plenty of food and rest to recover. Akhane didn't need to know that, and he wouldn't want to either.

Akhane didn't seem to notice Kullervo's hesitation. "What is it like, then, to be a griffin?" He smiled, and added, "I would never ask an ordinary griffin, of course. Only a griffin who has been human would be able to answer."

Kullervo preened his wing, and thought. It was an interesting question, and nobody had ever asked it before. Now that someone had, he wondered how he should answer. "I feel things less," he said eventually. "There's less emotion. There's less . . . thinking as well. I get angry faster and do things without thinking first. There's more instinct, I suppose. And," he went on, realising it for the first time as he said it, "it's more peaceful. Griffins don't worry about things the way humans do. They don't care about things they can't control, like what other people think." He chirped a laugh. "But if I smell food, I can't stop myself!"

Akhane listened closely. "Fascinating!" he muttered. "I must write this down at once and draw a picture of you as I saw you changing. If I have your permission, of course."

"Of course." Kullervo repeated. He yawned again. "I think I'll stay this way for a few days, maybe until Tara comes in sight. Right now, I want to go and see someone, so you can go and write if you want. We can talk again tomorrow."

Akhane nodded, eyes shining with excitement. "Whenever you choose, Sacred One."

Kullervo flicked his tail by way of reply—his griffish mind was already growing bored of all this human talk—and scooped his clothes up in his beak before he left.

He went up on deck again and returned to his own quarters.

Senneck was there, and she looked even more beautiful to him through griffin eyes.

"Kullervo," she said abruptly, looking up from her grooming. "You startled me."

He dropped the bundle of clothes and stepped over them carelessly. "I missed being a griffin," he said.

"I understand," said Senneck. "How long will you stay this way?"

Kullervo shrugged with his wings. "As long as I feel like it. But I'll change before we get to Malvern."

"That would be a good idea," said Senneck. "I cannot return there without my human."

"No, you can't," said Kullervo, not really listening. He sat back on his haunches and stared at her in silence.

If that bothered Senneck, she didn't show it. "When we

return, I think it will be time to ask your sister to reward us. She should be glad to give us an official position; a Mastership for you would not be much to ask. But you will need to decide which one would be best."

Kullervo finally blinked. "None, probably. Masterships are for men who can read, and I'm only half a man, and half-literate as well."

"Then we shall ask her to create a new post just for you," said Senneck, with complete seriousness. "Think it over when you are human again."

"I will." Kullervo moved closer. "You're beautiful, Senneck. Have I ever told you that?"

She put her head on one side. "I am beautiful, and you are small and ugly."

Kullervo didn't flinch. "Yes, but I fought Skarok, just for you. I'd do it again if you wanted me to."

"You fought him and lost," Senneck pointed out.

"I didn't," said Kullervo. "I fought him to stop him from mating with you, and he never did. So I won."

"I refused him because he hurt you."

"So I won," Kullervo said stubbornly. "He didn't deserve you."

"And you think that you do?" said Senneck.

"No," Kullervo admitted. He rubbed his head under her beak. "But I'll never leave you, and I'll never give up on you, no matter what. Would Skarok have done that for you? Would any other griffin do that?"

"No griffin would," said Senneck.

"But I will," said Kullervo.

"You will not!" Senneck said fiercely. "It is not the way. Griffins do not do that, not for each other. We do not need to."

"But you do," said Kullervo. "We do. Everyone else left you, Senneck. Even your human left you. Nobody's ever tried to protect you."

"I can protect myself," Senneck said at once.

"I know. But if you ever need someone there to protect you, I'll be there. That's what I'll give you, Senneck. That's all I have to offer, but it's the best I have." He pushed against her as he said this, not aggressively but affectionately, nibbling at her neck feathers and purring deep in his throat.

Senneck jerked backward away from him, rasping in

irritation, and even lashed out at him with her talons. But the
blows were gentle since she didn't want to hurt him, and
Kullervo's response was to rear up and bat at her with his own
talons. She knocked them away, and before she knew it, her
rebuff had turned into a game.

Tail whipping vigorously from side to side, Kullervo darted
around her like a giant kitten, cheeping and mock-pouncing.

Senneck leapt back at him, and in a moment they were chasing each other, bounding recklessly around the cabin before
Senneck led the way out onto the deck and they continued,
weaving in and out around the masts and hopping onto the railings, which promptly broke and tipped the pair of them off the
side of the ship.

The two griffins unfurled their wings before they hit the
water and glided away over the waves, side by side. Senneck
pulled up, and Kullervo followed, and they flew together around
the ship and above it, looping and diving and darting between
the sails, with Senneck always in front and Kullervo keeping up.

Not only was he keeping up, Senneck realised suddenly, but
he was gaining on her. He was smaller, and that made him
faster, and until today she had never seen what he could really
do in the air when he wanted to. He was flying after her, he was
probably going to catch her, and . . . and . . .

And this, Senneck saw abruptly, this was not a game. They
were chasing, showing off their skills to each other, and
Kullervo was proving his strength by keeping up with her. All
of that made this a mating flight, whether he knew it or not, but
he probably did. After all, he wanted her. He had even fought
another male for her.

And when Senneck realised that, for the first time she seriously considered whether Kullervo could be a mate to her. Not a
lifelong partner; griffins never mated for life, and he was already
a partner to her in a different way, but a partner for one night and
maybe the day after it . . . ? Could she do that? Could she *mate*
with her own human? Of course, he wasn't a human now, he was
a griffin, but still . . .

Part of her said no. To her, he was human, more or less, too
human to be a mate. But he was griffin, too, and he wanted her,
and he had proven himself . . . and besides, there was something he might be able to give her, something she wanted.

She had had chicks once, and she had lost them. Now she had the chance to lay another clutch, and if she wanted to do it, then she would have to do it soon. If she waited much longer, she would become too old for eggs.

And if Kullervo was here, and he was a griffin, and they were flying a mating flight together, then maybe he could give her the eggs that she wanted.

Not that Senneck had ever cared about motherhood, at least in the human sense. For a female griffin, chicks were important. A strong female was a fertile one, who knew how to hatch healthy chicks and raise them properly. Senneck had lost her last opportunity, and here she had found what could be another one.

Kullervo wouldn't understand that, of course. He might be an adult, but in many ways he was more like a chick, and he loved like one, too.

But chicks learnt, Senneck thought. And a female's task was to teach them.

She slowed her flight, and as he got close enough to touch her, she headed back toward the deck and let him catch her there on solid ground.

Kullervo landed, and pounced on her. He said nothing, and instead hissed and rasped excitedly as they tussled again. Flying had pushed most of the humanness out of his mind, and he acted much more like an ordinary griffin now. When he and Senneck were both tired, he groomed her the way a male would a female—roughly and powerfully, not hurting but trying to dominate.

He was weaker than her, but she let him do it anyway, sinking low under his talons and finally pressing herself against the deck. She had forgotten every objection that was still left, and now she raised her tail and turned her head sideways, waiting for him to take what he wanted from her.

But he didn't.

He lay down beside her and put his head on her shoulders, snuggling against her and purring to himself. "That was fun," he said, with a yawn.

Senneck did not move. "What are you doing?" She was bewildered.

"Resting," he said. "I shouldn't have done so much flying right after the change. But it was worth it."

He did not understand. Senneck lifted her head, pushing his

away. "Kullervo," she said, impatient and aroused. "We are not finished."

He huffed softly. "We can go again, if you want. I just need to rest first."

"No!" Senneck rasped, and shoved at him. "We have flown the mating flight. Now is the time to couple."

Kullervo's head went up. "What?"

"You must mate with me," she said, throwing caution to the winds. "It is time." And she pushed herself against him, offering herself in the hopes that he would finally understand.

Kullervo stood up and moved back, staring wide-eyed—humanlike again. Then he bowed his head. "I can't."

"You can. Do it now, before it is too late."

"You don't understand," said Kullervo. "I *can't*. I can't . . . do that with you, Senneck. Even if I wanted to, I couldn't."

She stood too, angry with confusion. "Do not be a fool! You are male, I am female, we are both griffins. Mate with me now, and give me eggs."

But Kullervo only turned his head away. "I can't," he said again. "I never have, and I never will. I'm sterile, Senneck."

"You told me that you suspected it, but you will not know until you have tried," said Senneck, staying close to him. "Come."

But Kullervo only bowed his head. "I'm sorry," he said. "But I . . . I can't . . . I mean, I can't try either. I'm not properly formed. Do you understand? My . . . I never developed properly. Do you understand?"

Senneck stared, then looked away dismissively. "Then I was wrong," she said, turning back into her usual abrupt self. "You are not a true griffin after all."

"No, I'm not. I never was." Kullervo came to her, and touched his beak to hers. "I don't mind, though. Senneck, even if I can't give you what you want, I'll always love you. Always and forever. No matter what. I know you want to have eggs again, and . . . if you want them, then you can have them. You can find a proper griffin to give them to you. I know I stopped you before, but I shouldn't have. It wasn't fair of me—I wasn't thinking straight."

"I do not need your permission," Senneck said coldly, but behind the coldness there was despair. She had been so desperate for eggs that she had made a fool of herself with Kullervo, and just now, here on the ocean with no sight of land, it felt as if there really was nothing else. Where was the mate she wanted, that she had wanted her whole life, ever since she was a youngster just turning into an adult? She had imagined a big, magnificent male griffin, but she had never found him, and now she knew she never would. Instead, she would have another young fool like Skarok, or an old one like herself. And Kullervo, poor pathetic Kullervo, who would never be a father and so never be whole.

He must have sensed what she was feeling because he came close and started to groom her gently. "You'll find someone, Senneck," he promised. "You'll be one of the most powerful griffins in Malvern, and everyone will want you. I'm sure of it."

"Yes." Senneck closed her eyes. "Perhaps."

11

Fugitives

Several long, painful months after the destruction of Skenfrith, Caedmon huddled down by a campfire. Myfina sat beside him, and Garsh and Shar were nearby, talking in quiet but rapid griffish.

Both humans looked ragged and grubby, and tired. Neither of them had slept under a roof more than once or twice since the war ended, and nowadays the only new clothes they got were stolen for them by Saeddryn. They looked like the fugitives they were now, and both of them knew it.

Caedmon glanced up again at the roof that sheltered them. It wasn't much of one; half of it had fallen down sometime ago, and the part that hadn't was rotting and full of holes. Over the last few months, they'd camped in many different places, knowing it would be safer to stay on the move, but despite the shelter here, this one was probably the most depressing so far. A ruined farmhouse in a ruined village, where nobody had lived for nearly twenty years. Eitheinn wasn't just an old village; it was a dead one. Griffiners had come from Malvern and killed it. Malvern's griffiners had all been Southerners back then, but nothing had really changed. Malvern still sent out griffiners to persecute rebels and destroy the places where they hid. The only difference now was that it was Laela doing the sending.

She was sending other kinds of people now, too.

Malvern—and griffiners in general, in fact—had never bothered with a very large human army. Why bother, when a handful of griffins could wipe out an enemy just as well and be much faster and easier to use? It had been the key to griffiner domination for a very long time.

But now Malvern had a new army, a human one, and Laela was using it well. Amoran had sent over shiploads of Northerner slaves, some as gifts and some traded for goods. Laela had freed every single one of them the instant they set foot on Northern soil, and since they were used to obeying and needed something to do with themselves, she had employed them, paying them for jobs not much different than they'd done as slaves. And what many of them had done was fight.

She had sent them to occupy every one of the major cities, some to work as guards, some as builders, and the educated ones, who spoke different languages and knew how to read and write, were given places in the towers. Soon every governor was surrounded by new assistants, and in Warwick and Skenfrith, where one governor had been killed and the other run away with the rebels, former slaves had been appointed to replace them.

It was a brilliant strategy, and it had worked painfully well. Every city was now all but controlled by Laela's new minions, all of whom had been trained since birth to be absolutely obedient. They were free now, but habits like those never really died, and the chances of getting any of them to turn on their new master were very poor. And with Skandar and the Unpartnered still on Laela's side . . .

With all that against him, Caedmon was nothing but an outlaw with an impossible dream, and a handful of supporters that he had all but lost contact with.

The only blessing he still had left was Saeddryn, but with the wretched Oeka in Malvern and Skandar by Laela's side everywhere she went, she couldn't get close enough to kill the one person whose death would make a real difference. Not that she hadn't tried, but so far she had failed, and Caedmon knew better than to even mention it to her any more.

He glanced sideways at Myfina. In her own way, she had taken the situation worse than he had. She had never really recovered from the loss of Heath. And the truth was that Caedmon missed him, too.

Myfina turned her head and caught him looking at her. She gave him a smile. "A copper for your thoughts."

Caedmon shook himself. "They're not worth that much. D'you want something to eat?"

"No thank you." Myfina looked past the fire, toward the empty doorframe. Beyond it there was nothing but darkness. "When is she ever going to come?"

"When it suits her," said Caedmon. His voice sounded indifferent to himself, but the truth was that these days, Saeddryn was the only person who ever gave him hope. Not much hope, but at least her visits meant news, and sometimes messages from the others.

Myfina shuffled closer to him. "I'm not sure I want her to come," she muttered. "She scares me."

"You shouldn't be scared of her," said Caedmon. "She's on our side, remember?"

"That doesn't make any difference. Doesn't it bother you too, how she . . . is now?"

"Not that much," Caedmon said honestly. "I spent too much of my time with Arenadd before; I'm used to it."

Myfina, who had never met the King face-to-face, shivered. "What was he like?"

"Not much different from how my mother is now," said Caedmon. "Except he was younger. In spirit, I mean."

"What does that mean?" Myfina put her head on one side.

"I mean he was like a younger person. More reckless, and he liked taking risks. Do you know he used to sneak out of the Eyrie at night? There was a back passage he used, and he'd go out into the city in disguise."

"Really?" Myfina exclaimed. "Honestly?"

Caedmon nodded. "He took me with him a few times. We explored the city, went to watch the theatre with the commoners, got drunk together . . ." He smiled at the memory. "When we were out there, he stopped being like a King. He was more like my brother, talking me into sneaking off and getting into mischief behind our mother's back. We even looked the same age."

Myfina laughed. "Good gods, I had no idea!" She leaned over unexpectedly and grabbed his hand. "When you're King, promise we'll do that. Promise!"

"I—" Caedmon stared at their clasped hands. Then he smiled. "Of course. You and me."

"And Heath," Myfina added. "When we find him again."

Caedmon lost his smile. "Yes . . ."

It was all a lie, of course, all a fantasy. But there was no reason to say so. There was no harm in cheering each other up.

"But you and the King argued, didn't you?" Myfina said softly, once the silence had gone on too long. "That's why . . ."

Caedmon's face hardened. "He was a killer, Myfina. He was always a killer. The Night God made him to be that way. I think with me he liked to pretend he was still the way he was before he died—just a boy with his whole life in front of him. He made me believe it, too. But he killed every woman he tried to love."

"So that's true, then?" said Myfina. "Did he really poison them, like people say?"

"Yes," said Caedmon. "But not in the way people think. He didn't *mean* to do it."

"I don't understand," said Myfina, not letting go of his hand. "How can you poison someone without meaning to?"

"He wanted children," said Caedmon. "He wanted an heir of his own. Those women he took as his lovers . . . all of them were meant to be his brides. He decided, you see, decided that if he took a lover, and she gave him a child, then he would marry her. Make her his Queen. That's why they all came to him, one after the other. They were afraid of what might happen, but none of them could resist."

"But none of them conceived," said Myfina. She tightened her grip on his hand. "They all died."

"No, they did," said Caedmon. "Not many people know it, but they *did*. They all did. Sooner or later, all of them conceived. And that's what killed them. None of them could carry a child of his to term."

Myfina cringed. "But why . . . ?"

"Because a child is made when the father's blood mixes with the mother's inside her body," a voice answered from the darkness outside. "And his blood was poison."

Caedmon stood up sharply. "Mother!"

Saeddryn appeared, stepping into the firelight. "Caedmon," she said formally. "An' Myfina. It's good to see ye. An' ye, Shar, an' Garsh."

The two griffins bristled instinctively at the sight of her but said nothing.

"What's the news?" asked Caedmon, knowing his mother cared even less about formalities now than she had before.

Saeddryn brushed a few bits of leaf off her dress and sat down opposite him by the fire. "There's no news," she said brusquely, and lapsed into icy silence.

Caedmon wisely sat down again and waited for her to speak in her own time. She sat quite still, staring into the fire. The light played over her face, showing every crease and hollow and filling the ugly scar over her eye with shadow.

Saeddryn had been dead for months now, and it showed. It showed as it had showed on Arenadd toward the end of his time as the Shadow That Walked, when he had withdrawn from living humans and stopped imitating their ways. When Caedmon had known him, he had still lived more or less like an ordinary man and had mostly looked like one, but Saeddryn had chosen to forget the habits of the living immediately after her death. She had stopped eating or sleeping, and ignored things like heat and cold. It had enhanced her powers, she said, but it had also begun to leach the humanity out of her, and Caedmon noticed it even if she didn't seem to care.

Her face was gaunt and pale as death, the one eye red-rimmed and soulless. On the rare occasions that she sat down to rest, as she was doing now, she didn't fidget or move her head around like an ordinary person would, but sat as still as ice, scarcely breathing. Caedmon wondered if she even needed to breathe any more. Probably not.

"I got to the new governor of Warwick," she said suddenly.

"Did you kill him?" asked Caedmon.

"No. No point. He's just doin' his job. Doesn't know or care about any of our troubles. I left a message instead. Left more in the city. Talked from the shadows. They think there's a ghost there now. Did the same in Skenfrith. That's the best place t'go. The people there won't ever forget what the half-breed did."

"What about the half-breed?" Caedmon interrupted. "Did you get to her? See her?"

"Tried," said Saeddryn, scowling. "She was supposed t'be visitin' Fruitsheart, but then at the last moment she goes to Caerleon instead. It's the third time this has happened. Every time I think she's gonna be in one place, I find out she's gone to another." Her fists clenched. "It's startin' to feel like she can read my mind. An' even I can't travel fast enough t'catch up with her when she does that."

Caedmon looked bleakly at her. "What are we going to do, Mother?"

"Don't know," said Saeddryn. "It's a bloody stalemate, an' it's gonna take more than just us to break it." She gave Caedmon a sharp look. "But maybe ye should be the one doin' something."

"Like what?" said Caedmon, more sourly than he meant to. "Should I challenge her to single combat? Invade Malvern with three griffiners and a dead woman?"

To his surprise, Saeddryn's answer was a dry cackle. "No, but maybe another mad Southerner with a dagger would do the trick, eh? Don't ye think? Worked well last time, didn't it?"

Caedmon stared and then started. "What—?"

"Aye, I know it was ye who sent that man after Arenadd," said Saeddryn. "Ye planned it well, too. Shame ye forgot it takes more than a dunking in the canal t'kill the Shadow That Walks."

Caedmon felt as if a hand had wrapped around his throat. "How did you know . . . ?"

"I didn't. Didn't know a damn thing about it until yer father told me. Yer little assassin fell into his hands after the half-breed pulled Arenadd out of the canal. When yer father got a confession out of him an' realised whose head would roll when Arenadd found out, he made sure he'd never say a word." Saeddryn's eye narrowed. "Ye had good sense t'be miles away from Malvern when that happened. Meant all the suspicion fell on me instead."

Caedmon had gone pale. "I didn't mean . . ."

"Hah." Saeddryn waved his guilt away. "It didn't make no difference. Arenadd already knew I was plottin' against him, an' said so before he ran off. It's just a shame yer plan didn't work, or we coulda had the half-breed safely out of the way an' ye on the throne before things got so out of hand."

"I thought *you* wanted the throne," Caedmon growled, embarrassment making him angry.

"Not for long," said Saeddryn. "I knew I wasn't gonna live much longer. But if I'd had the throne, it would've taken the uncertainty away, made it easier for ye when the time came. Anyway, that's in the past now. An' I lied."

"Eh?" The sudden change in topic had caught him off guard. "Lied about what?"

"About there not bein' any news. There is some."

"What is it?" asked Myfina, who had stayed sensibly quiet up until now.

"I've just come from the coast," said Saeddryn. "Last place I visited. A ship's just arrived there, an' guess who's on it?"

"More slaves?" Caedmon guessed.

"Some, but not that many," said Saeddryn. "No, it's the half-breed's crony that's come back. The one they call man-griffin. Him an' the griffin, Senneck—the Bastard's old partner."

"Oh." Caedmon had heard of these two even if he had never seen them. They were the half-breed's spies, and had proven to be surprisingly dangerous enemies given that one was an age-ing griffin and the other one a deformed freak. "Did you find out where they'd come from?"

"Aye, Maijan," said Saeddryn. "There on some secret mission. They've brought someone back with them."

"Who?" asked Myfina.

"An Amorani Prince," said Saeddryn. "Prince Akhane. The same man what the half-breed married in Amoran."

"He hasn't brought an army with him, has he?" said Caedmon, his heart sinking.

"Not that I know of. Just a few friends, nothing special." Saeddryn shook her head. "I couldn't figure out what he'd come over for. Obvious answer is it's t'be her royal consort. Guess she couldn't find a Northern man who'd touch her with a ten-foot pole."

Myfina laughed unkindly. "Still, that doesn't change much."

"It changes everything," Saeddryn snapped. "For one it means a stronger alliance with Amoran. For another, it means she could soon have an heir. It also means she's just made a big mistake."

Caedmon nodded. "Marrying an Amorani—a *sun worshipper*, when she's surrounded by good Northern men? And she'd get a half-breed heir from him, too . . . more than that. It'd be more Southerner and Amorani than Northerner. You know what people will say when that happens."

"Leavin' the throne to be taken by a foreigner," Saeddryn resumed. "Givin' it to an heir who's not one of us. We fought a war that tore the North apart so we'd have the right t'be ruled by our own kind. With this, she'll undo everything."

"Oh no," Myfina groaned.

Caedmon, however, smiled a grim smile. "No, Myfina—this is a good thing. She's just stabbed herself in the foot. If the people see her sharing her throne with some dog-eating Amorani, what do you think they'll do then?"

Myfina finally caught on. "Start thinking you'd be a better option?"

"Exactly." Caedmon's mind was already racing. "We'd need to move fast, to take advantage of the outrage this is going to create. Mother, what do you suggest?"

"We need griffiners," she said immediately. "An' that's what I'm going to get us. I'm gonna start making contact. Every time one leaves Malvern, I'll be on his tail. I'll talk to him, see what I can do. Plant a few ideas, make a few threats maybe."

Nobody dared ask her how she would know who was going where, or when.

"Do that," Caedmon said. "And spread the word to the others. In the meantime, we're going up to the Throne for a while. It should be a good enough hiding place for a few days, and Shar and Garsh should find better hunting."

Saeddryn nodded. "Pray in the circle. It'll make ye feel better, if nothin' else. I'll come an' meet ye up there when I've got more for ye."

She stood up and left the ruined house without another word.

Outside, she slipped away from Eitheinn without a backward glance. "Did ye hear all that?" she murmured aloud once she was out of earshot.

I did, Arenadd replied at once. *It's a good plan. Let's go.*

Saeddryn couldn't stop herself from adding, "An' now ye know I never sent that man after ye. I never did try an' kill ye . . ."

Your friend Penllyn tried in Amoran, Arenadd said tonelessly. *It doesn't matter now. Go to Malvern. We have to spread the truth, quickly.*

"Yes, yes." Saeddryn slid into the shadows, and was gone.

After Saeddryn had gone, Caedmon half expected Myfina to say something about her having exposed what he had done to Arenadd. But she didn't, and only wished him good night before they both snuggled down by their partners for warmth.

Caedmon lay on his side, taking comfort from Shar's deep breathing and the warm smell of her fur and feathers. Another griffin might have abandoned him by now after all his failures, but she hadn't. She still believed in him. Like Myfina did, and Saeddryn as well, and all the others out there who were still keeping faith and waiting for their day to come.

Silently, he vowed to himself that no matter what happened, he would not fail them again. Arenadd had failed them, first by disinheriting his rightful heir, then by naming the half-breed instead. But Caedmon knew with all his heart and all his soul that he was the one that the Night God had always meant to be his successor, and he would learn from Arenadd's mistakes. He would not repeat them. He would not run away from his duty the way Arenadd had, or betray his people to Southerners and half-breeds. Not for anything.

The promise made him feel better, and he drifted off to sleep.

The following morning, Caedmon and Myfina scattered their campfire and left before the sun had finished rising. Shar and Garsh were impatient to be off, and the moment their humans were mounted, they flew away from the remains of Eithe- inn and up into the mountains. Winter was over, but there was always snow on the tops of the First Mountains. By now, though, it had melted away from the plateau where the thirteen stones of Taranis' Throne stood. Shar and Garsh landed there and left their humans to find a camp while they flew away to hunt.

Caedmon stood for a moment by the altar stone in the centre of the circle and admired the stones. He had been here before sev- eral times, the first time when he was only a boy, and his mother had brought him to see the most holy place in the North. Once, she said, there had been many circles like this one. But the invad- ing Southerners had pulled them down when they began to sup- press the old ways of the Northerners and so make them lose their unity for good. But the sacred stones of Taranis' Throne were too high and far away to reach, and so they had been left alone by the Southerners, who must have thought nobody would bother com- ing this far into the freezing mountains just to worship at them. They had been wrong, and Northerners had come back to the

Throne. This was where the refugees who had survived the uprising led by Saeddryn's mother, Arddryn, had come to hide with their leader. This was where Arenadd had found them, years later, and been groomed to succeed Arddryn as the leader of the rebels, with Saeddryn as his wife and second-in-command. He had done everything that was asked of him, except for marrying Saeddryn. Instead, he had found another husband for her and conducted their wedding here, in the circle.

Caedmon stood where his parents had once stood and felt the weight of history pressing down on him. It was a long way away from the magnificent Eyrie in Malvern, but this was still his inheritance. Maybe, in its own way, it was a more important part of it than Malvern ever would be. After all, Malvern had been built by Southerners, but the Throne was a place for Northerners.

Myfina joined him. "I've lit a fire," she said. "Come on, let's go and lie low. If you want to pray, we can wait until night."

"Right, right." Caedmon followed her absently back down the slope and into the little hollow in the mountainside where she had begun to set up camp. There they ate a small breakfast from their supplies and worked together to set up beds for themselves, just as they'd done a dozen times before. After that, Caedmon went to gather firewood.

They had nothing much else to do here but wait and make themselves comfortable until Saeddryn brought news, so once the camp was secure, Caedmon left Myfina to work on it and went in search of food.

There wasn't much to find. He had a bow, but he had never really hunted before, and at this time of year there was very little in the way of edible plants. In the end, he found some mushrooms, and climbed laboriously back up the mountainside to where Myfina waited.

She was kind enough not to comment on the handful of shrivelled brown mushrooms; it was more than they usually got in the places they had camped so far. There was a chance that the griffins might bring them something, of course. But not a good one.

Sure enough, Garsh eventually returned empty pawed. He said nothing but settled down in an irritable kind of way and let Myfina clean his talons.

Caedmon left them to it and sat on a rock upslope from the camp, watching out for Shar.

She arrived a little while later, landing neatly by Caedmon's side. She shook out her wings and put her head down close to his. "There is a griffin coming," she said.

Caedmon stood up sharply. "Where? How close?"

"Do not panic," Shar advised. "It is only one, and smaller than I am. But it is coming this way, from the lowlands. I think it must be coming here."

"Right." Caedmon leapt down from the rock. His boots hit the ground just beside the campfire, startling Garsh, whose head shot up to hiss at him. Caedmon ignored him. "Someone's coming," he said. "A griffin."

Myfina bit her lip. "Just one?"

"Yes," Shar put in from overhead. "It has a human with it. I saw it as I came back here, but it did not see me."

Myfina looked at Caedmon. "What should we do?"

"You do not need to do anything," Garsh interrupted. He stood up. "I will kill the intruder before he arrives."

"No," said Caedmon. "We should let them land. Try to find out who they are—make sure they can't escape, and talk to them. For all we know, they could be looking for us. If not, then maybe we could persuade them."

"And if they do not decide to serve you?" asked Garsh, tail twitching in annoyance.

"Then we'll have to kill them," Caedmon said reluctantly.

"It is a good plan," said Shar. "It would be easier to kill him in the air since he is carrying a human, but his submission to us would be more useful than his death."

Garsh made an ugly rasping noise in his throat. "We will see, then." He was a big griffin and obviously tired of hiding. He'd always preferred to fight before anything else.

Caedmon checked that his sickle was still safe in his belt. It was, so he pulled his hood on and headed off up the slope toward the stones. If the strange griffin was planning to land here then the Throne would be the most obvious place for it since it was the only flat land for a long way.

Shar followed, sticking to the ground for now. Behind them, Garsh took off and flew to a perch on a mountainside overlooking the Throne. From there, he would be able to swoop in and ambush the stranger the moment it looked necessary.

Myfina came with Caedmon. As they neared the top of the plateau, the strange griffin came into sight. Caedmon's stomach lurched—it was much closer than he had expected, and it was indeed headed straight for the Throne.

Keeping calm, he motioned to Myfina to hide behind one of the stones. He chose one for himself, and Shar took another—it was big, but could only hide her if she stood head-on to it. Hopefully, the stranger would be too busy concentrating on his landing to notice her.

Their luck was in. The strange griffin landed by the altar stone, one forepaw catching it by the corner. Caedmon, watching, quickly summed up what he saw.

The griffin was male, and fairly large, but in a lean and sinewy kind of way. His coat was rough and shaggy, and made it obvious that if he had ever lived in a city, then it had been a long time ago. He turned his head, yellow eyes sharp, and yawned as his human nimbly dismounted.

Caedmon stared in bewilderment. The other griffiner looked about as tall as he was, but beyond that not much could be made out. He—if it was a man—wore a huge animal skin that covered almost his entire body. Feathers covered his upper torso, and the hood over his head, and below that a furry tail and legs dangled.

Holy gods, that's a griffin hide! Caedmon thought in shock.

The stranger turned, adjusting the hood, which Caedmon now saw was made from the animal's head with part of the skullbone and the beak left on to give it some shape. The tip of the beak curved down over the stranger's nose like the guard on a helmet, but Caedmon saw that he was indeed a man. With most of the rest of his face hidden by a long black beard, it wasn't much of an intuition. The forelegs of the griffin hide were mostly gone, but the feathered parts remained and had been sewn back together to serve as sleeves. Under that the man wore an assortment of other furs and skins, which made it impossible to tell what build he had underneath or whether he was carrying a weapon.

Caedmon had been staring for so long that he hadn't even noticed Shar leaving her hiding place. The other griffin did, however, and when he started up aggressively Caedmon came to his senses and emerged as well.

Moving to stand by Shar, he held up his hand in a sign of peace.

"There's no need for fighting," he called. "Welcome to Taranis' Throne. Please, tell us who you are and why you've come here."

The griffin only hissed angrily, but the man's reaction was very different. He stood very still, then took a step forward. "Caedmon . . . ?"

Myfina had come out as well, and she too stared at the stranger. "Who *are* you?"

The man's face split into a grin. "Myfina! Great gods, it *is* you. I don't believe it!"

Caedmon reached for his sickle. "Who in the Night God's name are you?"

The man looked surprised. Then he reached up and pushed his hood back. His hair was long and tied into a ragged braid, and his face was scarred and weather-beaten. He looked forty years old at least. "It's me," he said. "It's Heath."

Myfina nearly shouted his name. *"Heath!"*

Caedmon went toward him, disbelieving, but as he got closer he started to see what he had missed. Behind the thick beard, behind the scar that went from his eye to his cheek . . . behind all that it *was* Heath, grinning at him in the same way he always had.

Myfina had already seen it. She ran past Caedmon and hugged Heath so fiercely that the griffin with him almost reared up to attack. But he relaxed again when Heath hugged her back, and when Caedmon burst out laughing and went to hug him as well.

"Heath!" he exclaimed, slapping his old friend on the back. "My gods, I don't believe it! You were supposed to have died!"

"Oh, I wouldn't go and do a thing like that," Heath said easily. "There's no money in it. But I didn't think I'd find *you* alive. After all, you're the sort of noble person who'd go and die heroically. Us criminals aren't good enough for that!"

Myfina hadn't let go of his hand. "Heath, I'm so sorry we left you like that. There was no time . . . I begged Saeddryn to bring you with us, but she said it would kill you if she did. We couldn't go back after that. I kept asking her to look for you, but she said she never found you."

"I think I'd have noticed if she did," said Heath. He looked up warily—Shar had approached and was eyeing his partner.

The shaggy griffin kept his distance but didn't back down when Shar stood over him, her feathers puffed out aggressively.

For a few tense moments the two griffins faced off, until the male relaxed and looked away. "I am Eck-hoo," he said. "This human here is mine, but he is not a threat to yours. I am not here to intrude on your territory; my human and I came to find you so that we could join your cause. We have a common enemy."

"Which enemy?" Shar asked, apparently not satisfied by this little speech.

"The Unpartnered, who destroyed Skenfrith, which was my home where I had hatched," Eck-hoo said. "I could not risk staying there once they had overrun it, so I found this human to help me leave. A griffin cannot travel alone, and this human has been useful to me."

"I don't believe it," Caedmon murmured to Heath. "You, a griffiner."

"I know," Heath said ruefully. "The whole world's gone mad."

"I didn't know you spoke griffish," said Myfina.

"I don't," said Heath. "Echo here's taught me a few words, though."

"He cannot say my name," said Eck-hoo. "But that does not matter. Is there food here? Shelter? We have travelled a long way, and we need both."

Shar huffed. "You may hunt here; this is not yet my territory. But you will need to make peace with Garsh, who is hiding nearby ready to kill you if you are an enemy."

"I understand," said Eck-hoo, ignoring the threat. "I will stay until my human is sheltered, then hunt."

"Yes, come with us," said Caedmon. "We don't have much, but there's a fire."

"Can't wait," Heath said cheerfully.

The moment they were at the camp and Heath had made himself comfortable by the fire, Myfina spoke.

"Tell us everything," she said. "Where have you been? What happened to you? And where did you get that outfit from?"

Heath huddled closer to the fire, holding his hands out. "Haven't had a fire in a while," he mumbled. "It's good to be warm . . ." He coughed on the last word, and for the first time Caedmon and Myfina saw how frail he had become. Myfina moved closer to him to try to help him, and he tried to say something, but he went into a coughing fit that stopped him speaking for some time before he got his breath back.

"No, no, it's all right," he said as soon as he could. "It's just a bit of a cough; I've had it for a while. So, what have you two been up to all this time? You look like a couple of beggars."

"Thank *you*." Caedmon grinned. "Nice try, Heath, but we asked first. Tell us what happened to you, then we'll answer. We'll even pay you."

"In what?" Heath asked at once.

"A cup of hot wine should do it, I think," said Myfina. She brought out the wineskin and squirted some of its contents into a pot. "I've been saving this for a special occasion, and I think this is it."

"Definitely," said Caedmon. "Does that sound like a good deal to you, Heath?"

Heath chuckled. "I'd say you were being robbed, but it's a very good story. It's also long, so I'd better start now . . ."

12

In Pairs

Kullervo returned to Malvern as a human again, riding on Senneck's back. Inva and Skarok flew just behind them, with Vander and Ymazu, but Prince Akhane and Zekh led the way during the last stretch. Before then, Skarok and Senneck had led, since they knew the way to Malvern, but once the city had come in sight, they fell back and let the superior Zekh go ahead.

Kullervo was glad to see Malvern's walls again. It had been a long time since he had left them behind, and now that he was back, he realised just how much he had missed the city. It had become his home, he reflected, but it hadn't really started to feel like one until he had been asked to leave it.

The Eyrie already knew they were coming —Vander's little messenger dragon had seen to that, and it had returned with instructions for them to land on top of the Council Tower.

Sure enough, there was a welcoming committee waiting for them. Zekh landed in the open space provided, and Senneck and the others were close behind. Kullervo dismounted and nearly panicked when he saw the massive creature that came forward to inspect the Amorani griffin.

A male griffin, bigger than any griffin he had ever seen. A griffin whose feathers were silver and whose fur was pitch-black. A griffin who was horribly familiar.

Kullervo cringed backward, almost trying to hide behind Senneck's wing. "The Mighty Skandar!" he hissed.

Skandar, however, paid no attention to the man he had once

tried to kill. He sniffed at Zekh, who sensibly adopted a submissive posture, and once he was satisfied that he had intimidated the newcomer, he turned his attention to the others there. The griffins who had come with Akhane's friends all dropped their heads respectfully, and so did Skarok, who was native to Malvern but was still a stranger to Skandar.

Then it was Senneck's turn.

Later on, Kullervo was honestly surprised that he didn't run away when he saw the dark griffin coming toward him. He moved back, feeling his stomach twist, and nearly fainted with relief when Skandar ignored him completely and instead began to inspect Senneck. She made the proper signs of respect to him, but there was a hint of excitement there as well. Her tail flicked from side to side, a feathery fan making a dry brushing sound on the stonework. "Mighty Skandar," she purred. "It is an honour to meet you after so long."

He bit the back of her neck. "You female. What name?"

"I am Senneck," she said. "And I come before you as your inferior in every way, glad to do whatever you ask." It was traditional for a griffin to say something like this when hoping to be admitted into another's territory, but the promises weren't usually this servile.

It seemed to please Skandar, at least, and he moved away with a rasp of "You stay."

Kullervo, coming back to Senneck's side, saw the human he went to stand with, and felt his eyes widen again. Laela! He had almost expected it to be his father, and Laela certainly looked like him. She was wearing one of his finer robes, and the crown as well, and for once her hair was neat and glossy around her shoulders. But it wasn't just her clothes that made her look like her father; there was something about the way she stood, and the steady look on her face, that made Kullervo think of his father as he imagined he must have been. Laela had found authority.

Behind her there were other griffiners, all Northerners, of course. Kullervo only recognised one or two of them, but he found out later that they were Laela's new councillors.

The griffish formalities over with, Laela came forward. "Prince Akhane," she said in a loud, clear voice. "Welcome to Malvern, an' welcome to the Kingdom of Tara. I'm glad to see yeh here." She had been practising with her voice, too, Kullervo thought—it sounded much smoother than before even if she hadn't quite shed her crude, peasant accent.

Akhane seemed to appreciate it as well. He was wearing his own ceremonial clothing, complete with a small gold circlet, all of which made him look even more handsome than before. "Queen Laela," he said. "I am honoured to be here in your beautiful country, and in this Eyrie, which I have longed to see. And I am honoured to see you again."

Laela smiled at him, in a sweet way that Kullervo had never seen before. "Thank you for comin' here. An' you, Vander, it's good to see you again too. Now," she went on, as Vander nodded politely in response, "Prince Akhane, I have somethin' to ask from you."

He must have been expecting this because he only inclined his head pleasantly, and said, "Ask whatever you wish, Queen Laela."

Her smile turned a little shy. "I rule Tara, but I can't rule alone. Prince Akhane, you're my husband in Amoran—will yeh be my husband in the North as well, an' rule with me?"

"I will," he said gravely.

"Good!" And now Laela *did* take him by surprise, by taking him in her arms and kissing him. Akhane kissed her back, and several of the nobles there smiled to themselves.

Kullervo smiled, too, mostly with relief. He had always wondered what arranged marriages were like, and he had wondered whether this one would work. But Akhane had sounded affectionate when he talked about Laela during the voyage, and Laela had been the same when she talked about him, so maybe it wasn't really arranged at all. After all, arranged marriages in stories were always thought up by parents, but this one had been thought up by Laela and Akhane themselves.

"I've arranged for a celebration tonight, here on the tower-top," said Laela, once she and Akhane had parted. "If that's all right with you?"

"It is, of course," he said. "Once Zekh and I have rested, we will be glad to come."

"There's plenty of time," said Laela. "Let's go inside, an' you'll be shown to yer rooms."

The two groups broke up and filed over to the ramp that led down into the tower. The griffiners there who lived in Malvern flew away instead, returning to their homes via the outside entrances. Senneck and Kullervo went that way, too. Kullervo wanted to see Laela, but he knew she would be too busy for the time being, and he and Senneck should rest and tidy themselves up first anyway.

Their rooms hadn't been used in a long while, of course, but someone had been in and cleaned them out. There was fresh nesting material for Senneck and clean sheets for Kullervo, and a good fire burning. There was even some food laid out for them both, and water boiling for Kullervo to have a bath.

He bathed, and ate, and had a nap, glad to be in his own bed again. In her own room, Senneck attended to her needs and slept, too. She had flown a long way, and she would have to be alert tonight.

Kullervo was well rested and had just finished putting on some clean clothes when a servant arrived with a summons to go and see Laela in her audience chamber.

Senneck had woken up by now, and she and Kullervo went up together at once.

Laela was waiting for them in the marble chamber, but thankfully Skandar wasn't with her. She hugged Kullervo. "I'm so glad yer back."

"Me too." Kullervo grinned shyly.

Laela was looking up at him. "Holy gods, were yeh always this tall?" She exclaimed again a moment later, as her brain caught up with her eyes. "Good Gryphus, what happened? Yer a bloody giant! Tell me yeh weren't always like that, please."

"I wasn't," said Kullervo. "I grew a lot while I was away."

Laela raised an eyebrow. "You ain't gonna keep on doin' it, are yeh? Yeh won't be able t'get through doors if yeh do."

"No, it's all right, I'm finished now." Kullervo felt himself blushing. "But you've changed, too, you know."

"Yeah, I know," said Laela. "Everyone's changed. C'mon, sit down an' let's talk."

Kullervo took the chair she offered him. "Laela, why is Skandar here? Where did he come from?"

"I would like to know this as well," said Senneck. "I heard that he had left Malvern with his human. Why is he back?"

"He decided to," said Laela. "An' I talked him into helpin'

me. He wanted t'rule again, he needed a human t'do it, an' . . . well, there yeh go. Plus he's angry with Saeddryn. She made Arenadd run off, after all."

"And Oeka?" said Senneck. "Where is she?"

Laela's mouth tightened. "Well . . . her *body's* down in the crypt. Nobody knows where her mind is."

Senneck had become very still. "She has finished working her magic?"

"I s'pose," said Laela. "Couldn't get much sense out of her. She drove poor Yorath insane. He locked himself in the library an' filled a book up with horrible stuff. Wouldn't sleep or eat or do anythin' except write nonsense. He died when he was finished. Just put his head down on the book an' died. As for Oeka . . . we see her every now an' then. As a vision, I mean. She talks sometimes, but it's all gibberish. She talks to people who ain't there, griffins who died years ago . . . last time it was the Mighty Kraal, an' before that it was someone called Hemant, whoever that is. Was."

If Senneck felt any triumph at that moment, she didn't show it. "I warned her," she said. "She did not listen, and now she has paid the price. The griffish mind and body were never meant to contain so much power. No living creature can do that. Your partner is insane now and will never recover. She has lost everything."

"I know," Laela said grimly. "Now, Kullervo—tell me about yer trip, why don't yeh? An' tell me how yeh got so big while yer at it!"

Kullervo nodded cheerfully. "I'll do my best!"

He described his and Senneck's journey, leaving nothing out. Laela listened with interest, particularly when he talked about his unnatural growth spurt. She asked a few questions, but not that many until he reached the part about the Temple in Maijan.

"Wait, yer sayin' yeh couldn't go in there?"

"I could, but I didn't like it," said Kullervo. He rubbed his hands nervously. "If I had any doubt about whose son I was, it's gone now. You told me about how he couldn't go into holy places. Now I know it has a bad effect on me, too."

"It didn't hurt yeh, did it?" Laela looked anxious, and some of her old accent had come back.

"No, I'm fine. I just felt sick and nervous." Kullervo took a deep breath and continued with his story. He even told her about Vander and Inva becoming a couple. The only part he left out was his love for Senneck. It was too complicated and strange, and he was too shy about it anyway.

Laela took all this in and smiled when he told her about Inva. "That's nice. I always thought she was lonely here. An' if Vander's retired, then maybe he'll stay with her. I'm glad Vander's back, too."

"Why?" asked Kullervo.

"I've met him before," said Laela. "He was a big help in Amoran. I'm thinkin' he'll give us more good advice now if we ask. Do yeh know, he knew our father? Before they met in Amoran, I mean."

"Really?"

"Yeah. He knew him when he was just a boy, back in Eagleholm. I dunno much more than that, but they had a history. I listened in on 'em once, an' by the sounds of it, Vander saved his life. So, is that everythin'?"

"I think so," said Kullervo.

"Good." Laela clapped him on the shoulder. "It's good t'have yeh back, Kullervo. I've missed yeh. Livin' here like this gets lonely."

"I know," said Kullervo. "I mean, I guessed." He looked proudly at her. "But it looks like you didn't need my help much. You've done so much while I was gone!"

"Done this an' that." Laela shrugged. "It's all just busywork when all's said an' done. But the cities are secure, Caedmon's disappeared, an' everything's just about how I'd like it t'be. But not quite."

"Not quite?" Kullervo put his head on one side, griffin-like.

"No. It ain't gonna be right until Saeddryn's dealt with. As long as she's out there, we'll never be safe."

"Isn't she doing anything, though?" asked Kullervo.

"She is," said Laela. "She hasn't tried comin' back to Malvern, but she's been seen in the cities. She's killed a lot of people. Some of 'em were my officials. She scared the shit out of two of my new governors—got to 'em from behind locked doors or in front of other people who never saw her."

Kullervo shuddered. "That's horrible!"

"Scare tactics," said Laela, almost dismissively. "They're

workin', though. It looks bad, see. Makes us look weak for not
bein' able to stop her or even find her. But there's nothin' we
can do about it that I've been able t'figure out. I thought maybe
Skandar could do somethin', but fat chance of gettin' him t'do
anythin' he doesn't want to." She scowled.

"Why wouldn't he help you fight her?" asked Kullervo.
"She's his enemy as well, isn't she?"

"I dunno," said Laela. "It doesn't make much sense. He's gotten this bad habit of not goin' where I ask him to. I make plans
t'go to Skenfrith, he flies to Fruitsheart. I say let's go to Warwick,
he flies to Wolf's Town. Even if he says he's gonna go where I
decide, he changes his mind at the last moment. There's not a
damn thing I can do about it. Anyway, I don't reckon he could
find her even if he wanted to. Shadows That Walk ain't that easy
to find, not even for him."

"That's a shame," said Kullervo. "But maybe Akhane can
help you."

Laela smiled. "I'm sure he will, one way or another."

"What about me, then?" said Kullervo, getting straight to the
question he wanted to ask the most. "I've done what you asked
me to."

"An' yeh did a good job of it," said Laela. "If yeh want a
reward, name it."

"Well . . ." Kullervo looked at the floor. "Well, er . . . Senneck was saying maybe . . . er, that maybe we could have an
official position of some kind."

"Done," Laela said immediately.

Kullervo looked up. "What, just like that? What position is it?"

"Don't be daft," said Laela. "You've already got an important
position—the position of bein' my brother. Do yeh really think
yer inferior to all them Lords and Ladies what yeh saw up there
today? They're just griffiners. Masters, sure, but you're a Prince,
ain't yeh? You're higher'n the lot of them put together."

"Oh," said Kullervo. "Yes, I suppose so."

"No yeh don't," Laela said firmly. "You're King Arenadd's
son, so that makes yeh a Prince. An' don't think I've forgotten
that. While you were away, I drew up some documents recog-
nisin' you as my brother and Prince of Malvern. And if anythin'
happens to me, an' I die without an heir, you'll be King. If I
have any children, an' they're orphaned, you're their guardian,

an' you'll be regent until they're old enough. There. Hope that makes yeh feel important enough." She grinned.

Kullervo reddened. "I'm not sure I—"

"Yes yeh are," Laela cut him off. "Yer a Prince, so yeh can damn well act like one. I ain't havin' none of this I-ain't-worthy crap, understand?"

"Of course." Kullervo rubbed his forehead. "And . . . thank you. Is there anything you want me to do now, though?"

"Yeah. Rest an' recuperate, an' come to the feast tonight for some grub."

"And after that?"

"Sleep it off an' hope yeh ain't too hung-over the next day." Laela cackled.

"I don't drink," Kullervo said rather primly.

"Suit yerself." Laela saw his expression and caved in. "Oh, all right. There's somethin' else I was thinkin' I might ask yeh to do. I was gonna leave it for a bit before I asked, though, let yeh rest a bit first."

"Tell me about it now," said Kullervo. "And I can think about it while I rest."

"All right." Laela looked uncertain. "Now look, yeh don't have to do it. It's a risky plan, an' I can send someone else if you don't think yeh can."

"Try me," said Kullervo.

"Right, then." Laela took a deep breath. "I've had plenty of time to think while yeh were away, an' one of the things I'm thinkin' now is this. I've stayed Queen here 'cause my father wanted me to, but also because I knew that if Saeddryn ever took the throne, there'd be war. She was pushin' for Arenadd to invade the South, see, but he wouldn't do it. Everyone else disagreed with him, but he never backed down. I think that's why he made me his heir, 'cause he knew I was born in the South, an' I'd see to it that the invasion didn't happen. The honest truth is, if I lost out here, an' Saeddryn or Caedmon took the throne, they'd probably go ahead with the plan. The South ain't ready to be invaded, an' if it was, it'd be terrible. Thousands of people would die. Right now, I'm just about the only thing standin' in the way of that. An' maybe, one day, it'll be your turn. Any case, the South owes us a big favour."

"So?" said Kullervo.

"So I'm thinkin' it's time we let them know about it," said Laela. "You an' me ain't immortal like our dad. If the South is gonna stay protected, then the only way t'keep it that way is with a treaty. Bring them into this an' let them help us."

"You want me to go to them, don't you?" said Kullervo. "And make this treaty."

"Yeah, I do," said Laela. "Someone's got to do it, an' even if I don't like sendin' yeh out there, there's nobody here who'd be better. You was raised in the South, so yeh know their ways, an' there's the winged-man thing too if yeh have to use it. But more than that, yer my brother, an' a promise from you's worth more than anything I could send with Inva. Of course, if yeh don't want to go, I won't force yeh, but that was the idea I had."

Kullervo thought about it. "I'd have to visit all the capitals. Canran, Wylam, Withypool, and Eagleholm, if it's still there."

"Yeah," said Laela. "If everythin' goes right, yeh could get them to send griffiners here as ambassadors. I'm gonna tell them that if they make peace with us, then I'm gonna grant them permission to come back here an' live if they want to. Even commoners could come back to their old homes. Our lot won't like it much, but it's gotta be done. Otherwise, we'll just go on hatin' each other from a distance an' get more an' more scared of each other until the whole thing falls apart."

While she talked, Kullervo thought of a place he had visited and never forgotten. Gwernyfed, where Northerners and Southerners lived together in harmony. He had found Senneck there, and had met friendly, honest people who had treated him as an honoured guest and given him everything they had to offer. He had never told anyone about it, not even Laela. Gwernyfed was a secret place, and it had to stay that way. If the Southerners there were ever discovered, then they would probably be killed.

Now, though, he found himself picturing a future where Gwernyfed would not have to be a secret, a future where the two races lived peacefully side by side all through Tara. All through Cymria, even. A future where there would be no more need for pointless hatred, and where his father's story would never have to be repeated.

A wonderful excitement and joy rushed through him. "I'll do it!"

Laela smiled at his enthusiasm. "If yeh think yer up to it, then good luck. But yeh oughta talk to Senneck first."

"Oh, right." Kullervo turned to see what she thought, but she had disappeared.

For once in her long and ambitious life, Senneck hadn't wanted to stay and listen. Even though she knew they would be discussing important things, like rewards and advancement, she left the two humans to talk and slipped away through the chamber. An entrance, hidden behind a tapestry, led to a corridor that ran around the outside of the chamber and into a luxurious nesting chamber. Senneck had never seen it before, and she marvelled at the tapestries on the walls, the golden drinking trough, and the shining gemstones scattered among the nesting material.

At the moment, the nest was unoccupied, but even though she knew she was intruding, she crouched near the entrance and began to groom. She did so slowly and methodically, preening every feather and licking her fur flat.

She pretended that she was grooming only to make herself neat, but the truth was that she was doing it out of nervousness as well. And no wonder, given whose nest this was. But despite the danger, she would not leave it, and in between bouts of grooming, she thrust her beak in among the dry straw and reeds and inhaled deeply, filling her nostrils with the rich, musky odour that had been left there.

It excited her so much that it made her want to roll and wriggle around in it like a youngster, but she restrained herself. She was too old to let herself be that undignified.

And then . . .

And then *he* came.

He came with almost no sound at all—just a sudden, slick whoosh of wings, and his paws touched the stone with a faint click of talons. One moment she was alone, and the next the stars she had been watching through the archway were blocked out by a massive shadow.

Unable to stop herself, she moved back and pressed herself to the ground. Fear made her heart beat faster.

Skandar had already seen her. He came forward, feathers puffed aggressively, and made an ugly rasping hiss.

For an instant, Senneck nearly panicked. Old memories came back, of a time when she was younger and stronger, but when this griffin had been her enemy—and more than that, he had been the only thing she was afraid of. In all that time during the war, she had never met him, or even seen him more than once at a distance, but that had only made him bigger in her mind and more terrifying.

Thankfully, though, she managed to stop herself from running away. If she had, then he would probably have chased her down and killed her. Instead, she stayed where she was and kept her submissive posture, only raising her head a little so he could see her better.

"Mighty Skandar," she hissed back. "I am Senneck." She knew the name wouldn't mean anything to him.

Skandar stopped briefly. "Why you here?"

"To find you," she said. "But not to fight." Her voice lowered as she spoke, and took on a soft, purring tone.

"No griffin fight Mighty Skandar," he said roughly, but his feathers had begun to go down.

"Not many," she said. "And I am so small beside you." Her confidence began to return, and the fear seeped away. She moved closer, still keeping flat, and took him in properly for the first time. His huge size, the powerful muscles on his flanks and legs only hinting at the enormous strength he could unleash when he wanted to. And the scent as well. It was too dark to see much here, but she could smell him. He smelt of strength and virility, and overwhelming maleness.

In that moment, as she took in that scent, Senneck knew that she had finally found what she had wanted her whole life. *This* was the male who embodied everything she had wished for in a mate, *this* was the one who should give her a new clutch to raise, *this* was the one she would claim as her own, not to manipulate him or to learn from him, but just to pair with him because she wanted to. It was the closest thing a griffin ever found to true love, and Senneck found it now.

She advanced on him, lifting her head to rub it under his beak, and purred a rough griffish purr. "I am here for you, Mighty Skandar," she said. "I want you."

She didn't need to say it; she could smell her own odour as it strengthened and changed, sending a signal to him that said more than words ever could.

Skandar was more than male enough to pick it up. He rubbed against her in return, snuffing at her feathers, and purred as well, though it sounded more like talons on wood.

"Come," he said, with surprising gentleness. "We fly now. Fly with me."

He turned and took off from his balcony, and Senneck went after him.

It was dark outside, with no moon in sight. Normally, a flight like this would happen in daylight, when ordinary griffins like Senneck could see better. But Skandar was a creature of the night, and darkness was where he felt at home. He led her on a chase between the towers of Malvern's Eyrie, rushing past the openings where candles and lamps cast light over his sleek coat for an instant before he returned to the shadows.

Senneck forgot to be afraid and followed him. She was faster in the air than him, and more agile, but the darkness made up for that, and for most of the time she had to chase him rather than the other way around.

It made sense anyway; she had come to him in the first place, and now she had to catch him if she wanted to make him hers.

They flew the mating flight together, passing over the tower-top where the human celebration was being prepared, and when they were tired, they landed on top of one of the smaller towers. There they groomed each other, then mated at last.

Caught up in the oldest animal ritual of all, Senneck completely forgot about her ambitions and her plans.

She forgot about Kullervo and what he might do when he found out about what she had done. She never even thought of Erian, and how betrayed he would have felt if he were alive. But she had never looked to him for approval, and besides, he belonged to the past now. This was the present. And the future would be even better.

13

Liars

As Heath told it later to Caedmon and Myfina, Echo the spotted griffin, having effectively kidnapped him from Skenfrith, obviously had no intention of listening to him when it came to where they would go next. He skilfully avoided the other griffins loitering on the city walls, dodging two of them who decided to chase him. He had never flown with a human on his back before, and Heath was very lucky not to fall off and die right there and then. He hung on in desperation, until his knuckles whitened and his fingers began to go numb.

It didn't take him long at all to conclude that he was much weaker than he had realised. Echo banked sharply and flew upward, beating his wings hard for extra height. The sudden motion threw Heath sideways, and for one heart-stopping instant, he thought he was going to fall.

Other sounds dimmed as his heart thudded deafeningly in his ears. His vision swam. A grey haze filled his mind, and he began to feel a strange disconnection from his body. Somewhere below him, he was vaguely aware of a man pulling himself back into place on a griffin's back, babbling incoherently and snatching at the harness, but as the haze thickened, it didn't feel as if that man was him, or related to him, or had anything to do with him at all.

The feeling passed eventually, and he found himself hanging on to Echo's back with hands that had gone as hard and rigid as steel while the rest of him was limp and useless. Groaning, he forced himself to take control of his own body again and did his best to sit properly. Wind dragged at his clothes and hair, and flying drops of moisture made the wound on his face sting.

Very slowly, he managed to make his hands relax their grip and tried to take stock.

He was too confused to realise much, but when he thought about it later on, he understood that he had fainted, probably from a mixture of fright and lingering fever. Thank gods, his survival instincts had made him keep holding on even while he was unconscious.

The much clearer thought of what would happen if he fell off kept him awake after that, and he breathed deeply and did his best to adapt to Echo's movements in the air. Riding a griffin, he soon learnt, wasn't just a matter of sitting there like an idiot and letting the griffin do the work. Flying was much more delicate an activity than it looked, and if he, a human, was going to be a part of it, then he had to work with his partner.

With that in mind, he quickly picked up on how he should lean when Echo did, and keep his legs forward so they wouldn't get in the way of the griffin's wings. Matching Echo's rhythm in this way helped to calm him down, and when he felt safer, he leaned sideways slightly and risked a look down.

His stomach lurched when he saw how far up they were.

Shadows save me, he thought, what have I got myself into this time?

This whole situation was insane. He, the thief and professional cheat, who had been born in a slum and spent his whole adult life lying about one thing or another, was now flying on a griffin's back. Why, he wasn't quite sure, but the important question now was this: Where was Echo taking him, and why? Was Heath his prisoner now, or, even more insanely, his partner?

An idea came to him, and he looked around for the sun. It was just about right overhead, but not quite. Noon was close, then. And he was fairly certain that it was morning . . . yes, he decided, he'd seen the sun farther down in that direction before. Therefore, if he followed the path it had taken with his eyes, he would be looking east. So that made the opposite direction west, and therefore Echo was heading . . .

"South!" Heath said aloud, though the rushing wind in his ears meant that he barely heard himself.

What was south, then? Lots of things. Farmland, mostly, and the Northgate Mountains beyond that. Heath had spent most of his life travelling, so he knew where all the major cities were. Skenfrith was the second-southernmost of them, built by the River Nive.

Heath looked down again, and saw the river. It had to be the Nive—it was flowing southward. South toward the Northgates—and Malvern.

His stomach lurched. Malvern! Where else could Echo be going? Griffins didn't bother with farmland or villages. Unless they were wild, they lived in cities. And the only city in this direction was Malvern. Malvern, where he would land at one of the Eyrie's towers, then . . .

And then?

Heath's quite colourful imagination painted awful pictures of what might happen then. And he was in no state to fight.

Another man might have panicked, or even tried to fight Echo and make him land, but Heath hadn't survived this long as a criminal by accident. Fear trickled through his brain, but it was a familiar fear—the fear of every criminal, the fear of being caught and punished. Every time he had felt it in the past, he had fought it down and found a way to survive. He fought it down now and let it invigorate him, helping his devious mind to race ahead and start to plot.

Heath's suspicions had been absolutely correct. Echo flew on steadily, following the river, and made straight for Malvern. He flew on straight over its walls and toward the Eyrie, ignoring the other griffins who immediately took an interest. He went in among the towers as if he knew exactly where he was going and touched down neatly on top of the Council Tower, where arriving griffins always landed to announce themselves. Those that didn't were liable to be attacked.

Malvern's griffins were quick to respond. Echo had scarcely folded his wings before they arrived, landing around him and rushing in aggressively to confront him. Echo quickly lurched sideways, throwing Heath off his back, and snarled back at them. They stayed out of reach, unwilling to risk an injury, but seemed content to wait and make sure the intruder didn't escape.

Echo didn't try, and only moved to keep Heath close to him, rasping something that sounded like a command. Heath, who had long ago seen that the spotted griffin was his best chance for survival, was more than ready to obey. He stood by Echo's flank and did his best to smooth down his hair and clothes while he waited for whatever happened next.

Then Skandar arrived, and he nearly spat out his own heart.

The massive dark griffin landed with a thud, scattering the others, and advanced on Echo. He was so huge, and his reputation was so terrifying, that even though he only walked and didn't hiss or threaten, Heath saw his approach as an attack. He put his arms over his head to try to protect himself, and darted around to hide behind the nearest cover—Echo.

Luckily for him, Skandar wasn't paying attention. He was more interested in Echo, who, to his credit, didn't run away. The spotted griffin crouched low and bowed his head, saying something in griffish. Skandar replied, and a short conversation ensued, none of which made any sense to Heath at all. Finally, Skandar shoved Echo roughly with his beak and flew off.

Heath risked straightening up. "Where did he go? Is he coming back?"

Echo glanced at him, and sat down to nibble at his talons. *"Eeeeesh,"* he hissed by way of reply.

Heath considered running off just then but decided against it. He'd never get through the Eyrie unnoticed. And besides, when he moved too far away, Echo immediately herded him back with an angry hiss.

Skandar returned a little while later. This time, he had a human with him.

Heath's insides withered. Skandar had brought a young woman with long, curly hair. She would have looked like any other Northern woman if it weren't for the blue eyes glaring straight at him.

Queen Laela.

"Who're you?" she demanded unceremoniously. "Hurry up, I ain't got all day."

Heath straightened up, and offered her his most charming smile. "My Lady. It's an honour to meet you."

She snorted. "Thanks. Now get on with it; I'm a busy woman."

Heath kept the smile in place. "My name is Gwydion," he said, amazed once again by how confident he sounded, and how truthful. "I'm from Warwick. And this is Echo."

Laela did not smile back. "And?"

Heath coughed and allowed some nervousness to show. "Er . . . well, I'm really not sure how to begin. I think I've just become a griffiner."

"So I heard," said Laela. "How? Start with who yeh are."

"Of course." Heath fidgeted and glanced at Echo. "My father was a merchant in Warwick, but I don't suppose you'd have heard of him. He died not long before the Unpartnered captured the city—the rebel Saeddryn had him executed for speaking up in your support. I had to go into hiding until the Unpartnered arrived. When the fighting started in the streets, I did what I could, but I was hurt—you can see it here, on my face. My mother cared for me, but she was ill and died not long afterward. And while I was wondering what to do next, this griffin came to me. I can't understand what he says, but he made me go with him. I bought him a harness, and he brought me here, and I think he wants me to swear loyalty to you as a new griffiner. I think that's how it's done when someone becomes a griffiner. My Lady." He bowed, feeling sick to his stomach. Before Laela could speak, he let himself blunder convincingly on. "I—I can understand if you don't want us, and I'm really not sure . . . I'm not a noble after all, and I don't know what Echo really wants. I'm just guessing. But I've always supported you, my Lady, and you, Mighty Skandar, and I suppose if I don't swear loyalty to you, then that would make me a rebel or something." He shuddered. "I don't want to be like one of them. They killed my father, and destroyed my home. If I could find a way to fight them, I would."

There. He'd done his best, and now looked at Laela with a hopeful expression that wasn't all acting. She stared back stonily.

Then, joy of joys, she smiled. "That's one damn fine story, Gwydion. A new griffiner, eh?" She looked at Echo. "An' that's one special-lookin' griffin, too. Spots! I never saw a thing like it before. So, yeh want t'be my man, do yeh?"

"Yes," Heath said at once. "If you'll have me. But I don't know what I'd have to do . . ."

"Easy," said Laela. "Swear loyalty in front of the council, an' we'll see if we can't find an apprenticeship for yeh. One of the Masters would take yeh on an' teach yeh what yeh needed t'know. Got any skills?"

"Oh! Er, yes, skills. I'm good with numbers." Heath nodded quickly, deliberately letting his words come out in an eager rush. "Good at counting money and working out measurements and things. My father sold cloth, and I was learning to follow in his footsteps, so he taught me everything he knew."

"Money, eh?" said Laela. "I'm pretty sure the Master of Gold was lookin' for an apprentice. Well." She nodded to herself. "We can worry about that later. What yeh just said matches what yer partner here said, an' that sounds about right. Come on down, an' we'll see if we can't find a room. Yer obviously in pretty bad shape, an' I reckon a hot meal oughta do wonders." She looked at Skandar, who had already lost interest in the pair of them, and beckoned Heath to come with her.

So Gwydion and Echo got their room, and were left in peace there to rest.

Once they were alone, Gwydion turned to his partner. "Listen," he said. "Echo, if that's your name. I can't speak griffish, but I've heard most griffins can understand human anyway, so I'll just talk."

Echo had turned to look at him and inclined his head as if to indicate that he was listening.

"Now, I don't know what you said up there," Gwydion went on, "but it must have fitted with what I said, and thank gods for that. If I could have discussed a plan with you beforehand, I would have, but you didn't give me a chance. I had to improvise, and if you want to survive here, then you'll have to go along with it."

Echo didn't move.

"I know why you brought me here," said Gwydion. "I had plenty of time to figure it out on the way. Skenfrith's destroyed, and Caedmon and the others are probably dead. The best chance for both of us is just to settle down here. Become partners and join up with the Queen? Yes?"

Echo said nothing, but as Gwydion spoke, he inclined his head ever so slightly. *Yes.*

Gwydion felt sadness eat at his heart, but he didn't show it. "You probably saved my life by getting me out of there. I owe you one. And if this is what you want, then so be it. You can trust me to carry it off; I've . . ." He hesitated. He had never discussed it openly with anyone before, but there was something about Echo's silence that made him feel safe to do it now. "I've spent my whole life being whoever I wanted to be. I haven't used my real name once in twenty years. Even my closest friends didn't know what it was. It works for me, and I'm good at it. You want me to be a griffiner who's a loyal subject of the Queen. So I am." He shook himself. "Since we're both from Warwick, I'll have to tell you what it looks like, and anything else you might need to know, just in case someone asks questions. I've never done this with an accomplice before, but . . ." He grinned. "I think you'll do well. You don't give anything away. Does all that make sense to you?"

Echo clicked his beak briskly. From the way he stood and held his head, it was obvious that he was playing close attention.

Gwydion glanced toward the door and kept his voice low. "I'll teach you some tricks of the trade, if I can. There are ways of making people want to believe what you tell them. Be cheerful, and play the fool if you have to. Act harmless and friendly. Tell plenty of jokes and stories, keep people talking. Entertain them, and they'll end up liking you without even realising that they don't really know anything about you." He shrugged. "It works on humans. It might work on griffins. You'd know better than I would! Anyway . . ." His face was aching horribly, and greyness had returned to his mind. "I need to lie down for a while. I hope you understood me and get some use out of it."

He looked hopefully at Echo. The spotted griffin gave no sign, and Gwydion finally gave in and made for the bed.

Echo's chirp made him look back. The griffin had stood up and jerked his head in a beckoning kind of way.

"What is it?" Gwydion asked.

Echo stayed silent. He stretched his head out, and went rigid. A moment later his beak opened, and pale mist drifted out— so pale it was almost invisible. It was magic, but unlike the magic Gwydion had seen griffins use once or twice, it wasn't bright or forceful, and it didn't spread out from its maker to affect the world around it. Instead, it drifted back over Echo's body before soaking into his coat.

Echo's rigid stance disappeared, and he relaxed and shook

himself vigorously. A cloud of fur and feathers fell away from his body, but underneath it a new coat had already sprouted. But this one was grey and white, with attractive silver ticking around the neck and face.

With it, Echo looked like a completely different griffin. But the eyes had stayed the same. They looked straight at Gwydion's face, and as he looked back in wonder he knew what that look meant. *Don't worry about me. You're not the only one who can be whoever he chooses to be.*

When Gwydion saw that look, he knew for certain that he was going to be all right. It might not be rational, but he decided there and then that he was going to trust this griffin. From now on they were a team.

He was used to hiding his thoughts, so none of this showed on his face. He only smiled and nodded back at Echo before he removed his boots and flopped down on the bed.

Echo left for his nesting chamber, carelessly trampling his shed fur into the carpet on the way.

Gwydion slept like the dead and suffered from unpleasant dreams. The only one he remembered afterward was more of a fragment than anything else. He saw Caedmon, standing somewhere on the other side of a massive chasm. His mouth moved, but he made no sound, and his eyes were wide as he beckoned, pleading with Gwydion to come to him. But the darkness between them was deep and freezing and full of death, and Gwydion was not Heath and had no courage left to try to cross it.

The next day came, and Gwydion and Echo were both provided with a hearty breakfast. Gwydion's clothes had been taken away for washing, but he was given a new set—not overly fancy, but well-made and comfortable.

They had the morning to do whatever they liked, so Gwydion took the opportunity to bathe and groom. Gwydion wasn't a beard-wearer, so he shaved as well, and trimmed his hair—something he'd done himself plenty of times.

He inspected himself in his cherished mirror, and nodded to himself—he looked like Gwydion now. Gwydion was younger than Heath, and much more innocent. He'd never committed a crime in his life, or left his home city before. He knew nothing of the world, and griffins and griffiners intimidated him. But he was proud of everything he had done so far and determined to prove himself worthy to both his new partner and the Queen he had come to serve.

Someone knocked on the door.

"Come in!" Gwydion called.

The door opened, and a servant bowed. "My Lord. Ye are summoned to see the Master of Gold. I'll show ye the way when yer ready to leave."

"Oh!" Gwydion stood up. "Er, yes, I think . . . wait a moment." He went to the entrance to Echo's nest chamber and peeked through. Looking nervous and hesitant when he did this was easy.

Echo was there in his nest, idly grooming a wing. He looked up when Gwydion coughed, and made a noise that sounded vaguely like a question.

"Er, there's someone here saying we've been asked to go see the Master of Gold. I think it's about an apprenticeship." Gwydion fidgeted while he waited for a response.

Echo stood up and shook himself down. He was wearing his spotted coat again, and every hair looked beautifully neat and glossy. No wonder, considering that they were all brand-new. Gwydion moved aside to let him come through the archway, but once he was through it, Echo didn't move to go on ahead. When Gwydion walked toward the waiting servant, the griffin followed silently.

"We're coming," Gwydion told the servant, who nodded back politely and set off.

They were fairly low down in the tower, in one of the smaller and plainer of the griffiner quarters. Their route led them upward now, into the levels where the richer and more powerful griffiners lived. As a council member, the Master of Gold owned one of the best suites at the very top, just above the council chamber itself.

During the walk, Gwydion kept his eyes busy, taking in as much as he could. They met a few griffiners on the way past, and he paid extra attention to them, noting their faces and the outfits they wore, whether they carried anything, and whether they were accompanied by their partners or not. Most of them weren't, which wasn't that surprising. When they were at home, griffins generally left their humans to their own devices, unless something important was going on, or if they felt there might be some danger about. Clearly, the inhabitants of the Eyrie felt safe now.

The servant stopped at an open door and ushered them through it into a richly decorated chamber. Like all rooms used by griffiners, it was hugely oversized and had plenty of floor space, so a griffin could move around easily, and the furniture was sturdy and placed close to the walls. But the furniture was nicely carved from expensive woods, and the big floor was decorated with thick carpets. Tapestries hung on the walls, along with a ceremonial sickle and a painted shield. Unlike Gwydion's own quarters, the main room here wasn't also the bedroom—a door in one wall probably led into one, while this chamber was furnished as an office, with a big desk and shelves full of books and papers. An archway in a different wall led to the griffin nest and the opening to the sky beyond it, but the griffin who owned it was lying on his belly in the middle of the office floor, staring balefully at the newcomers.

The Master of Gold had been sitting at her desk, but she got up when she saw them and came over, holding out a hand in greeting.

"Ah!" she said, on seeing Gwydion. "You're the new one, aren't you?"

Gwydion smiled shyly. "I suppose I am. I'm Gwydion, and this is Echo."

Echo, seeing the other griffin wasn't threatening, entered the room beside his partner and stepped over to introduce himself. The Master of Gold's partner, a slim young female, stood up and huffed at him in a businesslike kind of way.

The Master of Gold watched the two griffins and relaxed when neither of them looked about to have a disagreement. "I'm Arwydd," she said, to Gwydion. "But you can call me Wydd if you like; everyone does."

She wasn't quite what he had been expecting. For one thing, she was young—possibly younger than himself. She had a pretty face and a friendly smile, and she was looking at Gwydion with interest and, he noted, admiration.

He smiled back. "Pleased to meet you, my Lady."

She laughed. "'Lady'! Just barely. I've only been doing this job for a month, you know."

"Really?"

"Oh yes." Wydd laughed again. "Oh bother, I shouldn't have told you that, should I? How am I going to get any respect out of you now?"

"Easily," Gwydion said stoutly. "You're a griffiner, and I'm . . ."

"Another griffiner," she said at once. "Don't worry, I've been told your story, and believe me, I don't think any less of you just because you're new. Everyone's new at least once in his life. Now, why don't you come and sit down, and we'll have a chat?"

"I'd be honoured."

"Don't be." Wydd showed him to a chair in front of the fireplace and dragged over another one for herself. There was no fire in the grate, but the room was warm enough anyway. "Now then," Wydd said once they were settled. "I'm told you're good with numbers?"

"Very good," said Gwydion, who had spent plenty of time making less intelligent people feel confident by explaining their own finances to them, and plenty more time afterward counting up his profits. "And I was the best dancer in Warwick," he added, thinking a light joke would work well here.

It did. Wydd chuckled. "And modest, too, I see."

"Honest," Gwydion corrected, without a trace of irony. "I used to help my father sort out his money. He owned more than one shop, you see, and it took some work to decide how much to invest, and in what, and when."

"That's good," said Wydd. "That's excellent, that's just the sort of experience we need. Honestly, it's a real blessing that you've turned up. Since I took over from my master here, I've been run off my feet trying to handle everything on my own. A good assistant is exactly what I need."

"You'll take me on, then?" asked Gwydion.

"Well," said Wydd, "The proper procedure is that I try you first— give you some minor work and see how you handle it. But the truth is that I don't think we're likely to find anyone else any time soon, and frankly I'm not in the mood to wait around and see who turns up. We'll do the trial anyway—I'd get in trouble if we didn't—but don't worry too much. I won't give you anything too hard!"

Gwydion looked relieved. "You'll teach me, too, though, won't you?"

"Of course. That's my job, as your master." Wydd blushed.

"I mean, it will be. Once it's all sorted out. You'll have to be officially sworn in as a griffiner first. There's a ceremony, and you'll take an oath to the Queen, and Echo will do the same to the Mighty Skandar. But don't worry about that; it's easy. Since you're untrained, I'll be given the official duty of training you as a griffiner, so I'll have a part in the ceremony, too. Once that's all done, we can start work together!"

Gwydion glanced at Echo. "When's the ceremony? Nobody's told me anything about that yet . . ."

"Oh, probably soon," said Wydd. "There's usually a party afterward."

"Oh good," said Gwydion. "I love parties."

"Me too." She grinned. "You'll have to teach me how to dance."

Gwydion laughed, and only someone watching very closely would have noticed the sly gleam in his eyes. But as he promised Wydd that he would dance with her and settled down to chat and joke with her now the important things had been discussed, he could not push away the guilt that had begun to grow in his stomach. He had rarely felt guilty before, but he did now, and no matter what he did for the rest of that day, he felt it grow steadily, like a tumour, eating away at his triumph and turning it into something bitter and ugly.

Guilt or no guilt, Gwydion's official acceptance as a griffiner went ahead a few days later. He spent the intervening time with Echo and his master-to-be, exploring the Eyrie, meeting people, and learning the first few basic lessons about how to work with his new partner. Wydd wasn't, as it turned out, much of a teacher. She was barely more experienced than he was and had obviously never taught anyone before, which she cheerfully admitted was true. She was more interested in getting to know her new apprentice and in the process letting him get to know her. Gwydion was fine with that. The last month or so had been more than stressful: It had nearly killed him.

So despite his need to learn griffish and prepare for his new life, he was happy to spend his time with Wydd, eating the fine foods she offered, chatting with the other griffiners she introduced, and deliberately losing at *grove*, the latest table game that had caught on in Malvern. He enjoyed it, too. It was good to lead the high life again.

Finally, the day of the ceremony arrived. Gwydion was given a new outfit: a griffiner's ceremonial costume, which all griffiners were expected to wear on occasions like this one.

It was made from rich brown fabric, and the chest was covered with hundreds of feathers sewn on so thickly that they made the wearer look as if he had a feathered chest like a griffin. Below that, a patch of grey rabbit fur extended into a hanging "tail" whose tip had been covered with more feathers—tail feathers this time, arranged in a fan shape just like on a griffin's tail. On the back and shoulders, huge wing feathers had been attached to hang down like a cape.

Normally, the outfit would have been made especially for him, with feathers donated by his partner. But there hadn't been enough time to have one made, so this one had been loaned to him by a friend of Wydd's since its colours were fairly close to Echo's.

It fitted quite well. Once he put it on—not an easy task— Gwydion inspected himself in the large mirror he had found in his new room.

He was playing at being younger than he was, but he thought that he looked older, and thinner as well. His illness had hollowed his cheeks, and the scar was fading, leaving a line of pale, shiny skin where it had once been red and swollen. He ran a finger over it, and grimaced. His looks were ruined. They'd been replaced by different looks, which some people might still find attractive, true, but the scar would be something more important than a blow to his vanity. From now on, changing his identity would be much harder. He had never had to hide something like it before, and he wondered how he would do so when the time came.

Then again . . .

Then again, maybe there would never be a need to change again. With Caedmon gone and the war almost certainly finished for good, this new life in Malvern would be the best he could hope for, and better. And there was no way Echo would ever let him leave it.

So . . . this was it, then. Live in Malvern. Be Gwydion the griffiner forever, and leave Heath the rebel behind. And why not? He'd shed a hundred other names and personalities before—why should this one be any different? Hadn't he always used his talents for his own benefit, to do what he liked and take whatever he wanted?

And now, of course, it was even better than before. He had a partner now, one who could change his coat just as easily as he, and shown that he knew how to play Gwydion's game quite well. Once Gwydion had learnt how to talk to him, it would become even easier. He could become rich and powerful here in Malvern, just as he had always wanted.

Gwydion adjusted the feathers on his outfit and tried not to meet his own eye in the mirror. "What's wrong with me?" he muttered aloud. It had never felt this hard before. He tried his best to push it away, but it was futile. He had a horrible feeling that he had grown a conscience.

But, in the end, what other choice did he have?

He sighed miserably and left the room to face the real beginning of his new life.

14

One Face Too Many

Despite his regrets, Gwydion still felt glad later on that, just once in his life, he got to see the great council chamber in use. The entire council had gathered, and many griffiners had come to sit in the galleries to watch with their partners. On the platform in the very centre, which was painted silver to look like the moon, Queen Laela stood with the Mighty Skandar. The council stood in a ring around the platform, each one standing between his or her partner's forelegs in the proper spot for official occasions. Several of them had their apprentices there with them, standing behind or to the side of their masters.

Gwydion and Echo entered the chamber from the floor and walked side by side to the platform, passing through the gap left by Wydd's empty spot. She walked ahead of them with her own partner, Essh, and recited the ceremonial words to Laela.

"Eyrie Mistress Laela Taranisäii, I am Arwydd Hafweni. In my position as Master of Gold for this Eyrie, I hereby present Gwydion of Warwick. He has been chosen, and seeks to become a part of this Eyrie."

Next it was Essh's turn. He came forward and spoke to Skandar, and though Gwydion couldn't understand it, it was obvious that his partner was taking a vow of his own.

Gwydion came forward when Wydd gestured at him, and knelt to Laela. "Eyrie Mistress Laela Taranisäii," he said, having memorised the words that morning. "I am Gwydion Warwicki. I have been chosen, and have obeyed the law of all griffiners by coming to swear myself to you."

"Then take the oath," said Laela.

Gwydion recited it, without standing up. "I, Gwydion of Warwick, hereby swear that I will obey my Eyrie Mistress in all things, that I will serve my apprenticeship faithfully in readiness for the day when I will be needed to fulfil the duties of my master before me, and that I will always and forever put the needs of my country and my Eyrie before my own. I swear that when danger threatens, I will fight at my Eyrie Mistress' command, and that I will never betray, or neglect my duties as a warrior of Malvern, or leave my Eyrie without permission or command. I swear this by the holy name of Scathach, the Night God, sacred guardian of Tara and its people, and may she strike me down if I have lied or if I ever break my oath."

There, it was done, and Gwydion felt his heart shudder. Not that he truly and honestly believed the Night God would strike him down for the lies he had just told, but he could not shake off the memory of Saeddryn's snarling face, or the pain when she had slashed his own face open from eye to jaw. If the Night God's anger and judgment had a face, then that was it, and he silently prayed that he would never meet Saeddryn again. Not now, when she would have every reason to kill him.

But she wouldn't dare enter Malvern again . . . would she?

He was too busy worrying to pay much attention to the rest of the ceremony, but his part in it was over anyway—all he had to do was stand there while Laela recited the proper words to welcome him and name him a griffiner of Malvern. Then Wydd came forward again and formally claimed him as her new apprentice, vowing to teach him everything he should know.

After that, the councillors held out their hands to him in a gesture of welcome, and the griffiners up in the gallery cheered and applauded—possibly because the tedious ceremony was now over, and everyone was now free to go up onto the tower-top and get drunk.

Gwydion and Echo followed Wydd and Essh out, as was customary. Once they were well away from the council chamber, Wydd smiled at her new apprentice. "Well done. I was wondering if you'd remember all the words properly—not easy, is it? How long did it take you to memorise the lot?"

Gwydion shrugged easily. "I recited them to myself all morning until I had them right."

Wydd chuckled. "Good idea. Don't tell anyone this, but when *I* had to do that I got nervous and trailed off halfway through. My master had to whisper the next bit into my ear! I nearly *died*."

"Don't worry about it," Gwydion said kindly. "Nervousness can make anyone stammer. Odds are no-one was paying attention anyway."

"Hope so." Wydd glanced at her partner. "Anyway, never mind about that. It's time to have fun! I'm going back to my room to get out of this outfit—no way am I going to try dancing with it on! You'd better do the same. One wine-stain and it's ruined, and you don't want to know how much those things cost."

"Oh, I don't know. If I'm going to be working for you, I'll probably wind up knowing the cost of *everything*. But I'll take your advice anyway. See you up top!" Gwydion nodded and headed off back to his quarters.

Echo arrived ahead of him and paced impatiently while he carefully put the ceremonial outfit away and put on a much plainer tunic he had been given along with it. "Plain" was a relative term; the tunic didn't have any feathers on it, but it was still made out of fine velvet trimmed with fur. Only the best for griffiners.

Once he was dressed, Gwydion took a moment to comb his hair, and told Echo he was ready to leave. The spotted griffin came over immediately, offering his back.

Gwydion's heartbeat sped up. "Er, no thank you," he said. "I can walk."

Echo didn't like that. *"Kkkssshl"* he hissed, shoving his human none-too-gently with his shoulder.

Gwydion would have argued, but despite the unpleasant prospect of flying again, he knew he was expected to do what his partner wanted and arrive in style. So he fetched Echo's harness and put it on him, and got onto his back once they were out on the balcony beyond the nest. Echo, thankfully, had apparently decided to accommodate his human's fear and inexperience because he took off with a surprisingly gentle motion and flew in a slow spiral up toward the tower-top where he had landed on his arrival at Malvern. Back then, it had been almost

completely bare, other than for a few plants growing in stone
pots, but now it had been turned into a dance floor. Tables had
been brought up and stocked with plates and bowls of food for
the guests to help themselves. They stood at one edge of the
space, and on the opposite side carcasses had been laid in a neat
row for the griffins. In between was a big open space for dancing, and a troupe of musicians were already playing a jaunty
tune. The small fruit trees that grew in their outsized pots
among the other plants were decked out with flowers and silver
bells, and several barrels had been brought up and opened, with
cups and ladles on hand.

Echo landed in the middle of the dance floor, and Gwydion
dismounted. Plenty of other griffins and griffiners were already
there, and they greeted the two pleasantly.

Now that Gwydion and Echo were there, the celebration
could begin, and the guests went to the tables to eat, or to the
barrels for wine or mead, or clustered together to talk.

Gwydion looked around for Wydd, but didn't see her, so he
headed off to investigate the food. The feast was a modest
one—accepting a new griffiner was more a minor point of
interest, and most of the people there had probably just come
for the free food—but there was still plenty on the tables that
looked good. Gwydion scooped up a handful of his favourite
honey-crusted nuts, and went to the barrels for a cup of mead to
wash them down.

He had just eaten the nuts and a very tasty cheese pastry
when Wydd arrived. She had put on a green gown that suited
her very well and looked just as cheerful as she always did.
"There you are!" she said. "How's the food?"

"Good," said Gwydion, swallowing hastily. "The drink's
not bad either. D'you fancy some? Er—" He made an exaggerated show of stopping himself. "I mean, shall I bring you a cup
of wine, Master?"

She giggled. "Yes, thank you."

He duly filled a cup for her and handed it over. "Do they
always have their celebrations up here?"

"Usually, unless the weather's bad, and then we use one of the
dining halls or even the council chamber if we need a lot of
space. Now, come with me. There're some people you should
really meet . . ."

Gwydion followed at her elbow, and paid close attention to names, faces, and titles. In quick succession he met the Masters of Building, Farms, and the new Master of War, who had just recently been promoted to replace the late Lord Iorwerth. The new High Priestess was there as well. Most of those he met were new to their positions, he noted, and many of them had collar scars and Amorani accents, which didn't match their Northern features at all.

"Former slaves, of course," Wydd said when he remarked on this. "Some of the ones the Queen brought over from Amoran. Just between you and me, some people don't approve of them. Not raised in the North, and slaves as well—former or otherwise. But that's because most people are used to the blackrobes around here being slaves from the *South*, where slaves were used for mindless things like mining and building. Amoran's different, though. They have slaves who just build and so on, too, of course, but they have other classes that the Southerners didn't have. Some of their slaves are very educated; they use them as teachers and healers, and translators, too. So some of that sort came over here, and most of them got given important positions and became griffiners. The Queen looks for talent, not birth. And she's right."

Despite himself, Gwydion had to agree that was true, and his curiosity about the half-breed Queen that Caedmon and Saeddryn both wanted to kill increased. To begin with, after his first meeting with her, he'd dismissed her as coarse and uneducated. She certainly *sounded* that way. But now he was starting to wonder if there was more to her than there seemed. Privately, he decided that if he got the chance to talk to her face-to-face, he would take it.

"Oh, here comes the Master of Law," Wydd resumed. "Hello! Druson, this is my new apprentice, Gwydion of Warwick. Gwydion, this is Lord Druson, Master of Law."

The Master of Law looked about thirty and had a shrewd look about him, but he sounded polite enough when he held out his hand and said, "Pleased to meet you, Lord Gwydion."

Gwydion had learnt how to greet a fellow griffiner. He linked fingers with the Master of Law and tugged briefly before letting go. "Pleased to meet you, too, my Lord. I hope that one day I can sit on the council with you."

The Master of Law smiled. "Not likely, with your master being as young as she is!"

"No, I suppose not," Gwydion said ruefully. "Still, apprentices have all the fun and half the responsibility, right?"

The Master of Law hadn't looked away from his face. His eyes narrowed. "Yes, that's true," he said, sounding slightly distracted. "It wasn't so long ago that I was an apprentice myself."

"I thought so," said Gwydion, not liking the way the man was staring. "Your master didn't die all that long ago, did he?"

The Master of Law tensed. "What are you talking about?"

"Oh. Er." Gwydion winced. "I'm sorry, that was probably a bit insensitive. It's just that I heard about what happened to the old Master of Law, and I thought . . . he must have been yours. Your master, I mean."

The Master of Law looked away. "Yes, Lord Torc was my master. But I prefer not to talk about that."

Gwydion grimaced internally. "I'm sorry," he said again. "I'm new at all this; I didn't mean to offend you."

"It's fine." The Master of Law nodded formally and left.

"Damn!" Gwydion didn't try to hide his dismay. "I should have known I'd say the wrong thing at least once tonight."

"Ah, don't worry about it," said Wydd. "He's not easy to get along with. He always was a bit prickly, and after his master got himself executed, he's only become even worse."

"Lord Torc turned traitor, didn't he?" asked Gwydion.

"So they say. I wasn't around at the time, but that's the story, and I believe it. Besides, with his wife and children openly rebelling, there was no way he could be trusted. The Queen didn't have much choice."

"I heard she gave them an ultimatum," said Gwydion. "Surrender or . . ."

"Yes, she did," said Wydd. She drank some wine. "But let's not talk about that now. We're supposed to be enjoying ourselves!"

"Of course!" Gwydion shook himself and polished off his own drink. He offered Wydd his arm. "Shall we?"

"We shall!" She finished her drink and put the cup aside, and the two of them took to the dance floor.

Heath was an excellent dancer, but Gwydion wasn't, so he tripped and stumbled a bit before getting into the rhythm of things with Wydd's help. She was more than happy to help, with several good-natured jabs at him for not living up to his boasts.

Gwydion danced with her, and then with one or two other women, but returned to Wydd quickly enough. Not so much because she was a better dancer, but because she was his master and the one he should be trying to please. And he liked her, anyway.

Once they were tired and had built up an appetite, they went back to the tables and ate some more, washing the food down with fine cymran juice wine all the way from Amoran.

Gwydion was just wondering if he should have another apple tart when someone called his name.

He turned, and found the Master of Law standing beside him. "Yes?"

The Master of Law was not smiling. "Tell me," he said. "Have you ever been to Malvern before?"

Gwydion eyed him a moment, and decided that despite his awkwardness, the other griffiner was just trying to make conversation. "No, unfortunately," he said. "I'd barely been out of Warwick before Echo chose me."

"Are you sure?"

Gwydion raised an eyebrow. "Fairly sure. Why do you ask?"

"What about Skenfrith?" the Master of Law pressed. "Have you been *there*?"

"No. Just Warwick and a couple of the villages around it. I'm hoping to see the other cities one day, though."

"And your partner?" asked the Master of Law. "Has *he* been to Skenfrith?"

"That I don't know," said Gwydion. "I can't understand him yet. He's around here if you want to ask him yourself," he added, by now quite uncomfortable and hoping to get rid of him.

The Master of Law ignored the hint. "What was your job before you were chosen? What did you do in Warwick?"

"Sold fabric," said Gwydion. "It was my father's business, and I helped him in the shop. Ran it for him, too, sometimes, when he had to go away."

"Hm." The Master of Law's eyes had gone narrow again. "For a commoner from Warwick, you seem to know a lot about what's been happening in Malvern."

"Only what I picked up from people in the marketplace," Gwydion said easily. "News gets around."

"I see. What about that scar on your face, then? Where did you get it?"

Gwydion touched it. "It's a bit of a story, actually . . ."

He launched into the same story he had told Wydd and others in the past few days, embellishing it slightly as any young man trying to impress would, but as he went on he began to realise that the Master of Law wasn't really listening. He was inspecting Gwydion's face, taking in every detail as if he were trying to memorise it.

"Have you ever heard the name Moren before?" he asked sharply, dropping the question on him without any warning when he was in mid-sentence.

Gwydion had. He started to sweat. "Er . . . Moren, did you say? I don't think so . . ."

And then, quite unexpectedly, the Master of Law laughed. "By gods, you're good. You're very good. Do you know what? I wish my master could have been here to see you, I really do. He admired you, believe it or not. He used to say that if he ever caught you, it'd be enough to make him think his time as Master of Law had been worthwhile."

Gwydion took a step back. "Listen, I don't know what you think you're talking about, but—"

The Master of Law only laughed again. "Hah! Lord Torc was right. I knew you were bold, but I never thought you'd have the balls to impersonate a bloody *griffiner*, and right in front of the council as well. I'm almost sorry that you didn't get away with it. But I suppose I should thank you. Catching you at last will do wonders for my reputation."

Past the pounding of his heart in his ears, Gwydion was amazed by the pure bewilderment and outrage in his own voice. "What? What do you mean 'catching' me? Do you think I'm a criminal or something? If this is a joke, then it's not funny."

The Master of Law grinned. "Give it up. Moren, also known as Anadd, also known as Heath, you're under arrest for theft, forgery, impersonation, and treason. If you don't want to ruin the party, I suggest you come quietly."

Gwydion's mask broke. "Oh *shit*," he said, and ran.

He dodged past the chattering griffiners, panic racing through his body. There were no guards here, but he would never get back down through the tower without being spotted, and the Master of Law had probably alerted the guards down there. His only hope now was Echo.

There were plenty of griffins around, and they didn't appreciate his rushing into their midst. Several of them hissed or reared up angrily, and when he got too close to one of them, she lashed out and sent him tumbling across the stonework.

By now the guests had noticed the commotion. The talk died down, and the dancing almost stopped, as people turned to see what was going on.

During the silence, the Master of Law shouted. "Stop that man! He's a criminal!"

In that moment, the mask of Gwydion finally fell away. He was not Gwydion the griffiner, the innocent servant of the Queen. He was Heath again, Heath the wanted criminal and rebel, and he was cornered.

"Echo!" he shouted. "Echo, for gods' sakes, where are you? *Echo!*"

And then, thank everything that was holy, Echo was there. He sprinted over, shoving other griffins out of the way to get to his partner. Heath ran toward him, relief soaring in his heart, but then it all crumbled. Echo suddenly stopped and darted away, as another griffin lunged at him.

Heath stopped, too, and moved out of the way with a yell of despair. If he went any closer while Echo and the other griffin fought, he would probably be killed. And he could already see people coming for him—men and women who had spoken so pleasantly to him only moments ago, some of them drawing weapons.

He backed away, looking frantically at Echo. His partner was doing his best, trying to knock the other griffin aside so he could reach his human, but the other griffin seemed to have anticipated that, and rather than attacking outright, he simply moved to stop him, hitting him savagely with his beak whenever he came close. Finally, unable to do anything, Echo ran for the edge and took off.

If he had been intending to swoop down for his partner, he never got to do it. The other griffin took off, too, and went after him, chasing him away from the Eyrie. Echo flew away, shrieking in despair, and took Heath's last chance with him.

Heath made one last desperate run for the opening that led into the tower, but he was already lost. When the Master of Law took him by the arm, he leapt at him in an attempt to fight him off, but his captor was far too well trained for that to work. He slammed a knee into Heath's stomach, so hard he doubled up and nearly collapsed.

Before he could recover, his arms were wrenched behind his back and chained together, and he knew it was all over.

As he was led off, he saw the griffiners all watching him. Some looked angry, others shocked. Wydd was there, pale-faced with horror.

Heath didn't try to fight back any more. He knew enough about guards to know that fighting back just meant being beaten until you stopped.

All his confidence and easy-going charm had deserted him, blotted out by a wall of blank, black fear. There would be no Caedmon to save him here, no Myfina to plead for his life, no Saeddryn to rescue him. He knew how ruthless Malvern's justice was. He would be tried, then he would lose a hand for his thievery, and possibly his tongue for his lies. And if they discovered that he had worked for the rebels, then he would lose his head as well.

If he had hoped to be given a night in a cell first to think and maybe concoct another story, he was mistaken. Down in the prison complex under the Eyrie, he was handed over to the head gaoler, who immediately had him escorted to a bare stone room with a chair that had been fitted with shackles. They made him sit in it and clamped both his wrists into place.

For a moment, he wondered if they were going to cut his hand off right here and now—but they didn't. When that happened, it would be in public, so everyone would see what happened to thieves.

Nobody talked to him until two guards had taken up station on either side, and the door had been locked. A third man, who had a heavy, angry look about him, came forward to confront him. "Your name?"

Even now, lies were Heath's first choice. "Heath," he said. It was the name he had been using when he had joined Caedmon and the one that sprang most readily to mind.

The man hit him. His face exploded in pain, splitting along the scar. *"Name?"* a voice roared through the ringing in his ears.

Heath gagged. He could taste blood in his mouth. "H-Heath," he gasped.

Another blow. "Your *real* name, rebel."

The word shot through Heath's aching head. *Rebel!* They knew, they knew, but how . . . ? "Heath," he said again, truly frightened now. "I'm *Heath*."

The blows continued to rain down, and so did the questions. "When did you join the rebels? Where are they? How many are left? What were you sent here to do?" *Thud, thud, thud, thud.*

Heath didn't answer. Or, at least, he didn't answer usefully. Before long, his eyelids were swelling, and his nose dripped blood onto a split lip. "Don't know," he kept saying, "Don't *know*!" And it was true, he didn't know. He had no idea where Caedmon might be, or even if he was still alive.

Not that it made any difference to them. He was a rebel, and he had come to Malvern and pretended to be a griffiner. Why else would he be doing it if not to get close to the Queen?

In the midst of it all, Heath had room to curse himself for his own stupidity. But it was Echo who had got him into this, wasn't it? He would never have come to Malvern if the spotted griffin hadn't forced him, but Echo hadn't known about him, had he? Hadn't known what he was, what he'd done, what . . .

Thought disappeared after that, swallowed up by fear and splashes of red obscuring his vision as he grew more confused and began to lose consciousness. His interrogator seemed to know that because he finally stopped hitting him. Heath felt himself being freed from the chair, and allowed himself to be half led, half dragged away.

After that, he was tossed onto a cold floor, and a door slammed behind him.

"That one won't last long," a voice said from somewhere above him.

Then silence.

Heath never knew how long he stayed in Malvern's prison. Nor did anyone tell him just how his captors knew that he was a rebel. Nobody told him anything. Here, he was the one who was meant to do the telling, nobody else.

They fed him and gave him some time to recover from the

first interrogation—but it was really just an opportunity to let him think about his situation and come up with horrible fantasies about what might happen next. Fear was as good a tool as any sort of punishment they could offer.

But they provided punishment as well, absolutely.

The next time Heath left his cell, it was to go back to the dreaded chair. But this time the burly interrogator didn't use fists. This time there was a brazier and a hot iron.

Heath tried to fight his way out when he saw it, but there was nothing he could do. He was outnumbered, and already weakened from the beating he had had. The chair claimed him, and he had to sit there as they tore his shirt open and . . .

Much later, crouching on a rock in Caedmon's camp, he shuddered and closed his eyes. "I'm sorry, but I'd just rather not talk about it."

Myfina put an arm around his shoulders and hugged him to her. "It's all right. You don't have to. Oh gods, I can't even imagine . . ."

Caedmon had gone pale. "What did they ask?"

"The same things as before," said Heath. His usually cocky face had turned grim and closed. "But you don't have to worry."

"You didn't talk, then?" asked Myfina.

"Talk? Of course I talked. I would have told them anything they wanted to know. But I didn't know anything, did I? I couldn't tell them where you'd gone—you never told me what the plan was if Skenfrith fell. I didn't know where Saeddryn was, or what you were planning to do next. I suppose I was away too long, and after that I was too ill for anyone to confide in me. Saved your hides, anyway."

Caedmon looked just as grim as his friend. "How did you get out of there, then?"

Heath managed to smile again. "Not because of anything *I* did, unfortunately. Seems I'm not as clever as I thought. But what happened was this . . ."

What happened was that one night, while Heath was in his cell, a message from a guard in a hurry brought the head gaoler to the door that led down into the prison complex. On the other side, he found a woman waiting for him.

She was dressed like a griffiner, and sounded like one, too. "Guard, come up here. Now."

He came at once. "What is it, milady?"

At the top of the stairs, in the featureless round chamber that made up the lowest level of the tower, a great, dark griffin was waiting.

The moment he saw him, the gaoler bowed low. He had never seen this griffin before, but there was no mistaking the silver feathers and the black fur. "The Mighty Skandar!"

"Quite," said the woman, while Skandar eyed the gaoler haughtily.

The gaoler glanced at her. "Is the Queen here . . . ?"

"The Queen is busy," said the woman. "The Mighty Skandar wanted to talk with you and found me on his way here. He asked me to come with him to translate."

"With me?" the gaoler exclaimed. "Er, I mean b . . ." He bowed again nervously, to the griffin. "Of course. What can I do for you, Mighty Skandar?"

Skandar rasped out something.

"He wants to see a particular prisoner," the woman translated. "The rebel who was arrested at the feast."

The gaoler coughed. "He's being interrogated."

Skandar snarled.

"He doesn't care," said the woman. "He wants this prisoner brought to him immediately."

The gaoler looked warily at Skandar. The prospect of arguing with him was far too intimidating, so he went for second best and argued with the woman instead. "Look, I'm sorry, milady, but I can't bring a prisoner up here without a direct order from—"

Skandar made a sudden rush at him and screamed in his face. The gaoler leapt out of the way and just barely avoided a blow from one of the dark griffin's flailing talons. Skandar came on, backing him up against the wall, and kept him there, hissing with his beak open wide, as if to demonstrate the fact that, if he wanted, he could easily fit the gaoler's head inside.

"Do it!" the woman shouted from nearby, panic edging her voice. "He says he'll kill you if you don't do as he says!"

All thought of duty and protocol evaporated from the gaoler's mind. "All right, all right!" he yelled. "I'll do it, I'll bring him up here right away!"

Thank gods, Skandar seemed to understand. He backed off and sat on his haunches, fixing him with a threatening yellow eye.

The gaoler made a hasty bow and retreated back into the prison corridors. Once inside, he summoned a couple of his men and ordered them to go and fetch the prisoner. They, seeing the look on his face, hurried off without argument.

While he waited for them to return, the head gaoler tried to make himself calm down and hoped that he wouldn't get into trouble for this. But what else was he supposed to do? The Mighty Skandar ruled the Eyrie as much as the Queen did, and in his own way he had the same level of authority. If he had decided to start throwing his weight around, then that wasn't the head gaoler's problem. Let the Queen deal with it.

The two guards returned, leading the prisoner between them. They hadn't put any chains on him; he wasn't in much shape to fight back.

"Good," said the gaoler. "Take him up top right away, and make sure he doesn't go anywhere."

The two guards nodded and made for the stairs, and the gaoler followed in the rear.

Heath went quietly. He was too exhausted to do anything but what they wanted. His entire chest was a mass of throbbing lines, and he could only see out of one eye. He had long since given up any hope of escape, or of dying with a single secret left. The only thing he had not told them yet was his birth name, and that was only because they hadn't seemed that interested in knowing. He had told them everything else he knew, and now, when he realised they were taking him back into the outside world, he thought they were finally taking him to his death.

He stumbled up the steps, head low, and stood still when his guards did.

"This is the one," said a voice. "Give him to the Mighty Skandar, now."

That voice . . .

Heath looked up blearily, and squinted in puzzlement when he saw that the face was familiar as well. "You?" he mumbled. "What are you doing . . . ?"

"Be quiet, you scum!" Wydd snapped. "You—guardsmen. The Mighty Skandar wants this prisoner. Don't keep him waiting."

"But, milady," one of them said, "We can't just hand over a prisoner like this, just because—"

He stopped abruptly, as Skandar approached. Heath, coming out of his stupor, looked up, and felt his heart freeze. The griffin's chest was in front of him like a big, feathered boulder, the head looming overhead. The feathers were silver and black. It was the Mighty Skandar, the dark griffin come for him, to kill him . . .

But . . . but . . .

Something wasn't right. Heath struggled with his thoughts, trying to get them back into some kind of order. There was something not quite right here, something he couldn't quite grasp.

Skandar, however, had no troubles. He struck, shoving one of the guards away. The man fell, dragging Heath with him, but as his colleague tried to interfere, Skandar smacked him aside as well and hooked his beak around Heath, dragging him away.

The guards knew better than to resist. They let go of their charge and retreated to a safe distance, unable to do anything but watch helplessly as Skandar hauled their captive off.

Bewildered and not knowing what else to do, Heath caught hold of Skandar's wing. Whether to try and fight him off or just to support himself he wasn't sure, but Skandar did not object. He walked off, pulling Heath with him, making for the door that led out of the tower. It was closed, but several brutal blows of the dark griffin's beak broke the wood into pieces, and he passed through the opening and into fresh air.

There, blocking the exit with his body, he finally shook Heath off.

Heath fell onto his back and lay there, gasping for breath as he looked up at Skandar and wondered if he was about to die. But Skandar only stared at him through impenetrable yellow eyes.

Yellow, Heath thought. His eyes were yellow. And his beak was grey, not black, and his forelegs, and he was too small . . .

The name finally rose in his mind. "Echo . . . ?"

Echo snorted at him and offered his back. He was wearing his harness.

Heath scrambled to his feet, his old grin finally returning. "Echo, you little . . . !"

Echo hissed and shoved him. No time for talk. Heath pulled

himself together and climbed onto the griffin's back. Echo straightened up and loped away from the tower. Fast, but not too fast.

Once they were away from the towers, and there was enough open space, Echo took off. He did it fast and roughly, and once he was in the air, he flew away from the Eyrie as fast as he could.

Heath, clinging to his back, was too tired and shook-up to feel much in the way of triumph. But what he did feel was gratitude. Gratitude toward Wydd, who had helped him for who knew what reasons, and gratitude toward Echo, but most of it was simply gratitude for the fact that he had found a partner like him in the first place, a partner who had both the cunning and the bravery to help him the way Echo had.

Before, he had been glad to have Echo with him because of the opportunities the spotted griffin offered. But now he had learnt just what a griffin's partnership really meant, and it made him feel the kind of awe that he had never felt before in his life.

15

The Lost Tribe

Heath paused again at this point in his story. Caedmon and Myfina had both been listening in silence, utterly riveted.

"So what happened next?" Myfina demanded when he went silent. "Thank gods you got away—but I'm so sorry you went through that because of us."

Heath shook himself. "It doesn't matter. Even if I hadn't been a rebel, I still would have lost a hand down there, and probably more. In fact, if I *hadn't* been a rebel, they probably would have just done that right away, before I had a chance to escape. I'll take a few burns over having to wear a hook for the rest of my life." He grinned.

Caedmon grinned back. "Nothing ever keeps you down for long, does it? But tell us what happened next! You didn't get that griffin-skin in Malvern, that's for sure."

"Right you are." Heath accepted the cup of hot wine from Myfina, and sipped it with a blissful expression. "Oooh, dear gods, if the manna from the Meadows of Heaven taste better than this, I don't want to know about it. Anyway . . . right, yes, the story. Well, as you've probably guessed, Echo and I didn't get away clean from Malvern. I never did find out what happened to Wydd, but I hope she got away. If they caught her, then she probably had the sense to say she thought Echo was Skandar and he just fooled her, too.

"In any case, the guards would have passed on the news that their prisoner had been carried off, and we didn't get far before people started chasing us. They sent griffiners, and a couple of Unpartnered came too—probably in the mood for some excitement. And we were in big trouble. We couldn't go to any of the cities, and if we went anywhere else, we'd be tracked down in no time. The Eyrie pays big money for rogue griffiners. I don't know what Echo had in mind, but he probably realised that, too.

"We did our best to stay away from people, but I was in a bad way. I needed food, and healing as well, so when it got obvious that I'd die without it, Echo took me to some village or other. I've forgotten its name, but I managed to get some help there. Peasants are always very quick to help a griffiner. We couldn't stay there long, so we ended up moving from place to place in bits and pieces until I was on the mend, and Echo decided it was time to head off into the wilderness.

"But we'd stayed too long. Word got out, griffiners came looking, and in the end they chased us northward for two weeks. Every time we thought we'd lost them, they'd show up again. Even when we were in the middle of nowhere, days away from the nearest village, they didn't give up.

"Eventually—and I'm pretty sure Echo was just flying at random, since he wouldn't have left Skenfrith before he met me—we wound up at the coast. We would have turned back from there, but those blasted griffiners showed up again. They were persistent, I'll give them that.

"They cornered us there, with our backs to the sea, and I thought we'd have to surrender, but Echo decided to do the only other thing we could do. He got me on his back and flew out over the sea. They chased us out there until we'd lost sight of land, then they finally turned back. I guess they thought we'd just keep on going until Echo ran out of energy and fell into the sea. And for a while, I thought that's what would happen, too.

"But it didn't. Echo kept on going, until I thought I'd freeze to death before I got to drown. And then I saw it." Heath paused dramatically.

"An island?" Caedmon guessed.

"Exactly," said Heath, looking slightly disappointed. "A big, icy island, hiding out there off the northwestern coast. Actually, I found out later on that there's more than one—there were two other, smaller islands just off the coast from the main one. You can swim between them—and I did, at least once. So Echo landed on the main island. Most of it is covered in pine trees, and there was snow everywhere even though winter had just about passed by then. I thought great, a hiding place, we'll stay here until those bastards have moved on, then we can go back to the mainland and find somewhere I can hide without freezing my balls off. But it didn't work out quite like that."

"Why, what happened?" Myfina rubbed her hands together in anticipation.

"I found out that there were already people living on that island, that's what," said Heath.

"Really?" Caedmon cocked his head. "Northerners?"

"Oh yes. But . . . it's not just that. The people there are . . ." Heath struggled for words, which was unusual for him. ". . . real Northerners."

The others looked blank.

"*We're* real Northerners," Myfina said eventually.

"No we're not." For once, there was no trace of mockery in Heath's face. "We're . . . well, we're civilised Northerners. We fought off the Southerners here, but we never did go back to our ways. We live like they do now. Cities. Books. Money. Griffins. That sort of thing. Things the Southerners taught us. But the people on that island, they don't have any of that. They wear furs and live in little huts buried under the snow. They don't even farm—everything they eat has to be gathered, or hunted. With stone weapons. They don't even have metal. None of them speak a word of Cymrian. They speak the old language, nothing else. And," he added with a grin, "they stink. Far too cold there for bathing, you see."

"Wow." Even Caedmon looked impressed. "That's incredible! A lost tribe!"

"Yes," said Heath. "And they're not used to visitors. In fact if it hadn't been for Echo, they probably would have killed me on the spot. But when they saw that him and me were working together, they were frightened, and then impressed. They still worship animal spirits as well as the moon, you see. Just the moon, mind you—they don't seem to have much concept of the Night God. Anyway, they know what griffins are—there are some living on the other two islands I mentioned—and they worship them especially; think they're extrapowerful spirits. So when they saw that I was friends with one, they assumed I was some kind of sorcerer. Luckily, I knew enough of the old language to understand some of what they were saying, and picked up on that easily enough. So I thought, wonderful, they'll help me, give me something to eat and maybe some of those furs to keep me warm.

"Unfortunately, it seems they had a different idea of what to do around sorcerers. They gave me food, sure enough, and a place to stay, but after that they wouldn't let me leave. They wanted me to stay with them and use my magic to help them, and, apparently, they don't believe a sorcerer can magic away stone spears when they're aimed at his throat.

"When Echo tried to put a stop to it, they didn't show much fear—they just drove him off. In the end, he flew off to the other islands and found a home with the wild griffins, and in the meantime there I was with the wild humans.

"Now, at first I thought, 'Great, I got out of prison and now I've taken shelter in another, completely different prison.' But after a while I realised they weren't that bad. The women certainly liked me! And I remembered the old stories about Arenadd and how he found your grandmother in the mountains, and she taught him the old ways. So I thought, maybe this is *my* time in the wilderness, and I've come here to learn without even realising it.

"And I thought about it some more, and realised that I wasn't likely to find a much better place to hide. For all I knew, you were dead, so there was nothing left for me on the mainland except a nasty death. The island wasn't much, but it could be a home, and at least nobody was trying to kill me.

"So I stayed, and let them teach me how to live like they did. And as you can see, I wound up looking like one of them as well. No razors over there, you know. Besides, the beard kept my face warm." Heath coughed again.

"And the griffin hide?" Caedmon prompted.

"I'm getting to that. So I stayed with the lost tribe for . . . however long it was, months probably. Eventually, the season changed—not easy to notice over there—and they started preparing for some kind of yearly ritual. In this ritual, it's expected that every young man must go out and hunt an animal. The animal has to be a predator, and the bigger it is, the more respected that hunter becomes. Of course, I was more than happy to go looking for a possum or something, but I was the griffin-man, and everyone there just sort of assumed that I would swim over to one of the other islands and hunt a wild griffin, which very few people were ever allowed to do." Heath ran his fingers through the feathers on his shoulder. "So I did."

"You what?" Myfina exclaimed.

Heath shrugged. "I hunted a wild griffin and killed it. Echo was on the island I chose, and he came to help me. Once it was dead, I floated it back to the main island, and Echo helped me drag it to the village. There was a big celebration, and the chief had a couple of men skin the griffin and prepare the hide for me to wear. You'd be surprised how good they are at tanning, but let me tell you this thing was damn smelly when I first put it on. I probably wouldn't have kept it, but it was so warm I couldn't resist. Besides, it made me feel pretty important, as you can imagine!" Heath grinned. "I never said I didn't have a weakness for other people's adoration."

"I never met anyone who didn't," said Caedmon. "So what happened next? How did you find us?"

"I didn't," said Heath. "Not long after the special hunt, things got bad on the island. There wasn't much food there to begin with, but it started to get even harder to find. I think they have famines like that fairly often because nobody seemed very surprised. But I'd been having a tough time of it this year as you might've guessed, and I didn't do very well at all. I started to get sick again, and my old wounds started opening up again. Most people start to feel a bit spiritual in these situations, and I started to think that maybe I wouldn't live to see the end of the year.

"And then I decided that I'd left too much unfinished to just accept it, so I left. Echo seemed to want to leave, too. I said goodbye first, of course, but none of the tribe was too unhappy about my leaving. One less mouth to feed, and sorcerers are meant to vanish mysteriously anyway.

"We flew back to the mainland, and I was feeling in the mood for a little religion, so I asked Echo if we could come here. And here we are."

Caedmon clapped him on the back. "It's wonderful to have you back, Heath. I missed you."

"I missed you, too," Heath said solemnly. "I'm afraid it seems

I've lost my taste for just looking after myself. I must have spent too much time with you because I've apparently caught a bad case of loyalty and nobility and so on. And a bad case of being a griffiner, as well. You should've warned me all that was catching."

Myfina gave him a hug. "You were right, that was a great story. I'll make you some more wine—I think you've earned it."

"Yes please!" Heath looked at Caedmon. "But listen, Caedmon. I think . . ."

"Yes, Heath?"

"I don't know." Heath shook his head. "I never was a very religious man, but I have a feeling right now, as if there's a reason why I came back to you. Not just so I could help you again, but also so I could tell you all this. About the island, and the lost tribe."

"What about them?" asked Caedmon.

"I think you should go to them," said Heath. "I think you should fly to that island and stay with them the way I did. Learn from them, the way I did."

"Why?"

"You want to be King," Heath said seriously. "King of the North and all Northerners. Those people on that island are some of the people you want to rule. And besides, they're Northerners in a way that you and I aren't. It's a funny thing that I've been thinking since I went there, but I think it's true. We won the war against the Southerners, but we lost something as well. We never got back what the Southerners took from us, all the things they made us forget. Don't you see, Caedmon? We won the war, but we lost ourselves. Underneath it all, we're just glorified Southerners with different looks. We live like they live, we squabble among ourselves and fight for power, we partner with griffins . . . It's not our way, Caedmon. It's not our true way. The lost tribe are the only ones left who know what we used to be. I think that if you want to be King, then it should be your duty to make sure it doesn't die with them."

Myfina looked thoughtful and glanced at Caedmon, to see how he was taking it.

Caedmon looked at Heath with a new respect. "You're right," he said. "You're completely right. And I think that's what my mother was always on about. I never really understood it properly back then, but now I think I do. Yes." He nodded.

"I'll go there. When my mother comes back to see us, I'll tell her about all this. I'm sure she'll agree, and maybe she'll want to come with us." He looked to Myfina. "What about you, Myfina? Do you want to come as well?"

"If you go, then I will, too," she said at once.

"I'll have to come along," said Heath. "To show you the way. And I think I should probably be there to introduce you, too. There's no telling what they might think when they see you two."

"Good point," said Caedmon. "But for now, get some rest. You look as if you need it."

Heath rubbed his face. "I do. It's been a long day. D'you mind if I just curl up here?"

"Not at all."

Heath smiled and nodded and lay down on his side by the fire, curling up inside the ragged griffin hide in a way that suggested he'd done it plenty of times in the past. In a surprisingly short time he was asleep.

16

Kullervo's Vow

Kullervo did not attend the party to welcome Prince Akhane. He had never felt at home in a crowd, and besides, he wasn't in the mood. He felt a little odd.

Not exactly ill, but uneasy.

He went back to his quarters and had a meal brought to him but didn't have much of an appetite. Food had been brought up for Senneck as well, but she wasn't there to eat it. Kullervo wished that she was. Talking to her would have made him feel better.

From somewhere above, his keen hearing caught the sounds of music and laughter. He knew Laela was up there now, probably dancing with her betrothed. Vander and Inva would be there together as well, and everyone else with their friends and family.

Kullervo felt very alone. A lump rose in his throat, and he rubbed his hands over his face like a griffin would, and sighed. If only . . .

Time drew on, and the darkness seemed to increase. Still Senneck did not return, and Kullervo sat on the edge of his bed in a kind of trance, listening to the sounds of celebration high above and feeling as if the rest of the world had faded away from him, leaving only its sounds to taunt him with what he could not reach.

Eventually, realising that there was nothing else to do now, he lay down on his side in front of the fireplace, wings protruding from the slits in his tunic, and went to sleep like a cat in the firelight.

But his unease carried over into his sleep, and a dream came. Or, at least, *something* came.

It loomed over him, the fire burning low and dim in its presence. It was something utterly black and misty, nearly featureless, but . . . human. There seemed to be a shape hidden in there, arms and a head, and maybe eyes. Eyes watching him without expression.

Liquid ice ran through Kullervo's veins. He felt as if his whole body had frozen in fear. And this was a fear that went beyond a mere fear of death. It was in his soul, eating away at him like a madness from within. He wanted to curl into a ball and hide, but he couldn't move. And then the voice came. It was whispering and echoey, as if there were several voices trying to speak at once, but all saying the same thing.

Kullervo . . . ullervo . . . lervo . . . vo . . . vo . . . Kullervo Taranisäii . . . aii . . . äii . . .

It was barely a voice at all, and yet it sounded . . . urgent?

Kullervo managed to move his lips. "Who . . . are . . . you?" His own voice felt strangled, as if every word were an effort.

The reply came, but it was so faint and shifting that he could only grasp a fraction of it . . . *death . . . Night God . . . death . . . coming . . . she . . . coming for . . . you . . . Night God want . . . death . . . can't fight her . . . can't resist . . . spirit . . . slave . . . danger!*

"You're a slave?" Kullervo found himself saying

The spectre didn't seem to hear . . . *death, death coming . . . go or die . . .*

Its voice grew fainter and fainter even as it tried to speak, but something in that shapeless blackness fought back. Its form warped and darkened, and just for an instant Kullervo saw a face. Pale, angular, bearded, and terrified. *Kullervo!* it shouted. *Run! Ruuuun . . . !*

"Father!"

Kullervo's own shout woke him up. He sat up almost before his eyes had opened, every sense alert for danger. But he was alone in the room.

He lay down again and tried to relax. *Just a dream.* Senneck would scoff if she were there. But she wasn't, and Kullervo's unease had only increased.

He got up and started to dress, not sure of what he was going to do next but certain that he had to leave. Something about this room just didn't feel safe or cozy any more.

He strode out into the corridor, but the rest of the Eyrie felt just as unpleasant. All of a sudden, he started to feel cooped up. The griffish part of him wanted to be outside, where he could see the sky. The sky was freedom, and safety.

He almost ran down the ramps and stairways to the lowest level of the tower, and left through a door on the ground floor. Outside was a large open yard surrounded by a wall that protected the Eyrie from the ground—as a griffiner, and occasional griffin, he had rarely used it himself.

He crossed it now and found a gate that led out into the city. It was guarded, but the guards let him pass. It was only people coming in who might need stopping.

Kullervo entered the city and began to wander along its streets, lost in thought.

Even at night, the streets were bustling. People passed him on both sides and in both directions, many of them throwing curious stares at the hulking hunchback whose ugly face didn't match his intimidating size. But his slanted yellow eyes and broad shoulders were more than enough to make them keep their distance, even if they made him look less than Northern.

Kullervo scarcely noticed them. Stares were so familiar to him that they didn't even register with him much any more. Now that he was away from the Eyrie, he felt much better, or at least his irrational fear had died down. His troubles, though, had followed him.

He wondered if he should have told Laela about what he had seen. But no, she was busy now, and she wouldn't want to be bothered with his nightmares. She probably had enough of her own. And besides, it was just a dream, wasn't it?

But Kullervo wasn't so sure about that. It had felt real though dreams sometimes did, and how had he known the face he had seen was his father's? He had never met him, or seen a picture of him; all he had to go on were other people's descriptions. Everyone said Arenadd had had a pointed beard and curly hair. The face in his dream, though, had had a scar under one eye. Had his father had a scar like that one?

He decided that he would ask Laela. If Arenadd *had* been scarred like that, then . . .

But if it wasn't a dream, what else could it have been? A vision? A haunting of some sort? People said ghosts were real, but Kullervo had never seen one, or met anyone who had. Lots of things were supposed to be real, and he wasn't so certain that any of them were real—even the gods.

He walked on for a while, following the main street, and followed that line of thought. Were ghosts real? Could his father's spirit have contacted him in his sleep? Who would know about things like that?

Kullervo looked up, and saw a large building rising above the rooftops all about. Unlike the other buildings around it, it was made from white stone and looked brand-new. A silver crescent shone on top of its domed roof.

It didn't take a genius to guess what the building was. They must have finished rebuilding it while Kullervo was away. He had never been inside it, and with that thought he started to head toward it. Maybe one of the priestesses inside could tell him about spirits.

The big front doors to the Temple were open, and Kullervo walked through them, intimidated by the size of the space beyond. The Temple had no internal walls, and for sheer size and magnificence, it put the council chamber back at the Eyrie to shame. It was, however, surprisingly gloomy. Pillars stood here and there—not in rows, but placed seemingly at random, like trees in a forest—and were decorated by silver branches with blue-glass lanterns hanging from them. The light they gave off was cool and muted, like moonlight.

The Temple's exterior might have been finished, but the interior still needed some work. Kullervo could see that the mosaic underfoot had only been partly finished, and no wonder—the parts that were finished were made up of thousands of tiny tiles, creating a pattern of fallen leaves interspersed with streams and pools. There were no seats here, or tables, but everything about the design, from the placing of the pillars to the patterns on the floor, directed him toward the centre and the light that waited there.

He walked toward it, spellbound. In the heart of the Temple, a circle of thirteen standing stones had been erected. The stones were smaller and the circle narrower, but he knew what they were at once. The holy stones of Taranis' Throne, re-created here in miniature.

Unlike the stones of the Throne, whose carvings were old and weathered, the stones here were freshly cut with sharp, clear lines making complex spiralling patterns that weaved around a central circle on each one which featured a triple spiral. Kullervo had learnt enough to know that those represented the full moon, which was why there were thirteen stones—one for each of the thirteen full moons of the year.

He went in among them, and sure enough there was an altar in the circle. But this one had an attendant. Not a priestess, but a statue. It was bigger than most people—not huge, but scaled up enough to look impressive. It stood a head taller than Kullervo, who had already been scaled up himself.

The Night God.

She was carved from white marble, and looked horribly lifelike in a light robe that flowed along with her hair and left her breasts bare. But there was nothing sensual about her. Her face was sharp and commanding, the mouth and forehead set in lines of coldness and judgment. One eye was a black gemstone, glittering and pitiless. The other was a great silver disc that shone in the light of the silver-glass lanterns that stood on the altar below.

When Kullervo saw that face, which seemed to stare straight at him with an expression of utter dismissal, all of the awe that the Temple had made in him disappeared. He stood there in silence, looking up into the face of the Night God, and felt his former fear twist itself up inside him and turn into pure and overwhelming hatred. This was the face that looked down on humanity without love and whispered thoughts of warfare and murder. This was the face that was supposed to belong to a mother, but underneath was concerned with nothing but gaining power through ignorance and fear. Humanity had put all their darkness into this face without even knowing it, and Kullervo saw it now.

There was a silver dagger on the altar, beside a shallow dish set into the stone, filled with water. Kullervo knew that the water was for divining the future, but he didn't want to know anything that this face might have to tell him.

He picked up the dagger instead, and pressed it into his palm. One quick tug sideways made blood well up through the skin. He dropped the dagger and held out his injured hand, squeezing it into a fist until blood dripped onto the altar, adding another stain to the dozens of others there.

"With this blood, I call to you," he intoned as red splashed onto white, like a teardrop onto ice. "With this sacrifice of my body, I summon you now to hear my prayer."

He didn't know if they were exactly the right words, but they felt about right.

Nothing happened, but he had a feeling that the silence in the Temple deepened.

He knelt, bowing his head to that savage statue, and prayed. "Night God," he said. "Scathach. Mistress of death and darkness. I am Kullervo Taranisäii, son of Arenadd Taranisäii and Skade of Withypool. I've never prayed to you, or stood in one of your temples before. I've never prayed to any god in my life. But I call you to hear me now, just once, because I promise you that after this I will never speak to you again. There is something I must tell you." He stood up abruptly, facing the statue, and spoke directly into its face. "I reject you," he said. "From today and forever, I turn my back on you. I will never pray to you, never honour you, never obey you. I know you are powerful, and that your followers are powerful, but I don't care." He moved closer, hatred burning in his yellow griffin eyes. "I would rather die," he said. "And I will die. I will go to the void and be lost there forever, and do it gladly if it means that I can be free of you. You turned my father into a monster. You did the same to Saeddryn as well, and who knows how many others. You teach ignorance and hate, you tell human beings that they can never be anything more than what you want them to be. I tell you now, I will spend my life fighting against you. I will work to undo what you've done and make the world a better place to live—without you."

Then Kullervo did something he had never done in his life before. He bared his jagged teeth, and spat on the Night God's altar.

Then he turned and walked out of the Temple with rapid and powerful strides, and never looked back.

L aela was in love.

She knew it with her whole mind, her whole body, her whole spirit.

Not much of a dancer, she stayed around the edges of the

dance floor with Akhane and watched the others. She chatted with her betrothed every so often, but for most of the time she was happy to say nothing. It was enough just to be there with him, close enough to touch, and wallow in the fact that he was there with her.

During Kullervo's absence, she had wondered if her memory of the Amorani Prince had become exaggerated over time. After all, she had only known him for a day and a night, and that had been a long while ago—more than a year by now. But if anything, she found that time had only enhanced him. He seemed even more handsome, kinder, and sweeter than she remembered, his deep, accented voice even smoother and richer to listen to. And better even than his presence now was the knowledge that he would never leave her again. He was hers now, hers to keep beside her and share her bed with, and to make heirs with. Before now, she had never been that interested in having children of her own, but now the prospect excited her.

So did the thought of making them, she acknowledged to herself with a wicked smile.

She had never felt like more of a woman than she did now. In all honestly, it was a relief.

Akhane turned to her with a smile. "You look as if you are thinking deeply, Laela."

She pressed herself against him, and astonished herself by tilting her head to give him a flirtatious smile of her own. "I was thinkin' about you."

He put an arm around her in a slightly hesitant way, which only excited her even further. "That is not a peaceful thing to know, my Queen. You looked so fierce!"

Laela's excitement crumbled. "Really?"

"I thought that you were thinking of your enemies and had meant to calm you down, truly," Akhane said.

She sagged slightly in his embrace. "I didn't mean it. I'm sorry. I've been doin' that too much, yeh know. It's eatin' me up."

Akhane let go. "What do you mean?"

Laela looked gloomy. "I'm tired of it, Akhane. Tired of bein' angry all the time. Tired of havin' to make people scared of me."

"You do not have to do that."

"I do. Yeh don't know how hard it is for me, rulin' this place. I'm a half-breed. People don't trust me no more. My reign ain't based on loyalty, like my dad's was; it's based on fear. Not gonna get loyalty now, not after all the stuff I had to do t'get rid of Caedmon's lot." She was rambling a little now, slipping back into her old, crude accents. "So it's gotta be fear. Remindin' people of what happens if they don't do what I say. Livin' up to having Skandar as a partner. I can do it, but I dunno. I never thought I'd end up as this sort of person, yeh know? It makes me feel so tired an' lonely. It's nice t'get a chance t'just . . . be myself for a while."

Akhane listened seriously. "You have done well, to rule alone like this. In Amoran, a woman is not considered powerful enough in the spirit to lead. But we know that the women here in Tara are not like our own. You are carved from ice, it is said, and have the hearts of wolves. I know enough of you to know that you have lived up to this tale. But underneath that you are still a woman, and you should not have to live this way. Nor will you. I am here now, and I will love you as a woman should be loved, and rule by your side. Together, we will shoulder this burden."

Laela smiled at him—a smile that felt soft and sweet. "Thank you."

Not caring that they were in public, she kissed him on the mouth. He kissed her back, causing several of the onlookers to chuckle and nudge each other.

He glanced at them, and leaned down to whisper in Laela's ear, "What do you say that we retire now?"

She grinned evilly. "Yeah, let's."

Akhane gave her a slightly puzzled look but quickly deciphered her meaning and smiled again. "It has been a long journey, but I am not so tired. I am used to travelling."

"I heard. Spent half yer life runnin' from place to place, Kullervo said. Feel free t'stop by an' visit yer wife along the way, though." Laela grinned. "I'm gonna go get another drink before we go. Want one?"

"I would be grateful," he said gravely.

Laela laughed at his solemn expression and turned to leave.

As she took a step toward the wine barrels, her neck prickled. She stopped in her tracks, looking around quickly. Everything looked fine, but the tingle of fear had not gone away. Her hand went to the hilt of the dagger in her belt.

Akhane had noticed her behaviour and came toward her with a look of concern. "What is wrong?"

Laela held up a hand to stop him. "I got a bad feeling. Be on the lookout." Without waiting to explain herself, she drew her dagger and backed away from the partygoers, her blue eyes narrow and searching everywhere, as if looking for a target. Her free hand went to her neck, and adjusted the hang of the thick silver neck-ring she had taken to wearing during the last few months. It looked nice and decorative, but it was also solid metal, and it covered most of her throat.

Akhane was also looking around, puzzled as well as apprehensive. "What is it? What have you seen?"

"Nothing," Laela said grimly. "But if I've sensed right, nobody *will* see anything. Damn it, where's Skandar? I'm payin' a fortune to feed the bastard, but when I need him, where is he?" She tightened her grip on the dagger. "Have yeh got a weapon?"

"No, but I am strong enough without one." Akhane had already guessed what she was afraid of. He moved closer to her, taking up a protective stance in front of her. "You think that your enemy is here?"

"Yeah." Laela was still looking for Skandar. "She crept up on me before, outta nowhere, an' right now it feels like it did then. Damn it, I didn't think she'd have the guts t'come back here after what happened then." The fear tightened its grip on her throat. "Look," she said quickly, noting that several of the guests had noticed the disturbance. "If somethin' happens to me—*argh!*"

Even as she spoke, every muscle tensed ready to fight, the grip on her throat became a hand of ice, wrenching her violently backward and into darkness.

She heard Akhane shout something, then he was gone, and the void took her.

But the void was not death. It was icy blackness, full of nothing but fear and those freezing hands dragging her away. She tried to break free, but here those hands were stronger than iron, and the darkness was in her mind, paralysing her body.

Every moment she expected to die, expected those hands to break her apart, but they didn't. And despite the terror, she realised that she had travelled like this before.

But that time it had been away from danger, not toward it, and the icy grip had been protective. Even loving.

But Arenadd was gone now, and Saeddryn . . .

The sickening journey ended when she was thrown out of

the darkness and into light, landing hard on a floor. She rolled over, gasping, but had the presence of mind to grope for her dagger. But it was gone. She didn't even remember losing it.

A boot kicked her hard in the side, rolling her over onto her back.

Laela looked up into the face of the Shadow That Walked.

Time had changed Saeddryn, and for the worse. She had grown gaunt and sick-looking, and her eye had lost its brightness and gone dull and lifeless. But it was much more enjoyable to look at than the place where the other eye had been. Weight loss had made the skin draw in around the empty socket, deepening the hole and filling it with shadows.

If Saeddryn hadn't looked so otherwise mundane, Laela might have thought she was looking at the Night God herself once again. But the utter contempt written in every line of that face was exactly the same look she had seen that awful night.

Laela's own face twisted. *"You,"* she spat.

"Aye, me," Saeddryn rasped back. "Surprised?"

"Honestly?" Laela pulled herself to her feet. "Yeah. Didn't think yeh'd have the guts to come crawling back. Didn't you learn yer lesson last time?"

"I did," said Saeddryn, surprising her. "That's why I didn't try an' kill ye there. That's why I brought ye here instead, where that griffin can't find me."

Laela quickly took in her new surroundings: a room somewhere, not one she knew. It looked like she was in a building somewhere in the city. "What makes you so sure about that?" she asked in her most confident, sneering voice. The best strategy now would be to keep her talking. Play for time, keep her busy until . . . until nothing, but more time spent living was worth it.

Saeddryn did not rise to the bait. "Somethin' tells me she'd have struck by now if she could Goodbye, half-breed. The void is waiting."

She lunged forward with lightning speed. One hand caught Laela by the front of her gown. The other seized the neck-ring, and wrenched it off so hard the clasp broke.

A crash made Saeddryn look up sharply. She drew her dagger, but before she could strike, a powerful blow knocked her down.

Laela went staggering to the ground, but she rolled and recovered herself in time to see Saeddryn struggling against an enemy much bigger than herself and far angrier.

The shout burst joyfully out of Laela's mouth. "Kullervo!"

But this was a Kullervo she had never seen before; snarling and savage, hands sprouting talons to slash at Saeddryn's face. His wings had come free of the cape he had used to cover them and flailed weakly; they were featherless again and horrible to look at.

Saeddryn leapt at Kullervo; she had lost her dagger, but grappled with him anyway, and despite the big difference in size between them she held her own against him without much effort.

But Kullervo, for once in his life, did not back down. He was possibly too angry for that. He hurled Saeddryn to the ground and pounced on her, hands closing around her neck.

Saeddryn grabbed at his wrists but could not make him let go as he dragged her upright again. But there was no fear in her face. She grinned horribly. "Tonight was going well already," she rasped. "But now it's perfect. Both of ye here in one place. I can finish it in one go."

Kullervo's teeth were bared. "Curse you," he snarled. "I gave you a chance. I asked you not to make a war. Why didn't you listen? Why did you force me to do this?"

Saeddryn spat at him. "Take yer filthy hands off me, half-breed."

"No." Kullervo's eyes blazed. "I won't obey you or your master ever again."

"Fine." Saeddryn kicked out, catching him in the stomach. He let go in shock, doubling up as the wind thumped out of him. In an instant, she had darted away and retrieved her dagger, diving back into the shadows.

Kullervo ran to Laela, helping her to her feet. He shoved her toward the door. "Laela, run! Get out of here!"

She didn't let go of him. "No. I ain't leavin' you. We're stronger together."

"Are we?" Kullervo turned, lashing out at nothing. "Damn you, show yourself! You coward! *Argh!*" A wound opened on the side of his neck.

Laela moved closer to him, holding her hands up to his throat. "Kullervo, cover it! Cover yer neck! Don't give her a target!"

"Right." Kullervo wrapped his left hand around his throat and breathed deeply. "Laela, move away," he said. "Don't leave, just go over there."

"No. I told yeh, if we stay together—"

"Just do it!" Kullervo shouted. *"Now!"*

Laela, hearing a command in his voice that had never been there before, went to the other side of the room. Kullervo stayed where he was, following her with his eyes.

A moment later, they narrowed into slits. *"There* you are," he growled, and leapt. His hands reached out into the empty air, and for a moment Laela thought she saw them vanish.

Kullervo turned sharply, and hurled Saeddryn out of the shadows. "Got you," he growled. "You can't hide from me, *Kraeaina kran ae."*

Saeddryn dodged out of his reach. "Who *are* ye?" she screeched. "How . . . ?"

"I'm my father's son," said Kullervo.

Outside, beyond the shattered door, a screech came. Two griffins came with it, snarling and scrabbling to get in. Senneck and Skandar.

Saeddryn knew she was beaten. "The Night God will have ye," she said. "Yer souls will be hers, I swear it."

"Get out," Kullervo threw back. "Get out of here and go back to the shadows where you belong. And tell your master that when I die, she can send me to the void for all I care. But if I find her, I'll tear her throat out with my talons."

Saeddryn slid back into the shadows and was gone.

A few moments later, Kullervo relaxed and went to Laela. "It's all right," he said. "She's gone. We're safe." The rage had gone out of him now, and his usual diffident affection came back as he hugged her.

Laela clung to him, breathing harshly. "Oh gods, I thought she was gonna kill me, I thought . . ."

"It doesn't matter now," Kullervo told her. "She won't come back."

Senneck managed to force her way into the room, leaving Skandar frustrated outside. "Kullervo," she said. "I am so glad you are safe. How did *Kraeaina kran ae* find you here?"

"She didn't," said Kullervo. "I found her. Wait—" He looked at Skandar. "How did *you* know where we were?"

"I did not," said Senneck. "I only followed the Mighty Skandar."

Laela was in no mood for questions. She let go of Kullervo and went out through the doorway to Skandar's side. He huffed and sniffed at her, reassuring himself that she was safe. "You stay now," he told her brusquely. "Not leave again. Danger here."

"Yeh don't say?" Laela glared. She looked at Kullervo again as he came out after her with Senneck. "Kullervo, how did yeh know? How did yeh find us so fast?"

He looked slightly puzzled. "I don't know. I was out in the city, near the Temple, and I just . . . had a feeling that you were in trouble. And I just sort of followed it, and it led here."

"That doesn't make any gods-damned sense!" Laela exclaimed. "Skandar? How did *you* get here?"

Skandar cocked his head. "Have feeling. See something fly to here, and followed."

"'Something'?" Laela echoed. "What something?"

"See something," Skandar repeated stubbornly. "Come, we go back to Eyrie now."

Laela shook herself. "Good idea. They're probably all going mad back there."

She climbed onto Skandar's back. Kullervo got onto Senneck, and the two griffins flew back to the top of the Council Tower.

The party had long since broken up, and most of the guests had left. But Akhane was still there, looking very pale in the face. When he saw Laela, he ran to her.

She gave him a wan smile. "Don't worry, I'm fine. Where did everyone go?"

"They are searching for you," said Akhane, embracing her carefully. "The entire Eyrie is on alert, and the guards are scouring the city."

Laela looked pleased. "Good men, they are. I'll make sure they get a bonus for actin' that fast. C'mon, let's go and spread the word. Can't have everyone runnin' around like headless chickens when they oughta be in bed."

Kullervo smiled and nodded to her as she left, with Skandar loping along behind her. When they were gone, he and Senneck were left alone among the ruins of the feast.

Kullervo wandered over to the tables and helped himself to

some of the leftover food. The night's excitement had finally given him an appetite.

Senneck found a carcass with some meat still on it and ate as well. "I am glad to be with you again," she said eventually.

"So am I," said Kullervo. He finished off a cake and ran his talons through his hair. They had extended his fingers; he would have to trim them if he wanted to use his hands for anything delicate. "Where were you?"

"I was with the Mighty Skandar," said Senneck, unembarrassed.

Kullervo watched her, nostrils flaring as he took in her scent. "You mated with him, didn't you?" he asked quietly. "That's where you were all evening."

"Yes," said Senneck, almost carelessly.

"I can smell it on you," said Kullervo. He paused. "Do you think you'll lay eggs?"

"I hope that I will," said Senneck. "And I will pair with him again to be certain of it. He will give me strong chicks."

"Yes . . ." Kullervo sat down by the tables, looking somehow smaller than before. "I hope you do have eggs. I know you wanted some. If I could, I would have . . ." He trailed off and shook his head slowly, as if trying to dislodge a thought he didn't want to have.

Senneck watched him for a while, slightly confused, before returning to her food.

After a while, Kullervo seemed to find his voice. "We're going South."

Senneck dropped the bone she was attempting to crack. "What?"

"At least," said Kullervo, "*I'm* going South. You can come with me if you like, but you're not going to talk me out of going."

"Why?" asked Senneck.

"I've been given a mission," said Kullervo. "Go South and talk to the Eyries. Make a treaty. I'm Laela's brother and her heir; I'm the best choice of ambassador."

"It would not work," said Senneck. "You have black hair; they will call you a Northerner and kill you on sight."

"I know," said Kullervo. "That's why I'm going to go there with my wings uncovered."

"No," said Senneck. "Kullervo, this is foolish. They will see you as—"

"As myself!" Kullervo snapped. "Senneck, I'm tired of lying. I'm tired of pretending to be something I'm not. I'll let them see me for what I really am, and I won't pretend to be a prophet or a holy man because I'm not. I'll tell them who I am: Kullervo, son of Arenadd, Prince of Malvern, hybrid freak of nature. And they can say what they like; I'm not afraid of words."

"You do not need to be afraid of words," Senneck hissed. "You should be afraid of swords and talons. If they know you are Arenadd's son, they will kill you."

"Then as Arenadd's son, I'll ask for their forgiveness and offer them peace."

"No!" Senneck stood up, tail lashing angrily. "I cannot allow this. I will not lose another human to stupidity."

"You won't," said Kullervo. "Senneck, my father made hatred. He drove the races apart even further than they already were. I will bring them together again, and I'll do it without violence or lies. I've seen enough of that for a lifetime."

Senneck took an aggressive step toward him. "I will not allow you to leave. You will stay in the North, and if you try to leave, I will stop you, by force if I must."

Kullervo nodded curtly. "I understand," he said. "I'm going to my room now. I need to rest."

He walked off.

17

Journeying Again

Senneck didn't see much of Kullervo for the next two days after that. She still shared quarters with him, but when she saw him in the evenings, he was distant and distracted. He spent his days talking with Laela or hiding in his room.

Senneck was content to leave him to his own devices. Now that she was home again and felt secure there, she relaxed in her own way, spending her time flying lazily over the city or squabbling with other griffins who saw fit to try to pretend they were superior to her. But she spent plenty more time with Skandar. The dark griffin was happy to accept her presence as long as she stayed out of his nest, and as she had promised, she paired with him several times, until her body's natural cycles made her lose interest in that and therefore in him. After that, they parted ways without a thought, and Senneck was left to rest and imagine she could feel the beginnings of new life stirring inside her.

And then, three days after their return to Malvern, Kullervo was gone.

He was gone for more than half a day before she realised it. She slept late that morning, and when she woke up and found his room empty, she assumed that he had already gone off to see Laela or attend to some other human business. He had left food for her, so she had no reason to go looking for him.

She ate and spent a lazy morning roaming the city, and didn't realise that something was wrong until she returned to her nest sometime past noon. Kullervo was not there, and there was no scent to indicate that he had returned since the previous night.

Senneck began to look for other signs and found that some of his clothes had gone.

That was when she knew he had left.

She set out through the Eyrie, looking for a scent. But if Kullervo had left one on his way out, it had long since been covered up. She asked several griffins and griffiners she met along the way, but none of them had seen him. Nor was there much point in asking. She had already guessed where he had gone.

She went back to the tower-top where they had argued and sat down in the sun. Her human had ignored her warnings and gone South, alone. By now, he must be well on his way.

Senneck's course of action was clear: She must go after him and bring him back, before he crossed the border. But would she be able to catch up with him in time? And if he did enter the South before she found him, what then?

As she sat there and groomed to soothe her nerves, the sound of another griffin intruded on her thoughts. She looked up irritably, raising her wings in readiness to make a threat.

The other griffin, however, seemed intent on her. She came closer, moving tentatively with her head low in submission.

"What do you want?" Senneck demanded.

The other female crouched low. "Are you Senneck?"

"I am, and I do not wish to be disturbed."

"I am sorry," said the female. "But . . . I had heard that you were back in Malvern, and I wanted to see you."

"Why?" Senneck started up aggressively. "Why would you know my name?"

The female shrank back. "Because you are my mother."

Senneck stopped. "What?"

The female dared to stand up straight. "I am Seerae. I am your daughter. I did not know that you were alive."

"You . . ." Senneck came closer, sniffing. The scent was familiar. So were the eyes, and the line of the body. She had grown, of course, and her feathers had darkened, but . . . "You are Seerae. I thought that you were dead."

"I stayed here in Malvern after the war," said Seerae. "They did not know me. I joined with the Unpartnered and lived with them."

"And your brother?" Senneck asked sharply.

"He did not hide as I did," said Seerae. "He chose to try to fight the Unpartnered instead, and was killed. I survived to adulthood and chose a human. His name was Penllyn, and he chose to fight for Shar. Now he is dead, and I do not know what to do."

Senneck paused for a moment, thinking. "Come with me," she said at last. "I must go South with my human. Fly with us, and I will help you to find a new human."

"You would do this for me?" asked Seerae.

"I will, but in return you and your new human will help me in return one day, when I ask for it," said Senneck. "Do you accept?"

Seerae's tail swished over the stonework, and she turned her head away for a moment. But she soon faced her mother again, and huffed softly. "I will do this," she said. "For a new human."

"Then come," said Senneck. "It is time to go."

Senneck took off from the edge of the tower, and Seerae followed, flying southward out of the city. Senneck led the way, letting her daughter ride on her slipstream, and felt stronger knowing she was there. Humans were not the only ones who knew how to win allies, and with Seerae beside her, she would be stronger. Now it was time to find Kullervo and keep him safe, as she should have done for Erian. Time to find a way forward, to a better future.

Saeddryn left Malvern seething with rage.

"How did they do it?" she roared as she rushed through the shadows. *"How?"*

There was no reply.

Saeddryn left the shadows and ran tirelessly across country, bounding over rocks and logs and leaping streams without breaking stride. "How?" she said again, without any strain showing through in her voice. When there was no reply again, she snarled. "Arenadd!" her voice lashed out like a whip. "Answer me. *How did they find me? How did they know where I was?"*

I don't know, he said at last, voice murmuring in her ear. *Saeddryn, I don't know. I was watching out like you told me to, and I just saw them coming.*

"But how? Nobody could have seen us, not in the shadows!"

I told you, I don't know. Arenadd sounded harassed. *Skandar has the power, too; maybe he could sense you.*

"But Skandar wasn't the first to come," said Saeddryn. "It was that freak, the man-griffin."

He's not human, said Arenadd. *Who knows what powers he might have? There's never been anyone like him before.*

Saeddryn ran on, swearing. "I was so close . . . so *close*! I could've . . ."

Don't beat yourself up about it, Arenadd soothed. *You did your best. But you shouldn't have taken a risk like that. I warned you not to. You're not invincible, Saeddryn. If something happened to you, it would tear the heart out of the resistance.*

"I know, I know," she snapped. "But it wouldn't matter if I took the half-breeds with me. I shouldn't've run. Should've just killed them. Could've done it."

No you couldn't. Not with Skandar there.

"Not with ye in my ear, yellin' at me t'run away," Saeddryn growled.

Discretion is the better part of valour. Anyway, it would be better if their deaths were more public than that. Caedmon should do it himself. I keep telling you . . .

"I won't put him in danger, Arenadd. Not again."

He'll never be King if he lets you fight his battles for him. I have a suggestion . . .

Saeddryn slowed her pace. "Yes?"

Advise Caedmon to send Laela a message. He should challenge her to single combat. Finish this once and for all.

"No. I don't trust her."

But it's got to be worth a try. Better still, bring the griffins into it. That's how griffiners duel. Laela and Skandar against Caedmon and Shar. It's a tradition; no griffiner can refuse, and there are rules . . .

"Shar can't fight Skandar. She'd die."

Skandar's getting old. He's not as strong as he looks, you know. Just think about it. Ask Caedmon and see what he thinks.

"No. It's foolery, Arenadd."

Is it? I wouldn't be so sure about that if I were you. Listen, you know Caedmon can't rule just because you say so. If you killed Laela and placed him on the throne, what would that look like? He'd be the weakling who stood aside while his mother fought his battles for him. You know how our people see these things. The strongest rules. But imagine if Caedmon challenged Laela to a duel. They could fight somewhere public, and everyone would gather to watch. I started training Caedmon to fight when he was five years old. Laela's nothing next to him. She's a tavern brawler at best; she never mastered the sickle. And Skandar's old. Caedmon and Shar would win, right there in front of everyone. A glorious victory! Then Laela would be dead and Caedmon would have no-one to challenge his right to rule. He could take power without resorting to open warfare again. No more cities would have to be destroyed, and no more Northern lives lost. That would be it, over and done with.

"Hrm." Saeddryn had been listening closely. "An' what about the man-griffin?"

What, Kullervo? Don't be ridiculous. He's an overgrown child. A carnival freak. I heard him say himself he'd never want to rule. Besides, you don't know what he's just done.

"Which is?" Saeddryn prompted.

Rejected the Night God. He went to the Temple and prayed to her just so he could tell her he'd never worship her.

"He did?"

Yes, and then he spat on her altar.

Saeddryn's breath hissed between her teeth. "He never!"

He did. And you can bet he won't keep it to himself. And he's partnered to the Bastard's old griffin. The chances of those two ever taking the throne are right up there with Gryphus himself appearing and turning you into a custard tart.

Despite herself, Saeddryn chuckled. "It's an interestin' idea, now ye put it like that. I'll talk to Caedmon about it, then. We're goin' t'see him now."

Oh good, said Arenadd, with just the faintest hint of smugness.

A fter Heath's return, the three friends stayed up by Taranis' Throne for several days. During his time with the lost tribe, Heath had indeed learnt plenty, and his newfound foraging skills helped them find much more food than they would have done without him. Not that Heath did much foraging himself; he went with Caedmon a few times and taught him what he knew, but once Caedmon had picked up the important parts of it, he seemed content to let him do it alone while he stayed at camp. The trials of the last few months had slowed him down, and he spent much of his time just resting. He also took to visiting the stones, usually alone, and both Myfina and Caedmon noticed a new quietness about him, as if he had learnt to enjoy stillness as much as talk and excitement. Either way, they were both more than glad to have him back. Even if he didn't say much, he made Caedmon at least feel more optimistic. But, then, Heath had always had that gift.

As for Echo, he seemed happy to spend his time with Garsh and Shar. The three griffins had formed a little flock of their own and even teamed up to hunt more effectively, something wild griffins had never really been able to do. But they were doing more than hunting, as Caedmon soon found out.

One day, when he was up at the stones, he saw them flying overhead and stopped to watch. At first it looked as if they were just flying, looking for prey or just enjoying the wind in their wings as griffins liked to do. But then one of them suddenly broke away from the group and flew higher. The other two circled below.

Then the one who had gone higher made a dive. He struck one of the others in midair, and the two plummeted, grappling viciously with each other.

The third griffin folded his wings and dived after them, and in a moment all three of them were fighting beak and talon. As Caedmon watched in alarm, he saw them meet and break apart again, sometimes darting into attack, sometimes fleeing to try to gain height while the others went in pursuit, none of them letting up for a moment. Once, after a particularly heavy blow, a feather drifted down toward Caedmon. He watched it land in the grass by the altar and recognised the reddish colour as Shar's.

"Shar!" he yelled, now really frightened. *"Shar!"*

Above, the fight continued, but as Caedmon continued to call, one griffin finally broke away and flew down toward him. The others followed. They landed among the stones and continued to tussle with each other, and Caedmon saw that they were Echo and Garsh after all.

Shar came toward him, sides heaving. "Caedmon, what is this?" she huffed. "Are you in danger?"

"No," said Caedmon, feeling unexpectedly embarrassed. "I just thought . . . what were you *doing* up there?"

"We are preparing," said Shar. "We must be ready to fight when the time comes again; this is good practice for us."

"Oh." Caedmon reddened. "I'm sorry, I just thought . . . it looked real."

"We do not hurt each other," said Shar. "We cannot win if we do."

"Yes, I see. It's a good idea."

"It is, and you should do as we do. Now I must go." Shar loped off to rejoin the two males, who were waiting impatiently for her.

Caedmon headed back to the cave. Heath was there, sitting by the fire and looking rather glum. Saeddryn was sitting opposite him. She was so still and unobtrusive that for a moment Caedmon didn't even notice her.

"Mother!" he exclaimed.

Saeddryn nodded to him. "Hello, Caedmon. How are ye keeping?"

"We're doing all right," said Caedmon. "Myfina's just off looking for food; she should be back soon. But what about you?" He sat down beside Heath. "What's the news?"

"The Amorani Prince has arrived in Malvern," said Saeddryn. "They had a celebration t'welcome him. Couldn't stay in the city long, but I'd guess the wedding'll be soon."

"Anything else?" Caedmon pressed.

"Not really." Saeddryn watched him for a moment. "Been talking to yer friend here. He's filled me in on what's been happenin' to him. Interesting stuff."

"Very." Heath coughed.

"I was just about t'say that it's good t'hear ye met up with Arwydd. Been wondering how she's been holdin' on in Malvern."

Heath looked up. "You know her?"

"Aye, I know her. She's one of us. I met up with her in Fruit-sheart just after she was chosen. Had a talk with her, offered her a reward if she came around to our point of view."

"What reward?" Heath asked.

Saeddryn did not smile. "Mastership. The old Master of Gold wasn't about to see things my way. I haven't just been idlin' away my immortality, Caedmon. We've got a few friends in Malvern now. No tellin' how long they'll last, but Arwydd's already proven herself. Saved yer hide, didn't she, Heath?"

Heath smiled ruefully. "Wish I had time to thank her."

"Life's full of regrets," Saeddryn said, with a touch of sadness. "Nobody ever gets to the end without wishin' they could go back and do some of it again. Now, Caedmon . . ."

"Yes, Mother?"

"I think it's time we got down t'business. I've got a suggestion. Ye can make up yer own mind, but ye must do it quickly."

"I'm listening," said Caedmon.

"Right, then." Saeddryn rubbed her dead eye and sighed. "I can't get to the half-breed. She's too well guarded. First Oeka, an' now Skandar and Kullervo. Too much power. An' besides, I've realised I've been goin' about this the wrong way. How can ye claim victory if I kill the half-breed while you're hidin' away up here? The North won't have a King who sends an old woman t'fight for him."

"I'm aware of that," Caedmon growled.

"Here's the plan, then," said Saeddryn. "We've got no quarrel with Malvern, or the people. It's the half-breed who's our enemy, her an' a few cronies. If ye can kill her in a fair fight, somewhere everyone can see it, that'll be the whole thing over with. No need for open war."

"I see. And how do we do that, then?"

"Challenge her to a duel," said Saeddryn. "A griffiner duel. Ye an' Shar against her an' Skandar."

"She'll never accept," said Caedmon.

"She will. She wants this over with, too. If she won, there'd be no more nagging doubts, no alternatives left. Just her an' her heirs when she gets them, which is why ye should do this quickly."

"Hm." Caedmon stroked his beard, much as Arenadd might have done. "It's a thought."

"Aye, so think about it. Talk it over with Shar."

"I think it could work," Heath said unexpectedly. "I mean, what's to be gained from hiding out here? The longer you wait, the less people will care. They'll start calling you a coward and a failure."

Caedmon's jaw tightened. "Yes . . . you're right. I'll consider it."

"Go find Shar," Saeddryn urged. "She'll help ye."

"Right." Caedmon stood up. "I'll be back later."

Saeddryn watched him go and smiled confidently to herself.

"We will do it," said Shar.

Caedmon stared. "Are you sure?"

"I am," said Shar, who hadn't even hesitated once she had heard Saeddryn's suggestion. "We will send a message to the Mighty Skandar's human, and he will make her accept. He cannot refuse; it would be weak."

"But Shar . . ." Caedmon reached up to touch her face. "Shar, he's the Mighty Skandar. How can you fight *him*? No griffin has ever . . ."

"Silence!" she hissed. "I will fight him, Caedmon. I am not afraid. The Mighty Skandar is growing old, and I am young and strong. I am smaller than him, but faster. I will use that to my advantage. When I defeat him, the Unpartnered will be mine, and I will own his territory."

"I've seen him, Shar," said Caedmon. "He hasn't aged at all, hasn't slowed. No-one has ever beaten him in a fight."

"No griffin can win forever. In the end, every griffin must lose. That is how the young find their territories. You and I will do as every young adult must and take what our strength earns us."

It was griffish logic, but in its own way it made sense, and Caedmon knew that he couldn't argue with her once she had made up her mind like this. And in a way, the very simplicity of it appealed to him, too.

Besides, he thought, wasn't this what he wanted, too? To fight the half-breed and kill her was all he had wanted, ever since he had been told about the deaths of his father and sister. And his mother, too. If he made the challenge, then it would mean finally living up to the vow he had made to his followers way back at the start of the war. He had told them that his intention was to take the throne while shedding as little Northern blood as possible. And even now, despite everything, he had followed that intention. It had been the half-breed who massacred her own people, not him.

And for that, she had to die. If he could do it in the way

Saeddryn had suggested, it would mean the end of the struggle at last.

And really, what other chance did he have? Without the Unpartnered, open war would only lead to more pointless deaths.

The thought of that made Caedmon finally decide.

"We'll do it," he said. "When we're ready. When the time is right."

"And when will that be?" Shar demanded.

Caedmon smiled. "When our training is finished. Come on."

He went back to the cave. Saeddryn was still there, with Heath, and Myfina had joined them. All three of them looked expectantly at Caedmon.

"I agree with your plan, Mother," he said. "And so does Shar. We'll send a message to the half-breed. But not until we're both ready."

Saeddryn cocked her head. "And when will ye be ready, Caedmon?"

Caedmon shook his head slowly. "I've had time to think out here; plenty of time. I'm not ready yet. Not ready to rule. You saw what happened when I tried. I ruled Skenfrith, and look how long I lasted. I shouldn't end this until I know that I can do it."

"What's that supposed to mean?" asked Myfina.

"I never finished my training with Arenadd," said Caedmon. "I never went through my manhood ceremony."

"Then we'll do it tonight," said Saeddryn. "I might be dead now, but I'm still a priestess."

"No," said Caedmon. "Not yet. I know where to go now. Heath?"

Heath raised his head. "Yes, Caedmon?"

"We're going to see your lost tribe. You were right, Heath. If I'm going to rule the North, then I need to learn how to be a real darkman. They'll teach me how, and you're going to take us to them."

"When?"

"Tomorrow. Mother, you'll come with us, and you as well, Myfina."

Saeddryn looked at him with open pride. "Agreed."

"And me?" Shar interrupted. She did not look very pleased.

"I think you can learn, too," said Caedmon. "There are wild griffins on those islands."

"What of them?"

"Skandar was a wild griffin. If you can defeat them, you can defeat him. Practise."

Shar huffed. "It could be useful, perhaps. If you must go there, then so must I. There is no hurry."

"We all have things to learn," Caedmon said firmly.

18

Liranwee

Kullervo left Malvern in the same way he had first arrived long ago. Alone, in griffin shape, and with both fear and hope twisting in his chest.

He carried a small bundle on his back: food and a set of clothes wrapped in a blanket. And, protected by a roll of oiled leather, were several copies of a letter dictated by Laela and signed in her own clumsy hand. Kullervo had not brought the sword given to him in Maijan, or any other weapon. The letters were the only real defence he was taking with him.

There was no real way of knowing what the Eyries would do when Kullervo visited them, or even if he would ever reach them at all. But he was going to try. A huge, almost savage sense of determination filled him, smothering his fears and doubts. This was his purpose in life now. This was what he wanted, what he had always wanted, and what, at last, he was going to dedicate his life to.

He had fled from Withypool and gone North in the hopes of finding a family. But what he saw now was that he had wanted something even more primal than just the father he had never known. He had simply wanted to be loved, and that was what he still wanted.

Once again, Kullervo thought of his father and wished with all his heart that he could have found him in time. Would Arenadd have loved him if they had met? Would he have been a father to him if he had had the chance?

The certainty that he would never know made Kullervo's heart ache.

But even if Arenadd had never given his son love, he had still given him life, and Kullervo had chosen a path for it. He would give other people the chance to put hatred aside and so show them the way to make the world better for themselves. And if he had to die to do it, then so be it.

His new certainty was more than enough to keep him going, and he flew on doggedly toward the Northgate Mountains, or *Y Castell* as Northerners called them. They were the natural barrier between North and South, and only a griffin could get by them easily. But Kullervo didn't take the easy option.

Once he reached the mountains, he perched in a large tree and rested. When he felt stronger, he took to the air again and struck out again, following the road through the pass that had once been used by traders who travelled between the two territories. Now, though, with the North utterly cut off from the South, the only traffic the road saw was the supply wagons sent to the fort that guarded the pass.

Kullervo had seen it once before, from above, but had avoided going too close. Now it was his destination, and he watched out tensely for its towers to come in sight.

The fort was called Guard's Post, and its two griffiner towers controlled a great gate that blocked the pass. Anyone trying to use the road would be stopped there. Once Guard's Post had been a stop-off point for griffiners and ordinary travellers, and its garrison of men had been assigned to inspect goods and charge a fee to anyone wanting to go through. Later on, when war had broken out in the North, it had been reinforced by the addition of several griffiners and a cohort of soldiers.

They had not been enough. Kullervo's own mother, Skade, had come to Guard's Post after her return from the South. She had brought thousands of slaves with her. Trickery had opened the gates for her, and after that, she and the slaves she commanded had utterly destroyed Guard's Post.

Nobody had been left alive.

Nowadays, of course, Guard's Post belonged to the North and its occupants were all Northerners, with ten griffiners constantly in residence. Their job was to see to it that nobody entered the North unless they were themselves Northerners.

Supposedly, Kullervo had heard, Southerners were killed on sight.

Regardless, when he reached Guard's Post, he flew straight to one of the towers and landed on its flat top. There, he waited.

He didn't have to wait long. The resident griffins must have seen him coming from a long way off because he had barely folded his wings before three of them came bursting out of the tower, snorting angrily.

"Who are you?" one demanded. "A wild griffin?" His manner was curt but not overly aggressive; Kullervo's small size made overt signs of force unnecessary.

"No, you fool," a second griffin interrupted. "He has something on his back."

"But not a human," the first griffin said, hissing at him. "Be silent; I am the master of this nest." He turned to Kullervo. "Speak now, youngster. Are you a messenger, sent by the Mighty Skandar?"

Kullervo had flattened himself to the ground in the classic posture of submission. "I am," he said, not daring to straighten up. "The message is here." He uncurled his talons and deposited a small scroll in front of the griffin who seemed to be in charge.

The other griffin scooped it toward himself. "I will take this to my human. You will stay here. Do not come into our nest."

After that, Kullervo was allowed to settle down and groom while the dominant griffin left with the message, and his two companions stayed to keep an eye on the intruder. A human would have been both frightened and offended by this sort of treatment, but Kullervo knew griffins, and this was how they always acted. Civilised behaviour was all very well, but territory was territory, and instinct would always come first. He wasn't worried anyway; the message was from Laela and it instructed the griffiner in charge of Guard's Post to give the bearer food and shelter, and to let him go on beyond the mountains when he was ready.

It also stated that if Kullervo returned with griffiners from the South, then they should be greeted politely, given whatever they needed, and allowed to go on. But *only* if Kullervo was with them, of course. The griffiners in charge of Guard's Post wouldn't like it, but orders were orders.

Sure enough, after a short interval, the dominant griffin

returned with a human beside him. The griffiner had the letter in her hand, and she gave Kullervo a narrow-eyed look. "So you're the ambassador?"

"Yes," said Kullervo. "And you'd better follow the Queen's orders. If not, then I'm authorised to relieve you of your post immediately."

This wasn't the sort of thing a griffin would normally say, and the griffiner looked more surprised than offended. But she quickly pulled herself together. "Very well. You can come into the tower and use one of our spare nest chambers. Food will be brought for you."

"Thank you," said Kullervo. "But first I should warn you. I'm expecting another griffin to arrive here, probably today. She'll come here to join up with me, and she'll be going South as well. Her name is Senneck, and she has brown feathers and blue eyes. When she arrives, tell me straightaway. You're to treat her the same way you do me. Understand?"

"Yes, of course," said the griffiner. "I'll inform the others to be on the lookout."

"Thank you." Kullervo shook out his feathers and loped off through the opening into the tower, doing his best to look as haughty and dignified as a griffin should.

An empty nest chamber was quickly cleaned out and prepared for him, and he gladly ate the raw meat brought to him. As a human, he would have been revolted, but his griffin self adored it. He washed it down with water and curled up in his nest to sleep.

Travelling had worn him out. He slept through the night and into the next morning, and when he woke up he was content to laze around in his nest and idly pick through his feathers for ticks.

He had found one and was trying to pull it off, when someone called to him.

Kullervo looked around, and saw a man standing in the doorway. "Yes?"

The man was alone, but his clothes suggested that he was a griffiner. "Your friends have arrived," he said.

Kullervo tilted his head quizzically. "Friends?"

"Yes, both of them. They're up top waiting for you."

Kullervo stood up and gave himself a quick shake. "I'm coming, then."

He flew to the tower-top, and sure enough, there was Senneck. With her was another griffin—a young female who had a slightly gawky, long-legged look about her.

Kullervo went straight to Senneck, and rubbed his face against hers. "I knew you'd come."

She nibbled his neck feathers. "You are a fool, Kullervo Taranisäii."

"I know. Come on, let's go to my nest. We can talk there. And you . . ." Kullervo looked at the stranger. "Who are you?"

The female huffed at him. "I am Seerae. I am Senneck's daughter. I have come with her to find you."

"Daughter?" Kullervo looked at Senneck.

"One of my two young that I lost in the war," she confirmed. "Seerae lived and has found me again."

Kullervo chirped. "That's wonderful! Seerae, you can come with us, of course. There's food."

He took off and flew back to his nest, with the two females in tow.

It was cramped with three griffins. Kullervo sat in the doorway to give Senneck and Seerae room, and waited patiently while they helped themselves to his food.

Once they had eaten, they both lay down comfortably in the straw, flank to flank as only close family would.

Kullervo, watching them, felt unexpectedly sad. "Are you coming South with me?"

"No," said Senneck. "We are here to bring you back to Malvern."

"I told you," said Kullervo. "You're not stopping me. You can come with me, or stay, but those are your only choices."

Senneck hissed. "How dare you speak to me that way? I am a griffin! I am the one with the power in our partnership, and if I command, then you must obey!"

Kullervo hissed back. "I'm a griffin, too, Senneck. I'm also a Prince. I'm Laela's heir, not you. Without me, you'd be nothing. You'd still be living in Gwernyfed, with no human and no status. Think about that."

Incredibly, Senneck did not flare up. "Why are you so determined to do this? What benefit is there for you?"

"The benefit of knowing that I made the world a better place," said Kullervo. "The benefit of knowing that I repaired the damage my father did. The benefit of knowing that when I had a chance to change the world, I took it."

Senneck looked blank. "I do not understand."

"I could stay in Malvern," Kullervo conceded. "I could look after my own interests. I could spend my whole life worrying about my career. But why? Why bother? It's only one life, and one day it'll end. But the world will go on, and I want it to go toward something better than what it is now."

"And what does the world need?" Senneck asked. "What makes you think that you can change it like this, alone and without power?"

"I'm not going to argue about this, Senneck," said Kullervo. "I'm going to make peace. A treaty to end all treaties. And I don't need power or status to do that. All I need is to speak and find a way to make people listen. *That* will be my legacy."

Silence followed.

"Your human is mad, Mother," Seerae said at last.

Kullervo gave her a look. "As mad as my father was. It seems to run in the family."

Senneck heaved a sigh and rubbed her face with her front paws. "Then so be it," she said in a tired kind of way. "I cannot dissuade you, and I will not resort to force. Go South then, if you must. I will go with you. I do not believe that this plan of yours will succeed, but I must protect you. Seerae will come as well."

"I shall," said Seerae. "But to find a human. Your treaty means nothing to me."

"Then we're agreed," said Kullervo, feeling light-headed. He went to the trough and drank, and lay down beside it. "We'll leave tomorrow, once you've rested."

"We shall," said Senneck.

Kullervo left Guard's Post in griffin form. It was easier to travel that way, and he had expected to go a long way. The nearest griffiner cities he knew of, Canran and Withypool, were weeks away.

But the three griffins were scarcely three days out of the mountains when they saw something that took them completely by surprise.

A city. A new city.

Or, at least, the beginnings of one. When Kullervo led them closer to investigate, he saw the half-completed wall protecting a surprisingly neat cluster of tents and wooden shacks, and the clear signs of an Eyrie tower under construction. He could see tiny figures at work among the newly cut stone blocks, and griffins circling overhead.

Sensibly, Kullervo retreated before he got too close; three strange, unpartnered griffins entering the new city like this would be attacked on sight and probably killed.

Landing among some trees, he waited for the others to join him.

"Do you wish to enter this territory we have found?" Senneck asked at once.

"Yes," said Kullervo. "So I'll have to change." He unhooked the bundle from his back and put it down neatly on a root.

"Then I will keep watch," Senneck said briefly. Nearby, Seerae looked on curiously.

Kullervo sat on his haunches, and began to concentrate. Making the change as a griffin was much easier since his griffin shape was adapted to using magic in a way his human one wasn't. In his throat, in his crop where it hid, his magic gland pulsated, expanded, then contracted sharply. Magic escaped from it and spread through his body.

In moments, his skin began to tingle sharply. Fur and feathers drifted onto the leaf litter. Then the magic reached his bones, and the real changes began.

Kullervo flopped over onto his side, rasping in pain as horrible crackings and breakings came from inside his body.

Under his skin, his bones came apart and joined together again, forming new shapes. Joints shifted, muscle bulged or shrank. His beak pulled back into his mouth, splitting apart to become teeth.

The whole process took less time than it had before, but it was every bit as painful as it had always been. Still, it ended, and Kullervo lay in a heap of shed feathers, trembling involuntarily with the shock. Once the pain had receded, he slept briefly and woke up feeling better.

He reached for his bundle, and unwrapped it to get out his clothes. He pulled them on, glancing over at Senneck. She had seen him transform enough times to have lost interest and was idly grooming her wings. Seerae, on the other hand, had moved back a few paces, her tail twitching in alarm.

"I have never seen such a thing before," she exclaimed. "Is your magic always like this?"

"Yes, unfortunately," said Kullervo. He reached back awkwardly to touch his bald wings. "I'll have to try to regrow those feathers; they won't be so impressive like this!"

"Grow them on the way," said Senneck. "We should enter the city before dark."

"Good idea." Kullervo wrapped the blanket around the rest of his possessions, tied it up, and slung it on his back. Senneck offered him her shoulders, and he climbed on.

The two griffins took flight again, heading for the city. Kullervo hung on to Senneck's harness, feeling weak and shaky from the change. But there was enough magic left in his system to channel into his wings and tail. He did that now, focusing as Senneck had taught him, and felt his skin prickle as new fur and feathers grew.

By the time the city was back in sight, his wings were dragging in the wind, catching it as they would if he had the ability to beat them in this shape. His tail flew back behind him, the feathery rudder on the end making it flap about at random. As a human, he did not have the right spinal shape to control the tail, and once he was on the ground again, it would hang uselessly down over his backside and legs.

But it would look impressive. Along with the wings, it would signify to everyone who saw it that he was something other than human—something other than a stray Northerner to kill on sight.

Senneck landed on the outskirts of the new city without attracting too much attention from the people below, who probably thought she was one of their own griffins returning from somewhere. Kullervo dismounted and adjusted his clothes. His heart was pattering.

Senneck's own fear was an odour in the air. "Go," she said. "Walk ahead of me. Seerae, be ready in case of danger, but do not attack unless we are attacked first."

Kullervo nodded by way of reply. He squared his shoulders and set out toward the Eyrie.

As he went in among the shacks by the wall, a noise ahead

and to his left caught his attention. His neck prickled instinctively. There were voices up ahead, and even though he couldn't catch the words, the tone of them immediately made him wary.

Despite that, he impulsively went to investigate. A sound like this was trouble, and maybe someone needed help.

In an open space among the huts, a gang of boys had gathered. A fight had broken out, and those not fighting were standing back and yelling encouragement, jeering at the one they wanted to lose. Now, standing close by but not yet seen, Kullervo could hear what they were saying.

"Traitor's bastard!"

"Darkman lover!"

"Get him, Hess! Punch his teeth in!"

In the middle of the circle, the victim fought back. He was a sturdy-looking boy of about fourteen, with thick red hair, and though he was putting up a good fight, it was obvious that he was in trouble. His lip was split and swelling, and blood had begun to congeal around his nose. The bigger boy he was fighting clearly didn't have much interest in fighting fair; he gave the red-haired boy a shove, sending him stumbling backward toward a couple of his friends, who kicked his legs out from beneath him.

The first boy closed in, fist raised.

"Stop that right now!" Kullervo roared.

The gang faltered, turning quickly to see, and almost immediately it began to break up as Kullervo strode in among them, shoving them out of his way.

"That's a Northerner!" one boy shouted.

"No it ain't; he's got wings!"

Kullervo turned to look at the one who had spoken. His yellow eyes were narrow with rage. He bared his broken teeth and hissed at them like a griffin.

The bullies fled.

Kullervo stooped and offered a hand to the red-haired boy. "It's all right, I won't hurt you. Let me help you."

The boy stood, and gaped in open fear when he saw who had rescued him. "Holy Gryphus . . . !"

Kullervo offered him a reassuring smile, careful not to show his teeth. "Are you all right? My name's Kullervo."

The boy's eyes were wide with awe. "You're . . ." He took in the black hair. "A Northerner . . . ?" His gaze quickly shifted to the wings. "But you've got . . . are those *real*?"

"The wings? Yes." Kullervo twisted on the spot to show him. "What's your name?"

"People call me Red," said the boy. "What *are* you? Are you a Northerner?"

"I suppose so," said Kullervo. "My father was one. But my mother was from Withypool."

"But you've got *wings*," said Red, returning to the most relevant point.

"Yes, that's because my mother was a griffin. Listen, Red, can you help me? I've just come here, and I was wondering what this place is."

"Your mother was a *griffin*?"

"Yes. She got turned into a human. Please, can you tell me what this place is?"

"It's Liranwee," said Red. "We're building it. Why are *you* here? Were you sent here?"

"Yes, I was sent," said Kullervo.

"By Gryphus?"

"By my sister," Kullervo said, more sharply than he meant to. "I've never met Gryphus. I'm here to talk with the griffiners who rule this place—can you tell me where to find them?"

"'Course I can," said the boy. "They live in the tents around where the Eyrie's gonna be. There's only twenty of 'em now. Lady Isleen's in charge now, and Calder's her right-hand man. He's the best fighter here; they're sayin' he'll be Master of War once the city's ready."

"You seem to know a lot about them," Kullervo observed.

"I know them all," said Red. "Isleen an' Calder an' stupid Eadoin, who thinks he's clever, an' Gallia, who said she likes my hair, an' all the rest of them."

"Really?" Kullervo sized the boy up; he certainly didn't look much like a noble, but looks could be deceiving. "Who *are* you, anyway?"

Red's face fell. "My dad was one of them. He was gonna be Eyrie Master, he said, but . . ."

Kullervo remembered what the bullies had shouted. "But he didn't?"

"No. He's dead now. Lady Isleen says he was a traitor; he

was gonna sell us to the Dark Lord, but that's a lie." Red's scowl deepened. "He never!"

Kullervo patted him gingerly on the shoulder. "It's all right, Red. I believe you. Can you show me where these griffiners are? I want to talk to them."

"All right." Red looked past him, to where Senneck and Seerae were waiting impatiently. "Are they with you?"

"Yes. That's Seerae, and this is Senneck."

"Are you a griffiner, then?" said Red.

"No. Yes. Sort of."

"Are you partnered with *both* of them?" Red looked more than ready to believe it.

"No, no. Seerae is just . . . with us." Kullervo straightened up. "Will you show us the way, Red?"

"Yes, sir." Red wiped the blood off his lip, and scurried off through the huts.

Kullervo followed, frowning to himself. He was glad to have rescued the boy; aside from anything else, the sight or the thought of bullying like that had always put him in a rage. But helping Red out of his trouble had been more than just a good deed, it seemed.

Of course, impressing a fourteen-year-old wouldn't be much of a comparison when it came to dealing with twenty haughty, suspicious griffiners. Kullervo would just have to try and hope for the best.

Red took them on a winding and seemingly roundabout route through the makeshift homes, heading for the tents at the centre. Along the way, plenty of people saw the odd little procession, and in no time at all the exclamations of shock had begun to rise all around.

"Wings!"

"Darkman!"

"The winged man!"

Kullervo turned his head toward the people who called out to him, acknowledging them with smiles and nods but saying nothing. He could talk to them later, maybe—assuming there was a later.

Many of them, though, weren't content with just stares and shouts. Not wanting to miss the chance to see whatever might happen, they started to follow. Before long, Kullervo was leading what looked like a sort of impromptu parade of curious people, some of whom seemed to think he was indeed a divine apparition, as they started to chant or to sing sacred songs, some boldly coming closer to try to touch his wings.

Kullervo fended them off as gently as he could, shaking his head when they called him "Holy One" or "Messenger."

Ahead of him, Red had seen what was going on. He slowed his pace and walked closer to Kullervo, holding his head high with pride. Maybe he didn't quite know who this winged stranger was, but he did know that he, Red, was the one who got to walk through the city with him, and that was more than enough to be proud of. He even started waving to his friends when they saw him go by, just to make sure they noticed him.

Kullervo, watching him, chuckled to himself.

Above, the griffins must have noticed the commotion in the city because they started to land. Not by the crowd, but in among the tents, where their humans could join them.

By the time Kullervo arrived at the spot where the Eyrie's foundations had been laid, a group of griffiners was already waiting for him. At their head was a middle-aged woman, brown-haired and rather nondescript, with a compact, square kind of build. But from her fine clothes and her place at the front, it was clear that she was in command here.

Accordingly, Kullervo went up to her, then stood aside to let Senneck pass. The brown-haired woman's partner, a pale-eyed grey griffin, approached her.

Senneck crouched low in a sign of respect and allowed the grey griffin to scent her. Once he was satisfied, she spoke the ritual words of one griffin accepting the dominance of another. He seemed satisfied with that and moved back to stand protectively over his human.

Kullervo stepped forward. "Lady Isleen," he said, ignoring the listening crowd behind him. "Eyrie Mistress of Liranwee. I am Prince Kullervo Taranisäii of Malvern, son of Arenadd Taranisäii and Skade of Withypool."

Murmurs started at this.

"Arenadd Taranisäii?" Lady Isleen repeated sharply. "King Arenadd Taranisäii?"

Kullervo smiled sadly. "I don't know of any other people by that name. Yes, that was my father. 'The Dark Lord Arenadd' as your people call him. But I'm not here to talk about him."

"Aren't you?" Isleen's eyes narrowed. "You're a Northerner. But why are you wearing those wings?"

"Yes, I'm a Northerner," said Kullervo. "I have come here on behalf of my sister, Queen Laela Taranisäii of Malvern."

The mutterings grew even louder.

"Queen?" said Isleen. "Then your father . . . ?"

"He's dead," said Kullervo. "He died sometime ago. I came here to bring you that news."

Shouts rose from the crowd.

"King Arenadd is dead," Kullervo said loudly, cutting across them. "Now his daughter Laela has taken the throne, and she has sent me to talk to you, and to all the Eyries in the South."

"What about?" Isleen asked, looking warily at Senneck.

"Queen Laela offers you a treaty of peace," said Kullervo. He reached into his tunic and brought out the precious scroll. "Here."

Isleen unrolled it and quickly scanned the message. Once she had finished, she passed it on to her fellows to read.

"As you can see," said Kullervo. "My Queen is tired of keeping up a barrier between North and South. As a half-Southerner, she has no interest in making war on her mother's people. King Arenadd is gone, and his supporters have been banished. We want to remake the North as a different country, one that doesn't hide away behind those mountains. We want peace and co-operation. An end to hatred between our peoples."

Isleen's expression did not change though behind her it was clear that her fellows were doing a lot of thinking. "And how do we know this offer is genuine?"

"You have me," said Kullervo. "I'm my sister's heir, and the highest noble she had to send. I came here alone because I would be happy to die in the name of peace. But if that isn't enough, then let Laela speak for herself. Go to Malvern, and you can negotiate with her there yourselves."

Several of the listening griffiners snorted derisively.

"And be held hostage?" Isleen asked stonily. "Or killed?"

"Then send a message back," said Kullervo. "Negotiate long-distance. Or you can go there with me and have me as your own hostage if you're betrayed. But you won't be. You have my word."

"And what is your word worth to us?"

Kullervo growled. With a supreme effort, he unfurled his wings.

The crowd gasped. Several people actually screamed. Among the griffiners, every human took a step backward. The griffins reared up in surprise. Three of the humans there knelt.

"*Do—not—kneel!*" Kullervo bellowed. "I am not a holy man. I am not sent by Gryphus. I am . . ." His voice and face softened. "I'm Kullervo Taranisäii. That's all. My quest is mine, not Gryphus'. Listen . . ."

Absolute silence fell.

"I never knew my father, but I know what he was. I know the things he did. And . . ." Kullervo bowed his head. "And I'm ashamed for it. I would die to bring back the people he murdered; I would give up everything I care about if it could rebuild what he destroyed. But I will never deny the value of what he fought for." He raised his head. "All men are equal. All men should be free. North, South, what's human is human.

"Why do we need gods? Why should we have to love them when we have each other? Love humankind. Love each other, and so be free. Let go of fear and hate. There's so much we could do, so much we could make if we only let ourselves try. Who can say what we could become?" His voice had grown louder and more passionate as he went on, and now he reached down and opened his tunic, showing the scars on his body, twisting their way between hair and stray feathers, "I've seen and felt what the darker side of us can do. I've felt it myself and inflicted it on others. I've tasted my father's hatred. It was enough, more than enough. What I want now is love. What I want now . . . is peace. But I've realised that I can never have those things unless I give them to other people. So I came here, even though I knew I could be killed because of this black hair, this pale skin. I came here to offer those things to you. Whether you choose to take them . . . is up to you."

By the time he had finished speaking, a good part of the crowd were looking up at him with shining eyes. Even the stern-faced griffiners looked moved.

Lady Isleen spoke, her voice slightly hoarse. "You *are* the winged man . . ."

Kullervo stared, and sighed. "I'm *a* winged man. I'm not a god. I'm not holy. I'm just a man with a dream."

But nobody seemed to hear him say it. Behind him, people began to kneel again, bowing their heads. Others surged forward, reaching out toward him, their faces full of adoration. Many of the griffiners did the same.

"Winged man," voices murmured. "The winged one has come! Gryphus has spoken!"

"No—" Kullervo began, but the protest fell on deaf ears. Before he knew it, he was being touched from all sides, and people were bowing their heads to him, whispering prayers or asking for a blessing. "I'm not," Kullervo said helplessly. "I'm not . . ."

Lady Isleen pulled herself together. "Prince Kullervo," she said. "We will discuss this treaty overnight. In the meantime, you and your partners will be given a tent and provided with anything you need."

"A ring of guards would be helpful," Senneck muttered from somewhere behind the mass of worshippers.

Kullervo, seeing the ecstatic faces all about, felt despair eat into his heart. He had only tried to tell them what he had come to believe, and he had never expected it to be like this. He had wanted to inspire people to accept Laela's treaty, not gather a cult.

It was madness, all of it.

But there was nothing he could do.

He allowed himself to be shown to a spare tent, big enough for griffins. Despite the efforts of the guards who escorted him, the crowd followed, clamouring for attention, all wanting a piece of his imaginary holiness. Even when Kullervo went into his tent, they tried to follow, ignoring the commands of the guards on either side.

Helpless anger took hold of Kullervo. He turned in the entrance, and shouted. "I am *not* going to bless you! I am *not a holy man*. I'm *godless*, you hear me? I spat on the Night God's altar. Gryphus' temples make me ill. *Go away*."

But perhaps he shouldn't have mentioned the Night God.

"The winged man rejects the evil of Scathach!" one man yelled fanatically. "He spits on her altar!"

Kullervo let out an incoherent scream of frustration and retreated into the tent, pulling the flap closed behind him.

Thank . . . whatever, the crowd didn't come in after him.

Once Kullervo had finished tying the flap in place, he turned around and put a hand over his face. "Oh gods . . ."

When he looked up, Senneck was there. She came closer to him and rubbed her face against his. "Kullervo," she purred. "Forgive me. I have misjudged you."

Kullervo stared. "What?"

Senneck's purring grew louder. "Once I thought you were a fool," she said. "I did not believe that you had the power to scheme and to manipulate as humans must. I was wrong, and now I am prouder than ever that you are my human."

"What power?" Kullervo demanded. "I didn't scheme anything."

"But your plan was brilliant!" said Senneck. "I cannot believe I did not think of it before! To come here and say those things in full sight of the common humans, to show them your wings and to speak of unity . . . it is genius! In one day, you have fooled a hundred humans into believing you are a holy man. By the sight and scent of them, I think they would follow you to the ends of the earth already."

"But I didn't want—" Kullervo began.

"I see now that your desire to come South was a wise one," Senneck went on, ignoring him. "If you do this in the other cities, before long you will have gathered an army of your own. And with them, you and I could win such power . . ."

"I don't want an army!" Kullervo roared, losing patience with her for probably the first time since they had met. "Why won't anybody listen to me? I didn't come here looking for *followers*, I just wanted to inspire people! Persuade them into taking Laela's offer."

"And so you have," said Senneck, unperturbed. "The griffiners here were as impressed by your words as the commoners. Do not be afraid; by morning, they will come to you and tell you they have decided to accept the treaty. Those you won over will persuade the rest."

Kullervo calmed down. "But I don't want people to think I'm holy," he said. "I never wanted them to."

"What does it matter?" Seerae put in. "It is only another way to convince others. Use it to your advantage and let them believe what they like."

"No," said Kullervo. "I won't live a lie. Not again."

"But you do not need to lie," said Senneck. "You did not lie today; the fools lied to themselves. If they wish to do this, let them. It is not your idiocy. My daughter is right."

Kullervo found a chair, and slumped into it. "It wasn't supposed to be like this." He threw an appealing look at Senneck. "You heard what I said. Didn't you understand it? Did it mean anything to you?"

"No," Senneck said brusquely. "It is nothing but foolery and wishful thinking. All humans are not equal; the world is not made that way. The strong must always triumph over the weak; that is how it has always been. My kind know this, and that is why we choose only the best, the strongest, and the most dominant humans—or those we can make to be so. Without the ones we do not choose, who will be left to serve us and our partners?" She regarded him, her blue eyes almost serene. "You say these things because you are too afraid to allow yourself to be strong. You are not weak; you are powerful, but you will not admit it to yourself."

Kullervo didn't want to argue any more. Exhaustion had closed over his mind, but it felt more like an exhaustion of the spirit rather than the body. "Maybe that's why I care about the weak," he muttered. "Because I'm weak, too. I didn't think you'd understand . . . I need to rest."

"Rest, then," said Senneck. "You have done well."

But Kullervo didn't feel as if he had. He flopped down on the small bed someone had set up in a corner and pulled his wings over himself like a blanket. Not for the first time, he wished he didn't have them. They had saved his life many times, but sometimes they felt more like a curse than a blessing.

Despairing, he eventually sank into a troubled sleep.

19

A Choice

Kullervo dreamed of a flowery field under a magnificent blue sky. In the distance, forests and mountains loomed, but no matter how far away they were, they had no darkness to them at all. There were no shadows here.

He wandered through the field, intoxicated by the scent of the flowers. He had never smelt a flower as sweet and rich as these—or seen anything like them either. Their petals were pure gold, darkening to fiery red and orange at the centre.

Dreamily, Kullervo tried to pick one—but found he couldn't. The stem wouldn't break, and when he tried to twist it, a gentle urge struck him to leave it alone.

There can be no death here, a voice said from above.

Kullervo straightened up, but a part of him already knew who it was.

I am Gryphus, child.

The god loomed over even him, surrounded by a glow of sunlight. He looked like a man, but a giant one, massively muscled, his bare chest broad and bristling with hair. His face was a Southern one, wide and heavy-jawed, with bright blue eyes. Hair the colour of fire hung down over his shoulders, and a beard covered his chin. A golden circlet gleamed on his forehead.

"You." Kullervo backed away nervously. "You look just like the carvings . . . in the temples . . ."

I have appeared in dreams before, child, Gryphus said. His voice was deep and rich, full of power. *Here.* He held out a massive hand. *Touch me, if you do not believe I am real.*

Kullervo touched it carefully, and to his shock, it felt real. It was rough and coarse, a farmer's hand, but the skin was so warm it was nearly hot. "You *are* real. But . . ." He withdrew hastily, looking up. "What do you want with me?"

To thank you.

"*Thank* me? For what?"

Gryphus looked skyward. There was no sun overhead. *Tonight, I have heard my children singing my praises, in louder voices than I have heard for many years. They give thanks that their faith in me has been renewed. And this is your doing, Kullervo.*

Kullervo felt shame, yet again. "I didn't mean to do that. I wasn't trying to . . ."

But you have been among them today, and you have preached my word. I am the god of life, and it is I who command my followers to revere life.

"But they don't!" Kullervo exclaimed. "They . . ."

Yes. And that is why it is you who must remind them. Inspire them. Teach them, in my name.

"But I don't *want* to do that! I just told them that because that's what I think is right, and . . ."

I know this, said Gryphus. *That is why I have come to you now, to ask you that you do this again. Go to my great cities, and speak these words that give people faith in me. They are disheartened now, and they fight against each other. You will show them unity again, unity under my glory.*

Kullervo cringed. "And then?"

And then they will be as one once more and will go forward to do my will.

"Which is?"

Gryphus smiled. *Your father did a great injustice to my people. You will help them to undo it. Bring them back to their stolen homes in the North. Give them back the supremacy I have decreed is rightfully theirs.*

"What about the Northerners?"

Your father's people will also benefit, Gryphus rumbled. *They need the protection and guidance of my chosen. You have seen how they have used their supposed freedom to fight against each other, bickering over power. The Night God teaches them to be this way, and they need our help to control their natural violence.*

"But . . ." Kullervo faltered.

The Day God looked down on him, full of fatherly benevolence. *Do this thing for me, Kullervo, and I will not be ungrateful. You are the winged man, as my people have called you today. You have the power to show them a better way. Do it in my name, and I will reward you.*

"How?"

Gryphus shone even more brightly as he spoke. *I will take the darkness from out of your body. You will be at peace in my temples and will never again touch the shadows. Your hair will change to blessed gold, your wings to white. I will give you the gift of life. You will no longer be half a man but will be able to touch a woman with love and give her children. Temples will be built in your honour, and your name will be revered in Cymria forever. Go forth in my name, and all this will be yours, and more.*

Kullervo touched the coarse black hair on his head. "Why do I need to have gold hair?"

So that you will cease to look like your evil father. You will become like one of my people. Purity will be yours, child.

"I'm not a child," said Kullervo.

Gryphus smiled. *In the eyes of the gods, all mortals are children.*

His words were gentle, kind, and beguiling. But Kullervo felt something in his stomach twist. "Then maybe it's time we grew up."

You cannot, said Gryphus. *Full enlightenment and maturity of the soul are ours alone. You are spiritual children and need my guidance to keep you safe, as the love of a father protects his sons.*

Kullervo's eyes narrowed. "You're not my father."

I am the father of all life.

"But you're not *my* father," said Kullervo. Sadness filled him. "My father was Arenadd Taranisäii."

Anger showed through Gryphus' paternal smile. *Your father did not love you. He was a heartless man, incapable of love.*

"He loved my mother."

Hollow love. Twisted love, without my blessing.

As Gryphus spoke, his benevolent façade began to break down, and Kullervo saw hatred and contempt behind it. "Why did they need your blessing?" he retorted. "They weren't your people."

Enough! Gryphus growled. *You are not your parents. You have a good heart, Kullervo. A heart that is close to me. Swear to do as I have asked.*

But Kullervo's heart had already begun to close away from the god. "And what happens then?" he asked, throwing caution to the winds. "The griffiners come back and take over the North again? My father's people go back into slavery? And what about Laela? She's a half-breed—what would they do to her?"

Your sister has done me a great service, said Gryphus. *She destroyed your father. For that, she is under my protection.*

"And the others?" said Kullervo. "What about the children, in Gwernyfed? They're half-breeds, too. Are *they* under your protection?"

Silence! Gryphus seemed to grow taller, his light turning darker and hotter. *How dare you question me? I am the master of Cymria. The Night God cannot be allowed to reign any longer, or she will drive her people South, to burn and slaughter like the savages they are. Would you allow that to happen?*

"No," said Kullervo. "But there has to be another way to stop it."

Unity is the way, said Gryphus. *Unity under my light, under my blessing.*

Even in the dream, the god's rage was massive, fiery and terrible . . . and helpless. As Kullervo backed away in growing fear, it suddenly occurred to him that even though Gryphus' light had become flames around him, the heat was not hurting him. The god's huge hands reached out but did not touch him. And in an instant, Kullervo saw the truth: Gryphus could rage, he could threaten, he could shout . . . but he could not hurt him. The god was impotent, unable to touch the mortal world with physical force. All at once, Kullervo's fear went away.

He stood tall, yellow eyes blazing back. "Never," he snarled. "I'll never serve you. I thought you were different, but you're just like the Night God. You just want power. You want people to be your slaves. But you're not going to enslave me. I won't end up like my father."

Incredibly, Gryphus backed down. *You do not understand. Our desires are the same. I, too, want peace . . .*

"And I want freedom," said Kullervo. "I want other people to be free, too—from you. Both of you." He could feel his hands warping, talons extending. "So I'll go to the cities. I'll try to show people what I believe is right. But I'll do it because I choose to, and never in your name."

Gryphus' light began to fade. *Beware, Kullervo Taranisäii,* he said. *You have already turned your back on one god. When death comes, you will be lost without us.*

"Then so be it."

As you wish . . . Gryphus vanished. Without him, the grass of the field withered and died. The golden flowers shrivelled into brown husks. The sky went dark and cold, and there was nothing but an endless, freezing void.

As Kullervo drifted away into nothingness, he heard a laugh. It was harsh and deranged . . . and full of savage triumph.

K ullervo was not the only one with Gryphus on his mind. Sitting by a brazier in her own tent, Lady Isleen tried to concentrate on the book she was reading, more as a way to distract herself. It was the latest installment in the adventures of Alaric the Dashing, an implausibly handsome imaginary griffiner whose escapades were written out and copied by some anonymous person in Withypool and sold at inflated prices to anyone who wanted to read them. Plenty of griffiners, particularly women, loved the series and would go to great lengths to get their hands on the newest volume.

Isleen started on the next chapter.

Alaric rose with the sun, leaving Erisa to her peaceful slumber. He performed his morning rituals in silence in order to spare her delicate rest, but could not resist turning to watch her doze. Her purely dark eyelashes fluttered like the wings of a butterfly as magical visions moved across her sleeping mind, and Alaric sighed as—

Isleen sighed, too, and closed the book. She loved the *Adventures of Alaric*, but right now even they couldn't take her mind off things. She put the book aside and warmed her hands over the brazier as she let herself think over what had happened that day.

The council, makeshift as it was, had discussed Kullervo's arrival and the treaty he had brought. The arguments had gone on long into the night. Many of the griffiners, believing that Kullervo was a holy man, wanted to do as he said and to blazes with any danger. It was the will of Gryphus.

Others, more skeptical, pointed out that Kullervo was both a Northerner and had denied his supposed divinity repeatedly and in a distressed manner. And besides, trying to negotiate a treaty with the North was ridiculous. True griffiners did not negotiate with Northerners, and they had far more urgent things to worry about anyway.

Regardless of all that, though, as Eyrie Mistress-elect, Isleen had the power to make the ultimate decision. She had heard the differing viewpoints of her fellows, and now it was up to her to tell them what they would do. She had far too much good sense to do it on the spot, so she had told them she would go away and think it over. She was supposed to be doing that now.

For herself, Isleen believed that Kullervo was the winged man—believed it utterly. Nor did it matter to her that he had said otherwise. He had wings—what more was there to discuss? He could try denying that he had eyes as well, but that wouldn't change anything.

The truth, Isleen decided, was that he must be the messenger of Gryphus without knowing it. He denied it out of fear and modesty, but that didn't matter. His words were Gryphus' words, even if he didn't realise it. What other explanation could there be for what had happened? That Gryphus had sent his messenger to them was fantastic, but the idea that there could be some other winged man preaching love and tolerance purely by coincidence was ridiculous. No, Kullervo was a divinity, and therefore what he said they should do was nothing less than the will of Gryphus. And a true Southerner would never deny Gryphus.

All that meant that her course of action was completely clear. Gryphus wanted her to make a treaty with the North.

. . . Or did he?

Isleen looked up. "Arak, what do you think about all this?"

Over by the wall of the tent, her partner turned his head. "I have thought carefully," he said. "And I think I have seen what we must do."

"What, then?" asked Isleen. "Do we go North?"

The grey griffin yawned. "I have spoken with the partner of this winged human. She has told me that she means to take her human to all the griffiner cities and say these words to every Eyrie Master who will listen. We have seen now how they will react; they will feel the same as our griffiners do. I think that many of them will choose to go to Malvern."

"Agreed," said Isleen. "They'll see he's Gryphus' messenger. So what do we do?"

"We go North," said Arak. "But not yet. We will tell this one's human that we will wait for his return. He must come this way to go back to Malvern. When he does, we will join him. By the time we arrive, there will be many other Southern griffins there. They will be our safety in case of treachery."

"And then we make the treaty?" Isleen prompted.

"We will begin our negotiations," said Arak. "But we will draw them out. We will argue, we will delay. We will make time for ourselves and use it to our advantage."

Isleen blinked; this wasn't what she had expected. "And then?"

"We will speak with the other Southerners there," said Arak. "And form a secret alliance. If we feel we are strong enough, and the situation is to our advantage . . . we will strike together. Seize Malvern. From there, we will be ready to take back the North. Without the dark griffin and *Kraeai kran ae*, they will not defeat us again."

Isleen gaped. "But Liranwee . . ."

"We can leave our territory to our inferiors; they will care for it while we are gone. The North is a far better prize." Arak said all this quite blandly.

Isleen's mind raced. "A chance to have it back . . . revenge for the war . . . and Gryphus . . ." She gasped, as the truth finally dawned on her. "Of course! That's it! By Gryphus' talons, I see it now. *That's* why the winged man came. *That's* why he was sent to us. That was his real message. Gryphus used him to tell us that it's time to take the North. Win back our supremacy in Cymria. That was what he really said. Go North, now. Make peace. Once we rule the North again, we'll make peace. Peace under us, just as it was before the war. A strong hand will keep the Northerners in check." Her voice had become low and fervent as she went on, growing more excited as her mind painted pictures of the glory to come. A Northerner had destroyed her home once, and that was why she was trying to build a new one. Now, Gryphus had shown her the way to a better life—and a way to have revenge at last.

Impulsively, she folded her hands and began a rapid prayer over the fire, whose flames were Gryphus' power. "Holy Gryphus, father of my people, thank you for your guidance. I have seen your will, and I will see it done. I swear it by . . ."

Nearby, Arak listened to her ridiculous babble and rasped quietly to himself. Humans were such fools. But they were a way to power, and he would put up with plenty more foolery for the sake of that.

And now he had seen a new doorway to power, and it was something far more alluring than ruling over this unhatched egg of a city. Oh yes . . .

Arak laid his head on his talons and dreamed of Malvern, and mastery of something that many would kill to own. And he would kill. Oh yes, he would kill. His talons were twitching already.

The North, he thought, and closed his eyes. *Mine.*

20

The Island of Wild Northerners

The first time Caedmon saw the island, he was almost shocked by its size. To him the word "island" had suggested something small, but Wild Island, as Heath had dubbed it, had enough space for a small town. Or it would have if the landscape had been more hospitable.

It rose out of the ocean ahead, dark among waves the colour of slate. Jagged rocks and spiny conifers gave it an uneven, dangerous-looking outline. The air out here was icy, not helped by the ocean, but as the three griffins flew closer, Caedmon couldn't spot any of the snow he had been half expecting. He was relieved about that.

Echo flew ahead to show the way. A long journey had made his wing-beats slow and heavy, but they were close now.

Once the island was below, the spotted griffin spiralled downward to land. Shar and Garsh followed.

Echo's landing spot was an open area—"field" would have been too generous even though there was some ragged grass about. He crouched to help Heath dismount and lay down on his belly to rest, apparently feeling safe enough here not to stay on alert.

Shar landed close by, snorting when Saeddryn decided to leap off her back before she had crouched. Caedmon, more sensitive, politely waited for the proper moment to get off before going over to help Myfina get down off the hulking Garsh.

Saeddryn, as always, was on the alert. She landed in a hunched posture and kept it as she slunk around the clearing, sniffing the air like a griffin, with one hand on her sickle. "Smells of people," she growled eventually.

Heath was standing by Echo, steadying himself with a hand on the griffin's shoulder. "They'll have seen us by now," he said. "They keep watch for the wild griffins. Don't want to get eaten." He looked rather pale, possibly from the cold.

Saeddryn's lined face was full of suspicion. "They'd better not try anythin' funny. I'm in no mood."

Caedmon and Myfina glanced at each other, and from Myfina's expression, Caedmon guessed she was thinking the same thing as him. Saeddryn was getting worse. Ever since her latest mission, which she hadn't said anything about yet, she had grown even more icy and aggressive.

Nearby, Heath looked at Saeddryn. His usual amused expression was absent; instead, he looked tired and rather sad. "They won't," he said hoarsely. "They've got even less of a sense of humour than you, milady. Just wait here, and they'll come. I should be ready . . ." He reached up and adjusted his griffin-hide hood.

Caedmon had already begun watching the trees all about, along with Myfina. But it was Saeddryn who saw them coming first. She turned sharply and pointed. "There."

Caedmon looked, and after a moment or two he saw them. A group of people were approaching, moving in an easy, loping kind of way. At first all he noticed about them was that they looked tall and emaciated, and ragged. But he was quick to notice the second thing: They were armed.

The tribespeople emerged into the clearing. There were four of them, and if the men hadn't worn beards, Caedmon might have had a little trouble telling them apart; they were all dressed in more or less the same way, in thick layers of fur. All of them carried spears, but the man who looked to be in charge also had a crude stone axe in his belt.

Heath stopped leaning on Echo and approached them, one hand held up. He called to them in the old language. "Llygad! I have returned, and brought my friends who are from the Griffin Tribe like I am. They are here to help you, as I was."

The leader, Llygad, looked at Caedmon and the others with great interest. But, curiously, it was Saeddryn he pointed at. "What is this old woman who has come? She has no griffin with her, but she is like a starving beast in a woman's skin."

Saeddryn came toward him, and Caedmon tensed instinctively. But she surprised everyone there by bowing her head to Llygad and speaking in the old language—much more fluently than Heath. "I am Saeddryn of the blood of Taranis, and I am sent by the moon itself to do justice in the name of all our race. I have come to your land, wise Llygad, to learn what I can from you and to ask that you give your strength to my son, who is the rightful ruler of Tara."

The tribespeople there started to chatter animatedly among themselves at this, gesturing at each other and at Saeddryn in great excitement.

Llygad silenced them with a look. "You are welcome to be among my tribe, Saeddryn. But for as long as you stay here, you must accept my judgments. If your children stay, they will do the same. We will not give them food. Every man here hunts, and every woman forages. Do they understand this?"

"We do," said Caedmon.

"Llygad, is there enough food here now?" Heath interrupted.

Llygad glanced at him. "There is, *conqueror-of-griffin*. The thin time is over. Come."

With that, the discussion was over. Caedmon could scarcely believe it had been that simple. Just what had Heath promised them, he wondered, as he followed Myfina and the others after Llygad and his friends.

The lost tribe's home was hidden among the trees and consisted of a cluster of small shelters that didn't really qualify as huts. They were made from wood and bark, in odd, humped shapes that would have made them look like heaps of dirt from above. Thick layers of pine needles covered each one, probably put there deliberately for insulation, and a thin column of smoke rose from a small hole in each roof.

As the newcomers arrived, the rest of the tribe emerged to see them. Caedmon counted about twenty of them; men, women, and a handful of emaciated children. The children ran excitedly toward Heath, whose familiar smile finally returned. "Hello! It's good to see you again, too. Look at you, you're nearly as tall as I am now!"

Caedmon chuckled. "You're popular."

"Oh, I can't help it," Heath said gravely. "I just seem to attract people like this, you know. Anyway, you'd better talk to Llygad. He'll get you settled in."

Sure enough, the thin-faced chieftain was already waiting patiently for them to turn their attention back on him. A woman had come to join him, and he spoke quickly to her before he addressed Caedmon. "You will come with me on the hunt. This is my wife, Gwladus. The women will go with her and learn the things women must know."

Myfina gave Caedmon a slightly sour look, but she went along politely with Gwladus, a weather-beaten woman who reminded Caedmon of Saeddryn.

Meanwhile, Shar and Garsh were looking to Echo. The spotted griffin, satisfied that the humans had been accepted, flicked his tail. "I am going to my island," he said. "Come with me."

"We shall," said Shar. "But we will see which of us owns this island by nightfall." She was already tensing in anticipation.

"We will see," Garsh agreed.

Heath seemed to have guessed what was being said. "I'll go with you, Echo," he said.

Myfina overheard him. "Aren't you going to stay with us?" she asked. "You should at least get some rest and have something to eat before you go."

Heath shook his head. "I'm not hungry. And I don't want to intrude. I feel like some time alone now." Echo had crouched to let him remount. He did, with some effort, and the spotted griffin flew away with Shar and Garsh in tow.

Saeddryn watched them go, and her eye narrowed. "I'm in the mood for some explorin'," she said. "I'll be back by nightfall."

"You must not wander," Llygad interrupted. "It's too dangerous."

Saeddryn inclined her head toward him. "I go where I want, Llygad," she said, politely but firmly. "There's no danger for me." Without waiting for an answer, she strode off into the trees.

Caedmon shrugged awkwardly. "She's stronger than she looks," he said. "Now . . ." He turned to Llygad. "I'm ready to learn what you have to teach me and do what I can to help."

"Then we will begin now," said Llygad.

Saeddryn was in her element. She slunk through the forest, drinking in the scents and sights. With her newly heightened senses, any environment was a feast to her, but she had come to prefer natural places like this. They made her feel safer, and closer to her master.

Just because she could, she broke into a run. Even though she had been able to do it for a long time now, she still thrilled at the speed and grace of her running. The rough ground passed effortlessly beneath her. On a whim, she slipped into the shadows and felt her speed and strength double instantly. She ran all the way to the other side of the island in no time at all, and when she reached the channel between it and its neighbours, she impulsively leapt straight into it. She landed in the water, not noticing the icy shock of it at all, and began to swim. This was the first time she had swum like this, and it was as easy as running.

She reached the other side and stepped out onto the shore, leaving the shadows to inspect the new island. It was one of the two smaller ones Heath had described—she could see the first one behind her, and the third off to her right.

The one she had reached was high and rugged, nearly mountainous, and as thickly forested as the one where Llygad's tribe lived. The air was heavy with the scent of conifer trees—and something else. A wild, musky odour reached her nose, faint but striking. It was a smell she knew very well.

"Griffins," she said aloud, looking up to see the huge, winged shapes that circled overhead.

I didn't think there were any wild griffins left in the North, Arenadd remarked.

"Me neither," said Saeddryn. "But it's good. Our griffins will learn from them. Nobody fights like a wild griffin, not even city griffins."

Exactly. Why did you think Skandar is so powerful?

"He's huge," Saeddryn pointed out with a smile.

He's wild. Always was. Arenadd sounded proud.

"If only he were on our side."

If only, said Arenadd. *But you probably shouldn't keep talking to me. You're not alone.*

Saeddryn fell silent and moved further inland to investigate. Sure enough, a human scent soon caught her attention. She followed it and found Heath sitting on a rock further along the beach, looking out to sea. He was alone, wrapped in his griffin hide.

Saeddryn stood and watched him for a while. Heath, not realising she was there, rested his chin on his hands and muttered something to himself. His shoulders were hunched. Saeddryn took in the smell of him, but she didn't need to. She had already long since noticed what was there in it.

"Heath," she called.

He glanced quickly over his shoulder in surprise but just as quickly returned to his former posture. "What can I do for you, Shadow That Walks?"

Saeddryn made up her mind and moved closer. "Caedmon an' Myfina have noticed how yer acting nowadays. They're worried about ye."

"Kind of them," said Heath. He didn't sound as if he was joking.

"I think ye should spend more time with them," said Saeddryn. "They need ye. They're both troubled, an' afraid—Caedmon especially. Ye make them feel better, Heath."

"I'm good at that," said Heath. "And I would, but . . . I'm not feeling up to it just now."

"But ye need them, too," said Saeddryn. "People need people."

"Yes, yes, you're right. I'll go back there later, once they're settled in. I've got things to think about first."

"I don't think yer going to find the answer yer after, Heath," Saeddryn said, with unaccustomed gentleness. "Not here."

"No, I don't think I will," said Heath. His voice was full of despair.

Saeddryn could see the shape of him under the heavy griffin hide, could see the frail tremble that Caedmon and Myfina had missed. "You're dying," she said.

"I think I am," said Heath.

"Ye are," Saeddryn said flatly. "I can smell it on ye. There's poison spreading through yer blood. It's killing ye."

"I know," said Heath, without turning around. "You'd be the expert, I suppose."

"I am," said Saeddryn.

Silence, for a time.

"People seem to die a lot around you," Heath said suddenly, and bitterly. "But I imagine you're used to it by now. I just wonder who's going to be next. Caedmon? Myfina? It's already happened to everyone else you threw your lot in with." He turned now to stare dully at her. "I thought you were a blessing for us, but I was wrong. All you ever brought us was death. Death for your partner, death for everyone in Skenfrith, death for me, too, now." His voice started to crack. "I'm twenty-nine years old. I loved being alive." His fists clenched. "I'm not ready to die."

For almost the first time since her death, Saeddryn couldn't find anything to say. She looked at Heath, full of shame, and despair that matched his own.

Heath turned away again. "If I'd known how you would repay me, I never would have saved you. I would have left you to rave in that cellar. This is why I never wanted anything to do with heroism before—it gets people killed."

"Heath." Saeddryn went to him, and put a hand on his shoulder. "Heath, I'm so sorry . . ."

"Don't touch me!" Heath threw her hand off. "And you're not sorry, so don't lie. I know how to read people, and I can read you. You don't care about us. Death's a joke to you. When I'm gone, you'll forget me just like you've forgotten everyone else you've killed." He looked at her with hatred. "You said it yourself: People need people. And you're not a person. You're not human. So leave me alone."

Saeddryn took a step back. "Heath, I . . ."

"My name's not Heath. Go away, Saeddryn."

Saeddryn shook her head slowly. "Heath, whatever yer real name is . . . I know I've never shown it, but . . . I'm grateful to ye. Ye saved me. One day every man an' woman in the North will know yer name an' know that without ye, they would never have been set free from the half-breed's reign. This is a poor way to thank ye, an' yer right—I bring death with me wherever I go. But I'm gonna do what I can to help ye now."

"You can't do anything for me," said Heath.

"I can," said Saeddryn. "I'm gonna speak with the Night God. She's the mistress of death. I'll ask her not to take ye. For the sake of all ye did in her name, I'll beg for yer life."

Slow amazement spread over Heath's face. "You will?"

"I will," Saeddryn promised. "I'll go an' pray to her now."

Don't waste your breath, Arenadd said as she walked away. *He's done for. Maybe if he'd had proper treatment for those wounds on his chest quickly enough, he'd have recovered. But he's too far gone now. The infection's in his blood. He'll be lucky to last a week. A body can only take so much.*

"I have to try," said Saeddryn. "I owe it to him. Even if the Night God won't save him, I can still ask her to take good care of his soul once he's gone."

When I was alive, I prayed to the Night God to save me, said Arenadd. *She heard me, but I died anyway. Don't get your hopes up.*

"Hope?" Saeddryn asked sourly. "What's that? Anyway, I've got a better use for ye than floatin' around here. Go back to Malvern an' bring back information."

Right away, beloved. Arenadd's presence disappeared.

Left alone, Saeddryn selected some rocks to make a circle and began her prayer.

Night in the North. Clouds had covered the moon, but something darker than even that shadow moved across the land. Arenadd was abroad.

He didn't know if he was truly Arenadd any more; he certainly wasn't a man now, or even a person. The words "evil spirit" kept springing to what passed for his mind. He wasn't even going to consider the possibility that he might be a good one.

For others, death might mean rest. For him, there was nothing but an eternity of slavery and no hope of oblivion.

Arenadd flew across the land that had once been his Kingdom, seeing everything. He had done this many times since his master had sent him back, and the novelty had long since worn off. Still, at least he was fast now.

Malvern's walls appeared ahead of him. He passed through them effortlessly and moved on toward the Eyrie. Inside, everything was as he expected, full of new people. Laela's followers, all of them. Most of the griffiners who had lived there when she had come to power were now gone—demoted, or killed during Caedmon's uprising, or executed for making their own plots against the Queen. Loyalty, it seemed, was not something she had been able to win easily.

He could also sense another, much more disturbing presence in the building. Oeka was still there, or her mind. As he walked unseen through the rooms and passageways, bizarre sounds and visions occasionally flickered around him. Ghostly figures appeared and were gone, sometimes frightening some unfortunate mortal. Once he even saw *himself*, large as life, walking straight toward him.

Arenadd turned to watch his past self carry on down the corridor before vanishing.

Did my hair really look like that from the back? he muttered to himself.

Either way, there wasn't much point in lingering over it. Oeka was still here, and she was still causing random flashes of past events to appear in the Eyrie. Arenadd could sense her mind wandering invisibly, much as he was doing, no doubt still alert for thoughts of treachery. No wonder Laela had been able to root out any remaining opposition so quickly; Oeka might be mad, but she could still do enough to a traitor to mark them out.

Fortunately for Arenadd, he no longer had a mind to be assaulted.

Still, no chance of Saeddryn's lasting long here if she ever decided to return. It was a miracle she had managed to abduct Laela at all; maybe all the unfamiliar minds around her had distracted the mad griffin. Arenadd didn't know, and didn't care enough to try to work it out. Magic wasn't his area of expertise.

He kept on going up the Council Tower. Now he'd scouted a bit, it was time to see what Laela was doing.

She was in her private chamber at the top, in Arenadd's old bedroom. Arenadd slipped inside to spy on her as he had done many times before. Laela wasn't alone, but this time there wasn't likely to be any conversation to listen in on—she was with her new husband, and they were well past the friendly chatting stage.

Arenadd left quickly, surprised that he could still feel embarrassed.

Trying to make me a grandchild, are you? he said aloud. *Enjoy it while it lasts, my girl. Maybe you'll even live long enough to be a mother.*

He left Laela and Akhane to enjoy themselves, and went to look in on the only other mortal there who interested him: Skandar.

The dark griffin was in his nest, fast asleep. Arenadd stood over him for a time, watching the massive shape of what had once been his greatest friend. In life, Skandar had been more than a partner: He had defined Arenadd's entire existence— brought it about, even.

Arenadd had no face for a sad smile. *You sleep, Skandar. Sleep and be glad for everything you are. Be glad the Night God never twisted you the way she twisted me. Be glad that you can die.*

He wished that he could leave the griffin to his rest, but he knew he couldn't. Yet again, he reached out and into Skandar's dreams. Yet again he spoke to him inside his head, whispering to him to join with Saeddryn. The Night God had failed to persuade him, but Arenadd was the only one Skandar had ever trusted.

Arenadd did as his master commanded, knowing that it wouldn't work. It never did. Skandar did not listen to his dreams any more, and with good reason.

Arenadd said the Night God's words anyway. Then, he whispered his own. Softly. Urgently. Maybe Skandar would listen.

Once Arenadd had said all he had to say, he rested a while in Skandar's nest. It was the only place he felt at home now. In the morning, he would spy on Laela again and pick up whatever information he could. He had to bring something back for Saeddryn or she would just send him away again.

Arenadd did not sleep any more. But he still felt weary. Endlessly, deeply. Somewhere inside himself, at the core of his being, he could feel the will of his master always pulling. She owned his existence now, and what remained of his ability to love. She had taken all his hope. How ironic that she had sent him all those years ago to bring freedom to others but had denied it to him in far deeper ways than mere chains.

No rest. And no-one to mourn.

The old familiar feeling of self-pity welled up inside him. But there was self-loathing with it. *I did this to myself. I let her have me.*

But besides misery, there was one other thing of the old Arenadd Taranisäii left.

The dark spectre drifted aimlessly around Skandar's sleeping form and allowed itself to dream.

One day, his silent voice sighed. *One day I will be free. One day . . .*

21

Back to Where It Began

Surprisingly enough, given the dream he had that night, Kullervo slept long and deeply. A change following a long flight, and the emotional distress that followed had well and truly worn him out, and he didn't wake up until long past dawn. And even then it was only because Senneck woke him up with a rough nudge of her beak.

Kullervo's eyes opened slowly, and he groaned. "Wsthat?"

"You have a visitor," said Senneck.

"Urgh." Kullervo sat up and rubbed his face. Senneck's words finally caught up with him, and he thrust the blankets off himself and turned to see who she had brought.

It was the boy, Red, looking pale and rather red around the eyes. But he sounded alert enough when he said, "I'm sorry, sir, I shouldn't've woken you up. I wanted to wait."

Kullervo shook himself. "No no, it's all right. It was probably time for me to be up. What's wrong?"

"I caught him sleeping beside our shelter," Senneck interrupted. "The guards chased everyone else away, but this one hid."

Red looked ashamed. "I'm sorry, sir. I couldn't think of anywhere else t'go."

Kullervo frowned. "Don't you have a home?"

"Well . . ." Red turned even paler. "I mean, no, I . . ."

"It's all right," Kullervo said in his gentlest voice. "You can tell me. I won't hurt you."

Red appeared to pull himself together. "Are you gonna stay

here, sir? I mean . . . people are sayin' you're here to live with us. Are you?"

"No. I'm going to move on as soon as I've finished talking with Lady Isleen."

"Oh." Red looked relieved.

Kullervo smiled. "Why, don't you want me to stay?"

Red flushed. "Oh! Er, no, I don't want you to go, it's just that . . ."

Senneck finally lost patience. "Answer him, you little red rat, before I throw you out!"

Red jerked in fright. But to his credit, he didn't move away from Senneck. "I'm sorry, I'm sorry," he babbled. "It's just that this was my dad's tent an' I was living here before you came, and . . ."

Kullervo stood up and touched the boy reassuringly on the shoulder. "All right. It's all right. Calm down. I didn't know this was your tent, and now I do, I'll give it back. Senneck and I will find somewhere else to stay."

Red looked horrified. "But I couldn't make you *leave*."

"It's fine. Don't worry about it; I'm choosing to leave. Isleen will probably have made her mind up by now anyway, so I'll most likely be leaving Liranwee today."

Red finally relaxed. "Then that's all right. But if you *do* stay, you can use my tent."

"I can't do that. It's not mine."

"I'll *share* it with you," Red insisted. "There's plenty of room."

Kullervo grinned. "Thank you, Red."

Red cringed. "What happened to your *teeth*?"

"Oops." Kullervo quickly hid them again. "Sorry. They got broken a while back, and sometimes I forget I shouldn't grin any more—it scares people!"

Red giggled. "It didn't hurt, did it?"

"Not any more," said Kullervo. "Now then, I should probably find something to eat. Is there anything around here that's soft?"

"I think there're some eggs. I'll go see!" Red hurried off to search the tent.

Senneck had already long since lost interest. "Groom yourself; it is time for us to see the Eyrie rulers again."

"Right." Kullervo unrolled his bundle of possessions and found a comb. "Where's Seerae?"

"She is exploring the city," said Senneck. "Learning about the griffins here. I am teaching her, and she is learning well." There was a note of pride in the brown griffin's voice.

"Do you think she'll find a new human while we're out here?" Kullervo asked as he tried to do something with his always unruly hair.

"I do," said Senneck. "She will stay with us as long as she chooses, and when she is ready, she will leave. Until then, she will be helpful to us. I am her mother, and she wishes to impress me."

Kullervo sighed. "Yes . . . I can imagine."

Red returned at this point, proudly clutching a small basket with some eggs in it. "I found 'em! Do you want them boiled? Why do you look so sad?"

"Yes, please," said Kullervo. "And I was thinking of my mother."

"Mine's dead," said Red. "She died when I was little. Is yours dead, too?"

"Yes, but I never knew her. Never knew my father, either."

Red looked solemn. "Where are you going after you leave?"

Kullervo gazed thoughtfully at the comb in his hand. "I think . . . I think I'd like to go to Eagleholm. That's where my father came from."

"Mine, too," said Red. "And my mum. But Eagleholm's a dead place. They say it's full of ghosts. Murdered men walk the streets." Since he was fourteen, Red looked ghoulishly delighted by the idea.

"Yes, I know," said Kullervo. "And I know I probably wouldn't find anyone to negotiate with there. But I'd like to see it anyway, if I can. I think . . . maybe I'd find some answers there. About my father, and how this all began."

"Kullervo!" Senneck was standing by the entrance. "Stop talking and come! We must not keep them waiting."

"Right, right." Kullervo dropped the comb and hastily pulled on his boots. He had slept in his clothes.

Red, quickly picking up on the situation, went off to boil the eggs. "I'll have 'em ready when you get back," he promised.

"Thanks, Red." Kullervo smiled gratefully at the boy and darted off after Senneck, with his wings dragging at his back.

Senneck loped out briskly into the sunlight. "It is good to have a servant here," she remarked.

"Host," Kullervo corrected.

Senneck ignored him. "The council has spoken again this morning, while you were sleeping. They will be ready for us now."

"Good." Kullervo could already see people coming toward him. He gritted his teeth, and decided to pretend they weren't there. "Senneck, I was thinking about where we could go once we leave here, and I thought . . . would you like to go and see Eagleholm?"

Senneck turned her head sharply. "Eagleholm? Why there?"

Kullervo started. "I know there's not really any point in it, but this might be my only chance to see it. It's my father's birthplace—ever since I found out for certain who he was, I've wanted to go there and find out where he came from."

Senneck walked in silence for a few moments. Then, without looking at him, she spoke. "I have not thought of Eagleholm in many years. But I am connected to it as well. I was hatched there, and it is where I met Erian—and your father as well."

Kullervo frowned. "You mentioned that before, I think. Where did you meet him?"

"He came to work in the Hatchery where I lived, after his disgrace," said Senneck. "He even tried to present himself to us to be chosen a second time. I bit him for his insolence. He was there when Erian came to us—he tried to trick him into making a fool of himself, but he underestimated my Erian. He presented himself, and your father watched in dismay as I chose him." Senneck sounded almost dreamy. "We pushed him aside with contempt as we left together, and my future looked clear. How could we have guessed that the ragged blackrobe would destroy our city only one night later? *Kssssshhh* . . ." She hissed a slow, weary hiss.

Kullervo walked beside her, frowning as he tried to imagine that fateful day. So odd to imagine his infamous father as a grubby Hatchery employee, cleaning up after the griffin who now walked beside him.

"I see no profit in it, but I, too, would like to return," Senneck said abruptly. "I feel a need. And perhaps it is fitting. I was hatched there, like my mother and all the mothers before her who made me. I would honour them by doing as they did."

Kullervo glanced at her. "What do you mean?"

Senneck's tail flicked. "I am going to lay eggs. My time will come in three full moons—enough time to reach Eagleholm."

Kullervo felt the warm sun soaking into his bones. "That's wonderful, Senneck. So we're agreed?"

"Yes. We will go to Eagleholm, and I will lay my eggs there. But for now, we must speak with this council."

"Right." The Eyrie's foundations were ahead, and the day's construction on them was already in full swing. The councillors had gathered in the open space just in front of the half-completed doorway, and were standing in a semicircle, waiting patiently.

Lady Isleen stood in the centre and received Kullervo with a big, overly bright smile. "Prince Kullervo," she said, without waiting for Senneck and Arak to greet each other in the proper way. "Welcome in Gryphus' holy name. Did you sleep well?"

No, Kullervo thought. "Yes, thank you, my Lady," he said. "I'm sorry if I kept you waiting."

"There's no need for apologies, my Prince," said Isleen, still smiling. "My council and I have spoken and have reached a decision."

"Give it, then," Senneck said tersely.

The smile flickered briefly when Isleen looked at the brown griffin but returned in full force when she returned her attention to Kullervo. "We accept your Queen's offer of a peace treaty, and we will send a message to Guard's Post, to be passed on to Malvern. But while we will send emissaries, we have decided that we must wait. Our city needs its leaders here while we finish our planning and build our new government. So if we can, we would like to request that you come back here on your way back North. When you leave us again, our emissaries will go with you. Is that acceptable?"

Kullervo tried not to let his delight show on his face and failed. "I accept. I can't say exactly when I'll be back here, but I will come back once I've visited the other Eyries."

"We can wait," said Isleen. She glanced at her fellows, all of whom looked happy with this state of affairs. "Can I ask when you'll be leaving, Prince Kullervo?"

"Soon," said Kullervo. "I have a long way to go. If there's nothing else you want to discuss, I think I'd prefer to leave today."

Lady Isleen nodded politely. "Of course, you're more than welcome to stay for as long as you want."

Behind Kullervo, a crowd had already begun to gather,

presumably hoping for more "divine revelations." Kullervo felt himself starting to sweat. "Thank you, but I want to leave today."

"We understand," said Isleen. "But before you leave, there is someone who wants to speak with you."

Kullervo put all his willpower into stopping himself from looking around. "Send them to my tent, please."

"I will." Isleen bowed slightly, giving Kullervo permission to leave.

He did, very smartly. Senneck had to hurry to keep up with him.

"It would have been more polite to stay," she said.

"I don't care," said Kullervo, using griffish. "I'm not spending one more day here with people trying to worship me. *Stop that!*" This last shout was in Cymrian, and aimed at a woman who had just made a grab for his wing. She let go very quickly and cringed when Kullervo glared at her.

Thankfully nobody had invaded the tent—probably thanks to Seerae, who had returned and was waiting. Red was there, too. He had boiled the eggs as promised and made up a platter of bread and cheese to go with them.

Kullervo sat down very gratefully to eat. Nearby, Seerae chirped at Senneck to come to her, and offered her a rather gruesome lump of meat.

"Thank you for this," Kullervo said to Red. "Here, you have some, too."

"Thank you, sir!" Red took some bread.

"You don't have to call me sir," said Kullervo.

Red nodded shyly. "All right."

The four of them had just about finished eating, when a call from outside made Senneck look up.

"Holy one?" The voice was muffled.

Senneck hissed. "What is it now?"

"May we come in?" the voice called.

Wearily, Kullervo got up and went to lift the flap aside. "Yes?"

The visitor was a young griffiner, plainly dressed, wearing his fine brown hair in a small pony-tail. "My name is Resling. You asked for me to come and see you here?"

"Er—" Kullervo remembered. "Oh, right."

Resling's partner, a female with yellowy feathers, lifted a

forefoot to scratch her face. "I am Keera." She seemed content with that because from then on, she said nothing else.

Kullervo wasn't in the mood for pleasantries. "What do you want?"

Resling coughed nervously. "Uh . . . Holy One, I just wanted to say that—"

"I'm not holy," Kullervo said flatly. "Call me Kullervo or go away."

The young man reddened. "Er . . . sorry. Prince Kullervo—" He bowed hastily. "I saw you yesterday when you arrived, and listened to what you said. I saw your wings. Afterward, I thought that I had never felt so inspired in my life. I prayed to Gryphus, and now I believe he has spoken to me and given me a purpose."

Kullervo scowled. "What purpose?"

"To follow you," said Resling.

Kullervo gaped at him. "What?"

Resling bowed again, with more certainty this time. "My Lord, with your permission, I want to go with you. Keera and I could be your escort on your sacred pilgrimage to bring Gryphus' word to—"

Kullervo hissed at him. "Go away."

Resling looked shocked. "What—?"

"Go. Away." Kullervo pulled the tent flap down and went back inside.

"Who was that?" Senneck asked.

Kullervo stalked back to his seat and slumped into it. "Nobody." He picked up another egg and started to peel off the shell.

"I heard a griffin's voice," said Senneck. "Who was it?"

Kullervo growled to himself. "Some young griffiner. He wants to be my *disciple*, for gods' sakes. The sooner I get out of here, the better."

"Disciple?" Senneck repeated. "What is that?"

"You know, a follower," said Kullervo. "He wants to come with us."

"What?" Senneck stood up. "Kullervo, you must call him back, now."

"I don't want followers," said Kullervo.

"Fool!" Senneck snapped her beak. "Are you blind? Do you know how hard it is to win the loyalty of another griffiner when you have no Eyrie of your own? Go and find this griffin at once, and tell her human they may both come with us. They would be invaluable."

"My mother is right," said Seerae. "This journey of yours is far too dangerous. Another partnered griffin would be a powerful ally. She could fight for us when we are attacked and make the Eyries trust us more for having such a follower."

"But I . . ." Kullervo trailed off.

"Think of it," said Senneck, almost gently. "This human wishes to learn from you. He is wrong now, to think you are holy, but you could teach him the truth."

Kullervo opened his mouth and shut it again. Senneck's idea wormed its way into his mind, and he rubbed his chin thoughtfully. Yes . . . she was right. A whole crowd was too big and unruly to truly listen to him, but one man alone could hear him properly. Maybe he *could* explain things properly to Resling. And maybe then Resling would want to help him. Two were always better than one.

"You're right," he said at last. "It could be good to have him with us. I'll go and find him."

He hurried out of the tent.

Kullervo returned a little while later. "They're coming with us," he said shortly. "Once they're ready, they'll come back here."

"Well done," said Senneck.

Red had been watching silently. "What's going on, s—Kullervo?"

"Hm?" said Kullervo. "Oh, a griffiner asked if he could come with us. I just went to tell him yes."

Red nodded. "I heard Lord Resling wanted to join you. He's very religious."

"I noticed." Kullervo rubbed his eyes. "But I'm not going to teach him anything about Gryphus."

"Kullervo?" said Red.

"Yes, Red, what is it?"

"Can I come with you as well?"

"What?" Kullervo put his head on one side. "Why would you want to?"

Red looked nervous, and sad. "My dad's dead, and I dunno

if they're gonna let me keep his tent. I got nowhere to go. And I thought maybe if I went with you, I could help. Do stuff for you, like making food."

Kullervo opened his mouth to say no, but one look at the orphan boy's hopeful expression made his mind up for him. "Of course you can come. But it might be dangerous."

Red grinned. "I ain't scared. My dad taught me how to fight since I was little."

"All right then," said Kullervo. "But no running off or doing anything silly. And don't get in the griffins' way. They bite."

"I know about griffins," Red said confidently. "My dad's partner even let me touch her once. They're not so scary."

"I could scare you if I wanted to, human pup," said Senneck. "Kullervo, he cannot come with us. He is not a griffiner, and I will not carry him."

"Nor will I," said Seerae. "I will only carry the human that I choose."

"Then *I'll* carry him," said Kullervo.

"You are too small," said Senneck.

"He's not so big," said Kullervo. "I can do it. He's coming with us, Senneck. I'm not going to leave him here to starve."

Senneck sighed. "Very well. Bring him if you must. Perhaps he will be useful to us."

"Right. I should make the change now, then—give myself some time to recover before we go." Kullervo mulled it over and turned to Red. "Red," he said, breaking into Cymrian again, "Do you know somewhere I could find some privacy?"

Red looked puzzled. "Why?"

"I'm going to change my clo—" Kullervo began to lie and stopped. He should probably explain it now. "I'm going to use my magic. But I have to do it somewhere people can't see me."

Red's eyes widened. "What sort of magic?"

"I'm going to turn into a griffin," said Kullervo.

"You can *do* that?"

"Yes. These wings aren't just for show, you know! But it's best if nobody watches me do it."

"Why, do they go blind or something?" asked Red.

"No, it's just not very nice. Do you know somewhere I could hide? I'd rather not have to leave the city. People would follow me, anyway."

"Er, well, you could use this," said Red, going over to a corner and unfolding a wooden screen. "You go behind it to change your clothes if there's someone else there."

Kullervo inspected it. "Yes, this should work. How do I set it up?"

"I'll do it." Red opened the screen all the way and stood it up in a zigzag shape so it wouldn't tip over. "And then you just stand behind it, see?"

"Thanks." Kullervo sat down to take off his boots and put them with his other belongings on top of the unrolled blanket. He put that behind the screen, and turned to Red. "Now you're going to hear some nasty sounds while I do this, but don't be scared. It's not dangerous. But I'd be grateful if you'd make sure nobody came into the tent. If Resling comes back, just tell him to wait outside."

Red nodded excitedly. "I'll stand guard."

"One other thing," said Kullervo. "While I'm a griffin, I won't be able to talk to you—griffins can understand human speech, but they can only speak griffish. But it'll still be me in there; I'll just look different. I'll do my best to tell you things in other ways, so just do your best to understand. When we leave, you'll have to fly with me. Do you think you can do that?"

"You mean you'd *carry* me?" said Red.

"Yes. Actually, is there a spare griffin harness around here?"

"My dad had some," said Red. "I know how to put them on."

"Good. You can put one on me, then. I'll do my best to fly gently, but you'd better hold on tight!"

"I will!" said Red.

"That's the spirit!" Kullervo smiled to reassure him and went behind the screen. Safely out of sight, he took off his clothes and rolled them up in the blanket. Once the bundle was securely tied, he crouched low and let the change begin.

As the pain enveloped his senses, he distracted himself with thoughts of what lay ahead. But there was less reassurance there than fear. Not fear of physical danger—he wasn't much afraid of that. This was a deeper fear, one that felt almost like a fear of the spirit. As if a part of him already had some idea of what was coming.

Eagleholm.

22

A Friend Indeed

Myfina was not enjoying her new life.

When Heath had talked about the island of wild Northerners, in typical Heath fashion, he had made it sound exciting and magical. Myfina wasn't sure exactly what she'd been expecting, but in her head it had been special. She had at the very least expected some sort of special treatment, to be hailed as magical or something similar.

The reality was that they treated her the same as they treated each other—at least at first. Once they realised how ignorant she was of their ways, they stopped treating her like an equal and started treating her like a child instead. Gwladus had taken charge of her, and she had to follow her around and help her with whatever she did—gathering food, mostly, and making things. Gwladus taught her mostly by not trying to teach her and instead forcing her to try things she was unfamiliar with until she worked it out.

Foraging wasn't so hard. Myfina soon learnt how to recognise which kinds of moss and lichen were edible and how to dig up roots that could be boiled into a kind of gruel. But with other things she was hopeless.

The worst task was basket-weaving. With almost no instructions and freezing hands since she had to take her gloves off, she could barely string two reed stems together. Nearby, Gwladus would work away steadily, producing a whole row of neat little jug-shaped baskets, while Myfina tried pathetically to make just one—and failed.

Gwladus was no help at all, and only looked at her protégé's efforts with a kind of distant pity in her black eyes. Nor was she interested in making conversation. Like most of her tribe, she was untalkative to the point of taciturn, and Myfina doubted that she had seen her smile even once.

On the first day, she and Caedmon had been told to build a shelter together that they would share. It was customary for the islanders to have shared homes, simply because it was easier to keep warm at night. But nighttime was the only time she could spend with Caedmon, and by the time they reached their shelter, they were both too tired to do much more than snuggle down together and sleep. It left Myfina feeling perhaps even more friendless and isolated than she might have felt if she hadn't been able to see Caedmon at all.

Nor was Heath any help. Myfina dearly wished that he had stayed around; his presence would have done a lot to cheer her up. But Heath had been almost completely absent since their arrival. Like Saeddryn, he had set off into the wilderness and was rarely seen in the village, often not even returning for meals. Myfina had no idea what he was doing, but he was wan and grim whenever she saw him, as if the island had robbed even him of his sense of humour.

As for Saeddryn, she was around even less than Heath and far more depressing to be with. Not that Myfina wanted to spend time with her; she had never felt comfortable near the heartless woman. Even Caedmon was uneasy around her nowadays.

The end result of all that was that Myfina had barely been on the island for a week and already wanted to leave. But without Garsh, whom she hadn't seen since the first day, she was trapped.

She wished she could spend time with Heath and Caedmon. It might be hard here, but time with the two of them would have made it much easier to bear. She missed Heath's cleverness, his funny stories, and his charming smile. She wished she could tell him how she felt about him, but the truth was that she wasn't completely certain. She felt a fierce affection for him whenever she saw him, and more than once she had wanted to reach out and touch him. But she never had. Every time she had come close, something warned her off.

She wondered why. Was she afraid of her own feelings? Or of him? She didn't know.

It was different with Caedmon, of course. She was never afraid to be close to him; he might be her leader, but he felt like a brother to her. He was vulnerable in a way Heath never was, and that had always made Myfina want to stay close to him. She wished she could say that to him, but how could she? He was her future King, wasn't he?

Feeling miserable and confused, she made one last attempt to tie the bundle of twigs that would form a framework for her basket. And, yet again, the length of dry, twisted grass she was using came apart in her fingers. Groaning, she reached for another piece and found it had all been used up. She would have to go and get some more grass and prepare it.

Myfina stood up, trying to avoid Gwladus' stare, and trudged off into the trees.

She was less interested in finding more grass than in having some time to herself, so she ignored several promising clumps and moved on toward the river. She could pretend she was getting a drink if anyone saw her.

There was already someone sitting by the bank. Myfina's heart leapt when she saw that it was Heath. But he looked different now. Unaware that he was being watched, he had dropped his normal confident air. She caught a glimpse of his face, and now it looked younger and gentler than usual. It made her heart ache.

Smiling properly for the first time in days, she hopped nimbly from rock to rock until she reached the other side and went straight to him. "Heath!"

Heath looked up, and to her joy she saw him smile in that easygoing way she remembered so well. "Hello, Myfina."

Myfina's happiness soon faded when she took a good look at him. He had grown thin, she realised—painfully so. His face was unhealthily pale, and his eyes had gone dull. Impulsively, forgetting her former hesitation, she put her hands on his shoulders. "My gods, you look awful!"

Heath coughed, deeply and painfully. "Y-yes, I know," he wheezed. "Feeling a bit under the weather right now."

Myfina sat down beside him, as close as she could in the hopes of warming him up. "You shouldn't be running around in the woods like this," she said. "You should stay in the village and get more rest."

"Yes, I know," said Heath. "I was planning to come back today. I needed some time alone, and now I feel ready to be with people again."

Myfina put an arm around his shoulders. "I'm glad. I missed you, Heath."

He hugged her back. "I missed you, too, Myfina. And Caedmon as well. How is he?"

"I think he's trying his best," said Myfina. "He has to go out hunting with Llygad and the rest every day. He comes back all bruised. He told me he has to use a spear for everything, and he never trained with one, so he's the worst hunter on the island."

"It takes a lot of practice," Heath admitted. "I—" He broke off into another coughing fit.

Myfina held him all the while, feeling fear in her heart with every painful jerk of his body. "Yes, like all the things I have to do," she said, trying to sound cheerful. "I can't even make a basket. And the food here is awful."

"It is, isn't it?" said Heath, after taking some deep breaths to recover himself. "But it's just food."

"Yes, and people are just people," said Myfina. "What I wouldn't give for a good solid meal, and a warm room with a good fire and a soft bed . . ."

Heath grinned. "Makes you appreciate things, doesn't it? Let me tell you, in my old life I loved living the good life so much that I didn't care about the risks. It made it all worthwhile. I never even thought of going back to how I started out."

"How *did* you start out, then?" asked Myfina. She didn't expect a straight answer; Heath was very good at avoiding those when he felt like it.

But he took her by surprise. "I was born poor," he said. "Actually, not poor—more like whatever comes below poor, if they have a word for it. And trust me; people might tell you that poverty makes men better, but the people who say that have never tried being poor. So once I was old enough, I decided I'd had enough of having nothing and went off to do something about it."

"And never looked back, eh?" Myfina grinned. "Where did you come from, then? What's your real name?"

"Whatever I want it to be, mostly," said Heath.

Myfina lost her smile. "Why won't you just tell me? Is it so much to ask?"

"No, but if I did tell you, I'd lose my mystique." Heath laughed. "And then I wouldn't be half as charming."

"That's just silly," said Myfina. "I'm your friend, aren't I?"

"I like to think so," said Heath. He took her hand in his and held it gently. "I'll tell you one day. When I'm ready. I promise."

"Then I'll wait for that day," said Myfina.

They sat together for a while in companionable silence. Myfina thought she could feel Heath shivering ever so slightly under his griffin-hide robe.

"I really missed you," she said eventually. "Everything's gone. Everyone I ever knew except for Caedmon and you."

"Don't you have a family?" asked Heath.

Myfina shook her head. "I've never told Caedmon this, but I came from the South. I was one of the slaves Lady Skade brought back with her. I was only about a year old—they used to give away the children of slaves if they were too young to work. After the war, I grew up in Caerleon—they sent orphans like us to different cities to be raised together. When I was old enough, I got a job teaching orphans like me. I still don't know why Garsh chose me. Maybe it was just because I could read."

Heath chuckled. "So that's why you like me, eh? You know another jumped-up commoner when you see him."

Myfina had to laugh, too. "You're right, that must be it. Or . . ." Her heart beat faster, and she couldn't believe it when her voice sounded just as casual as she went on. "Or maybe I like you because you're clever, and funny, and . . . well, not bad-looking either."

Heath coughed. "It's true, I do have plenty to recommend me."

"Yes, especially your modesty," Myfina teased.

"People like confidence," Heath said coolly.

"Bragging," said Myfina.

"Confidence!" Heath corrected. "And honesty, of course. Can't forget that."

"Hah, yes, of course," said Myfina. "But I think we know more about telling the truth than you do, Heath."

"'We'?" said Heath, suddenly serious. "I'm a part of 'we' now, Myfina. Aren't I?"

"Yes, you are." She hugged him. "But you've got a lot to learn about being honest."

"I think I'm learning it," said Heath.

"You are." Myfina tensed. It was now or never. "Heath, I . . . I just wanted to tell you . . ."

"Yes?" said Heath. He sounded as if he had already guessed.

Myfina held his hand in both of hers. "I love you, Heath. I have for a long time. I should have told you sooner . . ."

"No you don't," said Heath.

Myfina froze. "What?"

He put his other hand on top of hers, and smiled. "You don't love me, Myfina," he said. "You don't know me. You don't know who I am; you've never known. All you've known is the mask. The person I pretend to be."

"Then be yourself," said Myfina.

"I can't." Heath looked rather sad. "A mask is all I am. I've been so many people and worn so many names and faces, I lost track of what was underneath a long time ago. And anyway . . ." he said, trying to sound lighthearted, "I'm a bad catch. I've loved women before . . . for one night, maybe. I can't stay the same person long enough to be with anyone."

"I don't care about that," said Myfina.

"But I do," said Heath. "And maybe if I was as much of a scumbag as I used to be, I'd let you go on believing you were in love. But you've taught me how to tell the truth, so I'll tell it now. And Caedmon taught me how to be loyal, so I'll do that now. I didn't betray him in Malvern, and I won't betray him now. And I certainly won't break his heart."

Myfina pulled away from him. "What do you mean?"

Heath grinned his old, familiar, dazzling grin. "Haven't you seen it? Weren't you paying any attention? I was. I always do— it's a survival instinct for someone like me. Caedmon's in love with you, Myfina. I've seen the way he looks at you, like he'd give anything to be able to say something—but he won't. He's scared to. After what happened to Sionen, it's not surprising. He lost her to Arenadd, and he's terrified that he's going to lose you to me. Whenever you were close to me, he looked miserable. He knows you want me—he probably knew we'd talk about it on this island. It's hurting him, every day."

Myfina sat frozen, her heart aching. "Caedmon? I never . . ."

"Don't be daft," said Heath. "You love him, too. You're just a bit confused about it. You should go to him. Tell him how you feel; tell him about me if you want to. He needs you. He's even more alone than you are, Myfina."

Myfina wanted to cry. "But he's a Prince . . . my leader . . . *our* leader. One day he'll be King."

Heath smiled. "And you'd make a wonderful Queen. I'm sure of it. Don't be afraid."

"I . . ." Myfina stood up. "I don't know . . ."

Heath stood, too, and gave her a hug. "Don't be afraid," he said again, and kissed her on the forehead. "You'll be fine."

Myfina pushed him away. For a moment, it looked as if she was going to say something, but in the end she only let out a great, rough sob and ran away into the trees.

Heath watched her go and felt close to tears himself. He knew he had done the right thing, but it hurt anyway. Just now, he would have given anything to be close to someone again.

He winced and put a hand to his chest, where his wounds throbbed and burned. Nothing could cure them now. After Saeddryn had promised to plead with the Night God for him, she had never spoken to him again. Her silence told him all he needed to know. There was no chance left for him, no miracle.

Heath looked into his own future and saw only death. He was moving closer to it every day, with aches and pains and weakening limbs, and a cough that felt powerful enough to break his ribs. He had eaten nothing all day, but he had no appetite.

He felt dizzy and nauseous.

Heath sat down shakily on his rock, and huddled down inside his griffin hide. Best let Caedmon and Myfina sort themselves out first. Tonight, he would return to the village and the shelter he had built there before. Before long he wouldn't be strong enough to go anywhere, and he was ready to be with other people again. At least his friends would be there to look after him at the end. Right now, the thought of being alone scared him more than death.

But to die was to be alone, he thought.

Heath buried his face in his hands and thought of Myfina and Caedmon together. It made him feel a little better.

Time passed as if in a dream. One moment he was sitting there and feeling the hot shiver of the fever invading his body, and the next it was growing dark. Had he slept? He couldn't even tell. Standing up made him so dizzy, he nearly fell, but he recovered himself and started to walk slowly back toward the village.

In the end, there was nothing noble or dignified, or easy, about Heath's final decline. After his return to the village he stayed, but it soon became plain that he was too weak to do anything but the lightest work, and before long he had lost the strength to do even that.

Once the tribe discovered just how ill he was, Llygad insisted that those of them who knew something about healing should try and help. But the tribe's medical skills were hopelessly primitive, and by now even the Master of Healing at Malvern wouldn't have been able to do anything beyond giving him something to ease the pain. He had simply suffered too much to ever recover. Torture, stress, and starvation on top of an illness he had not had proper time to recover from added together, and he no longer had the strength to fight off the infection that had spread through the wounds on his chest. It continued to move into his blood, and once it had taken hold, his descent was frighteningly fast.

In just a few days, he was confined to his bed by a fever ten times more powerful than what he had suffered at Skenfrith. Caedmon and Myfina, ignoring their duties to watch over him, listened to him mumble and sometimes cry out at whatever he thought he was seeing. He seemed completely unaware that they were nearby, and sometimes spoke to people who only existed in his mind. Once, Caedmon heard him suddenly start talking in that same confident, easygoing way he had done on their first meeting, and he sounded so lucid that for a moment Caedmon thought his friend was awake. But when he moved closer to listen, he saw that Heath's eyes were unfocused and bright with fever.

". . . and, of course, being situated so close to the Eyrie would provide *excellent* views, not to mention make you the envy of all your friends!" he was saying. "I know it's expensive, but some things are worth more than money. A good home . . ."

After that, his voice weakened back to a mutter, and he fell silent again.

This sort of thing continued through the next day and night, and nobody could reach him any more. Sleepless, Caedmon and Myfina listened helplessly as their friend relived old memories and suffered through nightmares of savage griffins and cold shadows that he said were taking his life away. Those were the worst.

But something more mysterious and strange happened through it all. As Heath dreamed of the things he had done and the people he had met, his voice changed. With every memory, it was different. Sometimes he sounded like a native of Skenfrith, sometimes Warwick, sometimes even the South, as if he were reliving all his old identities in his mind. But behind those, emerging more and more frequently, there was one voice that didn't quite fit. It sounded younger and lighter than the rest, and far less refined. When he used it, he spoke to people who didn't seem to be the usual victims of his trickery.

"I'm leavin', Ma," he said once. "There's better things out there, ye know, an' a better life. I got the wits, I'm gonna take it. Gonna . . ."

After that, he slept.

When morning came again, Caedmon woke up and saw that Heath was still asleep. Myfina was asleep beside him, keeping him warm. Caedmon rose silently and crept away to the river for some water.

He brought it back and refilled the clay bowl that held the cloth they'd been using to try to cool Heath's forehead. There was some water left over, so he drank part of it and left the rest for Myfina.

As he was sitting down again, he saw Heath stir and moved closer to check on him.

Heath's eyes opened a crack, and he peered upward. "Caedmon," he whispered. "C . . ."

Caedmon managed a smile. "Are you feeling better?"

"A bit." Heath's voice had become a faint rasp.

Caedmon touched his cheek—it was burning hot. "You'll be all right."

Heath didn't seem to hear him. "Caedmon. Wanted to . . ."

"What is it?"

Heath lay still for a while, breathing raggedly. "My name . . . name's . . . Henwas Malverni. Real name."

"Henwas?" Caedmon repeated. He paused. "'Malverni' . . . didn't you know your father, then?"

Heath managed the ghost of a grin. "No. Your dad hanged him for burglary. Just a child of Malvern, me. Henwas . . ."

"I'm glad you told me," said Caedmon. "I'd have wondered for the rest of my life if you hadn't."

"Friends know friends' names," said Henwas, his eyes closing again. "Listen. Mother's still in Malvern. Adain. Lives alone. My brother's about, too. Little brother. Morgan. Tell them, Caedmon. Tell them what happened to me. Help them. They're good people. Not bad like me."

"I will, Henwas. I promise. But you're not bad, understand?"

Henwas coughed feebly. "You . . . good man. Good King one day. Be good to Myfina. I'm sorry I couldn't stay . . ."

"But you will," Caedmon told him. "I'll never forget you. One day, everyone will know your name. I'll put up a statue to you in front of the Eyrie."

Henwas laughed for the last time. "Handsome statue. Goodbye, Sire . . ."

After that he said nothing more. He slipped away back into sleep, and Caedmon knew with cold certainty that he had spoken his last words.

Myfina woke up a little while later, and she and Caedmon shared some food that Gwladus brought by. They both knew that they had things to do, but neither of them would leave.

The day dragged on, and Henwas did not wake up again. He lay utterly still, and his face slowly drained of the last of its colour. The heat of the fever had gone away, but coldness came in its place.

Caedmon and Myfina sat beside him in silence, listening to his breathing grow steadily slower and slower until, almost imperceptibly, it stopped altogether.

Neither of them moved, but both of them saw it, and after a moment Myfina began to cry silently. Caedmon reached out to take her hand, and she clung to his dead body but did not look away from what they both knew was a dead body.

"Goodbye, Heath," she said at last.

Caedmon looked down at the still face, too, and smiled sadly. "His name was Henwas."

"What?" said Myfina.

Caedmon turned the smile on her. He felt light-headed. "His real name was Henwas Malverni."

"How do you know?"

"He told me this morning. You were asleep."

Myfina's tears came faster. "Did he say anything else?"

"Yes. He asked me . . ." Caedmon touched her face. "He told me to be good to you, and he said he was sorry he couldn't stay."

Myfina stared at him for a moment. Then she threw herself into his arms and started to sob. Caedmon held her, and felt his own tears harden inside him.

"He taught us both so much," he said, not so much to her as to the presence that still lingered there around them. "He was a true friend, and a true Northerner."

"He was a hero," said Myfina.

"Yes." The tears trapped inside Caedmon burned at him, but he could not let them go. They stayed there as a torment. "The half-breed has taken everything from me. My home. My throne. My father and my sister. Even my mother. And now Hea— and now Henwas as well." He loosened his hold on Myfina, and looked down into her tear-streaked face. "You and Shar are all I have left. But I swear that I won't let it end this way. I won't let Henwas die for nothing. I'll stay here and become a real Northerner and a real man, the way he wanted me to. And then I'll go back. I'll challenge her, and I'll win. For Henwas. For the North. For the Night God. For you."

"You will," said Myfina. "Henwas believed in you, and so do I, Caedmon . . ."

"Yes, Myfina?" Caedmon's voice sounded deeper to him now. More certain.

"Before he came back here, Henwas told me you loved me," said Myfina. "I didn't see it, but he did. Was he right, Caedmon?"

The tears were in Caedmon's heart now. "Yes. I do love you, Myfina. I always have. And if I never said anything . . ."

"Then don't." Myfina took him in her arms, and held him close. Caedmon held her in return, his heart fluttering. Maybe it wasn't love yet—maybe this wasn't the time. But she was there, and that was all that mattered now. She was there.

23

Eagleholm

The journey to Eagleholm was a long one, and it was made longer by several things. One was Red. Despite Senneck's predictions, Kullervo did manage to carry him. But only with difficulty. He had to fly low and had to stop to rest much more often than a full-sized griffin would have. Despite that, he utterly refused to abandon the boy, who had latched onto him as something of a father figure despite the obvious obstacles—such as the fact that Kullervo was now a griffin and stayed that way through the entire journey.

Resling was the only human in the group apart from Red, but he showed no interest in talking with the boy and in fact treated him more or less like a servant, expecting him to prepare the food and build a shelter for his superior whenever they stopped for the night. Red obeyed without complaint; it seemed he was too excited at having been allowed to come along to mind much. Naturally, Resling wouldn't let him share the shelters he built, so he would use Kullervo's blanket and snuggle down under his wing for protection.

Both Senneck and Seerae were displeased by Red's effect on their progress, but of course they both refused to carry him themselves, and so the state of affairs continued as they struck out into the very heart of the South and the lands that had once belonged to the proud city of Eagleholm.

There had been war; they could all see the evidence even without Resling's and Keera's accounts. They saw farms and villages, and griffiner outposts. Some were still occupied, but many lay in ruins, seemingly abandoned long ago. The outposts, however, had very clearly been deliberately destroyed. Most had been burned, or simply broken apart by massive forces—forces that had had talons. In some places, the travellers even came across bones left abandoned. Human bones, generally, and in some cases one or two that were definitely griffin. Resling explained that any griffin remains would have been cannibalised by people—in both senses of the word. There had been a famine, and griffin feathers and bones were worth a fortune.

The few people still left in the territory were thin and nervous and rarely seen except as they ran to hide from the band of griffins that flew overhead. Once upon a time, a griffin and its partner would be something to welcome and revere. Nowadays, it would mean danger and dark memories.

The more Kullervo travelled through this landscape, the more depressing he found it. It was sobering to think of what must have happened here, but it also gave him an unexpected and powerful sense of guilt. All this, all of it, had been begun by his father.

"Terrible business it was," said Resling, looking more resigned than unhappy. "Every Eyrie in the South sent in its armies. After the fighting over the city tore it to bits, they gave up and pillaged whatever was left. They fought each other all over this gods-forsaken territory, then Withypool actually resorted to attacking Canran on its own land. Wylam joined in, and they sacked the city. For a while, Withypool owned a huge chunk of Canran's lands, but they couldn't govern it from so far away; and then the plague started, so they pulled back."

"So who owns this place now?" Kullervo asked.

"Nobody does. Well . . . Withypool owns the eastern part. They're building a new city down there, people say. A new capital of a new territory. Wylam took part of the West, but the central part, right here—it's no man's land. And, of course, while that was going on, the Wild Woman of Withypool came along and made off with all the slaves."

Kullervo's tail started to twitch. "How?"

Resling scratched his shoulder. "Bought them at first. Everyone wanted to get rid of his slaves; they'd realised they were outnumbered in most places, and if they got ideas from that lot up in the North, we'd have another uprising here as well. Then once she had enough of them, she started using them like an army. Fought off anyone who got in her way and started stealing any slaves she couldn't buy. Before long, others of them turned on their owners and ran off to join her. It was anarchy, I tell you. Complete chaos. If the Dark Lord had come through those mountains back then . . ." Resling shuddered.

"And Liranwee?" asked Senneck. "Who owns it?"

"We do, of course," said Resling. "Liranwee is a city of refugees, but don't let Lady Isleen hear you say that. Most of our people came from here originally, commoners and griffiners. Some of our griffiners even came from Eagleholm itself, in its last days. Not me, though; I was born after that, during the war. Others came from Canran. Our land used to belong to Canran, you see, but since it was unclaimed after the Withypool and Wylam fight, we took it. Nobody else wants it that badly; we're right on the North's doorstep. But it doesn't look like the Dark Lord's going to come through the mountains any more, so that's our greatest fear gone."

"Lady Isleen must be glad to make a treaty with the North now," said Kullervo. "So close by; Liranwee is in the perfect place for trading."

"Yes, I suppose we are," said Resling.

It was an interesting story, and a chilling one, too. Kullervo took it as a reminder of what people could do under the right circumstances. So much for Gryphus' claim that only Northerners squabbled over power—Kullervo felt disgusted at the mere thought of it. No, Gryphus was as mad as the Night God, and Kullervo had no regrets over rejecting him.

And so, with tale-telling and hard flying, the journey toward Eagleholm continued over two slow months. And, as the third month advanced, it became more and more obvious that there was now another reason for them to advance slowly.

Senneck, as she had claimed, was pregnant. Kullervo saw her slim shape form a bulge that grew steadily despite the poor food and heavy exercise along the way. She became tense and lethargic, and toward the end of the third month she was flying as slowly as he was. It was clear that if she was going to lay her eggs at Eagleholm as planned, they would have to reach it soon.

For a while, it looked as if they might not reach it soon enough, but with hard flying, they just managed it. At the heart of what had become nearly a wasteland, Eagleholm waited.

Senneck had predicted they were close when they came across a much larger ruined village than they had seen so far. Part of it had fallen down, but some buildings were still standing, and there were people still living there, though once again they had no welcome for the travellers and only hid away at the sight of them. Kullervo and his companions stopped there anyway, and finding a wild and overgrown orchard bordering the village, they rested there and gathered some apples.

Senneck wandered among the trees, her former graceful lope now distinctly heavier and clumsier. Rotten apples littered the ground under her paws, and she awkwardly batted one away.

"I know this place," she said, as she lay down at the base of a dead tree. "I have been here once before. This village is Carrick."

"When were you here?" asked Kullervo.

"On the day following Eagleholm's destruction," said Senneck. "When Erian and I left, we stopped here so that he could say farewell to his grandparents, who raised him, and show his friends that he had become a griffiner."

Resling had been listening. "You mean this is where he was born?"

"It is," said Senneck. "And in those days, it was a strong home. Many people lived here. They sold their honey and apples to Eagleholm, and they revered us as humans should." She looked unexpectedly sad. "And now it is all destroyed, like so many other places."

Kullervo heaved a griffish sigh. "I wish I could have met Erian."

"I do not," said Senneck. "He would have hated you, and possibly teared you as well, as he hated and teared your father."

Resling looked slightly puzzled at this remark, but he said nothing. Like everyone else in Liranwee, he seemed unable to understand or accept Kullervo's parentage, and so ignored it whenever it was brought up.

"Are we close to Eagleholm, then?" said Kullervo.

"We are," said Senneck. "If we were not burdened, we would be able to reach it before nightfall. As it is, we should stay here until morning and move on then. It would be better to arrive in daylight."

"I agree," said Resling.

So they spent the night in the village, undisturbed by the locals, and Kullervo and the other griffins ate a dead cow they found abandoned in a field near what Senneck said had once been Erian's home. By now, it, too, was abandoned; no doubt Erian's grandparents had died long ago, along with anyone who might have claimed their old home. But the adjoining barn was big enough to provide shelter for Kullervo and the other griffins, and Red even managed to light a fire in the crumbling fireplace.

None of them had much energy for talking that night. They slept huddled together for protection, all preparing for what might happen the next day.

But Kullervo, even warmed by Senneck's beloved flank, found himself too nervous to sleep and stayed awake there until well after moonrise, feeling his oversized griffish heart pattering away as if it had forgotten how to slow down.

Morning came at last, and the travellers prepared for the final push toward the city. Kullervo waited patiently while Red climbed onto his shoulders, and when he and Resling were both ready, they both looked toward Senneck.

"Show us the way, Mother," Seerae urged.

Senneck stretched her wings. She looked nervous. "Yes . . . Kullervo, Seerae—Keera . . . follow me now. But do not expect to like what you will find."

She went out through the gaping hole in the barn wall and took off heavily. Kullervo followed with equal difficulty, envying Seerae's and Keera's ease as they rose alongside him.

Flying as a flock once again, the four griffins moved away southward one last time.

Both Kullervo and Senneck needed to rest before long, but both of them seemed equally determined and pushed themselves harder than they had before. And when Eagleholm came in sight at last, even Senneck sped up.

When Kullervo saw the ruined city for the first time, even as a griffin, he felt sick to his stomach.

Ahead, a massive stump of stone rose out of the earth. It was so big it was more of a plateau than a mountain, and its sides were sheer and rocky, nearly unclimbable. On its flat top, the city stood, silhouetted against the sky. Kullervo could see the outlines of the buildings, black in front of blue, but the closer he came, the more he saw that they weren't buildings any more, but ruins.

At the centre, a jagged spire of a fallen tower spiked upward, and he knew that it must have been an Eyrie once upon a time.

At the edges of the mountaintop, huge wooden supports jutted outward to expand the city's street space. But now they were rotting and falling apart, and in one place had broken away and caused a devastating rock-slide down the mountainside.

Behind him, Kullervo heard Red exclaim in horror as they came close enough for human eyes to see the devastation.

If Senneck felt the same way, she didn't show it. She beat her wings harder and flew high enough to fly over the city, where she circled for a time before choosing a landing place and spiralling toward it. Kullervo followed, taking in much more of the city. Everywhere, he could see houses and other buildings broken apart or looking as if they were halfway there. A huge patch had clearly been burned in what must have been a devastating fire, leaving only blackened foundations to tell the tale. At the centre, the Eyrie was little more than a heap of rubble, with only a crumbling section of wall somehow still standing.

There was no sign of life anywhere, and Kullervo couldn't fathom how anyone could survive here either.

The area where Senneck chose to land was toward the edge of the city and didn't seem to have had much on it even before the disaster—there were no signs of buildings or their remains, only a large open space scattered with garbage. Somewhere in the midst of it, though, a building was still standing, and it looked to be in better shape than most.

Senneck landed near its entrance and immediately began to huff aggressively and look about for any sign of danger. Kullervo touched down beside her, feeling both tired and apprehensive. "Senneck, what is this place?"

Senneck was looking at the building now. "This is my old home," she said, and if there had been a hint of sadness in her before, now it was open and obvious. "This was once the Hatchery. I was hatched and raised here."

Red dismounted. "What was this big space here for?" he asked.

"Yes, what was it for?" Kullervo echoed.

Senneck watched Seerae and Keera land. "They penned the goats here for our food. Every day some were slaughtered for us. Now they are all gone, like the griffins I grew up with."

"Not all," said Keera. "I was hatched here as well. But I was too young to remember it."

Red seemed to be listening even though there was no way he could understand them since they were speaking griffish. "I wish I coulda seen it when it wasn't wrecked."

"So do I," said Kullervo. He had got into the habit of talking to Red as a griffin despite the obvious reason not to bother. Red seemed to appreciate it.

Resling looked both disgusted and sad. "You see?" he said. "This place is finished. Worse than finished. There's nothing here for us."

"I would like to see the inside of the Hatchery again," said Senneck. "There may be a good nesting place there, and if I do not lay today, I will lay tomorrow. I cannot afford to go anywhere else until I have."

"I understand," said Kullervo, going to her side. "I want to see it, too."

Together, he and Senneck walked toward the building, with Red keeping close to Kullervo, and the others bringing up the rear.

At first glance, the Hatchery looked as abandoned as the other buildings they had seen. But it was in good enough shape for them to see signs of what it had once been like. The roof was high and peaked, with openings that must have always been there, made big enough for griffins to fly through. The entrance, too, was oversized; naturally, as this was a building meant for griffins. The doors were still there, or rather one of them was; the other had broken off its hinges and was now propped up against the doorframe, leaving a gap big enough for a human to walk through. Senneck, however, couldn't, so she unceremoniously hooked her beak into the big slab of wood and tossed it aside.

Beyond was a big open space, big enough for griffins to move about. Dozens of small pens lined the walls, and Kullervo, who had been in a Hatchery before, recognised them as homes for griffin chicks.

"I lived in one of these," Senneck said, sure enough. "But I cannot remember which by now." As she was speaking, she tensed suddenly. Her head went up, and she sniffed roughly at the air. Her talons curled. "Human!" she exclaimed.

Kullervo had already caught the scent. "Look there," he said.

Sure enough, a young woman had appeared through a back door and frozen to the spot when she saw them.

"Griffins!" And then, again, "Holy Gryphus . . . *griffins!*"

"Who are you?" Senneck demanded. She sounded almost angry at being intruded upon.

"Er, I'm . . . my name's Liantha," the woman faltered.

"She knows griffish!" said Kullervo.

"I do," said Liantha. She must have also known about griffins themselves, because she didn't try to run off, or show fear—in fact, she only looked astonished. She bowed hastily. "I'm so sorry, but I never thought . . . wait here." She hurried off back through the door she had entered through, shouting in Cymrian. "Dad! Dad, there's griffins out here!"

Senneck had calmed down. "I do not believe it," she said. "Humans still here, and one who knows griffish. I did not expect that."

Kullervo suddenly wished he had taken the time to become human again. "Neither did I." He looked back toward the entrance, and saw Keera, Resling, and Seerae entering.

While they stood there in a little group, confused, Liantha returned. She came much more slowly this time, supporting an old man.

At first, the old man looked as if he were too confused and weak to do anything except lean on his helper, but as he came out into the open he looked up and saw Senneck. His eyes were faded and looked nearly blind, but he must have seen her, because his face slackened slightly in apparent shock.

Then, shuffling but eager, he let go of Liantha and came on toward the brown griffin. "Senneck?" he said in a wheezy voice. "Senneck, is that really you?"

"It is," said Senneck. "But who are you?"

The old man laughed, and suddenly seemed a lot younger. "Senneck, it's me. Roland."

Senneck hissed softly. "Roland?"

"I'm afraid so." Roland grinned. "You haven't changed a bit, even if I have. Hah, I remember raising you in here with Eluna and all the others. You always liked your rat in the morning."

"Yes . . ." Senneck crouched low, and put her beak down toward the old man, with a gentleness that Kullervo had never seen in her before. "I did not think that I would find you here."

"Neither would anyone," Roland said cheerfully. "But they do anyway. How's young Erian getting along, then?"

"He is dead," said Senneck. "He has been dead for twenty years."

"Oh." Roland's face fell. For a moment, he looked a little lost. "Oh, yes, I remember now. Yes, I remember when the news came about that . . . they said Arren did it, of course, but they said so much about him after he left, and I never could quite believe it all."

While he spoke, Kullervo quietly withdrew. He left Red where he was, and stole into the adjoining room. All his instincts told him that now was the time to change. This old man knew important things, and Kullervo had to be human if he wanted to understand them properly.

In the next room, he found the quarters that had once belonged to the adult griffins like Senneck. There were more pens here, but open ones this time, some of which looked as if they had been used as beds by people. Kullervo chose one and began the change. It was as if his magic knew how urgent this change was because it worked much faster than it usually did. But it still took longer than he wanted it to.

When it was finished, he was too exhausted to even dress. He fell asleep next to his bundle of clothing and stayed that way for a good chunk of the afternoon.

When he woke up, it was nearly nighttime, and he still ached all over. But his urgent desire to talk to Roland gave him energy.

He dressed as quickly as he could, leaving his wings and tail uncovered as before, and limped slowly back to the chick room.

The others were all there, resting from their journey. Roland and Liantha were there, too, and someone had lit a lantern. They were sharing some food with Resling and Red, and Senneck and the other griffins were eating what looked like dried meat.

When Red saw Kullervo, his face split into a smile, and he ran toward him. "Kullervo! I didn't think you was ever gonna be human again!"

Kullervo smiled back. "It was just for travelling, like I said. Anyway, now's the time to be human."

He walked into the circle of lantern-light, straight toward

Roland, who was in the midst of telling Resling some story. "And so they started coming to me for . . ."

Kullervo screwed up his courage. "Roland," he said. "I want to talk to you."

Roland looked up sharply. "What?" When he saw Kullervo's face, his reaction was sudden and almost frightening. He jerked as if someone had hit him, but before Liantha could try to calm him down, he stood up, with surprising strength. He took a step closer to Kullervo, reaching out slowly, and his face was full of utter shock. "Arren . . . ?" he faltered. "Arren, it can't be . . ."

Kullervo wanted to cry. "No, Roland, I—"

Roland looked close to tears himself. "Arren, why have you come back here? You know they'll kill you if they see you. After what you did . . ."

"I'm not Arren," said Kullervo.

"Yes, so you said before," said Roland. "But that was madness! No matter how badly they hurt you, you didn't ever stop being yourself. You know you can't run away from that, don't you, lad? Don't you?" He looked away. "I know I failed you. Ever since I've never forgiven myself. I tried so hard to teach you, tried to keep you away from what your father wanted you to be. Rannagon never believed it could be done . . . damn fool that he was. If they had let you be what you wanted to be, none of this would have happened. But if I'd never . . ." Roland shook his head. "I always wondered what I'd say if I ever saw you again, but I never did find it. Arren . . ."

Kullervo didn't know what to say while Roland spoke, and only stood there, feeling his throat tighten with emotion. But as he saw the old man grow more distressed, he reached out and stopped him with a gentle touch to the shoulder. "Roland, I'm not Arren."

Roland finally seemed to hear him. "Not . . . ?"

"I'm his son," said Kullervo.

Liantha started violently. "*What?*"

"His *son*?" said Roland. "You're Arren's son?"

"I am. My name's Kullervo."

A weak smile appeared on Roland's face, and he reached up to touch Kullervo's hand. "Kullervo Arrenson. Then you're Flell's child?"

"No." Kullervo managed to smile back. "Flell's child was a girl. Her name's Laela. My mother was someone else."

"Then Flell had her baby," Roland muttered. "I never . . . we all heard she was dead."

"She is," said Kullervo. "Roland, Arren's dead, too."

Roland's shoulders sagged. "They're all dead," he said. "Everybody's dead except me. Rannagon, Flell, Arren, Eluna. Even that lad Bran, most likely."

"Who was Bran?" Kullervo asked.

"I know who he was," Resling interrupted before Roland could answer. "Branton Redguard. Bran the Betrayer. The one who destroyed Eagleholm."

"But Arren . . . Arenadd did that," said Kullervo. "Everyone knows that."

"But he never would have had the chance if it weren't for Branton Redguard," Resling spat. "The fool was friends with him and decided to help him escape from prison. Afterward, the blackrobe scum was free to take his revenge."

"He never!" To the surprise of everyone, it was Red who spoke up. "Bran never did! He wasn't no betrayer; I'll punch you if you say so!"

Resling looked furious. "How dare you? What do *you* know about anything, boy?"

"I know lots," Red retorted. "My dad, he was from Eagleholm. He was Bran's sergeant before the burning. He was friends with him, and *he* said Bran would never betray nobody."

Resling snorted. "Well, that proves it."

Roland shook his head. "Bran was Arren's best friend. It tore him apart to see him turn traitor, but he was always loyal to the city. I should know; I trained him here after the fire. You remember him, don't you, Arren?" he looked at Kullervo. "He became a griffiner, you know. The unpartnered here needed humans to leave, so they chose whomever they found."

"I'm not Arren," Kullervo reminded him.

"Yes, yes, that's right. You're his son." Roland waved his hand vaguely. "Let's sit down. I should tell you what happened after the fire."

Kullervo sat down, ignoring Liantha's gasp when she saw his wings. Roland didn't seem to have noticed, possibly because of his failing eyesight.

"What *did* happen here?" Kullervo asked the old man. "You say this Bran was chosen?"

"Yes, and not because he was a noble," said Roland. "As I said, the griffins needed partners urgently, and they had no time to wait for the Springday ritual or look for nobles. They chose anyone who looked strong enough. Bran was one, and afterward I offered to train him. I trained the others, too. New griffiners who needed help and didn't have elder griffiners about to teach them. No apprenticeships left in a city with no more officials or even an Eyrie Master, you see. So I taught them. When Bran was ready, he married Flell, and they left the city for good. Chasing after Arren, so they said." Roland actually laughed his wheezy laugh. "They didn't know the truth about that then, and neither did anybody. If they had, they would've known it was a fool's errand."

"Yes, because when they found him, he murdered Flell," said Kullervo, who knew that part of the story at least.

Roland shook his head. "No, no, that wasn't Arren who did that. Not him at all. Arren wasn't a murderer, not my Arren. No, they never found him because he never went North at all."

"What do you mean?" asked Resling.

"Arren's still here," said Roland. "He never left. And we know it, we all do, and that's why this city never recovered. We never forgave ourselves for what we did to him, even after the Dark Lord took his revenge." The old man half laughed, half cried, and Liantha touched him and murmured to calm him down.

"Don't worry about it; he gets like this sometimes," she said aside to Kullervo. "It was all too much for him."

Roland looked as if he had already forgotten his frightening little speech. "I clung on here, anyway, somehow or other. Helped people however I could. The goats, you see. Didn't have to feed griffins any more, so I gave the meat to people who needed it, and the hides, too, and even milk. But they're all gone now. All killed, all stolen. The people here, they've all gone mad. The curse on our city . . . too much for ordinary people to live with. But Liantha keeps me safe here."

"Your daughter?" Senneck asked.

"Adopted," said Liantha. "I was an orphan. From the Eyrie fire."

"No, I never had children of my own," said Roland. "Never

married, either. Arren was the closest thing I had to a child of my own before Liantha came along. I taught him all I knew. Her, too."

"So there are no griffins left here?" asked Seerae, speaking up for almost the first time.

"No. No griffiners either. In the fighting here, someone broke into the Arena. They let out all the wild griffins there, and they went on a rampage. Killed dozens. After that, they flew away, back to the wild, I suppose. The civilised griffins went away, and the griffiners with them. Even the ones I trained here all left."

"And her?" said Seerae, meaning Liantha.

"Trained her as a griffiner, even without a griffin," said Roland. "But I suppose if she had one, she'd leave me, too."

"Never," Liantha said quietly.

"Roland," said Kullervo. "I wanted to ask you a favour."

"Eh?" Roland rubbed his eye. "What is it, Arren?"

Kullervo's heart ached. "Can you tell me where my father used to live? I'd like to see it for myself."

"Oh, I can if you've forgotten," said Roland. "But you won't want to live there any more, lad. It was never rebuilt, and what they've done to the ruins . . ."

"I want to see it anyway," said Kullervo. "If you don't mind."

"Of course, lad." Roland gave his directions, but they were rambling and confused, referring to landmarks Kullervo didn't know and people he would never meet.

"Maybe a map would help," Liantha finally suggested.

"Yes, yes, I suppose it would," said Roland. "I never was that good with directions. Run and fetch it would you, there's a good girl."

Liantha went off into the back room and returned a little while later with a roll of thin leather. She handed it to Roland, who unrolled it and peered at the black line drawing inside. "Oh, curse these eyes . . . where's the Market District?"

"Here." Liantha helpfully touched it.

"Thank you. Yes, so that would put it right . . . uh . . ." Roland ran his finger over the area indicated, and finally stopped over a spot right on the edge. "Here, along a bit from the guard tower and with a lifter on the other side. I always thought it was brave of you to live on the edge like that, lad— we all know how you were with heights."

Kullervo didn't try to correct him again. He accepted the map and pressed his talon into the spot Roland had shown him, leaving an indentation. "Thanks, Roland. I think I'll go and see it now."

Roland looked slightly alarmed. "You mustn't let anyone see you. They'll kill you, Arren. You know they will."

"All right. I'll make sure I stay hidden," Kullervo said sadly.

"You should not go alone," said Senneck. "I must come with you . . ." She tried to stand up, but sank back again, wincing.

"It's all right," said Kullervo. "I can defend myself if I have to. Anyway, I want to do this alone."

He walked off back toward the entrance. Behind him, unseen, Red crept away from the others and followed him at a distance.

Kullervo was too distracted to notice him. He paused briefly outside the Hatchery and checked the map. The Market District was right alongside the Hatchery to the south, so if he followed the city's edge, he should find the spot without too much trouble.

Satisfied with his plan, and hoping he would recognise what he was after when he saw it, he tucked the map into his belt and set out into the gathering gloom.

24

The Ghost and the Ruins

Kullervo walked through the streets of Eagleholm, picking his way through the rubble and refuse that had clogged what had once been open areas. Here, at the edge of the former Market District, he was walking on planks and moved very carefully, constantly afraid that they might break under his weight. Luckily, they didn't even though a couple of them shifted alarmingly—Kullervo's light griffish bones made him less heavy than he looked.

There was enough sunlight left for him to see where he was going, but as darkness fell, he started to see other light sources: fires, burning here and there inside buildings that looked empty and abandoned. Clearly, there were still people around here somewhere though he didn't see any directly, and only saw their shadows and sometimes heard movement.

He decided to keep quiet and avoid drawing attention to himself even though he made no attempt to hide his wings. If he looked like just an ordinary Northerner, it would be far more dangerous if anyone saw him. His wings, at least, might make attackers hesitate.

His map had been drawn a long time ago, when the city was whole, and it proved almost completely useless beyond having shown him that the house would be on the edge. Nowadays, it was almost impossible to recognise any of the landmarks shown on it, and in the end it was more thanks to luck that he found what he was after. And when he did, it wasn't because of anything he saw, but from the smell.

As he walked along the edge of the city while the stars started to shine above and on the horizon, a stench hit his nostrils. He had already smelled bad things—rotting food, sewerage, and sickly fires—but this new odour was something much worse, enough so to make him cringe when he noticed it.

It was the putrid stench of rotting meat, and not just any meat.

Kullervo's nose was sensitive enough to tell him that what he was smelling was human corpses. It was a smell he had only encountered once before: in a cave high up in the First Mountains, where his father's body had been laid to rest.

But this time the smell was far stronger. He would have avoided it, but he soon found that it was coming from a spot on the edge of the city, and he would have to walk right past it if he wanted to stay on course. So he followed the stench, remembering that word healers used to describe odours that were bad enough to cause illness. "Miasma."

Kullervo clambered over a heap of rotten wood and found an appalling sight.

Right on the very edge of the city, still perched precariously on the rickety planking, was a house—or the remains of one. Two walls were still standing, opposite each other, but the one that had run along the city's edge was gone, and Kullervo could see over the darkened landscape beyond.

In the middle, between the jagged, half-burned walls, were the bodies. Dozens of human corpses in various states of decay, deliberately piled up on what had once been a floor. Only one of them was outside. It was a smaller body, a child, laid in front of the doorframe that was still standing.

Kullervo stood there, dumb-struck. He couldn't imagine why anyone would do this. Why carry the dead all this way, right to one of the most dangerous spots in the city, just to put them here? Surely, people would leave their dead friends somewhere holy, like wherever the city's Temple was or had been. But instead, they'd brought them here, to what looked like nothing more than somebody's burned-out house, and not even a very big house at that.

Grim insight took hold of him then. Holding his breath, he went closer and peered at the ruins. The light was nearly all gone, but his eyes were strong enough to make out the faint marks of letters on the walls.

He couldn't read very well, but he knew enough Cymrian letters to work out some of what had been daubed or cut into the charred wood.

BURN FOREVER.
A cuRSe on yoU.
freeze in the void Aren Cardokson

Kullervo clasped his hands together and lowered his head as if in reverence. He had found his father's old home, and now he saw what Roland had meant. The people of Eagleholm knew who had destroyed all their lives, and they had come to curse his memory and to desecrate his home. Laying their dead at his doorstep, where they belonged. And this was what Kullervo had come so far to find.

Despair overtook him, and not caring if anyone saw him, he knelt in front of that horrible temple of death. He tried to say something, maybe even pray—though not to the gods, not even now. But his words died in his throat, where the lump that had been there ever since his talk with Roland finally came loose.

Kullervo covered his face with his big, clumsy hands, and cried.

"Kullervo? Are you all right?" a nervous voice intruded on him.

Kullervo raised his head, and turned it to see Red picking his way through the rubble. The boy looked very pale, but he was determined enough to keep on toward his friend. "Oh Gryphus . . . gods . . . what *is* this?" he mumbled, looking as if he were about to vomit.

Kullervo managed to stand up. "Don't look at it, Red."

But Red came to his side anyway and looked up at him with concern. "What were you cryin' about? Did you know any of them?"

"No." Kullervo rubbed his face. "Did you follow me here?"

"Yeah. I wanted to see where you was goin'."

"Here," said Kullervo. "I was going here. But I wish . . ."

Red couldn't quite bring himself to look at the corpses. "*This* is where your dad lived?"

"Yes." Kullervo shuddered.

Red made himself look, and immediately started to retch. "Oh Gryphus . . . it stinks!"

"I know. You don't have to stay here, Red."

"Then let's go!" the boy said at once. "Let's go back to Roland's place."

"In a little while," said Kullervo. "I want to stay here for a bit. I need to . . . think. But you don't have to stay with me. Why don't you go over there and wait for me? I need to be alone for a while."

"All right," said Red.

"But don't go too far," said Kullervo. "This place isn't safe."

"Don't worry; I ain't stupid," said Red. "Anyway, there's nothing but rubbish around here, and it's too dark. I'll go . . . there." He pointed to the pile of wood Kullervo had climbed over before. "Liantha said it would be good if we had more wood, so I'll look an' see if any of it's good for burning."

"You do that," said Kullervo.

Once Red was out of sight on the other side of the woodpile, Kullervo turned to look at the house again. Night had all but come, and only the faintest grey glow was left in the sky. Ignoring the stench, he went as close as he could and reached up to touch the doorframe. It swayed alarmingly when his fingers brushed it, but didn't fall, and he guessed it must have been very sturdy once upon a time. As for the walls, they were thin and rotting, full of holes, and the small talons he had in place of fingernails scratched away flakes of charcoal. He wondered when the house had burned and who had lit the fire. Most likely, after the Eyrie had been destroyed and people had found out who had done it, a mob would have gathered here. Maybe they had been hoping to find the wretched Northerner who lived there, but by then he was already dead, so they must have burned his house by way of revenge.

Kullervo tried to imagine what his father might have been like in those days. He couldn't have always been the blood-thirsty monster he had become. Nobody was born that way. Had Arren Cardockson ever been a good man? Roland had made it sound as if he had. But something had happened to him, something so horrible it had driven him mad, something that had put so much hatred into him that the Night God had found him worthy to be her creature.

Roland had said that the entire city had been what destroyed Arren, or the people that lived in it maybe. Laela had told Kullervo what she knew about their father's background, but it wasn't much. Just that he had once been called Arren Cardockson and had lived here. And died here, too.

It was all too easy, Kullervo thought, to think of his father as just a monster, or as an evil man. But once, Kullervo had killed people, and even though he hated the memory of what he had done, it was a dark reminder of how easily it could happen. In the right circumstances, anyone could become a murderer. And the circumstances here had been terrible. They must have been.

"I wish I could have known you," he said aloud. "I wish I could have understood. I'm trying to."

He didn't know what he should do, but despite the darkness that had made the house nothing but an outline, he couldn't bring himself to leave just yet. He had come so far, but now he didn't quite know why, or what he had planned to do when he got there.

Moving slowly for fear of bumping into something, he went back toward the front of the house.

He stood there by the doorframe for some time, almost as if he expected something to happen. But nothing did, and by the time an impatient Red came to check on him, he had realised that nothing was going to happen. He had come here for nothing.

Red had an armload of wood that must have passed muster, and he kept a good distance away from the defiled ruin. "Can we go back now?" he asked.

Kullervo shook himself. "Yes . . . yes, we should go. I'm sorry I kept you waiting."

"It's all right." Red almost fled from the stench.

Kullervo cast one last glance at the house he could barely see any more, and followed. *That was my inheritance,* he thought. *All my father left me was a heap of dead.*

But it wasn't in Kullervo's nature to mope for long. He hurried on after Red, not wanting to lose track of him when they could both get lost in the dark. Fortunately, Red seemed to know which way he should go because he headed straight back toward the Hatchery without much hesitation.

It was only a short journey, even in the dark, but along the way Kullervo quickly noticed that he was being watched. On both sides of the road, people had begun to appear in doorways and windows. Most of them carried burning pieces of wood from the fires he had seen, and their faces looked glaringly pale in the gloom. Gaunt faces, hollow-eyed from starvation, some of them pockmarked by disease. The eyes looked like black holes, all staring straight at him without expression.

Kullervo tried not to look back at them, but it was all he could do not to run the rest of the way back to the Hatchery.

There, thank goodness, the lamp was still burning. Resling and Keera were still there, both asleep in a corner. Seerae had moved away to the opposite corner and was talking to Liantha in a low voice. Roland was still sitting in the spot where he'd been before, but there was no sign of Senneck.

Kullervo went straight to Roland. "Where's Senneck?"

Roland jerked slightly, as if waking up. "Eh? What's that, lad?"

"Senneck," said Kullervo. "Where did she go?"

"Oh, she's gone next door," said Roland. "Back to her old quarters. But she needs to be alone now. Don't go over there, Arren, or you either, lad."

"Why not?" asked Kullervo. "She's not sick, is she?"

"No, no, but she's laying her eggs now, and we all know how dangerous it is to disturb a female when she does that." Roland looked sternly at Red. "And don't you go thinking you can sneak a look either! She'll attack to kill if she sees you."

Red shivered. "I won't."

Kullervo sat down beside the old man. "I hope we can carry the eggs with us; she didn't say if she wanted to hatch them here, too, but there's no way she could. There's not enough food here."

"No, not at all," said Roland. "But eggs can be carried if you need to. In fact . . ." He struggled to his feet, supporting himself with a stick, and shuffled off into the back room where he lived.

He was gone for so long that Kullervo started to worry, and even moved to go and see if he was all right, but he returned at that moment, carrying a misshapen leather object.

"Here," he said, handing it over. "An egg-bag. Hadn't used it in so long, or not for eggs—had to empty out some books first!"

Kullervo examined it. It was indeed a bag, but a huge, square one, whose insides were divided into six heavily padded compartments. The flap that closed it was even more padded, and fitted with no less than ten buckled straps. Clearly, nobody wanted the contents to even shift around.

"See, it's insulated to protect the eggs," said Roland. "One in each space, so they don't crack together. You warm it up by a fire first; the padding holds the heat very well, I've found."

"Can I have it?" asked Kullervo.

Roland laughed his wheezy laugh. "Not likely I'll ever need it, lad!"

"Thank you." Kullervo put the bag aside. "Listen . . . when we leave, I want you to come with us."

"What?" Roland shook his head slowly. "No, no, I can't leave. Too old now, not strong enough for travelling, and old Keth died a long time ago, so there's nobody to carry me."

"I'm sure Senneck would agree to carry you," said Kullervo. "You shouldn't stay here; it's too dangerous right on the edge, and you can't have much food left."

"Not much," said Roland. "Only what still grows up here in the rubble. But this is my home, lad. Been my home now for eighty-odd years. Too late for leaving now."

"But don't you want to meet Flell's daughter?" said Kullervo. "She's still out there, you know, and I'm sure she'd love to hear you tell her about her mother. She never knew her. And besides, she could give you a better home."

"I don't know . . ."

"At least think about it," said Kullervo. "I really don't want to leave you here in this place when I could help you get away. And Liantha could come, too," he added.

Roland rubbed his eyes. "I know she'd like to go. She always says she wants to see a proper city again someday. I suppose I could think it over, maybe. But for now I should probably get some rest. Old men need their sleep!"

"Of course." Kullervo smiled. "Do you want me to help you to your room?"

"I'd appreciate it," said Roland. "I never was too proud to ask for help, not like you, Arren. Pride always was your downfall, you know."

Kullervo almost laughed out loud at the irony of that as he helped Roland up. Arren might have been too proud for his own good, but Kullervo had almost no pride at all.

Roland leaned on his stick with one hand and let Kullervo support his other arm, and the two of them made a slow and careful trip toward the back room.

And then, a scream came from the adjoining room. Kullervo and Roland both froze. The scream came again.

"Senneck's in trouble!" said Kullervo.

Roland gave his arm a reassuring squeeze. "Laying troubles, lad. They happen all the time, but we aren't allowed to help. It's an insult to the mother's pride, you see."

Kullervo reluctantly agreed, and might have gone back to helping Roland, but then the scream came a third time. This time it was louder, and this time it was a word.

"Kullervo!"

"She needs me," Kullervo said sharply. "Red! Come here, now!"

The boy came running. "What should I do?"

"You look after Roland," said Kullervo. "I have to go help Senneck. Don't come after me, any of you!"

Resling and Keera had woken up, and both looked anxious. Liantha and Seerae, breaking off their conversation, glanced at each other.

"Stay here," Kullervo told them fiercely, and ran into the other half of the Hatchery.

But what he found there was not what he had expected at all.

People had invaded the building, a whole group of them. They carried burning torches, and many of them had weapons. They were closing in on one of the nesting places, where Senneck lay, and Kullervo heard her hissing a warning at them.

He ran forward. "Get away from her!"

The people ignored him. They entered the nest, as if they couldn't hear Senneck's threats at all, and their weapons plunged downward.

Simultaneously, Kullervo heard a shout from behind him, back in the chick room. Panicking, he darted back to the entranceway and saw more people, coming in from the street outside. They, too, were armed.

Old Roland took a step toward them, and held up a wrinkled hand. "Stop!" he said. "I don't have any food for you, I swear—"

A heavy wooden club hit him, hard, in the face. He fell backward, and in an instant, chaos broke loose. Keera and

Seerae both charged at the intruders, bounding straight over
Roland's body as if he weren't even there. But the ragged people did not run away, or even show much fear. More of them
were coming in.

Back in the adult chamber, Kullervo could hear Senneck
screaming as she tried to fight in the midst of her laying. He
saw Red try to run for cover, yelling for help. Liantha, madly
diving into the mass of attackers to rescue Roland. Resling,
drawing his sword as two scrawny men advanced on him. So
far, nobody seemed to have noticed Kullervo.

He never knew why he thought to do what he did next.

Rushing forward, he shouted at the top of his voice. *"You!
Southerners! I'm here! Here!"*

People turned to look at him.

Kullervo hoped that the torchlight was enough to show his
bony features, and his black hair.

"It's me!" he yelled wildly. "Arren Cardockson! I've come
back to kill you all!" And he even laughed, wildly, as he imagined his father might have laughed. "Come and get me!"

It worked. Hands rose to point at him, and shouts began.

"It's him! He's here!"

Hatred rippled through the mob. Forgetting whatever they
had come here to do, they came straight at Kullervo.

Kullervo ran back into the adult chamber and charged at the
people attacking Senneck. "I'm Arren Cardockson!" he shouted
at them. "Come and fight me, you Southern scum!"

Then they, too, were after him, and he put his head down
and ran straight out of the building and into the street.

There were more people out there—the same people who
had watched him in the street.

They closed in on him.

Kullervo had no weapon or much knowledge of how to use
one. But he didn't need one. His mouth stretched into a mad
snarl, and for the first time he gathered up his new strength, and
unleashed it in full force.

The starving survivors were no match. Kullervo lashed out
with his talons, and followed it up with massive punches. He
grabbed people in his oversized hands and hurled them aside,
and as others struck back with their weapons, and he felt the
pain, his griffin side took hold, and he went berserk.

Losing himself in a haze of fury and fighting madness, he slashed with his talons as a griffin would, and even bit with his jagged teeth, drawing blood more than once.

He was barely even aware of it when the others came out of the Hatchery to help him. Keera and Seerae charged in, and Resling and Liantha as well. Even Red came, wielding a knife he had picked up somewhere.

But Kullervo's madness was his downfall. Heedless of any need to protect himself, or do anything but mindlessly hurl himself at anyone who came near, he couldn't keep going forever. A blow to his leg made him stumble, and in that instant something flashed and tore down the side of his face.

"Blackrobe!" voices screamed, as mad as he was.

Something else hit him in the back of the head, and he fell.

He felt other blows strike his body as he lay there, and knew with a distant, serene certainty that they were killing him. Taking their revenge at last.

After that, there was only fading pain, and a darkness that seemed to pull him in with icy hands.

Come to me, a voice whispered. *Be with me now, now . . . claim your inheritance now . . .*

No, Kullervo whispered back. *Never . . .*

Then be dead, said the voice.

25

Endings and Beginnings

Light returned to Kullervo in a thin sliver, and his sense came back confused. Pain shuddered through his limbs and face, but despite his confusion and the knowledge that he was hurt, he made an effort to get up.

"He's awake!" someone yelled. The voice felt painfully loud.

Hands had him by the shoulders. They were lifting, dragging him backward. The griffin side still thought he was under attack, but he was too weak just then to put up much resistance.

Other hands tried to lift his legs. "It's all right," another voice said. "We're taking you back inside."

Kullervo's eyes opened fully, and made pain lance downward. The whole right side of his face hurt. But his head was clearing quickly. He mustn't be as badly injured as he had thought.

He coughed, and managed to speak in a thick mumble. "Let me try and get up."

The people dragging him let go and moved to lift him into a sitting position. He peered at them, and relief made him feel much better. Resling was there, and Liantha, and Red. They were all alive, and none looked badly wounded. Only Red had a shallow cut on his forehead.

Kullervo tentatively touched his own face, and winced. Something had laid his cheek open from his eye to his mouth; blood was already congealing on the skin around it.

But though there were numerous throbbing bruises and cuts

on his chest and arms, and a nasty ache in his leg, he seemed to be more or less fine. The blow to the head that had knocked him out must have been the worst injury he'd collected.

He managed to stand up, wobbling slightly as dizziness made the world spin briefly around him, and massaged the back of his head. A lump bulged under his hair.

The others all looked relieved. "We thought you might be badly hurt, sir," said Resling.

"I'll be fine," said Kullervo. He tensed as recollection came back. "What about the others? Senneck?"

"Senneck's a bit cut up," said Liantha. "We could only look at a distance; she's still trying to lay. But she can't be that bad. None of them were very well armed, and they were all very weak. If not, we'd probably all be dead."

"And Roland?"

The others looked grim.

"He's unconscious," said Liantha. "We've put him in his bed, but I don't know . . ."

Kullervo's head had started to ache savagely, but he ignored it and made for the building. There was no sign of any of the people who had attacked him. "Why did they do that?" he asked. "What *happened*?"

"They're desperate," said Liantha. "Starving. We have a store of food here; we've been sharing it, but it's never enough."

"But why attack Senneck?"

"I told you; they're desperate," said Liantha. "Starvation does that to people. Makes them want to eat anything they can find."

Kullervo gaped. "They wanted to *eat* her . . . ?"

Liantha did not look shocked, only resigned. "They eat each other sometimes. But there's more meat on a griffin."

Kullervo tried to get his mind around her story—not an easy thing to do, and not just because of the headache. "But that's not why they came here, is it?" he said eventually. "It's because of me. They saw me in the street, and they followed me here. They thought I was my father."

"Well, you did *tell* them you were," Resling pointed out. "We all heard you."

"Of course I did!" said Kullervo. "They were killing Senneck, and all of you. I had to lead them away, or . . ."

"You were real brave," said Red.

The pain in Kullervo's head spiked. "I was a damn fool," he muttered. "Oh gods, I didn't kill any of them, did I?"

"No," said Resling. "You hurt plenty, but they weren't fool enough to keep on after you went into a frenzy like that! They only got you down by luck, and we drove them off you. They ran away after that."

Kullervo sighed. "That's good."

"Why?" asked Resling. "They were lunatics. They would have killed us all if they could."

"That doesn't matter," said Kullervo. "I never want to kill anyone ever again, no matter who they are. Where did Seerae and Keera go?"

"Chasing the mob," said Liantha. "To make sure they don't come back. They shouldn't be gone long."

"Let's hope not, or we'll be undefended," said Resling.

"Yes . . ." said Kullervo. "But we'd better go and see Roland now."

The old man was in the back room of the Hatchery that had been his home for decades. It was a small space, and sparsely furnished, but so badly cluttered that there wouldn't have been room for any other furniture than what there was: a table with two chairs, two beds, and a cupboard beside a fireplace.

The mess, on the other hand, was everywhere. Books were stacked haphazardly on the table and more stood in dust-covered rows on top of the cupboard. A large wooden chest stood open, not so much out of laziness but because the spare clothes spilling out of it would have made closing the lid impossible.

In any other circumstances, it would have been an amusing and pleasantly eccentric sight, but when Kullervo saw the frail old figure lying in the bed closest to the fireplace, it felt more like a shrine, or a monument to a life that had fallen apart and would now never recover.

Roland was still unconscious, scarcely breathing, and on his forehead, blood had oozed and dried. The moment Kullervo looked at him, he knew that the old man would never wake up. He had seen the blow that had knocked him down, and now he saw the injury as well, he didn't need any more evidence to know it would be fatal. Roland had been weak enough already.

Kullervo knelt by his bedside, ignoring the resulting twinge in his leg, and touched the old man's forehead. It felt frighteningly cold.

He looked back at the others. "Do any of you know about healing?"

"I do," said Liantha. "But we have no medicines left or ingredients for making them. People come to us for healing, you see, and by now . . ." She shook her head, and said more softly, "And anyway, I know there's no point. Even if I had a full healer's kit, there would be nothing I could do for him."

"Yes . . ." Kullervo stood up, wincing. "I should go and check on Senneck."

"Be careful," Resling warned.

Kullervo nodded absently and went back into the chick room. Seerae and Keera were there, both visibly out of breath.

"So you did not die after all," Seerae said by way of greeting.

Kullervo tried to smile, but stopped when it made his face hurt. "Did you chase them all away, then?"

"We have seen them off," said Keera. She looked positively excited at having finally seen some action. "They will not return, and if they do, we shall kill them."

"They won't," said Kullervo, hoping he was right. "But you should keep a watch out."

"We shall," Seerae hissed in annoyance.

Kullervo went off into the adult chamber, limping slightly. He felt sick with fear for Senneck's sake, even after Liantha's assurance that she was fine.

Senneck was where she had been before, lying motionless on her side. Kullervo ran toward her, but as she came into proper view he saw a great convulsion go through her lower body and realised that she was lying that way from exhaustion, not injury.

Senneck didn't seem to notice him. There was congealed blood and muck on her hind legs, but Kullervo couldn't see any sign of eggs. But at least she did not look badly wounded; as Liantha had said, the only marks on her were some cuts on her face and one foreleg. Her attackers had been too poorly armed, and Kullervo had come early enough to save her.

Senneck's eyes were half-closed, and her breathing was convulsive. She opened her beak wide as he watched, and gasped sharply as another contraction moved through her swollen belly.

Kullervo was not afraid. He moved closer to her and called her name.

Senneck's eyes snapped open, and a faint hiss came from her throat. But she did not attack or even try to get up. Clearly, she was too exhausted to be a danger to anyone.

"Are you all right?" Kullervo asked.

Senneck's reply was as gasping as her breath, and even drier than usual. "You . . . are alive. I am glad. So glad . . . I thought . . . and could not go to you . . . "

"I'll be fine," said Kullervo. "And the others are fine, except for Roland."

"Roland . . ." Senneck's blue eyes rolled backward as she convulsed again. "He is hurt . . . ?"

"He's dying," said Kullervo. "I think they've cracked his skull."

Senneck's front paws scrabbled at the nesting material, as if for a moment she wanted to get up. "Cowards! If I had . . . could have . . . *aaaahk*!" She sank back with a rasp of pain, front talons curling in on themselves with yet another contraction.

Kullervo went to her and put his hands to her head. "Senneck, calm down. Don't worry about anything else; we'll be ready if they come back. Just concentrate on getting through this."

She bit weakly at his fingers. "I do not need . . . you must not . . ."

Kullervo ignored her. "I'm going to stay with you until it's over."

Senneck subsided again. "You cannot . . . help me."

"But I can keep you company," said Kullervo. "And anyway, I want to be here in case we're attacked again."

"Then stay," said Senneck, and fell silent.

So Kullervo stayed. He sat beside her the entire night, murmuring to comfort her when he saw she was in pain, sometimes stroking her face. The others next door left them both alone, clearly much too cautious to risk disturbing Senneck as he had done. But he could hear them moving around and the murmuring of their voices, and that was enough to tell him they were fine.

Most of the time, he kept his eyes on Senneck. It was troubling, but almost reassuring to see her so vulnerable. Since the
start of their journey South together, she had often been hostile,
and argued against him again and again. Kullervo had forgiven
her, of course—it was just her nature to be combative, and under
different circumstances, he would have bowed to her judgment.
But now he was reminded that even she could need help and
comforting, even if she was too proud to accept it easily.

It reminded him, too, of why he loved her.

Well before dawn, however, he had begun to fear for her as
well. She had continued to struggle with her laying, but not a
single egg had appeared, and she was growing steadily more
and more exhausted, often falling asleep for short periods in
between contractions. Kullervo had never watched a laying
before, but his instincts told him this was not right. One egg at
least should have come by now.

Dawn had begun to lighten the sky outside, and still Senneck had not laid. She had fallen asleep again, and Kullervo
watched her, not feeling tired at all himself.

While he sat there, watching in silence, lantern-light came
into the room and hurt his eyes.

He stood up stiffly. "Who's that?"

"It's Liantha. How is she?"

Kullervo shook his head. "She hasn't laid anything yet. I
don't know . . ."

Liantha's face was pale. "Roland just died."

"Oh." Kullervo felt numb. "I'm so sorry."

"He had a good long life," said Liantha. "I just wish it could
have ended differently . . ."

"I understand," said Kullervo. "And I'm sorry that I helped
it to happen that way. I never realised anyone was following me."

"Don't blame yourself," said Liantha. "You did your best."

"Thank you." Kullervo looked at her in silence for a
moment. "What are you going to do now?" he asked.

Liantha's brow furrowed in a determined frown. "I'm Roland's
heir," she said. "This Hatchery is mine now. So I'm going to take
charge and see what I can do to make things better."

"It sounds like a good plan," Kullervo said, as brightly as he could. He glanced over his shoulder, and took a step closer to her. "Look . . . I don't know if I should be asking this now, but is there anything you can do for Senneck? I'm sure it shouldn't take this long."

"Layings sometimes do take a long time, Roland said," said Liantha. "Though I've never seen one myself. But if there haven't been any eggs yet at all, that's not a good sign."

Kullervo's heart sank. "Then what can I do? Is there anything?"

Liantha thought it over. "You can try helping her to push," she said. "If you think she'll let you."

"I will, then," said Kullervo. "Thank you. Now I think you should probably get some rest—you look like you need it."

She smiled wanly. "Speak for yourself. Good luck."

Alone again, Kullervo went back to Senneck. She was still asleep, but he had barely sat down again when she came awake with a cry. Another contraction had begun, and her claws scratched hopelessly at the ground.

Kullervo acted on impulse. He leapt into the nesting pen and straddled the prone griffin, wrapping his arms around her midriff. He could feel the hard shape of an egg under her skin, even covered as it was by layers of wrenching muscle.

He braced himself, and pushed it downward as hard as he could.

Senneck screamed and jerked her head toward him, but couldn't reach him. Desperate now, Kullervo kept hold of her, and now, whenever a contraction came, he pushed with her, adding his strength to hers.

He was never quite sure whether his efforts did anything to help, but however it was, Senneck's egg finally came not long after the sun's first rays had begun to light the sky outside.

There was only one egg—but an egg so huge that it could just about make three. Kullervo gently rolled it into the shelter of Senneck's belly, and let her curl up around it and give it a weak sniff before she finally went to sleep—true sleep now.

Tiredness caught up with Kullervo then, but he had the strength to smile. "Rest now, beloved," he murmured. "You've done it."

He chose the pen next to hers for his own sleeping place, but before he went to curl up in it he took one last look at Senneck as a ray of sunlight lit up her wing and flank.

The light touched the egg, too, but while it made Senneck's feathers glow, it seemed to be sucked into the egg, as if nothing could ever truly light it up.

When Kullervo saw it, he felt his heart grow cold.

The egg was the biggest he had ever seen, and its shell was as black as the void.

26

Flying in Pairs

The little group at the Hatchery gathered together at noon that day and burned Roland's body on a pyre outside the building. Other people in the city, seeing the smoke, came to investigate, and Seerae and Keera immediately prepared themselves to fight. But these intruders were unarmed, and though they looked as gaunt as those who had attacked them the night before, none of them were aggressive. They only gathered around the pyre in silence, not to warm themselves but just to watch.

Liantha, standing by with a sword strapped to her back, began to recite a prayer in Cymrian. It wasn't one Kullervo knew, but Resling did, because he soon joined his voice to hers. And, around the fire, the new arrivals did the same, chanting the words in a kind of rough harmony.

> *Of earth born, and in fire forged.*
> *By sunlight blessed and by cool water soothed.*
> *Then by a breeze in the night blown away,*
> *To a land of blue skies and bright flowers.*
> *Gryphus the giver of life, accept this soul into*
>   *Your embrace.*
> *As life is given to us by You, so it shall return, but*
>   *well and faithfully used.*
> *Receive our noble brother Roland now, we pray . . .*

Kullervo, listening, felt almost ashamed that he was there to hear them. He who had met Gryphus and rejected him, and rejected this faith that gave these people hope even here. But even though he felt alone then, and afraid as well, and wished he could believe the way they did, he knew that he would never be able to. His capacity to worship had become as stunted as his ability to breed.

But he shed tears for Roland—and for Liantha as well. He could imagine how she must be feeling even though she herself didn't seem to be crying. She would do it later, he thought, in private. Some people were like that.

For now she led the others in their prayer, and in others after it, and even sang one of the sacred temple songs that Kullervo had heard when he was small.

But she finished with a speech, spoken to the pyre as it burned lower. "Roland, you were more than a father to me— you were a father to this city. Once you were even a father to griffins like Senneck, who flew all this way after so long just to lay her own eggs under your eye, like her own mother once did. All your life, you helped people, no matter who they were. You were even a friend to the worst of us, when he had no-one else left to turn to." Several people there muttered at this.

"I'm only young," Liantha went on regardless, "And I don't believe I'll ever be as wise as you were. But I'll carry on and remember what you taught me, and let them guide me for the rest of my life." She drew the sword from her back, and held it point down, so the firelight reflected off its rusting blade. "Once this sword belonged to your father. You passed it on to your apprentice when you were young, and after that it was lost. But it was found again, and now it has passed to me. I'll carry it in your name, and one day I'll pass it on to my own children, or to my apprentice, or whoever I believe is worthy to own it."

Silence fell. The pyre had just about burned itself out by now, but no-one had left.

"What will you do?" one of the crowd asked. "Will you share your food the way Roland did?"

"I will," said Liantha.

But before anything else could be said, someone else stepped forward, and not someone anyone would have expected.

Seerae. She pushed past Resling and Keera, and touched Liantha's head with her beak. "Human," she rasped. "Look at me."

Liantha turned. "Yes, Seerae?"

Seerae looked around quickly, as if making sure that all attention was on her. "I have thought long and hard, through yesterday and today, and through the night as well. I have decided."

"Decided what?" asked Liantha.

"I came here not to visit this foul ruin, or to guard my mother and her human," said Seerae. "I came here to find a human of my own. That human will be you."

"Me?" said Liantha. "But . . ."

"You," Seerae repeated. "Do not argue; the choice is mine, and it is made. You are a worthy human, and you are in the right place. I have seen a chance for us to make a future, and we will make it together."

"What future?" said Liantha. "What are you thinking of?"

Seerae looked toward the crowd. "You must tell them. Tell them as I tell you. They must know, for we will need their help."

Liantha hesitated. "All right . . ."

"People of Eagleholm," Seerae began. "You were once proud to call this place your home." She paused to let Liantha translate, and continued. "But now that time is gone. Your home is destroyed, and you have no hope of survival here. Before long, you will all be dead, and there will be nothing left to tell the world what Eagleholm once was. But there is still hope for you."

Liantha continued to translate, and people moved in closer to listen, sensing that something important was about to happen.

"Once," said Seerae, "humans like you made this city great. But you did it under the guidance and protection of griffins, and proud griffiners. Now a griffin has come again, and she has chosen a human. I am Seerae, daughter of Senneck, who was a mighty warrior in the days of the war in the North. Today, I have chosen this human, Liantha, to be mine, and therefore a griffiner. Together, she and I will lead you. We will take you from this accursed place, and we will gather others. All those who now live in these lands that have no ruler, will join under our leadership. And together, we will take back what was once ours! Together, we will make a new Eagleholm, and a new territory around it. And it will be greater than ever before! Griffins will come back, and griffiners, and they will serve us!" Seerae's voice grew louder as she spoke on, and more powerful, but she still stopped to let Liantha speak, too, and her own voice grew louder with her partner's, as she understood what she was being asked to say, and her own excitement grew.

"So join with us!" she said. "Join with Seerae and the Lady Liantha. Let us lead you now, and we will give you a new life, make a new beginning! *New Eagleholm!*"

Most of the people there shouted their approval.

Others were more cautious. "How will we get down from here?" one man yelled.

"I will carry you," said Seerae. "One by one, I will carry you down from this mountain."

"What about our neighbours?" someone else said. "What if they attack us again?"

"They won't," Liantha answered. "None of them want this land; that's why they abandoned it in the first place. Nobody wants this place except us. We still own it, so let's rebuild it! We were a great nation once—why should we let ourselves fade away?"

Kullervo listened to everything in disbelief, then awe. "They're right!" he said impulsively. "Follow them, and they'll show you where to go."

They seemed to notice him for the first time.

"Who's *that*?" someone asked. "Is that a Northerner?"

Resling gestured frantically at Kullervo to stay silent, but he didn't. "Yes," he said, almost fiercely, as if daring them to attack him again. "My name is Kullervo Arrenson."

"*Arrenson?*" a woman in the crowd yelled.

"Kullervo, don't!" said Red. "Shut up, before—"

Kullervo squared his shoulders. "I am Arren Cardockson's son," he said. "But I'm not your enemy. I came back here to try to understand who my father was, and to try and make amends for what he did. Now I know there's nothing I can do, but I brought Seerae here with me, and now she and Liantha can undo my father's crime."

Many of them looked angry, or afraid, but none tried to attack. Word had probably spread about the previous night, and with the griffins there, fighting must have looked like a bad idea.

"You can't stay here," a man spat. "Go away, blackrobe."

"I will," Kullervo promised. "I'm leaving today. Immediately, in fact." He felt he had risked enough, and took a step back in preparation to leave, but there was one last thing he felt he should say.

"I'm so sorry," he said, and hurried away back into the Hatchery.

Senneck had not come outside for the funeral. She was far too weakened from her laying, and had slept through the whole morning. She was still asleep when Kullervo went back to check on her, but breathing peacefully, one wing spread protectively over her egg.

Kullervo's gaze lingered on the egg. Even now he had half hoped that its colour—or lack of it—had been his imagination, but it was as black now as it had been at dawn. He couldn't see a single fleck of any other shade.

There was no way to tell what the dark shell signified, but Kullervo knew enough about griffins to know that their eggs always came in varying shades of brown, or occasionally white. Black was unheard of.

But then Kullervo knew what griffin had fathered this one. Were all of Skandar's offspring born from black-shelled eggs? Somehow he doubted it. Whatever else this hatchling would be, it would be very big. It was painful just to think of Senneck's having to lay this egg, which was so huge Kullervo would have had trouble carrying it even in his powerful arms. It was a wonder she had managed it at all, and Kullervo doubted she would be able to fly far for some time.

But he knew that she would have to fly at least a little, and soon. Staying in the city any longer would be insanity, especially after he had revealed himself to the crowd like that.

Kullervo sat down by Senneck's nest and thought it over. When she woke up, he would ask her if she felt ready to fly. If she did, then they would be able to leave at once. Red could ride on her back and carry his egg—she would accept him if he had charge of it—and Kullervo would go in griffin shape. They could just go as far as the foot of the mountain, and camp there until she had recovered enough to journey on.

He wondered if he should risk making the change again after the previous night's beating. Careful inspection hadn't revealed any serious injuries, but his limbs had stiffened horribly overnight, and his headache kept returning.

Maybe he would be better off asking Keera to take him down the mountain, and make the change later, when he felt strong enough.

For now, he went back to his nesting spot and went to sleep in it. Danger was all very well, but he was nearly as exhausted as Senneck must be, and he would need his strength for whatever lay ahead.

In the end, Kullervo and his friends did not leave that day, but they took care not to show themselves in the open until they did leave on the morning of the next day. Senneck had needed that time to recover, and nobody wanted to force her, least of all Kullervo, who was the most anxious to go.

Fortunately, though, it seemed Senneck wasn't as badly off as she had looked, and once she had had plenty of sleep and eaten whatever food was left for her, she was able to walk around again—though she was a little unsteady on her hind legs. It seemed female griffins were well adapted to this sort of thing.

As for Seerae and Liantha, they spent all their time together. Mostly they talked, discussing their plans for founding New Eagleholm. When people came to see them, as they did once word had spread about the speech they had given, they went out to meet them. This time, though, Seerae was content to let Liantha do the talking. She had said her piece, and from now on the tedious negotiating was for her human to do.

Liantha rose to the occasion without complaint. She had accepted Seerae's choosing of her with impressive calmness, and it was clear that she was more than eager to commit to her new partner's dream. Kullervo guessed it was probably a dream she herself had had at least once. Now she had the power to make it come true.

When Senneck was lively enough to talk, Kullervo went to her and described his plan. She listened seriously. "You think that this boy can be trusted with my egg?"

"Yes," said Kullervo. "But the choice is up to you. If you'd prefer, you can carry it yourself in your talons, or I can carry it. It'll only be a short trip anyway, and after that we can take time to recover and think of a new strategy if we need one."

Senneck thought it over. "Let me see this egg pouch."

Kullervo brought it, and showed her its features. "Of course the egg won't fit in these compartments, but they're just laced in—I can detach it here and here, and take out this bit. That should make a space big enough."

"It has a long strap," Senneck observed. "Long enough to loop around my neck. It could be held against my chest. That way it will be safe and will not hit the ground when I land."

Kullervo inspected the strap. "It feels sturdy enough. And Red could keep an eye on it in the air."

"Yes. I will trust him to do that," said Senneck. "Normally I would not allow him on my back, but he is only small, and I need him for this purpose. He has enough sense around griffins to be trusted."

"He does," said Kullervo, as proudly as if Red were his own son.

"Now," said Senneck. "I want to speak with Seerae."

"I'll go and get her," said Kullervo.

Seerae came back with him easily enough, and Kullervo left her and Senneck to talk. Senneck already knew about what her daughter had done, and Kullervo guessed that she wanted to offer her some advice on how to be a partnered griffin. And maybe she wanted to tell her something about Eagleholm as it had been once upon a time.

Either way, it was none of Kullervo's business.

Whatever they talked about, Seerae surprised him the next morning by offering to be the one to carry him away from Eagleholm.

"In gratitude that you brought me here to my human, I will do this for you," she said, sounding as dispassionate as her mother. "And I cannot have you here in my city any longer. My human followers want you gone, and while you are here, you may cause another fight."

Kullervo had enough sense to look flattered rather than insulted. "What about Liantha?" he asked. "Both of us would be too heavy."

"My human will stay here," said Seerae. She rarely called

Liantha by her name—mostly, Kullervo thought, because she got too much pride from calling her "my human" instead.

With that, the last detail was settled, and they made their preparations and left well before noon. With Senneck's egg safely bundled up and slung around her neck, and all three griffins harnessed, they went to a spot at the edge of the city that overlooked the northward plains they had crossed before.

Before he got onto Seerae's back, Kullervo stopped to say a last goodbye to Liantha.

"Roland would have been proud of you," he said. "I'm sure of it. And I know you can do this. You've done more than find a purpose for yourself; you've given it to everyone else here."

Liantha smiled. "You know, you're not what I would have expected Arren Cardockson's son to be at all."

Kullervo shrugged. "I'm only half him, you know. The other half is griffin."

"Yes, so you said before," said Liantha. "And I still don't believe it. But thank you. And send my partner back safely!"

"I will do that myself," said Seerae.

"I know you will." Liantha gave Kullervo a quick hug. "You saved all our lives, Kullervo Arrenson, and I'll never forget it. You're not like your father at all, and don't you ever let anyone tell you otherwise."

"I won't," said Kullervo. "Goodbye, Lian— I mean, *Lady* Liantha. And one day, Eyrie Mistress Liantha."

"Maybe, one day!" Liantha laughed. "Now get going!"

Kullervo got onto Seerae's back. Nearby, Keera and Senneck were both taking off. Seerae took a moment to give her human a gentle nudge with her beak. "Wait for me, but do not worry," she said. "I will be back before another day begins."

Then she, too, took to the air.

Kullervo hadn't expected that they would go much beyond the mountain, but the three griffins surprised him by going much further. Perhaps they had decided it together beforehand, because they went on toward evening, heading north, and even Senneck flew with impressive endurance.

They rested several times, on temporary perches, but did not allow their riders to dismount until that evening, when they finally touched down in the same ruined village where they had stayed before.

There, everyone got down and Senneck hobbled off into the tumble-down barn with her egg-bag hanging between her fore-legs. The others glanced at each other and followed, even Seerae.

Inside, Senneck had unhooked the bag and was trying to open it with her beak.

"Here, let me," said Kullervo. He undid the straps and checked on the egg—it was still nicely warm. But he lifted it out anyway and laid it down by Senneck, who curled up around it and finally allowed herself to relax.

"Here will be a good place for you to rest," said Seerae. "And perhaps the humans here will be willing to help if you ask them to. I will stay with you tonight and leave at first light."

She was as good as her word, and left before any of the others had even woken up, when dawn had scarcely even begun. But Kullervo, lying close to Senneck, woke up to the sound of talons on the ground.

He recognised Seerae's scent, and lay still, with his eyes closed, listening.

"Mother," her voice said softly. "I must leave now. I do not think we will see each other again."

"Go, then," Senneck replied just as quietly. "You have all the strength that you will need, and the cunning as well."

"You think that I have done well, then?" Seerae asked, with just the faintest trace of pleading. It was not a question any griffin would ever ask—except from her mother.

"You have," said Senneck. "Your choice of human was wise, and your opportunity could not be better. I am very proud that you came from my egg, and I know that one day you will be a ruler of a great territory."

"Thank you, Mother."

"Stay," said Senneck. "There is one other thing I must tell you."

"Yes?"

"I will not stay here, or in the South as you know," said Senneck. "I will return North when my task with my human is done. But do not be afraid of me. When the time comes, and my position changes, I will not oppose you. Do not forget that this was once my home territory, and that you are my daughter. My ambition will not extend beyond my borders."

"I believe you," said Seerae. "And thank you. I will be glad to remember your promise one day, and I will remember my own to you."

"Go now, then," said Senneck. "Go and protect your human, and begin your journey toward dominance. It will be glorious!"

"It will," said Seerae. "Goodbye, Mother."

Her pawsteps moved away, and Kullervo, still lying quite still, felt his heart pattering. He wondered what Senneck had meant.

He went back to sleep again a short time later, and by the time he woke up again, he had all but forgotten what he had heard. And surely it didn't matter, anyway. Seerae and Liantha had their purpose, and he had his. Now, he could truly begin.

27

The Shell Breaks

Kullervo's journey from that point on was a long one, and would be recorded in the histories of every town and city he passed through on his way. Nobody who saw him in those months ever forgot him. After all, who would forget a winged man, one who travelled with such an odd group of companions and seemed to have no fear even though he was clearly a Northerner? Kullervo certainly didn't make any efforts to hide who he was, even after what had happened at Eagleholm. Wherever he went, he introduced himself with both who and what. He was a half-griffin, he was a Prince, he was Arenadd Taranisäii's son, and he was travelling on behalf of his sister, Queen Laela.

Nobody telling a story that ludicrous could be forgotten in a hurry, wings or no wings.

After taking some time in Carrick to recover some strength, he and his companions moved on westward, to Wylam. It took just under three months.

At Wylam, which was an odd city built in and around the waters of Woodger's Dam, Kullervo once again demanded to speak to the Eyrie Master. The Master, the ageing Lord Kyron, was intrigued enough by this winged stranger to give him an audience. After that, he let him speak to the council as well.

Kullervo did, and spoke with as much passion as he had in Liranwee. The council listened, and, afterward, he and his friends were given quarters to use while they waited to hear whatever decision they made.

That very night, while the companions rested, Senneck's egg began to hatch.

She had carried it carefully through the entire journey, and with Red's help and Kullervo's as well, it had stayed warm—though there had been a couple of close calls. Now, Senneck had announced that the incubation period was over and they had all been keeping an ear out for the telltale sounds of cheeping.

Those had started sometime that afternoon, and the actual hatching started at about the same time as a gold-tinged half-moon reached its highest point outside.

Senneck watched over the hatching, in her nest, but she allowed Kullervo and Red in to watch—by now, she was used to their having contact with her young, and had lost the normal anxiety of a mother griffin.

Red brought in a lantern and sat at a respectable distance beside Kullervo, watching excitedly as the black egg began to crack. It took a while, but gradually, as it rocked around against Senneck's belly, it formed a crack that spread in an almost straight line, travelling back to meet itself on the other side. It was almost as if the chick knew the fastest way to escape.

Eventually, though, as the egg stopped moving every so often while the chick rested, Red grew impatient. "How long is it meant to take?" he asked.

"Not much longer, I think," said Kullervo.

"He is right," said Senneck, speaking for the first time. "This egg is hatching much more quickly than my first clutch. The chick must be a strong one." She looked and sounded very proud, and rightfully so.

The egg moved again, and the crack spread. A big piece of shell broke away, white on the inside, and for a moment the onlookers caught a glimpse of a small beak.

After that, the hatching was more or less done. The egg rolled over, and the top half split away, spilling the chick out onto the ground.

It lay there, half-in and half-out of its shell, shivering and gasping for breath.

"Ew, it's all slimy!" Red exclaimed.

Kullervo nudged him playfully. "So were you when *you* were born! Damn me, look at the *size* of it. That's the biggest chick I ever saw!"

The chick was as massive as its egg had been—longer than one of Kullervo's arms. Its eyes were big bulges on either side of its head, still sealed shut under dark, slick down. The skin, easily visible, was dark as well, and stayed dark under the paler fur on the chick's hindquarters. Kullervo caught a glimpse of a little black pad on one of its hind paws.

An inner chill made him shiver. "A dark chick from a dark egg," he said. "A giant one."

Senneck licked the chick's head and guided it back toward the shelter of her belly fur. "The Mighty Skandar has given me a fine hatchling," she said. "As big and dark as he himself must have been. One day, it will rival him in size."

"For sure," said Kullervo. He thought back to the griffins he had seen at Malvern and among the Unpartnered. There were plenty of big griffins there, all offspring of Skandar, but not one of them had been like this chick. None of them had inherited their father's full colouring, and Kullervo had a feeling that none of them had hatched from black eggs like this one had.

"This is Skandar's true heir," he said aloud. "If griffins have heirs. I wonder if it's male or female?"

Senneck was still grooming the chick, despite its squeaks of protest. "It is male," she said, without looking up from her work. "I smell it."

Red leaned in closer to look. "Are you gonna give him a name?"

Senneck snapped at him, causing him to reel backward in fright. But she sounded quite calm when she said, "We do not name our young. They name themselves. A name is not something to be given, even if some chosen humans give their partners new names. When my son is old enough, he will decide for himself."

"Well then," said Kullervo, trying to lighten the mood, "For now we'll just have to call him Skandarson."

"If you wish," said Senneck indifferently. "Now we should all rest. There will be important things tomorrow."

"She's right," said Kullervo. "Let's go, Red."

They left, one human and one half-human, and let Senneck and her son sleep.

The next day came, and so did word from Wylam's council. They had decided to accept Laela's offer. The city's Master of Diplomacy would go with Kullervo and accompany him back

North, along with no fewer than six apprentice griffiners who all claimed they wanted to follow Kullervo of their own free will—apparently thinking, like Resling, that he was holy. This time Kullervo didn't bother to try to dissuade them and accepted their requests.

It was a much larger band of griffins who left Wylam a few days later. Senneck carried her son—or rather she carried Red, who was under strict instructions to keep the little chick restrained. Senneck had not wanted to risk having him ride in the bag that had carried his egg, lest he climb out of it, and Red was eager to hold a griffin chick.

Together, Kullervo and his followers—which was what the band of griffiners had already come to resemble—flew on to Canran. It was a shorter journey this time, and ended at the valley that sheltered a rather run-down capital. The ravages of war were still visible in and around it, and parts of the city had even been left in ruins. It seemed Canran's Eyrie was too low on money and good leadership to rebuild everything that had been lost.

As it happened, the new and inexperienced Eyrie Mistress of Canran was more than happy to welcome friendly griffiners, and she and her depleted council listened to Kullervo with far more interest than Lord Kyron had shown.

Maybe the presence of Wylam's Master of Diplomacy helped, but Canran's council was much faster to accept the treaty and didn't even ask for time to discuss it. Even Kullervo guessed that since Canran's lands had shrunk to a fraction of their old size, it stood to gain a lot from being so close to a potential ally and trade partner.

There was no Master of Diplomacy in Canran, but the Eyrie Mistress instead offered her sister, Lady Burnet, who joined the party with a group of four other griffiners she called her escort though they were obviously just some friends of hers.

After that, it was time to move on. Most of the group seemed to think they would be going straight back to Malvern, but Kullervo surprised them.

"There's one last city we haven't visited," he said. "Withypool. I want to go there before we head home. But you don't all have to come with me. Kaine, Burnet—you can both go on to Malvern if you'd prefer, and anyone who wants to can go with you."

"I have no business in Withypool," Burnet said stiffly.

"Neither do I, and I want to return to Wylam as soon as I can," said Kaine. "I will go to Malvern with my colleague here."

"Then it's agreed," said Kullervo. "Queen Laela will be expecting you, but be careful."

"My Lord Kullervo, I know very well how to enter a city in a peaceable fashion," said Kaine. "There's no need to be afraid of that!"

Two of Burnet's friends, and two of the apprentices from Wylam chose to go with the diplomats. Resling and the remaining six stayed with Kullervo.

They parted ways within sight of Liranwee, and Kullervo and his remaining band even stopped there briefly, to visit Lady Isleen. She hadn't changed her mind about how and when she would go to Malvern, and she gave them a place to stay overnight and offered some provisions.

Here, Kullervo offered Red the chance to leave the group. "You've been flying with us for a long time now, lad. All this travelling can't be good for you. And this is your home."

"I know, but I don't wanna stay here," said Red. "I ain't seen Withypool yet, an' Skandarson still needs me anyway."

The baby griffin had continued to fly in Red's arms, and seemed to like him, happily accepting food from his hands. By now he had grown alarmingly; his down was already giving way to black feathers, and his kittenish fluff to pale brown fur with attractive silver ticking. His eyes were open now and had revealed themselves to be the same icy blue as his mother's. He had a lot of energy, and since he had no siblings, he liked to play with Red instead—the boy's arms were, of course, covered in scratches to prove it.

"You've certainly been a big help looking after him," Kullervo admitted. "Anyway, we'll be stopping here again once we've been to Withypool, so you can decide then."

"I will!" Red said, almost fiercely.

So when the group moved on toward its final destination, the boy from Liranwee went with them once again. It took them just under two months—less time than it might have done once upon a time, since by now they were all very well practiced in travelling.

Along the way, Skandarson continued to grow and develop. The last of his fluff disappeared, and his wings lengthened as his flight feathers developed. The grey scale on his forelegs thickened and hardened, and his talons grew long and sharp. He was now far too large to be carried by Red, but more than strong enough to hold on to his mother's back by himself. He had even begun opening his wings in the air and flapping them in time to hers.

Finally, when they were within sight of Withypool, he jumped off.

Kullervo, flying just ahead, heard Red's cry of panic. He wheeled around, and saw the boy waving his arms desperately from Senneck's back. Skandarson was gone, and Kullervo soon spotted him. He was below Senneck, not quite falling, but not quite flying either. His wings were flapping erratically, too uncoordinated to keep him steady, while his tail twisted from side to side rather than locking into a straight line to act as a rudder.

Kullervo flew frantically toward him, but amazingly, Senneck seemed completely unconcerned. She flew on as if nothing had happened, not looking down or changing her course at all.

As for Kullervo, he might as well not have done anything either. He did his best, dodging about to try and catch Skandarson in the air, but the small griffin's flight was so erratic, and precise movements in the air were so difficult for any griffin, that actually catching him was next to impossible.

Ultimately, Kullervo didn't have to do anything. Skandarson, apparently acting on instinct, held his wings out straight from his sides and went into a glide. The bones in his tail locked together as they should, and he stopped rolling.

After gliding a short distance, he began to flap again, steadily, gaining height. Kullervo stopped panicking and returned to a more steady flight, and Skandarson came toward him and rode on his slipstream, as easily as if he had been doing it his entire life.

He was too young to have much stamina in flight yet, but he didn't need it. Withypool was soon beneath them, and he came in to land with the other griffins, running over to prance around his mother and cheep proudly at her. She chirped back and shoved him with her beak, nearly knocking him over, and he got up and bounded in a circle.

"Thank Gryphus!" Red laughed. "I thought he was a goner!"

"He has made his first flight," said Senneck. "Soon he will be ready to choose a name, and after that, it will be time for him to leave me."

"Food!" said Skandarson. "Food food food!" It was the first word he'd learnt, and still his favourite.

Red knew it, too, of course, and obligingly tossed over a strip of dried meat.

Skandarson ate it and pattered along beside his mother as she went with Kullervo to meet the Withypool griffiners, who were already coming to confront the group of strangers that had arrived on their Eyrie roof.

Withypool's council was a harder challenge than the others. Kullervo spoke to them and their Eyrie Master, Lord Penrin, and showed them the treaty as before. He mentioned the fact that the other Eyries looked about to sign it and that so far Withypool was the only one not to be taking part. He even, in a fit of desperation, displayed his wings. But even though he was as astonished as everyone else had been, Lord Penrin stayed as unforthcoming as before.

Like the other Eyrie Masters, he asked for time to talk with his council. But the time here stretched out over three long days. Three days in which Kullervo, becoming oddly tense and sullen, refused to leave the Eyrie for any reason.

On the third evening, Lord Penrin summoned him and Senneck back.

"My council and I have talked about this matter, and we have decided that we will not be sending anyone to Malvern," he said baldly.

"Why not?" asked Kullervo.

Lord Penrin's expression did not change. "We know who you are, and you are not a Prince. You're a native of Withypool, and therefore one of my subjects."

Kullervo stiffened. "I'm a Northerner," he said.

"You were the griffin-boy who was put on show in the fighting pits," said Lord Penrin. "I saw you there myself when I was an apprentice. You lived in a cage and ate scraps that people threw."

A low hiss began in Kullervo's throat. But he sounded calm enough when he said, "I've gone up in the world since then. Like you have, Eyrie Master. You've seen my sister's letter. Worry about that, not the person who delivered it."

Penrin snorted. "Is that so? I should remind you, *Prince* Kullervo, that an Eyrie Mistress shows respect for her neighbours not just by what she says, but by who she sends to say it. And I am not in the habit of accepting treaties from sideshow freaks claiming to be the offspring of the Dark Lord Arenadd."

Kullervo's hiss grew louder and took on a snarl. "And my sister?"

"A sister only you say exists," said Penrin. "The answer is no, griffin-boy. Leave my city, and take your friends with you."

Kullervo nodded curtly and stalked out. He was in a foul mood for the rest of that evening, surprising his friends, who had never seen him like that before. But though the trip to Withypool looked like it had been a wasted one, it wasn't quite.

When Kullervo left the next morning, he had a surprise group of visitors. No less than seven griffiners came, most of them young, but one of them was an older woman who said she was nothing less than the Master of Law herself.

"We believe you, Lord Kullervo," she said. "We believe you're the winged man, and we want to go with you."

Kullervo didn't waste any time being surprised over this; he had heard similar things in Wylam and Canran already.

"Aren't you the Master of Law?" he said instead. "Don't you have to stay here?"

She waved a dismissive hand. "My apprentice is more than ready to take over from me once he finds out I'm gone. He's eager enough that I'm fairly sure he's been planning to get rid of me himself, in fact. They don't need an old woman like me. I want to spend my last years doing something more important than shout at guardsmen and hunt down poisoners, as if we didn't have three of them on the council!" She glared at Kullervo.

He laughed despite himself. "All right, then, come with us if you want to come that badly. We've got room."

Red was grinning. "Wow, we're almost like an army or somethin' now, ain't we?"

"Close enough, but we're not going to attack anyone," said Kullervo.

"A pity," Senneck said quietly.

They left Withypool together, sixteen griffins in a great flock. Senneck flew at its head, with Kullervo, and felt bigger and stronger for all the others behind her.

Red had been right: They *were* almost an army now. They would certainly put up a strong defence if it came to a fight. And even if he didn't seem to know it, Kullervo was their leader. This had been his quest from the beginning, and it still was, and everyone there was there because they wanted to follow him. Kullervo accepted it without complaint but hadn't given in to any temptation to become a bully. He probably didn't even know how. But leadership had changed him, Senneck noted.

He had grown calmer and more confident, and his voice had slowed and deepened. His face was scarred now, and that, combined with his newfound ability to lead others, made him remind her of his father more than he had ever done before.

When they got back to Malvern—and they would soon enough—Senneck felt certain that her human would be a much more powerful force there than he had been before. With time, and her help, he had learnt how to be. And that was all to the good.

It was everything she had hoped for, and more.

Everything was going to plan.

Their journey in the South ended as it had begun, in Liranwee. By now, after nearly nine months since their first sight of it, the new city had grown significantly. The walls were complete, and the Eyrie's outside was finished as well. Other buildings were growing around it, and proper houses had appeared further away. It had taken on a shape now, and several villages had even been founded on the lands around it.

Lady Isleen received them graciously. "So glad to see you again!" she said to Kullervo. "I was beginning to wonder if you would ever return."

"It's been a long time," Kullervo agreed. "But we're ready now, if you are."

"Much more ready now than I was before," said Isleen. "Rest here a while, and tell me when you want to leave."

"Soon," said Kullervo. "I want to get back to Malvern!"

"I understand. In the meantime, eat, drink, and sleep. The morning should be fine."

The tent that had belonged to Red's father was still there, albeit in rather bad shape, but some thoughtful person had gathered up its contents and locked them away in the Eyrie. They were brought back now.

"All yours," one of the bearers told Red. "The Master of Gold made sure your inheritance from your father was kept safe."

Seeing his father's possessions again made Red go quiet for most of that evening. He rearranged them in the tent and kept out of everyone's way, not saying much when he sat down to eat with Kullervo and Resling. Kullervo noticed his mood but left him alone. Red obviously had something on his mind.

Later on, when Resling had left for his own quarters and Senneck and Skandarson were asleep, Kullervo found Red hiding behind the dressing screen. He was crouching by an open chest, and as Kullervo watched, he lifted out a short sword in a leather scabbard and turned it over in his hands, half drawing it to check the blade.

Kullervo coughed politely, not wanting to spy.

Red glanced up but quickly relaxed again. "This is my dad's old sword," he said. "An' here . . ." He reached into the chest and pulled out a leather breastplate. "His armour, too. He always took good care of it, an' showed me how to look after it, too. Armour's no good if you don't take care of it, he said."

"You never really talked about him," said Kullervo, coming to crouch beside him and look into the chest.

"Yeah . . ." Red looked vaguely unsettled.

"What was his name?"

"He was called Danthirk, but everyone just called him Dan. He was a guard in Eagleholm before he was a griffiner. This was his guard armour an' sword, see?"

"Oh," said Kullervo. "So that's how he knew Bran?"

"Yeah, Bran was his Captain. They was in the same squad. Dad said they used to go drinkin' together after work, an' . . ."

"Yes?" said Kullervo.

There was nothing vague about Red's discomfort now. "An' there was . . . someone else, too."

"Who?" said Kullervo. "What do you mean?"

"Well, you know how Bran was . . . who his best friend was, I mean."

"He was friends with my father," said Kullervo. "I know."

"Yeah, so that means my dad knew him, too," said Red. "He told me about him an' what he was like. Said he knew him well, an' used to help him catch smugglers."

Kullervo frowned. "Why didn't you tell me this before?"

Red clutched the sword to his chest. "'Cause . . . 'cause I thought you'd be angry."

"*Angry?* Why?"

"Because my dad killed him, that's why," Red blurted. "My dad killed Arren Cardockson."

Kullervo started. "He what?"

"Killed him," said Red. "Everyone says that ain't true, like he got away somehow, but Dad said he died, and he knew because he was the one who killed him."

"How?" said Kullervo. "Why?"

"He got out of prison," said Red. "An' ran away. Bran an' my dad chased him with some other guards, an' they got him at the edge of the city. Dad said when they got there, he gave up. Said he surrendered. An' then Dad shot him. He shot him in the heart. Sent him off the edge of the city."

"Why?" asked Kullervo.

"I dunno," said Red. "Dad said he didn't know either; he just did it without thinking. But he said afterward he never felt good about it. Said he felt like a murderer, and he felt like what happened to Eagleholm was his fault, like if hadn't done it, then the Dark Lord wouldn't've come." The boy looked as if he were struggling for words now. "So he told me, 'Son, don't do what I did. Do yer duty instead. My duty was I should've arrested the bastard, not killed him. I ain't had nothing but bad luck since then.'"

"Your father sounds like he was a wise man," said Kullervo.

"Yeah, he was real clever," Red said proudly. "He told me a good an' honest man does like what a guard does, an' serves his home an' the people in it first. I've been thinkin' about that a lot after we left Withypool."

"And what did you decide?" asked Kullervo.

"I'm gonna stay here," said Red. "'Cause I've been around now, I've seen lots of different places, but I always knew I was gonna come back here. Liranwee's my home, an' I'm gonna stay an' serve it an' the people in it, like my dad said."

"So how are you going to do that?"

Red squared his shoulders. "I'm gonna join the guard. Every city needs good guards. But first, I'm gonna join the workers here an' help build the city. Then, when I'm older, I'll be a guard. My family's always been guards, you know. For generations."

Kullervo smiled. "That's a good plan. You'd be more use here than in Malvern, I think."

"Yeah, an' who wants some kid who's not a griffiner over there, anyway?" said Red. "Anyway, I'm a Southerner. They wouldn't like me much!"

"No, probably not," said Kullervo. "But maybe one day we'll change that. I'll do my best. Promise."

"You already are," said Red, quite seriously. He grinned suddenly. "Come back one day, Kullervo. Come back to Liranwee when you're done with your war an' looking after your sister. I'll be a big strong man by then, like my dad. You wait an' see!"

"I'm sure I will," said Kullervo. "And if this alliance with the South works out, I'll probably have to come back here for more negotiations. You'll see me then, for sure."

"Promise?"

"Yeah, I promise." Kullervo held up a hand in a solemn gesture. "On my honour as a Taranisäii."

It seemed the others had been expecting Red to leave, too, because none of them showed much surprise the next morning when he told them so. And of all of them, aside from Kullervo, only Senneck's son cared much.

"You were good to play with, red human," he said in his chirping youngster's voice.

"He said he liked playing with you," Kullervo translated.

"Me too," said Red. He patted the small griffin on the head—"small" was a relative term by now since Skandarson had grown bigger than Red was. "I wish you'd chosen a proper name while I was there."

"I have chosen."

"You've chosen a name?" said Kullervo, partly for Red's benefit.

Senneck rubbed her head against her son's flank. "Tell us your name then, little one, before we go back to your rightful home. It will make an adult of you."

The youngster raised his own head proudly. "My name is Kraego," he said.

"Kraego!" said Red. "It's a good name."

"It means 'thunder,'" said Kullervo. "A perfect name for a griffin as big as you, Kraego."

"It is," said Kraego, with typical griffish modesty.

"Goodbye then, Kraego," said Red. "I'll miss you, too."

"Maybe one day we shall meet again," said Kraego.

Red shared a farewell hug with Kullervo. "Don't you forget!" he said. "Come back one day. You promised!"

"I will," said Kullervo. "And you take good care of yourself until then."

"I will," said Red.

"Come, Kullervo," said Senneck. "We have waited too long."

"Just a moment." Kullervo pulled his shirt down, and plucked a feather off his chest. He handed it to Red. "Here. Something to remember me by."

Red took it eagerly. "Thanks! I'd better not tell anyone where it came from, or they'll want to put it in a temple or somethin'."

"Good idea," said Kullervo. He got onto the impatient Senneck's back and gave Red a final wave. Nearby, Kraego prepared to take off after his mother.

Red took a few steps back as Senneck took to the air, with Lady Isleen and all the others following. Kraego went among the flock, flying just beside his mother, and before long, they had gone beyond the city's walls and were off over the plains beyond.

Red watched them until they had disappeared from view, and felt very alone. But he was glad that he had finally told Kullervo the truth. Or, at least, part of the truth. He carefully tucked the feather into his pocket and walked back toward his father's tent.

With the help of the same griffiner who had kept his belongings safe while he was away, he sold most of what his father had left him, except for the tent itself. He would need that to live in until he could buy a house. He only kept a handful of other things, including the sword and armour, which he stuffed into the old chest. He took the money he had made and walked away, off toward the wall where a gang of builders was hard at work.

A tent had been set up close to the worksite, where the overseer had made a temporary office for himself. Red went inside, following a couple of other new arrivals.

The overseer sat behind a small folding desk, with an open book and a pen in front of him, and the two men already there spoke to him one after the other, giving him their names. Once the overseer had written them down, he sent them out to start work.

Red waited patiently for his turn. When the overseer nodded to him to come over he stepped up to the desk, dumping his bag on the ground.

The man eyed him briefly, then picked up the pen again. "Name?"

"Er, Red."

The overseer gave him an impatient look. "Not good enough. Give me your full name."

Red hesitated. "Why?"

"Just give it to me, or get lost," said the man, looking past him to the group of others who had already started arriving.

Red set his jaw, and stood a little taller. "My name's Kearney Redguard."

The overseer blinked. "You what?"

"You heard me," said Red. "It's Kearney Redguard."

"I thought the Redguards were all dead."

"Not all of 'em," said Red. "I'm the last one."

The overseer frowned as he wrote the name down, while the other men who had heard murmured among themselves. "I'd have thought you'd change your name rather than call yourself Redguard. I mean, aren't you ashamed, being related to that traitor?"

"Uncle Bran wasn't a traitor," Red snapped. "And my dad wasn't either."

"Wait," one of the new builders behind him interrupted. "Aren't you Danthirk's boy?"

"Yeah," said Red. "But my mum was Finna Redguard, so I've taken her name." He gave the man a fierce look. "You got a problem with that?"

Nobody argued, but he saw them giving him odd looks. The overseer took his name down and shooed him away.

Red left with his head held high. Even so, he could hardly believe what he'd just done. His father had always warned him not to mention that he was a Redguard on his mother's side. Once it had been a proud name—not any more.

But Red had learnt. Kullervo's heritage was even more shameful than his own, but Kullervo never lied about who he was, and he refused to be ashamed of it. Red only wished he had told the man-griffin the whole truth about who he was.

Even so, Red knew what he had to do now. He went out to

where the wall was being built, and took his instructions from one of the supervisors. As he started work, he made himself a promise. He would never lie about who he was ever again. His friends might call him Red, but he would be Kearney Redguard, now and forever, and he would never apologise for it. And he would find a way to make the name of Redguard a proud one again. He'd show everyone.

Red smiled to himself, as he lifted a heavy stone block onto his shoulders and started to carry it to the wall. "Thank you, Kullervo," he murmured.

28

Ready to Strike

Kullervo travelled back through the North with his new companions and was relieved to see that nothing had changed much. But even though the people he spoke to along the way all claimed that Laela was still alive and on the throne, his tension rose steadily higher as he grew closer to Malvern. He had been away for nearly nine months, and there was no way of knowing how much things might have changed in that time. Had Laela kept herself safe and the others as well?

When he finally saw his home again, however, he started to feel better almost before Senneck had flown over the walls. Malvern didn't look the same as he remembered—it looked better. People had clearly been at work on it while he was away; he saw numerous buildings that had been restored, including the brand-new Temple, which positively glowed in the sunlight.

The Eyrie itself looked even better. Brightly coloured banners hung from the walls, most of them decorated with the animal totems of the four tribes. But others had griffins, and others, the most striking, were pale blue with a black triple-spiral device. Kullervo thought he had seen it somewhere before.

At the top of the Council Tower, the plants and small trees that grew in pots and half-barrels were more numerous and healthy.

The Eyrie's inhabitants had long since spotted the large group of intruders, and a second group had gathered among the plants to meet them.

At their head was Laela, with Akhane by her side, both protected by Skandar and Zekh.

Laela wore the thin silver circlet she had inherited from Arenadd, along with a rather nice new gown. But those weren't what caught Kullervo's attention the most. She was heavily pregnant.

Kullervo, who had travelled the last leg of the journey as a human, jumped down from Senneck's back and approached his sister with a kind of wonder on his face. "Laela," he said. And then, again, "Laela!"

Laela looked back at him, smiling. But behind the smile she was almost shocked. Was this really her brother? He looked even bigger than she remembered, easily the tallest of all the people there. His wings hung down from his shoulders, fully feathered in mottled grey, and almost beautiful. She could see his tail, too, furred and feathered, trailing uselessly down the back of his legs.

But the biggest difference she noticed was in how he carried himself. He looked taller because he was standing straighter, without the apologetic hunch she remembered so well. His wiry hair had grown a little longer and taken on the hint of a curl. He had a scar now, too, thin and twisted, starting at his eye and ending near the corner of his mouth. She had only known one other person with a scar like that.

"Kullervo!" she exclaimed, forgetting formalities for a moment. "Ye gods, for a moment I thought you were our dad!"

Kullervo frowned slightly. "*You* look more like him than I do, Laela." He didn't sound as if he were completely happy about it.

Laela shook herself. "I'm so glad t'see you again," she said. "Those diplomats you sent back here told us you was all right, but I knew I wouldn't feel right until I saw you myself."

Her speech had improved even further, Kullervo noticed. "It was the same for me," he said. "But I should introduce my friends . . ."

Laela nodded formally. "Please do. Excuse me for not speakin' to you first, Lords and Ladies, but my brother and I haven't seen each other in a long while."

They looked suitably impressed by her good manners and were polite enough themselves to stand there quietly while Kullervo made the introductions.

Now Skandar came forward. He was as huge as Kullervo remembered, and unlike Senneck, whose feathers had begun to show a hint of white around her beak, he didn't look as if he had aged at all.

He approached Senneck first. "You back now," he said. "Back to bow head to me?"

"Yes," said Senneck, and bowed her head to prove it. "I am honoured to be back in your territory, Mighty Skandar."

"And you?" said Skandar, thrusting his beak at Kraego. "Who you?"

"Your son," said Senneck, ushering the youngster forward. "Kraego, this is your father."

Skandar sniffed his offspring suspiciously. "Big chick," he said. "Big and dark. Must be Mighty Skandar chick!"

Kraego faced his father boldly. "I have come back here to live in your territory, Father."

"Not have human," said Skandar. "Humanless griffin not welcome."

"Then I will fight you," said Kraego. "For my right to stay."

Everyone there breathed in sharply, even the Southerners. Horrified, Kullervo hunched down, ready to jump in and protect the youngster if he had to.

Skandar lashed out, but with the side of his beak, not the point. The blow sent Kraego flying. He landed against his mother's legs and lay there in a heap, shrieking in fright.

"Little warrior," Skandar boomed. "Come fight Mighty Skandar another time and maybe stand longer!" He chirped to himself and moved on, and Kullervo relaxed. If Kraego had been an adult, he might have been killed. But a challenge from a youngster was a joke to Skandar.

Satisfied, Skandar moved on to speak to each unfamiliar griffin and intimidate them in turn, and all of them sensibly retreated and promised to accept him as the dominant one.

After that, Lady Isleen was allowed to go forward and speak to Laela.

"Queen Laela," she said. "My name is Lady Isleen, Eyrie Mistress of Liranwee. I have come to accept your offer of a peace treaty between our territories, and would like to ask if I and my companions can stay here while the negotiations take place."

Laela inclined her head. "Welcome to my Eyrie, Lady Isleen. You an' your friends will all be welcome to stay for as long as you need to. Tomorrow we can start discussin' the terms of the treaty."

"Thank you, my Lady," said Isleen. She sounded quite satisfied.

The Master of Law from Withypool spoke up. "Excuse me, my Lady, but I'd like to say something as well."

"Go ahead," said Laela.

The old woman coughed. "My name's Della, and I'm the Master of Law from Withypool. But I've retired now and decided that I wanted to come here with your brother, Lord Kullervo. I'm not here to negotiate a treaty."

"Then what are yeh here for?" Laela asked, suspiciously.

Lady Della shrugged. "To see Malvern, which I've always wanted to do. But I count myself as Lord Kullervo's follower now, so if he needs anything from me, I'll be ready to give it. The same goes for my friends here."

Laela looked thoughtful for a moment. Then she nodded brusquely. "That's fine. In fact, I think he might soon have a use for you. But I'll leave him to tell yeh about that later on. For now, let's go inside." She nodded to her own companions, who took their cue and headed off back inside. Then she turned to Kullervo. "Come with me. We've got some catchin' up to do."

Kullervo went with her and Skandar, back toward the audience chamber. Senneck, of course, came too, and Kraego followed along beside her.

As for Akhane, he came with them for most of the way, but at the entrance to the audience chamber he said, "I have duties elsewhere, so I will leave you and your brother to speak in private."

"Thanks, love. See yeh later." Laela kissed him on the cheek and let him go. "Now, Kullervo, we've got a lot of stories to tell!" She smiled sweetly at her brother.

The moment Akhane was out of sight, however, the smile disappeared. Laela reached up and grabbed Kullervo by the ear. "Get in here," she snarled, and dragged him into the audience chamber.

Kullervo shuffled along beside her, protesting. "Ow! Laela, what the—? *Let go!*"

Inside the big, marble-lined chamber, Laela let go of him and gave his head a violent shove in the process. "You great git!" she yelled at him. "What where yeh thinkin', bringing that crowd here! Have you lost yer head?"

Kullervo stood there, clutching his ear and looking blank. "What? Laela, what's wrong? Why are you so angry?"

Laela ripped off her crown and looked about ready to throw it at him. *What?* Oh dear gods, he really doesn't get it. I said send back diplomats, Kullervo. I didn't say 'come back with sixteen bloody griffiners we don't know an' who've got no business bein' here.' Who the blazes are they?"

"They're my friends," said Kullervo.

"Friends?" Laela repeated, calming down slightly. "I sent ych on a peace mission, not to make friends. Why'd they come here?"

"Laela, please, let me explain," said Kullervo. "It's just . . . it's because of these." He indicated his wings.

"Yeah, an' another thing," said Laela. "Why're you walkin' around with them things hangin' out? Yeh want people to stare or somethin'?"

"You said to use my wings," Kullervo said sharply. "So I did. And that's what happened. People started wanting to follow me, and I let them do it."

"Why let them?"

"Because Senneck said I should," Kullervo said stupidly.

Laela glared at her. "Oh yeah?"

"Followers are always useful," said Senneck. "They gave us protection on our journey and made us look more legitimate to the Eyries. By now we have travelled with all of them for a long time, and they have been faithful and obedient."

"They believe in me," said Kullervo. "They all want to believe. How could I take that away from them?"

"By not bein' soft," said Laela, but she looked much calmer now. "I see, then. So my little brother's got himself some offsiders. Fair enough. But I'm expectin' you to keep them in line. Any trouble out of any of 'em, anythin' at all, an' it'll be your neck on the block. Got it? If they're as loyal as yeh say they are, they can stay. Otherwise, they're goin' right back where they came from."

"Understood," said Kullervo. "I trust them."

"Yeah, well, you ain't that good at not trustin' people," said Laela, mollified. "Now tell me about yer journey. What did yeh see? What happened?"

Kullervo told her. His story took some time, of course, as he outlined his journey, then went into more detail on anything he thought might be important, such as his failure in Withypool.

"Shouldn't be a problem," said Laela. "As long as they ain't openly hostile. Once all the other Eyries have signed treaties with us, they'll see more reasons t'do the same. Won't want to miss out on all the trade opportunities an' whatnot. So then what happened?"

Kullervo went on with his story and finally reached the end.

"Sounds like yeh had an adventure an' a half," said Laela. "Yeh got that scar in Eagleholm, then?"

"Yes. I wish I could have brought Roland back here; you would have loved to meet him."

"Probably would've," Laela said sadly. "But that's how these things go. Death stops us meetin' everybody in the end. It's a shame what happened to Eagleholm. I wish I coulda seen it when it was in one piece."

"So do I," said Kullervo. "But tell me about what's been happening here!" He looked down at her bulging middle. "Either you've been eating too many pies, or I'm going to be an uncle."

Laela punched him playfully. "Shut it, you. Yeah, you're gonna be an uncle. Inva's expectin', too. Her an' Vander got married. In the Moon Temple, no less. I bullied the High Priestess into it. Bet the Night God was thrilled."

Kullervo laughed. "Ah, who cares about what she thinks?"

Laela didn't join in his laugh. "I do, because Saeddryn does, an' she's no laughin' matter."

"She's still around, then?"

"Yeah. There's been no word of Caedmon in about a year, but Saeddryn ain't gone anywhere. She's like a bloody fly yeh can't swat. Keeps poppin' up in different places an' killin' people. Sometimes important people, sometimes just at random. I think she's gettin' frustrated and takin' it out on anyone what gets in her way."

"Have you been safe?" asked Kullervo.

"Just about, but there's been some close calls. She caught up with me twice while you were gone. Nearly did for me the second time, but Skandar came to the rescue again. It's like he knows where she is, like they're linked in the mind or somethin'."

Kullervo shivered. "I wish I'd been there to help you."

"You were helpin' me where you were," Laela said firmly. "But I'm glad yer back now, because I need yeh for somethin' else. With someone else I might've waited a while before I told yeh, but I know you don't like sittin' around at home."

"What is it?" said Kullervo. "You know I'll do whatever you need me to."

"Yeah, I do." Laela smiled. "You're the most valuable ally I got, yeh know. Even more valuable than Skandar, 'cause unlike him, you do what I tell you."

"Mighty Skandar not follower," Skandar growled. "Do what want to, not what human say."

"Yeah, right," said Laela. "Exactly. Oeka's still keepin' me safe here in Malvern, but I can't stay cooped up here forever."

Kullervo chuckled. "All right, Laela, enough suspense. What do you want me to do?"

Laela became serious. "It's time to get rid of Saeddryn. An' I need you to help me."

Kullervo leaned forward. "How? What are we going to do?"

"We're gonna catch her," said Laela. "We're gonna catch a shadow. An' you're the only one we have who can do that. An' you're also gonna be the bait. You an' Senneck." She looked over at the brown griffin. "You especially, Senneck. Saeddryn wants me an' Kullervo dead because the Night God told her to kill us. But she hates *you*. You're the one what killed her, an' that gives you power over her. Trust me, I know how it works now. When my dad came back from the dead, the first thing he did was kill the one he blamed for his death. My granddad, Lord Rannagon. Saeddryn wants t'do the same, an' I reckon not being able to's drivin' her mad. She'll run over flamin' coals to get at yeh, Senneck."

"I understand," said Senneck. "And I am more than willing to use this to lure her. Her destruction will benefit us all."

"You bet it will," Laela said grimly. "So both of you will bring her in, an' then you'll use yer little gift to catch her, Kullervo. I'm thinkin' after that, those friends of yours will come in handy. I'm sure *they'll* be more'n happy to bring in the Shadow That Walks. Southerners are her natural enemies, even more than us filthy half-breeds."

"And then?" said Kullervo.

"An' then you'll bring her back to me," said Laela. "Akhane's worked out a plan. You an' I both know the Shadow That Walks can't go into holy places. Not if they're holy to Gryphus, or Xanathus. She probably can't go into any place that's holy to a god who ain't the Night God, but that's neither here nor there. Our dad wrote that when he went into the old Sun Temple here in Malvern, he lost his powers an' got so weak an' sick he couldn't fight or even walk properly. An' I know that's true because I saw the same thing happen to him in Amoran. He nearly died from it."

"But how does that help us?" asked Kullervo. "There are no Sun Temples here any more."

"No," said Laela. "So we're gonna make one. Akhane's priest friends are gonna bless a room. Make it holy to Gryphus. We'll take Saeddryn in there, an' if it works, she'll be powerless. Then we can kill her, for good this time."

Kullervo sat there in silence as he thought it over. At first, as he imagined what the outcome of this plan would be like, he felt revolted. To drag someone into a place that hurt them, then to murder them there . . .

But then he remembered. Saeddryn was not human, not alive. She was a heartless murderer, the slave of the Night God Kullervo hated. She was . . .

. . . exactly what his father had been.

Kullervo banished that thought and felt the unaccustomed, icy burn of hatred in his heart. "We'll do it," he said. "I'll do it. Saeddryn has to be stopped. I won't allow her to hurt you, or Senneck. And the Night God has to be stopped as well. With Skandar on our side now, she won't be able to make a new Shadow That Walks easily."

"You're right," said Laela. "Once this is done, we'll be safe. If anyone else decides to rebel afterward, they won't stand a chance without Saeddryn or someone like her to help. We can get old here together, an' one day my child will be King, or Queen."

"And we can work on our alliance with the South," said Kullervo. "I've decided to spend my life making peace between our peoples. Once Saeddryn is dead, the Southerners will know they have nothing more to fear from us. Maybe I'll even live to see the day when we can open the borders again and make a united Cymria."

Laela looked a little surprised at this declaration. "Maybe.

After all, we don't know how long you're gonna live for. With our father's power in you, yeh could be immortal for all we can tell."

"I hope not," said Kullervo. "I don't want to live forever."

"Nah, don't worry about it," said Laela. "You got a heart-beat, so that probably means you're mortal like the rest of us."

"I hope so," said Kullervo. "So when are we going to start our plan?"

"Soon as possible," said Laela. "Here's an idea for yeh. How about you an' some of yer new friends get together an' head out to, say, Warwick? You can tell everyone yer takin' them out to show them the sights while we sort out the treaty here. We'll send word ahead that you're comin', make sure everybody an' their nosehair knows about it. Stay there a few days, an' if Saeddryn doesn't come, move on to Skenfrith an' make a big deal about that, too. But I don't reckon you'll need to. Saeddryn has a weird way of knowin' everythin' that's goin' on around here. Knowin' that not only you an' Senneck but a gang of Southerners are about will be too big a temptation for her to resist. Then when she does come, you catch her an' lock her up—in chains, for gods' sakes, don't let her disappear again—an' send word back here. We'll be along in a jiffy."

"It sounds like a good plan to me," said Kullervo. "Actually, Resling and some others were already saying they would like it if I could show them some of the cities around here. So I'll tell them that's what I'm doing. Only me and Senneck will know the real plan."

"Heh, you ain't as slow as yeh look." Laela grinned. "I was just gonna tell yeh to do that."

Kullervo grinned back, flattered. "Thanks! I'll give them a day or two to rest, then ask them if any of them are interested. They probably won't want to stay around here too long."

"Settled, then," said Laela. "An' meanwhile, you go get some rest, too! Can't have my best man too worn out for a little huntin' trip, can I?"

"No, no, understood," said Kullervo. "And you're right; I'm exhausted."

He and Laela parted ways, both cheerful and a little excited, and Kullervo went back to his old rooms with Senneck, leaving

Laela to go in search of her beloved Akhane. Neither of them were aware, or could be aware, of the presence that had hovered in the room all that while, taking in every word.

So they do take after me, Arenadd thought. *Lucky them. But cunning and cruelty won't save them now.*

Then he drifted away, flying back unhurriedly to find Saeddryn and tell her everything she had to know.

29

Out of the Shadows

"He did *what*?" Saeddryn roared.

Arenadd drifted anxiously around her. *I'm just telling you what I saw.*

"Southerners? In Malvern? In our land?"

Here to make a peace treaty, yes, said Arenadd. *About twenty of them. They're from all the different cities. But it looked to me like they were more interested in following my—in following Kullervo.*

Saeddryn's sickly-pale face was beginning to turn red. "That son of a bitch! Comin' back here with a band of those sun-worshippin' scum, lettin' them live in my Eyrie, tryin' to make a peace treaty?"

That's what they're aiming for, said Arenadd. *And that's what Kullervo thinks. But you know what those Southerners are thinking, don't you? You know what they really came here for.*

"To try an' take the North back," said Saeddryn. She was actually quivering with rage.

Exactly. That damn fool Kullervo just gave them the opportunity they needed. Now they're in the Eyrie, imagine the trouble they could cause.

Saeddryn took a few deep breaths. "They can't take over like this. Not with only twenty of them."

They can if they use Kullervo as a puppet, said Arenadd. *He's Laela's heir, remember. What if they found a way to persuade him into helping them? He's stupid enough for it.*

Saeddryn reached up and took hold of a branch that jutted out of the tree above her head. It was thicker than her arm, but she snapped it off with ease. "Well I ain't givin' them that chance," she snarled. "The winged freak dies."

As I said before, you'll have your chance soon, said Arenadd. *He's going to Warwick soon. And some of his new friends will be with him. But—*

"Then Warwick's where we're goin'," said Saeddryn. "I'll have his ugly head on a spear."

Of course, but—

"But nothin'!" Saeddryn spat. "When's he leaving?"

Tomorrow.

"Good. Then that gives me time for Caedmon's manhood ceremony. We'll leave the moment it's over."

Arenadd's vague, smoky shape gave a shrug. *Just as you say, beloved. I'll come along, too, and watch.*

Saeddryn took some time to compose herself, and as her fury retreated back inside her, she managed a smile. "I can't believe it. My son, finally gettin' his tattoos! Hope I remember how t'do them."

Don't worry, said Arenadd, rather sourly. *You still have all your memories.*

"Eh?" said Saeddryn. "What's that?"

Never mind. Yes, it's a proud day for you, isn't it?

"For us," Saeddryn corrected. "Caedmon's as good as a son to ye."

Oh yes. Always was.

"An' Myfina, too. I had my doubts about her, but she's gotten t'be a fine young woman."

I think Caedmon helped with that, Arenadd cackled. *Eh, Saeddryn? Makes you wish you were young again, doesn't it?*

"It does, aye," said Saeddryn. She smiled to herself. "Myfina will make a fine Queen when the time's right."

Just as you would have, said Arenadd. *And the time will be right soon, I think. Yes, very soon.* He laughed again, softly this time.

"I reckon so," said Saeddryn. "Now, we'd better get goin'."

Shouldn't you meditate first? asked Arenadd. *Get yourself closer to the Night God or whatever it is?*

"Once upon a time," said Saeddryn. "But nobody could be closer to her than I am now."

Speak for yourself, Arenadd muttered.

Saeddryn didn't meditate, but she did take a moment to neaten herself up. She had spent a good chunk of time during Caedmon's training roaming the country in search of people to kill, but she had spent plenty of time on the island, too, and had begun dressing in furs the way the tribespeople did.

The tribespeople were still cautious around her, but she had won their respect once she cared enough to try. Her powers meant she could bring back any animal she wanted to, even from the mainland—it had certainly helped whenever food became scarce. She hadn't planned to show them her powers, but Llygad had stumbled across her once as she emerged from the shadows. From then on, she had become the most revered person on the island. Clearly, she had great powers, and because she was a one-eyed woman, she must therefore be holy as well.

Thanks to that, it had taken no effort at all to persuade them that she should be the one to conduct the adulthood ceremonies for both Caedmon and Myfina, and the handful of young tribespeople who would be joining them in the ritual. In fact, Llygad had all but begged her to do it.

The work of a wise woman for the lost tribe was very different from being a High Priestess at Malvern, but the more Saeddryn learnt, the more she had seen the similarities between the two. Nearly every ritual the lost tribe practised had a counterpoint in the Temple, and Saeddryn had seen the roots of her own ceremonies in every one.

But the ritual of adulthood was one she had known when she was still a child herself. Her mother Arddryn had taught it to her, in secret, and when the time came, she had performed it for her daughter's own entry to womanhood. Later on, Saeddryn had performed it many times in the Temple, albeit in a stylised fashion, without the same trials as she had gone through.

Here on the island, all those trials were still complete. That morning, Caedmon had set out on his ceremonial hunt. Myfina and the other young people had gone with him. Each of them had to bring back something they had killed. Failure meant having to wait until next year.

Now, night was coming, and Saeddryn walked unhurriedly through the forest and to the coast of the island. There, she stepped into the sea and swam out to the other of the two smaller islands. The adults of the tribe would cross it on rafts, but Caedmon and the others would have to swim as well, and they would have to do it naked.

The water was deep and icy. As she swam, Saeddryn imagined she was mortal again and could almost feel the pain biting into her, crushing her lungs and making her heart patter with panic.

But the sensation was only a memory from long ago, when she was young and afraid, and had only thrown herself into the frozen pool when she thought of how angry her mother would be if she showed fear.

Never show fear. Never show pain. That was the true Northern way.

Saeddryn stepped out onto the shore of the island and moved inland. This island wasn't the one she had swum to on that first day. It was smaller and flatter, and no griffins lived on it because there were no good nesting places.

What it did have was something that brought a smile to Saeddryn's face: a stone circle, rising proudly against the horizon up ahead. Thirteen stones, like those that made up Taranis' Throne, but smaller and thinner. It was incredible to think that the lost tribe had managed to cut them and stand them upright like this when they didn't seem to have any metal tools or even much concept of proper rope. But nobody, not even the tribespeople themselves, remembered how their ancestors had made the stones. Some people even said the Night God herself had done it.

Of course not, Arenadd said when Saeddryn mentioned this to him. *Don't be daft. She can't touch the physical world. That's why she needs us. Give the poor mortals a bit more credit than that!*

Saeddryn chuckled. "I s'pose if they can build something like an Eyrie, they can build this."

Exactly. Hmm, I smell warm blood up ahead.

Saeddryn went on to the circle, and sure enough, she found some people there. Gwladus and Llygad and several other adults, all wearing simple fur kilts and nothing else, despite the cold wind. But they had lit a fire in the middle of the circle, at least.

Saeddryn nodded to Llygad. "Is it time to begin?"

He nodded back. "When the moon rises, they will come to the circle. It will not be long."

"Then we'll pray while we wait," said Saeddryn.

"We have a song that we sing on this night, wise woman," Gwladus put in. She was fierce enough to remind Saeddryn of her mother, but now she sounded almost timid.

"Then sing it for me," said Saeddryn. "And teach me."

Gwladus glanced at her friends. When none of them volunteered, she started the song herself. But soon, everyone there had joined in.

Saeddryn looked on, and listened. The song was in the old language, of course—the lost tribe didn't speak anything else. But it was too rich and complex for her to join in, and she was too afraid of spoiling it to try.

As she listened, however, she slowly realised why she couldn't make out the words properly. The language they were using was different. Not quite the old language, but something close to it. A different dialect, maybe, or an older form that had been forgotten everywhere else.

Saeddryn understood it just enough to know that it was a song to the stars, and the earth, and the moon above all, the moon that watched and gave life to every animal and bird. Maybe there was something helping her to understand, something inside her that was part of what she had become. Or maybe it went even deeper.

Quite unexpectedly, she felt her one eye start to ache with unshed tears. Everything here, the song, the stone circle, and the ragged tribespeople, carried her mind back to a time long ago, when her mother had been alive and she had been young, and life had been simpler and . . . happier?

Yes, she had been happy. Life had been hard, and her mother had been harder, but she had been happy then. She had had a purpose to believe in, and her whole life in front of her.

Saeddryn's tears did escape then, just a little. Her eye moistened. "Spent my whole life tryin' to be a real Northerner," she mumbled to herself. "But they were the real ones."

Just be yourself, Arenadd advised. *It's easier.*

The first of the adults-to-be arrived as the song ended. It was a young woman, naked and dripping wet, carrying the equally sodden corpse of a bird.

She laid the bird at Gwladus' feet, and said, "I have come to say farewell to childhood and become adult."

"Then say your name to the wise woman," said Gwladus.

The girl came to Saeddryn. She looked almost blue from cold, but her voice was quite steady. "Myfina."

Saeddryn did not smile. "Ye are welcome to come among the tribe, Myfina. Stand with them an' wait until the moon is bright."

In fact, the moon had already appeared in the sky, but that wasn't important. Stone-faced, Myfina took her place beside Gwladus and waited. The next of the supplicants had already appeared.

It was a boy this time, one of those who had trained with Caedmon. He also had a dead animal with him, but he presented it to Llygad instead before giving Saeddryn his name. She said the ritual words to him, too, with a touch of impatience as she watched out for Caedmon.

Three more arrived before Caedmon did, and when he came it was obvious why he had been slow: He had the carcass of a goat slung over his shoulders.

He dropped it at Llygad's feet before going to his mother.

"Caedmon," he said, as stone-faced as Myfina had been.

Saeddryn took a moment to look at him before she answered. Nearly a year on the island had changed him as much as it had her. He was lean and wiry now, with not a scrap of spare flesh on him anywhere. His hair had grown long, like his beard, which he had braided and tied with a bit of leather thong. There was no trace of weakness in his face or in the way he stood, covered in gooseflesh.

"Ye are welcome to come among the tribe, Caedmon," Saeddryn said softly. "Stand with them an' wait until the moon is bright."

Caedmon gave her a nod and joined Myfina. He finally smiled when he looked at her. She smiled back and laid a protective hand on the small bulge that had grown between her hips.

The moon was well up by the time the last of the young people had arrived. Saeddryn had been counting to make sure, and once she had formally welcomed the straggler, she began the ceremony at once.

The initiates stood in a group in front of her, by the fire, and she fixed them with her one-eyed glare, and asked in a loud voice, "Why have ye come?"

"To be initiated," they answered in ragged unison.

"Do ye swear this in the name of the moon an' the night an' the stars, an' the great god of the night that watches over us all?" asked Saeddryn.

"We do swear it," they said.

Saeddryn thought quickly. In the version of the ceremony she had been taught, she would now command them to submerge themselves in a pool of icy water. But they had already done that part by swimming to the island. So she skipped ahead to the next part. "Ye have bathed in the ice an' so washed away childhood," she said in her best High Priestess voice. "Ye have proven yer worthiness an' shown yer strength. Ye are ready to be marked as one of us."

She held out a hand, and Gwladus gave her a small leather pouch. Inside were a large pot of blue dye and a pair of long, bone needles. Saeddryn opened the jar and put the needles into the dye, point first.

Then she beckoned to Caedmon. "Caedmon of the Deer Tribe, come to me now an' receive the sacred marks."

He stepped forward and stood silently in front of his mother. She stayed where she was and held the jar, while Llygad took one of the needles out of it and took Caedmon by the chin.

When the needle went into his forehead, Caedmon flinched—but only slightly, with a flicker of the eyelids. Most likely only Saeddryn noticed it, and she watched with pride as he stayed still and silent for the rest of the time.

Llygad worked slowly and methodically, dipping the needle into the dye between every use. First he went over Caedmon's face, inscribing an intricate spiral pattern over his forehead, then down over his cheek to his jaw, stopping at the point where his beard began. After that he added tattoos to his neck and the upper part of his chest as well. In the background, the adults and some of the other initiates began a low, humming chant.

Ooh, this takes me back, Arenadd murmured.

Saeddryn ignored him.

Once Caedmon's tattooing was done, he was given a fur kilt of his own and allowed to stand with the adults by the fire.

Saeddryn called Myfina forward next—she didn't want to risk hurting her unborn grandchild by making her stand in the cold for any longer than she had to.

Saeddryn had expected Myfina to be less stoic than Caedmon, but the girl surprised her. She grimaced and shuddered under the needle—wielded by Gwladus this time—but didn't cry out or try to pull away. Eventually, she, too, was allowed to go with Caedmon. The adults around the fire had begun cooking the animals that had been offered up to them, and they shared the meat among themselves. Caedmon and Myfina ate, too, but the remaining initiates had to wait.

Saeddryn moved on through the others, five in all, but the whole process took such a long time that the sun had begun to rise by the time the last of them had received tattoos.

Then, at last, the whole tribe was free to eat the last of the food as one group, and joke and laugh among themselves. The formalities were done; from now on, it was time to have fun.

Saeddryn did not join in. She ate nothing, and, ignoring the invitations from the others, she moved away from the stone circle.

Oh, go on, said Arenadd. *At least have something to eat. Just because you're dead doesn't mean you can't enjoy yourself.*

"Shut up!" Saeddryn hissed once she was out of earshot.

No need to be like that about it, said Arenadd.

Saeddryn sighed. "What's gotten into ye, Arenadd? I never knew ye t'be like this when ye were aliv— when ye had a body, I mean."

Arenadd gave another ghostly shrug. *I don't feel pain or hunger any more, and I don't need to sleep. Also, I float everywhere. I'm just saying that sort of thing tends to change your outlook a bit.*

"Don't be daft," said Saeddryn.

All right then, said Arenadd. *You want to know the truth?*

"Go on."

I can't touch anything. I can't change anything. Once I was a King, and now I can't even speak with anyone, except you. You have no idea how powerless I feel. And so . . .

"So?" said Saeddryn.

So I've accepted that and I'm letting myself relax. I have to tell you, it's a lot more fun than worrying about everything all the time. Maybe dying was the best thing that ever happened to me.

Saeddryn shook her head. "I tell ye, Arenadd . . . joke about all ye like, but dying wasn't the best thing that ever happened to me."

No, I wouldn't have thought so. Arenadd drifted around her like a small black cloud, creating the faintest hint of a cold breeze. *Not easy, is it?* he asked softly. *Living with the memory of your own death. Unable to ever be a proper part of the mortal world, knowing you're not who you used to be. You can feel yourself twisting. Corrupting. Turning into something you would have hated and feared when you were alive. Becoming . . . evil.*

"Don't say that," said Saeddryn.

Why not? Arenadd asked mildly. *You've killed dozens of people since you came back, and not in fair combat. Slitting throats from the shadows when you can't be killed by your victims anyway—not really the accepted strategy, is it? And you enjoy doing it, too.*

"I don't!" Sacddryn snapped.

Oh, don't bother lying to me. I've seen your face. Killing's the only thing that makes you feel alive any more. Forget wine or those yellow toadstools they use in Amoran—that's the real rush for you now. Eh? Better than sex, isn't it?

Saeddryn said nothing.

Don't feel too bad, Arenadd added. *It's not really your fault. The Night God makes us this way. Makes our job easier, I suppose.*

Saeddryn turned away.

Not how you thought it would be, is it? said Arenadd. *And she's not how you thought she would be either, is she? But nobody but us could ever really understand that.*

"Stop it," said Saeddryn. "I don't want t'hear this now."

Arenadd didn't seem to hear her. His faint voice had become even more distant. *I remember when I was young . . . newly made, I suppose . . . I could still remember my life before I died. I thought I was still that man who fell, and I was so afraid. A mortal mind in an immortal body. Hadn't grown into my powers yet, didn't know who the Night God was or why she wanted me. But I'd discovered that I could kill, and felt my first bloodlust, and it scared me. I hid away on a hillside and cried like a damn baby.*

"Ye cried?" That wasn't a thing Saeddryn could imagine him doing.

Oh yes. Several times. I also whined. But people do that

*when they're scared witless, and they can't see any other way
to go. Just count yourself as lucky that you've got me, and the
Night God never left you in the dark the way she did to me. Are
we leaving now?*

The sudden question caught Saeddryn off guard. "Aye, I
suppose we are."

You should go back and say goodbye to Caedmon, said
Arenadd, with some of his old authority. *And Myfina as well.
This might be the last time you see them.*

"Yes, yes, yer right . . ." Saeddryn turned around distract-
edly, and started heading back.

But she didn't have to go all the way back to the circle before
she found Caedmon. He must have seen her leaving and gone
after her.

He looked sickly pale in the grey light of dawn, and the congealing blood on his neck and face stood out darkly. "There
you are," he said. "Aren't you going to stay and eat with us?"

"I don't need food nowadays, ye know, Caedmon," said
Saeddryn. "Best leave it for those that do."

"But it's the night of initiation," he said. "You could at least
stay and talk."

"Wasn't in the mood for it," said Saeddryn.

Caedmon just stared at her, frowning slightly, and she knew
she was disappointing him.

She smiled, and came closer to touch his forehead. "Ye did
well. Ye were brave."

Caedmon smiled back, hesitantly. "My skin was so numb
after that swim, I barely felt a thing. Maybe that's why they
made us do it."

Saeddryn chuckled. "I wondered the same thing when I was
yer age. How's Myfina?"

"She's well. Tomorrow we're going to go over to the griffin
island and see how Shar and Garsh are getting along. And what
about you? You're leaving again, aren't you?"

"I am," said Saeddryn.

"Where to this time?" asked Caedmon.

Saeddryn hesitated.

"Tell me." There was command in Caedmon's voice now. It
made him sound so much like Arenadd that Saeddryn started.

"I've had word," she said. "The man-griffin's come back

from his journey South. What's more, he's brought some new friends back with him."

Caedmon gaped. "Not Southerners?"

"Aye, Southerners. Griffiners, no less."

Caedmon swore. "That piece of filth! Bringing those damned heathens back here . . . what are you going to do?"

"What do ye think?" Saeddryn growled. "He's comin' to Warwick with some of them, an' that Senneck will be there too. None of them are leavin' alive."

"Good," said Caedmon. "Kill the man-griffin first."

"Oh, I will. Trust me, I will. He's been outta my reach for far too long." Saeddryn smiled horribly. "Been a long time since I've been able to kill Southerners. I'll be glad t'do it again."

Caedmon had never even seen a Southerner before. "Don't kill all of them," he said. "Let some of them get back to Malvern. They'll probably want to run off back to their homes once they've seen what you can do. And they'll take back the news that the North is still under the Night God's protection. That ought to keep them away."

Saeddryn smiled—a true smile this time. "Spoken like a true leader. I'll let one or two get away. But Kullervo an' Senneck are dead."

"Come back and let me know once they are," said Caedmon.

"I'll bring ye their heads," said Saeddryn. "A manhood ceremony present t'my favourite son."

"I'll be proud to have them," Caedmon said grimly. "Good luck."

"I don't need luck," said Saeddryn. "I have the shadows."

She slid away.

30

Steel Jaws

Saeddryn set out for Warwick at a leisurely pace—at least by her own standards. With her new powers, she could travel at least as fast as a griffin in flight and cover more ground since she didn't need to rest, and was, if anything, even faster at night.

It meant that there was no need to hurry, since if she did, she would probably reach Warwick before Kullervo did. But to make sure, she ordered Arenadd to go on ahead every so often and check.

Saeddryn was fast, but Arenadd was even faster, and he reported that Kullervo hadn't arrived yet.

Saeddryn had calculated her travelling time with care, and by the time Warwick had come within one night's walk, Arenadd let her know that Kullervo had just landed. Six of his new griffiner friends had landed with him.

Think you can handle 'em? Arenadd asked, teasingly.

Saeddryn had not stopped her effortless run while she listened to his news. "Easily," she said, and sped up.

She reached the walls of Warwick by morning, and went to ground among the shadows of a dirt heap just outside. "Go in an' tell me what they're doing," she ordered.

Right away. Arenadd drifted off.

He returned a short time later. *They're mostly asleep. Must be tired out from the flight. Want to go in and stab 'em in their beds?*

"What about Kullervo?" asked Saeddryn. "Is he asleep?"

Yes. Senneck, too. Are you sure you don't want to wait until they're away from help?

"No." Saeddryn's eye narrowed. "We've got nothin' to fear from guards." She drew her dagger. "Show me the way."

All right. Let's go.

The two of them slipped away, the one using the shadows and the other already invisible. The city's front gate had just been opened, and Saeddryn went in through it and on into the city. People were already up and about. Everywhere she went, she saw them. Bakers lighting their ovens ready for the first batch of loaves. Traders opening up shop. Guards arriving to take over a shift from their fellows who had stayed up all night.

But not one of them saw her, or even had an inkling that she was walking among them. A darker person than them, with a dark day's work of her own.

The governor's tower was locked at ground level, and guarded as well, by men who were far more heavily armoured than the ordinary guards out in the city, especially around the chest and throat. Saeddryn had visited this place plenty of times in the past.

But guards hadn't stopped her then, and they didn't stop her now. She ignored them completely, and began to climb the wall. There were gaps in the stonework just wide enough for her slender Northerner fingers. They weren't big enough for her toes, booted or bare, and the fingerholds would have been completely useless to anyone without unnatural strength and endurance.

Saeddryn had both, and she effortlessly pulled herself up the wall until she reached one of the lower openings meant for griffins and went in through it.

Hiding in a shadow, she whispered to Arenadd. *"Show me the way."*

He did, as he had done a hundred times before, floating through the rooms and passageways and up the inside of the tower, along a route he must have worked out for her on his last few visits.

Following one step behind him, Saeddryn felt glad yet again that he was there. Once she had obeyed his commands, but now he was her faithful servant, and far more loyal to her than she had ever been to him. He never argued or tried to dissuade her from anything, and did everything she told him to instantly.

And more importantly, he was there for her. Without him, she would have had no-one to talk to. By now, ordinary people felt irrelevant to her. They could never understand. But Arenadd did, and if he had not been there, she knew she would have felt terribly alone.

And now . . . now, at last . . .

Saeddryn gripped her dagger tightly, and swore a hundred times, to herself, to the Night God, that this time she would not fail. She would not leave Warwick until Kullervo and Senneck were both dead, even if she had to kill a hundred people to get at them. Her time as the Shadow That Walked had been far too long, and far too fruitless, and she would not let it go on any longer. Her eternal rest beckoned, and she would go to it having fulfilled her vow to her master. Then she and Arenadd would have peace at last.

Finally, Arenadd reached a door and drifted through it. Saeddryn opened it quietly and went inside.

It was a bedroom, and she didn't need to be told whose. The moment she stepped inside, the smell hit her nostrils: a musty, confused smell of both feathers and human skin. Nobody else in the world had a smell like that.

The room was utterly dark, but Saeddryn could see everything. She saw the bed, and the bulky shape of the vile hybrid asleep on it. She couldn't see Arenadd anywhere, but she didn't need him now.

She walked silently to Kullervo's bedside. The blankets covered his neck, so she carefully folded them back and pressed the point of her dagger into his throat.

Kullervo's eyes snapped open, and he jerked upright with a deafening yell of shock. Instinctively, Saeddryn jumped backward and into the shadows. While Kullervo freed himself from his bedclothes and groped for a lamp, she started to stalk him, trying to position herself in the right place to strike.

Kullervo found the lamp and lifted the covers from it. Instantly, light flooded into the room. Saeddryn hissed involuntarily, but confusion muddled her mind. Why had he kept it burning? Why keep it ready like this, unless . . .

Kullervo turned sharply. He was still fully clothed, and his yellow eyes were puffy with sleep, but wide open and fixed on her.

"I know you're there," he hissed. His was a griffin's voice, low and full of menace.

Saeddryn backed away silently, moving around behind him. Kullervo turned to follow her, but couldn't quite see her, and her confidence began to return. He could only just barely see where she was, and if she was careful, she could still hide from him.

A strange, low whispering sound filled the air. Kullervo shook his head confusedly and batted at his ear, as if a mosquito were bothering him.

Saeddryn took her opportunity and lunged at him.

And then a voice split the air, loud and commanding and furious.

NOW! Kullervo, now!

"Arenadd—!" Saeddryn began, but her moment of shocked realisation came too late. Kullervo came straight at her. His big, taloned hands thrust into the shadows and caught hold of her, and this time they did not let go.

He pulled her back into the light and slammed her against the wall, pinioning her arms.

"No!" she snarled, trying to break free.

But though she was strong, Kullervo was strong as well. His hands wrapped around her arms in a crushing grip, stunted talons cutting into her flesh. She kicked out powerfully, catching him in the stomach, but he only winced and tightened his hold.

But the shock of being caught was nothing next to what she saw then, and it was something so horrible that all the strength seemed to leave her.

She saw Arenadd's dark spectre hovering by Kullervo's side, whispering to him as he had once done to her.

Don't let her go, son. For gods' sakes, don't let go! Call for help, get those chains on her, fast!

"Arenadd!" Saeddryn screamed. "No!"

But he did not reply. He stayed by his son and spoke on.

Kullervo seemed vaguely aware of his father's voice. He yelled out for Senneck, and she came rushing into the room as if she had been lying in wait. She helped Kullervo pin Saeddryn to the floor, hissing in sickening triumph. Moments later, the door slammed against the wall, and others came running.

Southerners! Saeddryn saw their brown hair and pale eyes,

all alight with hatred. And worse, other Northerners were there, too. Guards, armed and obedient to the hideous man-griffin.

But it was the Southerners who put the chains on Saeddryn. Manacles snapped shut around her wrists and ankles, all of them attached to iron weights.

Once they were on her, Kullervo finally let go. "Take her to the dungeon," he said.

Saeddryn fought like a wild animal when they let her up. But the chains weighed her down unbearably. She tried to escape into the shadows, but they pulled her back.

The guards lifted the weights for her—each one needed a man to carry it—and dragged her away.

The Southerners came, too, and Kullervo, and Senneck as well, none of them letting her out of their sight.

And all the while there was Arenadd, the traitor Arenadd, watching calmly from his son's side.

Down in the prison under the tower, they put her in a small cell without a single piece of furniture and chained her to the wall by the wrists, neck, and waist. She couldn't even stand up once they were on her.

Kullervo locked the door on her and hung the key around his neck. "You guards," he said, "I want all of you to stay here—*all* of you. You can't leave unless someone relieves you, and I want you to keep your eyes on her at all times. Don't let her out of your sight for an instant. And don't talk to her, or listen to anything she says. I mean it. Is that understood?"

"Yes, my Lord."

"Good." Kullervo stayed a moment, looking in at her. His friends stood beside him. Most of them looked afraid, but all of them looked triumphant as well.

"I vowed I'd stop you," Kullervo said. "Now you'll never hurt anyone again. Laela will be here soon. In the meantime, you've got plenty of time to think about what you've done."

"So that's her, is it?" one of the Southerners asked. "*That's* the Shadow That Walks. The Dark Lord's successor."

"The Dark Lady," one of his friends suggested with a smirk.

"It is," said Kullervo. "But I don't want any of you coming down here to see her again. She's the most dangerous creature in the world, and don't ever forget it."

"We won't, sir."

"Good. Now let's go and get some proper sleep."

Kullervo left, taking his friends with him.

Senneck lingered, casting a contemptuous blue glance into the cell. "I killed you once, *Kraeaina kran ae*," she said. "Now, I shall watch you die a second time. Erian is avenged."

Saeddryn spat at her. "Coward! Fight me again, an' we'll see who finishes who."

Senneck looked amused. "I would turn you to stone as I did to the griffin who chose you, but the end that my human has worked out for you will be far more satisfying. I will see you then." She loped off after Kullervo.

Trapped, with only the stares of her guards for company, Saeddryn started to struggle against her chains. When that failed she subsided and started to examine them more carefully, looking for any sign of weakness she could exploit.

She found nothing. The chains and manacles were brand-new, and well-made. Even the Mighty Skandar himself would not have been able to break them.

Quivering slightly with anger, Saeddryn looked around the cell for something, anything, that could help her.

What she saw instead was Arenadd, standing by the doorway and watching her.

She lunged at him, falling back when the chains pulled her up short. "Ye son of a bitch!" she screamed at him.

I've been called worse, said Arenadd.

"Traitor! Filth! How *could* ye?"

How could I? Arenadd drifted closer. *I'm sorry, Saeddryn, but you had to be stopped.*

"*They* had to be stopped!" said Saeddryn. "The half-breeds—an' the Night God . . ."

Oh, burn her, said Arenadd. *I've had enough of her and her orders. I'd had enough of them a long time before she killed me, in fact.*

"But betraying her . . . and *me* . . ."

I really am sorry, said Arenadd. *But I had no choice. I told you back on the island. I'm not a King any more, or a Shadow That Walks, or even a man. But I'm still a father. I couldn't let you hurt my children.*

"But the Night God," said Saeddryn. "She taught ye . . . she said . . ."

Arenadd laughed softly. *Her? I fooled her, too. Haven't you guessed? I seduced her. Once I realised that was what she wanted from me, I took my chance. I told her everything she wanted to hear. She's not all-knowing, Saeddryn. Otherwise, she would have known I've been betraying her ever since I got back here.*

"Ye what . . . ?" Everything was falling apart now. Saeddryn's world was in ruins around her.

Who do you think warned Skandar about where you were going to be? said Arenadd. *Who brought him and Kullervo to stop you when you kidnapped Laela? Who knew this was a trap but didn't tell you? Who went into Kullervo's dreams tonight and told him to wake up? I did.*

"But they can't hear ye," said Saeddryn. "Only I . . ."

They both have the dark power in them, said Arenadd. *Kullervo has just a touch of it. Skandar can hear me as loudly as you can, and Kullervo can hear me, too, just a little. He hears me better when he's asleep. I found that out at Malvern when I warned him to get out of the Eyrie. After that, I followed him to the Moon Temple. It was me who whispered to him about what the Night God really is and what she's done. I taught him to hate her.*

"Why?"

Because if he let her do it, he could become like us. The seed's in him. But now he'll never trust her, and he's used his power to stop you.

Saeddryn felt close to tears. "Why?" she whispered. "Why?"

Why? Do you really need to ask me that now? Arenadd's voice had been quite steady, but now it grew louder and full of the passion she remembered so well. *There must never be another Shadow That Walks. Our kind should never have existed. All we do is destroy. Once you and I are gone, Kullervo will make sure that nobody else rises to take our place.* His form solidified, showing the scarred face she had once loved. *The world is meant for the living. We are the dead, and the only place for us is the grave.*

Despair twisted in Saeddryn like a knife. "Go away," she groaned.

No. I'm staying here to keep an eye on you. The instant you try anything, Kullervo will know.

After that, he said nothing more, and only moved silently around her, watching her every move.

Saeddryn did not rest. She fought on endlessly, nearly wrenching her arms out of their sockets in the process. She hurled threats at the guards, but they were as unyielding as the chains, and Arenadd would not answer her any more.

Finally, she tried to pray. The Night God had to know what had happened, had to be warned about Arenadd's treachery. But here in her prison even the Night God seemed to be out of reach, and deep down she knew that her master could not help her now.

She was lost.

Kullervo returned to his quarters with his heart pounding. Part of it was excitement, but there was fear there as well. To have been so close to Saeddryn, and to know she was so close now, even if she couldn't hurt him, made him afraid. So did the memory of her face glaring at him with more hatred than he had ever imagined could exist. It was the face of a woman who had no fear and no conscience. He knew that if she got the chance, she would kill him, and feel nothing.

The memory of his dream lingered as well. That face, the same bearded face he had seen in Malvern, shouting at him to wake up, wake up *now*. So he had woken up, and once again the dream had been accurate, and had probably saved his life.

Once was a coincidence. Twice meant something more. Kullervo knew that something, or someone, had come to warn him—and he had a good idea of who.

"Father?" he said aloud. "Was that you? Did you come to help me?"

But the insistent whispering in his ear had gone now, and it didn't come back. If Arenadd had been there, he was gone now.

Someone was waiting in Kullervo's room. Kraego, crouching on the bed and idly grooming a wing. He looked up when Kullervo entered and stood up to greet him.

"Where did you go?"

"She came," said Kullervo. "Just as we were hoping. Sennock and I caught her. She's chained up in the dungeon now. Didn't you hear all the commotion?"

"No," said Kraego. "I was flying."

"In the middle of the night?"

"Yes. I like the night." Kraego shook out his black feathers.

"You can see in the dark, then?" asked Kullervo. He knew that most griffins couldn't.

"I can," said Kraego. "Like my father." He hopped down off the bed. "You can have this back now. I am not tired yet."

"Thank you," said Kullervo. "Listen, Kraego—can I ask you to do something for us?"

"Perhaps," said Kraego.

"Now that we've caught Saeddryn, we need to tell Laela right away," said Kullervo.

"You want me to go to Malvern?" said Kraego.

"Yes. You're faster than any of us, and you wouldn't be carrying anyone, either."

Kraego purred to himself and scratched his cheek thoughtfully. "I have never flown alone before. It would be interesting."

"It would be," Kullervo agreed. "And your father would be impressed. Everybody likes someone who brings them good news."

"That is true," said Kraego. "I will go, then."

"When?" asked Kullervo.

"At once. I slept when we came here before tonight." Kraego strutted toward the door.

Kullervo knew better than to tell him he should wait until morning; Kraego was young, but he was as proud as any griffin. That pride, and his desire to impress Skandar, would be more than enough to assure that he would go straight to Malvern as fast as he could. He would make a good messenger.

Kraego left the room and walked on down the tower, tail swinging easily behind him. He fully intended to do what he had said he would, but not immediately. First he would satisfy his curiosity and go to look at this human that even his mother feared.

To Kraego, humans weren't something to fear at all. From the moment he hatched, they had been around him, all ready to feed him and to play with him. Not once had a human ever been unkind to him, or posed any threat. Some of them were dark and some of them were light, but both kinds were friendly and weak.

On his way down toward the dungeons, he met his mother coming the other way.

"Kraego," she said. "Why are you here?"

Kraego didn't need his mother's care any more, but she was still a protective figure for him, and he answered her politely. "Your human has asked me to fly to my father and tell him that *Kraeai kran ae* has been captured," he said.

"The human is *Kraeaina kran ae*," Senneck corrected. "Female. You must go to the Mighty Skandar quickly. The sooner she is killed, the better."

"I know," said Kraego. "I will leave at once."

"Go, then," said Senneck.

Kraego darted between her legs and went on his way, before she could ask why he was going down the tower rather than toward the nearest flight entrance.

At the place where the dungeons began, he found a pair of humans guarding the way. But he was too small and quick for them. He crept up on them and snuck past under their weapons, and because he was only a small griffin, they didn't try hard to chase him.

His confidence soaring, Kraego almost swaggered along the dungeon corridors, searching for the place where the dark human was trapped. Barred doors blocked his way, but he squeezed through them. Once a human tried to stop him, but he hissed at him and went on his way.

He knew that he had found the place when he saw it. Not because of the four guards standing there, but because of the scent. It was icy cold, metallic, and it made the feathers stand up on his spine. Nothing living should have a scent like that.

He crept closer, keeping low to the ground without realising he was doing it, and heard the dark human muttering aloud in her own language. It wasn't the human language he knew, but the other one, and he only knew a few words of that.

Caution told him he should leave, but his curiosity got the better of him. He went to the door, and peered through it, ignoring the shout from one of the guards.

And there she was. She was brightly lit by many fires, and he saw the iron ropes that stopped her from running away

She looked like just another human; an old, thin, sickly one with only one eye. But in that long moment that Kraego looked at her, he saw something in that eye that wasn't human at all.

It was a black eye, black and savage, and the look in it was not a human look. It was the look of a wild animal. A look that Kraego felt deep inside himself, as if it were a part of him.

Irrational shock gripped him, and he crouched low, extending his talons, and opened his beak wide to rasp at her. It was an animal reaction, one he had no control over, and it caught Saeddryn's attention at once.

Her head turned toward him, and he saw the human look of surprise appear on her face.

"Dark griffin," she whispered in his own language.

Dark human, Kraego thought.

And then something rushed at him, something shadowy and horrible, screaming a curse at him.

Kraego had had enough. He turned and ran out of the dungeon as fast as he could go, feeling as if the screaming thing were chasing him all the way.

It was.

In her cell, Saeddryn watched dully as Arenadd returned and started to float around rapidly, swearing in a low, feverish voice. *Shit! Shit, shit, shit. Gods damn it! She's made another one! She's given the power to another . . . shit!*

"Ye see?" Saeddryn hurled the words at him. "Ye can't stop her, Arenadd. So what if ye an' Skandar have turned traitor? She made Skandar; ye must have known she could make another griffin like him."

He saw me! Arenadd exclaimed. *He could* see *me. He heard me! He's got Skandar's power. Shit. I have to . . . gods, what am I going to do? Got to do something, something . . .*

"Give it up," Saeddryn said as smugly as she could. "Ye can't win."

Arenadd said nothing. Trying to ignore her, most likely.

"Ye've lost," she continued. "Ye know those half-breed brats of yours can't kill me. Nobody can. Sooner or later, I'll get away. The Night God's sent this griffin t'be my partner. One day he'll be as big as Skandar. He'll help me kill yer children, Arenadd. Both of them."

No. He won't help you. I won't let him. He won't hurt my children, and neither will you. They'll find a way to kill you first, I know they will. They're clever, and I'll help them. But Arenadd's voice was desperate now, panicky even. He wasn't certain of anything he was saying.

It gave Saeddryn some of her confidence back. She laughed cruelly at him. "Did ye really think ye could stop me?" she asked. "Yer nothing, Arenadd. Yer a puff of smoke that talks. An' yer children are nothing either. Mortals, half-breeds, heathens. Nobody ever stopped ye when ye still had a spine. An' nothing's gonna stop me. Yer children have killed themselves by lettin' me near them. The Night God will freeze them in the void forever. But I don't think she'll do that to ye. No, she'll punish ye far more painfully."

Shut up. I don't care what she does to me any more. I need to think . . .

"Help me," said Saeddryn. "Find a way t'get me out of here, then help me do what I was sent t'do. Maybe the Night God will forgive ye."

Not a chance.

"Ye've got until Laela arrives," said Saeddryn. "Think about it, Arenadd. Think very hard."

Oh, I will, he growled. *I will.*

31

Immortal Sin

Arenadd made his decision, and did not leave Saeddryn's side once. He stubbornly ignored all her attempts to persuade him and kept watch over her in her cell.

He needn't have bothered. Saeddryn's continued efforts to escape all failed. The chains would not give, the guards would not listen, and her cell door was not opened once, not even for food to be brought. Nobody brought her any food at all, or anything to drink. She wondered if they knew she didn't need to eat any more, or if this was an attempt to soften her up in preparation for whatever came next. She would never know.

The wait finally ended when Laela came. She arrived surprisingly quickly, and brought a small entourage with her to Saeddryn's cell. All of them were Amorani. A handsome, well-dressed young man who must be her husband, two middle-aged men with shaven heads, and a fourth; a sinewy, scarred woman of indeterminate age, whose face had an odd, faraway look on it.

Kullervo came, too, and stood by in silence while his sister inspected her captive.

Laela wore a plain dress, but the crown was on her head. She regarded Saeddryn with an insolent, blue-eyed stare.

"Not wantin' to open with the obvious, but I told yeh so," she said. "I said if yeh stood in my way, it'd come to this, an' now it has, thanks to my brother here."

"It was my pleasure," Kullervo growled.

Saeddryn stared back at her enemy and felt the hatred in her dead heart. "Yer time is nearly up, mortal," she said. "Ye can't kill me."

Laela shrugged. "Senneck already did that for us. What I'm plannin' here ain't death so much, but you'll probably wind up wishin' for it by the time I'm done with yeh."

"What do you mean?" Kullervo interrupted suddenly. "I thought we were going to kill her."

"When we're ready," said Laela. "But first we're gonna talk."

"I've got nothin' to say to ye," Saeddryn spat.

"No," said Laela. "Not yet you ain't." She gestured at the quiet, scarred Amorani. "This is a friend of mine. She used t'be a slave back where she came from, an' she did a very useful job there. Not many people'd want it, an' it wins yeh no friends, but she was damn good at it. Still is. So I thought I'd bring her here an' introduce yeh, see how yeh get on."

Saeddryn kept her word and only glared.

"We need t'find out some things from yeh," said Laela. "An' you're gonna help us. One way or another. Even if it takes a month. Which it won't."

Kullervo had begun to look alarmed. "But Laela, we can't—"

"Shut up," said Laela. She rested her hands on her pregnant belly and addressed Saeddryn. "I ain't in this for the fun, so I'll give yeh one last chance before we get started. Tell us where Caedmon is, an' we can get it over with right now."

Fear began to twinge in Saeddryn, but still she said nothing.

Laela did not look surprised. "Right then," she said. "Akhane, you an' yer friends can leave now. I'll see yeh later. But you—" She nodded to the scarred woman. "Stay. An' you, too, Kullervo."

Kullervo's face had gone pale. "I don't really want to . . ."

"But yer gonna stay anyway," said Laela. "I need yeh here, in case she gets back into the shadows. Stand guard an' be on the lookout."

"But—" Kullervo began.

"That's an order, Kullervo," Laela said sharply. "Do it."

Kullervo looked miserable, but he nodded his yes and silently handed over the key.

"Be careful," Akhane advised his wife. "I can all but smell the danger in this one."

"I'll be fine," said Laela, smiling sweetly at him. "With Kullervo here, there's nothin' to be afraid of."

Akhane nodded respectfully to Kullervo. "Agreed. The power of Xanathus will protect you both." His two friends were already leaving, but before he followed them, the Prince went closer to the bars and looked in at Saeddryn. "Be warned, heartless monster," he said. "There are no methods of torture more painful or more effective than those used in Amoran. You would do better to speak now and spare yourself, and recall that you cannot escape into death."

Saeddryn only snarled at him. He shrugged and walked away.

The four guards who had stayed outside the cell moved into position while Laela unlocked the door. She ushered the torturer inside, then locked her in and stood by with Kullervo, watching impassively.

Saeddryn eyed the scarred Amorani. She did not look very threatening, but everything about her, Saeddryn thought, hinted at a heart of steel underneath her bland expression.

Silently, the torturer unrolled a leather bundle and laid it out on the floor, exposing the metal instruments that had been stored neatly in individual pockets inside. She selected one, then straightened up, and tore Saeddryn's tunic open.

For a moment, the two women looked at each other, eye to dark eye. Neither one betrayed a flicker of emotion.

Then the torturer looked away and quietly and blandly began her work.

Saeddryn lasted a while in silence, vowing to herself that she would not betray herself, but it was the same hopeless vow that most prisoners in her situation made, and it did not last for long before she screamed for the first time.

Outside the cell, Laela watched with a look of hatred and distaste on her face. If she had any remorse for what she was doing, it didn't show.

Kullervo was far less restrained. His expression was openly horrified, and he often looked away but couldn't stop himself from looking back again. Before long, he started to retch, and even looked close to actually throwing up.

Inside the cell, unseen, Arenadd did not look away at all. He had turned on Saeddryn and so thrown away his last chance at redemption, but at least he had the courage to see the consequences of his actions and not flinch. This was the inevitable outcome of his betrayal, and he looked it full in the face and accepted it.

Just tell them, Saeddryn, he said eventually. *Don't do this to yourself.*

But Saeddryn did not talk. The only sounds they got from her were screams and curses, and finally sobs.

After an eternity, Laela finally said, "That's enough for now. I'm tired. We'll go again tomorrow. Yeah, that's right," she added loudly, as Saeddryn finally sagged to the floor. "This ain't over. We'll do it again tomorrow, an' the day after that, an' the day after that. We don't have t'give yeh time to heal, do we? No chance of killin' yeh, just as yeh said. We'll just keep on goin' until we get what we need. Have a think about that why don't yeh?"

She let the torturer out of the cell, and she and Kullervo left.

Saeddryn could not lie down. She hung from her chains, feeling her own blood drip onto the floor. Her body spasmed uncontrollably. She could not raise her head. But it was over, at least. For now. She was alone with her pain.

But no. Not alone. The guards were still there.

And Arenadd. He would not abandon her either. He was her enemy now, he was damned, but he would stay her companion, and he understood, yes he did . . . had to know how it felt . . .

Saeddryn coughed weakly, and nearly screamed again when the action made pain explode through her body.

"Arenadd . . ." Her voice came out as a bloodied rasp.

I'm here, Saeddryn. Always.

"Ye . . . Arenadd . . . ye won't . . . tell them where . . . ?"

No. Caedmon's secret is safe with me. I don't want him to be hurt. He was like a son to me.

Saeddryn managed a smile. "Shoul . . . should've been . . . yer son."

We all wish for impossible things, Saeddryn.

Speaking was agony, but Saeddryn could not stop herself. She had to know. "Was it all . . . lies? Did ye ever . . . ever love me?"

You? Arenadd chuckled. *You were the bane of my existence. You argued with me about every damn little thing. You nagged me for being drunk too often. You made a scene in front of the council at least three times because I wouldn't agree to something you wanted.*

Saeddryn's eye closed. "So . . . nothing . . . was true."

You were my rock, Arenadd said gently. *One of the only constants I ever had. I loved you for that.*

Saeddryn tried to laugh. "Thank . . . thank ye."

I wish I could have made things right, said Arenadd. *But I've spent my whole life wishing for things I couldn't have. And when I try to do what's right, things just get worse for everybody.* He made a soft, shuddering sound. *Whatever punishment the Night God has in store for me will just be what I deserve for doing this to you.*

Saeddryn tried to rise. "No," she gasped. "Ye did . . . right thing. Protecting yer children . . . I understand. If it was ye here in these chains, ye'd do the same, wouldn't ye . . . ?" She fell back again.

Yes. A hundred times.

"Then . . . ye understand why . . ." Saeddryn couldn't speak any more.

Just rest, said Arenadd. *If you give up or stay silent, it's up to you now. Do what you think you can do. The gods can't demand any less.*

No, Saeddryn thought. That wasn't true. The gods always demanded more.

But she said nothing and let herself rest there in the shadows that weren't hers to command any more. And even though she knew what lay ahead, and what the outcome would eventually be, she felt almost glad to be where she was, and glad that Arenadd was there. No matter what happened, she would feel better to know he was with her.

The days that followed were a nightmare.

As she had promised, Laela returned every day and brought Kullervo and the torturer with her. Brother and sister stood by and watched as the nameless Amorani did her work, neither one speaking to Saeddryn though every session began the same way, with Laela asking once again where Caedmon was.

Every day, Saeddryn said nothing, and every day, the torture continued.

It was torture unlike anything another prisoner would have suffered, since Saeddryn could not die or be injured beyond recovery.

Nor was she allowed to escape into unconsciousness. Her tormentor always seemed to know exactly when to stop, always bringing her just to the brink but no further.

Trapped underground, Saeddryn could not see the moon or the stars, and time soon melded together into an endless succession of punishment. Waiting for it to end, waiting for it to resume, and never being free of pain in all that time.

Pain and the memory of pain were her companions in that cell, along with Arenadd, who whispered to her sometimes. Sometimes he tried to console her, but more and more often he pleaded with her to just give in. Give in and end it, and spare them both.

She did not give in.

But Saeddryn wasn't the only one suffering; Kullervo was, too. Every day he had to go with Laela and watch what took place in that cell, knowing that there was nothing he could do about it. And worse, he knew that it was all his fault. He had brought Saeddryn to this. But what choice did he have? He couldn't let her go, but he couldn't bear to watch her agony, and the longer he had to, the more he wanted to do something. Even if he couldn't stop it, he wanted to be allowed to leave and not have to see it any more.

But Laela needed him there, and she wouldn't let him leave. Only she had the power to stop it, but she wouldn't, and when Kullervo pleaded with her in private, she was dismissive.

"If she got the chance she'd do the same to us," she said flatly. "Remember that. Don't ever ask me again, Kullervo."

"But can't we just kill her?" asked Kullervo. "She's not going to talk."

"It ends when she decides to end it," said Laela. "An' that's all there is to it. Now go an' get some rest."

So Kullervo gave in and continued to stand by in silence, hating himself for being so weak, for not knowing what to do other than what he was told.

He watched as Saeddryn's body was torn and mutilated bit by bit. He watched her scream and plead and try to fight back. But despite everything, she still would not give in, and when

Laela coldly refused to accept it and ordered for the torture to continue, Kullervo watched her finally descend into insanity.

When that happened, even Laela saw sense. She told the torturer to stop, and the three of them stood there and watched Saeddryn babble and moan to herself, sometimes sobbing softly.

"That's it then," Laela said in disgust. "We'll leave her for now. If she's still like this tomorrow, we'll get on with things. Caedmon won't be a threat without her anyway."

She let the torturer out of the cell and dismissively turned away.

But Kullervo's eyes had stayed on Saeddryn. He reached out gently and put a big hand on Laela's shoulder. "Wait."

Laela stopped. "What?"

"Let me in there," said Kullervo. "Let me talk to her."

Laela's eyes narrowed. "Why?"

"I just . . ." Kullervo looked past her into the cell. "She's family. Just let me talk to her."

"Fine." Laela handed him the key. "But Kullervo . . . don't do anythin' stupid."

Kullervo unlocked the door without replying and went into the cell.

Saeddryn half lay at his feet, held up from the floor by her chains. Her head hung downward, as if she were staring at the dried blood beneath her, and Kullervo saw her ruined hands shaking uncontrollably.

He knelt beside her and lifted her head into his hands. "Saeddryn," he murmured in his gentlest voice.

Saeddryn's trembling stopped for a moment. Then she started to cry—horrible, painful sobs which turned the trembling into ugly convulsions that made her wasted body jerk against its restraints.

Kullervo held her as well as he could, embracing her awkwardly and speaking softly to her. "It's all right, Saeddryn. It's all right."

The words were meaningless, and stupid as well. Nothing was all right. Everything was in pieces, just like her sanity. Even his own world felt as if it were coming apart.

Saeddryn's sobs died down eventually, and she relaxed against him, taking comfort from his presence.

Forgetting everything, even caution, Kullervo reached out and started to unfasten her manacles. He freed her wrists and her waist, ignoring Laela's warnings, and pulled her onto his lap, hugging her to him as if she were a child.

Saeddryn did not try to escape. She clutched at him, or tried to, and sighed a long, deep sigh.

Outside, Laela came up to the bars and banged on them with her fist. "Kullervo!" she said. "What the blazes are yeh doin'? Put them chains back on her right now, or I'll have yeh in a set of yer own!"

Kullervo glanced over at her. There were tears on his face. "It's all right," he said. "I need to help her."

"No yeh don't! She's tried to kill yeh three times!"

Kullervo turned away from her, and murmured to Saeddryn again. "It's all right. It's over. You're safe now. I've got you."

"Arenadd?" Saeddryn whispered.

Kullervo hesitated. But then he decided to let her believe it. If it made her feel better, it wouldn't hurt anyone. "Yes, it's me, Saeddryn," he said. "It's Arenadd."

Her eye had opened, and she looked up at his scarred face. "Yer back. Yer alive. I feel a heart . . . a warm heart beatin' . . ."

"That's right." Kullervo smiled. "I'm mortal."

"Good . . ." Saeddryn's eye closed. "It's all up with me, Arenadd. Leave me. Go back t'Caedmon. He needs ye now. Be a father to him."

"I will," said Kullervo.

Laela was pressed up against the bars, listening. "Where is he?" she hissed. *"Where is he?"*

"On the island," Saeddryn muttered. "Still with the lost tribe. He's got the tattoos now, but he won't leave till . . . till I go back an' tell him it's time. Ye go back, Arenadd. Go tell him . . . say his mother loves him, say it . . ."

"I will," said Kullervo. "But I don't know the way. Where is the island?"

Dead silence fell. Laela held her breath.

"North," Saeddryn said at last, eye still closed. "North . . . west . . . off the coast of the First Mountains, remember? Where the lost tribe . . ." She trailed off into silence, and something that might have been sleep.

"Come out of there now," said Laela, breaking the moment. "Bring her with yeh, an' keep hold of her. We ain't takin' chances, no matter what."

Kullervo removed the last of the chains from Saeddryn's ankles, and stood up with her huddled in his arms. "So now you know," he said weakly.

Laela's face was alight with determination and triumph. "Yeh did good, Kullervo. I'm proud of yeh. Now let's go. It's time t'put an end to her. No way I'm leavin' it any longer."

She led the way out of the dungeons with the guards forming up on either side of Kullervo, who carried Saeddryn out of there, feeling light-headed. It was over. At last it was over, and he had helped to end it.

You lied, his conscience whispered. *You lied to her and made her betray her own son.*

Kullervo's heart ached. But still he did nothing. He obediently took Saeddryn up and out into the governor's tower, and into the room they had picked out and prepared long ago.

Once it had been a simple storeroom, but its contents had been removed. The window had been enlarged, allowing sunlight to shine on a stone block that had been hastily carved with a sunwheel. A bunch of flowers stood on it, and incense brought in especially had been burned there every day. Akhane's two priest friends had blessed the room from wall to wall, performing all the rituals of purification in the name of the sun god several times. They had prayed there, too, along with Akhane and several of the Southerners staying in the tower. If any room could become a Sun Temple, this one had.

When Kullervo took Saeddryn inside, he knew immediately that their efforts had succeeded. The instant he stepped over the threshold, Saeddryn gasped in pain and went limp. He could feel her breathing become fast and shallow, and he knew that the room's influence must have stripped away her powers. He, too, felt uneasy here, and had done ever since the blessings had been made. That had been proof enough for Senneck, at least.

Akhane and the two priests came running shortly after Kullervo entered the room. Laela came with them, and so did Kraego, who went to crouch by the makeshift altar and watch.

Heart fluttering, Kullervo took the flowers off the altar and laid Saeddryn down there. The two priests stepped in and tied her down with some ropes that had been put in place long ago. Once she was secured, one of them stood aside and began to chant a prayer, while the other hurried to light a brazier.

Akhane picked up a long golden knife and looked expectantly at his wife and her brother. "Who will do the deed?"

"Not me," said Laela. "I'm no good with a knife. An' besides . . ." She looked uneasy.

Akhane turned to Kullervo. "You should do it, sacred one," he said. "You are the one with the power."

Kullervo blanched. "No. No, I couldn't . . ."

"Very well then," said Akhane. "I will do it. I have read many books about the human anatomy."

"Do not begin until my mother is here," Kraego piped up. "She wished to see this for herself."

"She won't fit in here," said Laela, glaring at him.

"She does not need to," Senneck interrupted from the window. Her head poked through, haloed with light. "Has she told you where her son has hidden himself?"

"Yeah, she has," said Laela. "We wouldn't be doin' this now if she hadn't."

"We must begin now," said Akhane. "The sun will not reach this room for much longer."

"Go on," said Laela.

The two priests took up station at Saeddryn's head and feet, and recited a verse from their own sacred book. It was in Amorani, but Kullervo had been told that it was to do with the banishment of evil and the protection of life.

Akhane stood between them, at Saeddryn's side. She was awake now, moaning softly as the power of the Temple burned inside her.

Using griffish, Akhane began to recite something he had written beforehand, making a ritual that had never been performed before—and hopefully never would be again.

"Years ago, a wise griffin of this land gave a message to humankind: Find the heart of the heartless one, and so destroy the creature the Night God sent. The one who heard those words tried to follow them but died for his courage. Today we remember him, and them, and we will carry them out as they were meant to be carried out. We will remove the heart of this abomination, and so destroy it forever. We do it in your name, mighty Xanathus, who is called Gryphus. We destroy this monster of the shadows, and so protect the life you create and bless. Bring your power to us now, and help us, we pray to you!" He held up the dagger so it caught the sunlight, making Senneck hiss angrily when it reflected into her eyes.

Then Akhane brought the dagger down, into Saeddryn's chest, and slowly and laboriously hacked out her heart.

Saeddryn came fully awake then. Her scream was unearthly.

It would stay with Kullervo for the rest of his life.

Akhane's face twisted with revulsion, but he didn't hesitate. He cut away until he had made a hole, ignoring Saeddryn's screams and struggles, and forced her ribs apart. He thrust his hand into the gap, and pulled out her heart with an almighty wrench.

The instant it came free, Saeddryn went limp. Her sufferings were over.

Akhane held up the heart. It was slick with blood, but underneath they could all see what it had become.

It was withered and shrunken, leathery, crossed with black veins. Anyone who saw it could tell that it had not beaten in a long time. This was the heart of a dead thing.

Akhane examined it with morbid fascination. "It is so cold . . . *argh!*"

He jerked his hand away, dropping the heart. It landed on the altar, by Saeddryn's arm.

Kullervo, stepping closer to see, saw Saeddryn's hand twitch. The broken fingers curled inward. He nudged the heart away with his talon, and the movement stopped the moment it lost contact with the skin.

Akhane was shivering, rubbing his hands. "It attacked me!" he said. "I felt it . . . it felt as if it were trying to take the life out of my body."

Kullervo breathed in sharply. "Look!" he said.

"It's horrible," Laela grimaced. "Like old boot leather."

"No, can't you see it?" said Kullervo. "There's mist . . . black mist coming out of it."

"I can't see nothin'," said Laela. "Destroy it, now."

Akhane nodded toward Kullervo. "This is your task, winged man. Destroy the heart. We cannot allow it to exist."

Kullervo picked it up cautiously, using his talon tips to stop it from touching his skin. But he still felt the hideous cold bite into him before he dropped the heart into the brazier.

The flames licked around it, making the blood sizzle and dry. For a moment, they rose higher, hiding the heart from view. But then they died down again, burning lower and dimmer until they went out.

The heart sat on the coals, untouched.

"Shit!" said Laela. "What the . . . ?"

Akhane, frowning, tried to stab the heart with his dagger. The blade bounced off its surface without leaving a mark. He tried again, harder, but the dagger only wrenched out of his hand with the impact.

"Indestructible," the Prince breathed. "By Xanathus . . ."

"All right then," said Laela. "If we can't destroy it, we'll just get rid of it. Hide it somewhere. An' we'll get rid of the body, too. We can't destroy the heart, but we can destroy the body, an' as long as they're not put back together, we're fine."

The people in the room all looked at each other, as if daring anyone to step forward.

"You take it, Lord Kullervo," said Akhane, still nursing his hand. "You should be strong enough to protect yourself from it."

"What should I do with it?" asked Kullervo.

"Just keep it safe," said Laela. "Never tell anyone yeh got it, never let anyone see it."

"But . . . me?" said Kullervo. "Isn't there someone else . . . ?"

"I trust you more than anyone else in the world," Laela said with a smile. "More than enough t'trust yeh with this."

"Here," said Akhane, offering Kullervo a leather pouch. "This should be large enough."

Very carefully, Kullervo lifted the heart out of the brazier. It was just as icy cold as before. He stuffed it into the pouch and tied it shut, feeling better the moment it was out of sight.

Laela looked happier as well. "Right then," she said. "Finished. Whew. Thank gods. You—" She turned to Senneck. "I got a job for yeh."

Senneck put her head on one side. "What do you want me to do?"

Laela pointed at Saeddryn's corpse. "After executions, the executioners always give the body back t'the family. Take care of that, would yeh? An' take some friends with yeh, too. Kullervo can stay here."

Senneck's eyes narrowed. "I will do it gladly, Queen Laela."

32

The End of All Hope

After the adulthood ceremony, Caedmon and Myfina stayed on with the lost tribe. Now that they had been initiated, they had full status and weren't forced to go with their teachers. Free to do more as they pleased, they spent most of their time together and used it to gather food and improve their lodgings.

Both of them felt ready to leave the island, but by now they had become so used to life with the tribe that staying was easier. And Caedmon wanted to wait for Saeddryn to come back.

"She'll tell us what the situation is and whether she managed to kill the man-griffin. Besides, if we leave, she won't know where to find us."

"I don't know about that," said Myfina. "She has a way of knowing where people are. Haven't you noticed?"

"Of course I have," said Caedmon. "But I told her I'd wait."

"I suppose." Myfina touched her belly. "But she'd better come back soon. I don't want to travel with a baby."

"You already are." Caedmon grinned.

"You know what I mean. We should go and see how the griffins are doing."

Caedmon nodded thoughtfully. He and Myfina had gone over to the griffin island as planned, after the ceremony, but only Garsh had come when they called, and even he had been reluctant.

"Shar will not come," he had said briefly. "Her young are not ready to be left behind."

"What young?" Caedmon had asked.

"She has laid my eggs," Garsh had explained. "Her chicks are still in the nest. She will not leave them."

So the two humans had left, with no idea of when Shar's eggs had hatched or how long it would take before she was ready to leave.

"I'm not worried about the chicks," Caedmon said now. "We can just carry them with us if we have to. It's not unheard of with partnered griffins, if there's a need for it."

"Maybe, but you'll have to do a lot of persuading," said Myfina.

Caedmon shrugged. "No time like the present. Will you come with me?"

"Of course." Myfina stood up and went to put on an extra layer of furs.

She and Caedmon crossed the island, following a track they had both come to know very well, heading for the sea.

"I wish she'd come back," Caedmon said along the way. "She's been gone too long. I hope something hasn't happened to her."

"Her?" said Myfina. "Don't be silly. Bad things happen to other people when she's about, not the other way around."

"Yes, but it still bothers me. If something did happen to her, we'd have no way of knowing about it." Caedmon frowned. "We should leave soon. We've stayed here too long."

"So you keep saying." They had reached the coast by now, and Myfina uncovered a bark canoe they had stashed among some rocks. "Help me with this, will you?"

Caedmon helped her drag it to the water, and the two of them climbed aboard and paddled out toward the island. Fortunately, the sea was fairly calm at the moment.

On the other side, they hauled the canoe out of the water but left it just barely out of reach of the waves. Staying close to the water themselves, they cautiously scanned the sky. Caedmon had brought his spear and kept it ready in his hand.

The moment a hostile griffin came near, they would both dive into the sea. It would make them hard to spot, and since griffins hated water, it would be unlikely to try very hard to get at them.

Myfina cupped her hands around her mouth, and screeched her own name like a griffin would. *"Myfina! Myfina!"*

Caedmon squared his shoulders and added his voice to hers. *"Caedmon! Caedmon!"*

They called for as long as they could and rested while they waited for a response.

Eventually, a faint call came back. It was difficult to make out the name.

Caedmon and Myfina both watched closely, still on the alert in case of danger.

Then Caedmon pointed. "There!"

Sure enough, a griffin had appeared in the sky. It circled overhead for a while until it spotted them, and came down toward them. Myfina tensed, but Caedmon nodded and smiled. "It's Shar!" he said. "I'd know her anywhere."

The griffin landed on top of a nearby sand-dune. It was indeed Shar, and she was not alone. Four youngsters landed more clumsily here and there on the sand, and scurried back to their mother's flanks. Shar held out her wings to cover them, and looked calmly at Caedmon.

"My human has become wild," she said.

"So have you, I think," said Caedmon.

Shar didn't look much like the griffin who had once lived in Malvern's Eyrie, with servants to bring her food and clean her nest. Her fur and feathers were grubbier but managed to look more glossy at the same time, even though there were visible scars on her haunches and a row of what had to be talon-scratches on her beak. Her eyes looked brighter, her talons sharper, and she looked leaner, but in a way that made her seem more powerful than she had ever looked before.

But she was more restless, too, as she soon looked away from Caedmon to check on her chicks and watch out for danger. She didn't lie down or sit on her haunches but stayed standing with her talons extended, like a wild animal ready to fight or run the moment she had to.

"I have learnt," she said shortly. "This place has shown me what a griffin truly is."

"And what's that?" asked Caedmon. He was genuinely curious.

"A wild creature," said Shar. "The most dangerous creature in the world." She looked proud, and fierce as well. "I have fought as a griffin should, and mated as a griffin should, and here are the young that I have raised."

Caedmon eyed them. They were more than old enough for

him to spot their genders right away—three females and a male, all showing various shades of brown and russet inherited from their parents. They eyed him back warily. He must be the first human they had ever seen.

"When will they be ready to leave?" he asked.

"They are ready to leave now," said Shar. "They will come with us when we leave this place. Garsh and I have defeated every other griffin on this island; we are the dominant pair now. We have won that challenge, and now we are prepared to battle for true supremacy."

"Where's Garsh?" asked Myfina.

"He is well," said Shar. "I will tell him that you have been here. He is larger than I am, but I am the more powerful fighter, and my human is superior to his. Therefore, I will be the one to fight the Mighty Skandar."

Even now, Caedmon shivered at the idea. "You really think you can do it?"

"I will fight him, and I will defeat him," said Shar. "The Mighty Skandar has grown old, and life among humans has made him fat and soft. He will be no match for me."

It was an impressive boast, and Caedmon had to nod, and say, "Of course. We're still waiting for my mother to come back. She'll have news for us. Once she's with us again, we can leave."

"She is not here?" said Shar.

"No, she left a couple of weeks ago. She said she was going to Warwick to kill the man-griffin."

"I do not like this," said Shar, eyes narrowing. "She should have come back by now."

Caedmon began to feel uneasy. "Maybe you're right . . . everything's so quiet here that I didn't really think that much about it. What do you think we should do?"

"The time for *Kraeaina kran ae* to guide us is past," said Shar. "She is not your leader, and if she cannot be here beside you when she should be, then forget it. We must leave the island now, before winter comes again. She will find us herself."

Caedmon shook himself. "Maybe you're right. My training is finished. I'm a man now, and I shouldn't still be worrying about what my mother thinks."

"Agreed," said Myfina. "We should leave. The tribe doesn't need us around eating their food any more."

"Yes . . ." Caedmon scratched the now-healed tattoos on his face. "It's time to take charge. Let's go back to the mainland, say . . . tomorrow. Why not? Is that all right with you, Shar?"

"It is," said Shar. "I have been prepared to leave for some days now and was only waiting for you to come and say you were also ready. I will go and find Garsh now, and we will come to the human island and meet you at dawn."

"Right," said Caedmon. "We'll wait on the easternmost beach. There's enough landing room there, and you'll be able to see us easily from the sky."

"Then we are agreed." Shar unceremoniously flew off, with her chicks close behind.

After that, there was nothing for Caedmon and Myfina to do but return to the tribe's island.

"We'd better go and tell Llygad we're leaving," said Caedmon. "But first . . ."

But first they returned to their hut. There, Caedmon unfolded a large fur that he had been using as a bedspread. Henwas' griffin-skin robe.

Caedmon put it on and found that it fitted him quite well. "I'm taking this with me when we leave," he said. "I know it'll make me look strange to everyone back home, but I'm not leaving it behind."

"It's the only thing we have to remember Henwas," Myfina agreed. She smiled sadly. "It looks good on you."

"It's smelly, just like he said." Caedmon chuckled. "Come on, let's go."

Llygad was out hunting, but they found him that evening when he returned to the village. When Caedmon told him they were leaving, he squinted and rubbed his nose.

"I had thought you would leave sooner."

"We were waiting for my mother to come back," said Caedmon. "But we can't stay here and keep being a burden. We're both grateful for everything you've taught us. When we've won our war, I'll send people out here to bring you food and good weapons. You'll be a part of my Kingdom, and can ask for anything you want."

He had already promised this long before, and Llygad nodded curtly by way of reply.

"We'll leave tomorrow morning," Myfina put in. "With our griffins."

Llygad regarded her, and finally smiled. "We will miss you. You both learnt well, and your powers have brought us good luck."

"Thank you," said Caedmon. "I'll never forget my time here with you. Llygad, if my mother comes back here looking for me, could you tell her where I've gone?"

"I will," said Llygad.

"Tell her I've gone to . . ." Caedmon paused. "Eitheinn. That should be a good starting place."

"I will tell her," Llygad promised.

Caedmon and Myfina excused themselves as politely as they could and whiled away the rest of the day doing some minor repairs and improving their hut for whoever moved in after they left it.

That evening, they shared their last meal with the tribe and sat up late around the communal fire, telling stories. Afterward, they retired to their hut and slept in each other's arms.

"You'll be Malvern's Queen soon," Caedmon whispered before he fell asleep. "I can feel it."

"With you, Sire," Myfina whispered back.

Morning came, and the two of them rose at dawn, just as they had every morning during their time on the island. Together, they gathered up their few belongings and dressed in their warmest furs before walking away toward the eastern beach.

There was no sign of Shar or Garsh there yet, so they sat down together on the sand and shared some dried meat.

"I'm going to miss this place," said Myfina. "I really am."

"Me too," said Caedmon.

"I mean," Myfina continued, "when I first got here, I hated it. I thought there was no way I'd ever get used to it. I even thought about just going and finding Garsh and leaving for good. But now I've been here for so long that it feels like home. I'm almost scared to go back."

"Only sensible," Caedmon said gruffly. "Once we're on the mainland, we'll be fugitives again."

"We're fugitives here," said Myfina. "More or less."

"True, but—hey, look there's Shar!" Caedmon stood up, shielding his eyes, and waved to Shar with his free hand.

"I can see Garsh, too!" said Myfina, waving to her own partner.

But Garsh stayed overhead, soaring in a tight circle over the two humans. The chicks stayed with him, leaving Shar to swoop down on her own.

She landed in a spray of sand, and bounded to Caedmon's side. "Quickly, there is a griffin coming," she said tersely.

Caedmon tensed. "Only one?"

"Yes, but it is not wild. It has come from the mainland, and it is carrying something."

"What should we do?" asked Myfina.

"If there is only one, Garsh and I can kill it easily," said Shar. "But we could also flee. Caedmon, you must decide."

He thought quickly. "It could be a friend. If there's only one, there shouldn't be too much danger as long as you're with us. Let's wait until it arrives and see what it does. What was it carrying?"

"I cannot tell," said Shar. "Something large and wrapped in cloth."

"Maybe it's those heads Mother promised," Caedmon said darkly. "But let's wait. When we see how it acts, we'll have a better idea of whether it's a friend or not."

They waited together in a little group, while Garsh watched from overhead. All of them knew that if the strange griffin decided to attack, he would be in a perfect position to hit it from behind. The griffin that flew higher always had the advantage.

Soon enough, Caedmon saw the stranger come into view. It flew slowly and wearily, weighed down by the large bundle that hung from its talons. Clearly, the beast had flown all the way from the mainland with it. Caedmon relaxed when he saw how tired the griffin was; if it decided to attack, it would be at a disadvantage.

But the griffin didn't seem interested in attacking. It saw Garsh and avoided him, instead coming in low toward the beach in a clear gesture of nonaggression. A griffin looking for a fight would have attacked Garsh first, not landed and put itself at his mercy.

Shar stood by warily as the stranger approached. It was female, middle-aged, her sandy brown feathers flecked with grey. She dipped her head respectfully to Shar.

"I have come to bring a message and a gift for Lord Caedmon."

"Where have you come from?" Shar demanded.

"From Warwick," said the stranger. "From Lady Saeddryn."

"You have a message from *Kraeaina kran ae*?" said Shar.

"I do, but I must give it to Lord Caedmon only."

Shar started up angrily, but Caedmon pushed past her. "I'm Lord Caedmon," he said boldly. "What do you have to tell me?"

"I have brought you this." The griffin lifted the bundle with her beak, and dumped it at Caedmon's feet. "A gift."

The bundle was wrapped in cloth. Caedmon drew his knife and slit it open.

Saeddryn's body fell out onto the sand.

"No!" Caedmon threw his knife down and fell onto his knees, turning the corpse over to look at it.

Saeddryn's face was ghastly white, the mouth hanging limply open in a silent scream. Even at a glance, Caedmon could see everything that had happened to her since her disappearance. The fingers crushed and broken, fingernails ripped out. Flesh burned and torn apart. And the gaping hole in the chest, filled with congealed blood that didn't hide the space where her heart had been.

"No," Caedmon heard his own voice say, from somewhere far away. "No, no, no . . . !"

The world seemed to spin around him. He looked up, and saw the griffin looking down at him with pitiless blue eyes.

"Before your mother died, she told us where to find you," she said. "But not willingly. It took many days. By the time we gave her death, she had already lost her mind."

Caedmon stood up slowly, letting Saeddryn's body fall at his feet. "You . . ."

"I am Senneck," said the blue-eyed griffin. "Senneck of Eagleholm, partner to Lord Erian Rannagonson. Now I am partnered to Prince Kullervo Taranisäii, the true heir to the throne of Malvern. Together, we have avenged Erian at last. And now I will protect my new human by killing you."

She lunged at Caedmon.

Shar hit her in the flank, knocking her down. But she recovered herself with surprising speed. Ignoring the other griffin completely—and ignoring Garsh, who had seen the attack and was already swooping down on her—she charged.

Caedmon stumbled away from her, desperately searching for Myfina. From somewhere to his left he heard her shout, *"The Unpartnered are coming!"*

Distracted, he looked up, and felt ice stab into his heart. The sky was full of griffins. Griffins, coming out of nowhere, confusing Garsh, who abandoned his attack on Senneck and wheeled around to try to face them.

Senneck had kept them all occupied long enough, and now her companions descended on the island in their dozens. It was enough to distract Shar as well. Seeing the enemy close in on her young, she screeched her rage and bewilderment.

Senneck took her chance and brought her talons down on Caedmon.

A scream tore the air. Senneck shuddered with the force of her blow, and hissed furiously as she pulled her talons out of her victim.

Caedmon stared dumbly. Myfina had moved so fast he had barely even seen her, and for a moment it was as if she had simply appeared on the ground, torn almost in half by Senneck's talons.

Senneck recovered herself, and trampled over Myfina's body to get at Caedmon.

He ran.

Forgetting Shar, and everything else, he ran inland as fast as he could, bounding over logs and stones and dodging trees until he reached the village, and ran through it, shouting at the top of his voice.

"Run! Get away! Griffins are coming! Run!"

Llygad appeared in front of him. "Griffins?" he exclaimed. "What griffins have come?"

"Enemies!" Caedmon yelled in his face. "Dozens of them! Tell everyone to get away—hide! Get to the sea! Don't try to fight!"

Llygad had too much sense to waste time with questions. He darted off through the huts, roaring warnings and orders to everyone he saw. Caedmon went in the other direction to spread the word.

It came too late. The Unpartnered were already landing. There was no room for more than one or two in the main clearing, so they landed wherever they could, some perching on tree-tops and sliding awkwardly down the trunks to get at their prey.

One griffin, more practical-minded, stayed where he was and simply used his magic to start a fire.

It spread through the village in moments, then to the forest beyond. The flames drove people away from hiding places, out into the open, where they were caught and killed.

Caedmon knew there was nothing more he could do. He ran out of the village, past his old hut. It was already burning. The forest was no good, so he made for the only other place he could think of that might be safe. The island of wild griffins.

He reached the shore where the canoe was hidden, and dragged it out into the water. He knew that trying to paddle it would make him an easy target, so instead he turned it upside down and began to swim, hiding in the air pocket underneath it.

It was the longest swim of his life. The water was freezing, and the canoe was a dead weight. The waves constantly splashed up under it and into his face, leaving him gasping for air and only just able to keep himself afloat.

Every moment he expected to be attacked. A griffin's talons could cut straight through the flimsy canoe, then they would pluck him out of the water like a fish. Whenever he closed his eyes, he saw the bodies of Saeddryn and Myfina, their blank black eyes staring at him, and the knowledge thundered sickeningly through him.

I'm all that's left. The last one. My child . . .

Even hatred wasn't enough to take away the agony of knowing that.

Eventually, when cold had numbed his body and grief had numbed his mind, he began to think of just letting himself sink. The ocean would take him into itself and let him forget everything.

But he kept on going. Somehow, he couldn't make himself let go.

Sand touched his feet. *Then* he let go, and dived out from

under the canoe. He surfaced within sight of the shore and swam the rest of the way, heart thudding painfully in his ears.

But the death from above never came.

Caedmon hauled himself out of the sea and stumbled up the beach toward the shelter of the trees and finally let himself look up.

They had followed him.

Two Unpartnered hovered above. They were already coming lower, ready to attack him now that he had left the water. He could see their talons extending, clutching the air in anticipation.

Despair weighed him down. Slowly, knowing that he had no chance, he staggered on toward the tree-line. There was no way he would make it in time. He was going to die, and he knew it, and with him, the last of the true Taranisäiis would be gone forever.

"Mother, forgive me," he mumbled to himself.

A screech came from above. Caedmon did not stop to look. He didn't want to see his death coming. He kept on going doggedly, thinking of what a pathetic ending this would be for the Taranisäii line. For its last descendant to die a failure, running hopelessly from his enemies.

But the trees opened up in front of him, and he entered their shelter and collapsed there, shuddering with exhaustion. And still death did not come.

He pulled himself upright, and looked out at the sky over the shore. The two Unpartnered were still there, but they weren't coming after him. They were circling around uncertainly— *Retreating!* he thought suddenly. That was it, they were leaving! Flying away from another griffin. A big, rangy wild griffin, coming at them from the island's higher reaches and screeching a territorial challenge.

It was one the two intruders didn't want to answer. They hung back, not quite fleeing outright but unwilling to come any closer.

The stalemate broke when a fourth griffin appeared from the main island. For a moment it looked as if it was about to join up with the two Unpartnered, and they acted as if they thought it would, but then it viciously assaulted them, taking them completely by surprise.

One of them took a blow to the head and another to the wing, and tumbled out of the sky. It landed in the sea and floundered there, unable to swim. The other Unpartnered flew away, back to the main island.

That left the attacker, who came on toward the griffin island, screeching a counterchallenge at the wild griffin.

A challenge that Caedmon recognised.

"Shar! Shaaaar!"

The wild griffin recognised it, too. He screeched back unenthusiastically and retreated when Shar came closer. This was a griffin he didn't want to fight again.

Shar landed on the beach, and Caedmon ran to her. Forgetting the proper behaviour around griffins, he flung her arms around her neck.

"Shar! Oh thank the Night God . . ."

Shar pushed him off her. "Stop that," she snapped. "Get onto my back. We must leave immediately. They will soon overrun this island as well."

"But Myfina—"

"She is dead. You cannot help her now."

"Garsh—?"

"He is also dead."

"Your chicks?" Caedmon faltered.

"I do not know," Shar said more quietly. "I think they are dead, too. But they are old enough to care for themselves. What happens to them now is for them to choose. Come."

Caedmon climbed onto her back. "Where are we going to go?"

Shar said nothing. The moment he was on her back, she took off with a big, rough motion that nearly threw him straight off again.

It had been a long time since he had flown with her, but all his time on the island had made him far stronger than he had ever been before. He held on tightly, and soon found himself moving in harmony with her, just as he had done a thousand times before.

Shar avoided the main island and flew straight over the third island, where the standing stones were. It was the same island where Caedmon and Myfina had buried Henwas, and if any of the lost tribe survived the massacre, they would bury Saeddryn and Myfina there. And with her they would bury Caedmon's child.

Caedmon closed his eyes against the wind and felt a massive

void open up inside him. It had been there already, with the loss of Sionen. But it had widened when his sister Arddryn died, and now with the deaths of both Saeddryn and Myfina, it consumed him.

He didn't try to take any more vows, not even to himself. He knew now that there was no point. Vows were for weaklings and dreamers. Nor did he make a promise.

Instead, he decided. It was as simple as that.

I will kill them all.

33

Rotten Core

Once Senneck had left with a group of Unpartnered, Laela didn't waste any time before returning to Malvern. Her pregnancy made her tired, and she didn't like Warwick.

Kullervo went with her. He went in griffin form, and flew at the rear of the flock that left Warwick. He spent the entire journey that way and barely spoke to anyone. When they reached Malvern, he retreated silently to his rooms and slept alone in front of the fire.

Once he would have become human again now that he was home. But he didn't. He had done everything he had been ordered to do for now, and there was no need to change. Besides, he didn't want to be human any more.

He lay on the hearth rug and stared dully at the fire, emotionless in his griffin shape.

I don't deserve to be human, he thought. *What I did was inhuman. I can't pretend to be a real man any more. Never again.*

Deep down, though, he still felt like a coward. He kept telling himself that he was staying a griffin as punishment, but the truth was that it was easier this way. The griffin shape did not feel anything half as powerfully as the human. It helped to protect him from the worst of his guilt.

But not all of it.

I am a monster, he thought, the words looping endlessly in his head. *A destroyer. I've become my father. I lied. I murdered. I saw something evil happen and did nothing. I am a monster . . .*

He fell asleep with those words torturing him, and fell into a dream of darkness.

A dream in which his father came to him.

Not as a faint, wavering impression as he had before, but as something solid and sharp, as real as if he weren't a dream at all. Kullervo saw him step out of the shadows and stand there, staring at him in silence. He was tall and thin, clad in a black robe that hid most of his body. His face was thin and scarred with a pointed beard, framed by long, curly hair.

Kullervo, can you hear me? his voice called. It wasn't the barely audible whisper of before. Now it sounded real, loud enough for Kullervo hear the accent. Not a Northern accent at all, he knew.

The voice of Arenadd Taranisäii had an accent belonging to someone who had been born and raised in Eagleholm.

Kullervo felt no shock. "You're Arren Cardockson," he said.

Not many people remember that name any more, said the dream.

"But it was your name," said Kullervo. "Wasn't it?"

Once. But that was a long time ago.

"I've seen the place where you lived," said Kullervo. "And the place where you died."

All gone now, Arenadd said sadly. *All ruined. I can't remember it any more. Kullervo, you know I'm your father, don't you?*

"Yes," said Kullervo. "And Laela's father as well."

No. Laela was Arren's daughter. He died before she was even born. You're my only child, Kullervo. The only child of Arenadd Taranisäii. The son of the only woman I ever loved.

"You can love, then?" said Kullervo.

Yes. Your mother was the last time I ever fell in love. Maybe that's why she survived long enough to give birth to you.

Kullervo watched him, feeling completely calm. "This isn't a dream, is it?" he said. "I saw you before, when I was awake. And I heard you, too. You came to help me."

I did, said Arenadd. *I thought I might be able to talk to you properly while you were asleep.*

"Why are you here?" said Kullervo. "Are you a ghost?"

Arenadd gave a twisted smile. *An evil spirit. The Night God sent me back to help Saeddryn kill you. She made me her spy and her advisor. But I betrayed her. If I hadn't, she would have killed both of you by now.*

Kullervo couldn't make himself look at that smile. "I didn't know what Laela would do. I thought . . . and I stood there and watched her be tortured, and did nothing. I lied to her so she would tell us where Caedmon was, I . . ."

Ah, Kullervo. Arenadd's smile softened. *You really aren't much like me at all. You didn't get my good looks, sadly. You don't seem to have much of your mother in you, either.*

"I know," said Kullervo. "I'm ugly and weak, and I know it."

You have a gentle heart, Kullervo, Arenadd said softly. *You're kind and loving, and you'll never be a monster like me. But you're not weak.*

"I am," said Kullervo. "I could have saved Saeddryn—"

No you couldn't have. Even if you had tried to interfere, Laela would have stopped you. She's the one who takes after me, not you. You're not weak. If you wanted to, you could be a leader every bit as powerful as I was. You could be a great fighter, too. It's all up to you.

"I don't want to lead," said Kullervo. "Or fight."

Then don't. Arenadd glanced around at the nothing that surrounded them. *I don't know how long I can stay. As soon as my master realises what I've done . . .*

"What will she do to you?"

I don't know. There was real fear on Arenadd's face. *I don't know . . .*

"Then leave!" Kullervo tried to reach out to him. "Run away. Get away from her."

I can't. You don't understand. I can't leave her. Arenadd's shoulders hunched. *She has my soul. I'm her slave forever. And now I've betrayed her again, I . . .* He shook himself. *Kullervo, listen. This might be the only chance I ever have to speak to you again. So before I go, I just want you to know this.* He reached out in return, so close, but still unable to touch his son. *If I had known you were out there, I would have done whatever it took. I would have torn the South apart just to get you back. I swear.*

"Then maybe it's better you didn't know," said Kullervo. "I don't want anyone else to die because of me, ever."

Arenadd looked slightly puzzled. *Why not?*

"Because people deserve to live. They're good—"

No. Arenadd spat the word. *People are* bad. *They try to do good, but at the end of everything, they'll always fail. Take it from someone who knows.*

"And how do you *know*?" Kullervo demanded.

Arenadd began to fade. *Because once I was good.* His voice faded, too, like his face, becoming faint and whispering once more. *Don't be me, Kullervo. Be safe . . . goodbye . . .*

Then he was gone, turning back into the shadow that was all that was left of him and disappearing into the darkness that had made him and would be his home now forever.

Kullervo woke up sharply, and for one instant he was convinced that there had been someone there with him, someone standing over him as he slept.

But there was no-one there, and no scent in the air. He was alone.

Misery wrapped itself around him yet again, like a predator that had been waiting patiently for him to emerge. He stood up and loped out of the room, hoping to escape, but it followed him all the way down the tower.

On an impulse, he kept on going until he was in the lowest levels of the building. From there, he went down the sloping passageway that led to the crypt.

It hadn't changed much since his last visit. Someone had finally been able to retrieve the bodies of those killed by Oeka's power, but Kullervo's skin still prickled. In his throat, his magic gland pulsated gently in response to the energy that still hung in the air.

Cautiously, he entered the crypt and looked around. Oeka's hunched body lay exactly where it had been before. It looked dead, and he went closer to investigate.

Over a year had passed since Oeka had destroyed her own mind in her mad quest for power. Her body had been left unoccupied in all that time, and that time had taken its toll. The blinded eyes had shrivelled away to nothing. The tongue, left hanging out of her beak, had turned into a strip of dried, leathery flesh. Oeka's small body had become so thin, there was almost nothing left of it but skin draped over bones, and everywhere the fur and feathers had moulted away in huge patches. She stank of decay.

But, incredibly, Kullervo could see her flanks still move in and out ever so slightly. Each breath came after a huge interval, but it was just enough. She was alive.

If she had still been able to use her body, she would probably have died. But by now her mind had expanded so massively that it had lost the ability to control a body and forgotten how to return to it. Wherever that mind was now, it had no idea where it was in time or space.

Senneck's warnings had been right. Oeka was worse than dead.

Kullervo stepped around the little griffin's pathetic shape, and went to the tomb he knew. On top it was carved to look like a woman lying down, apparently asleep. Her face was sharp and savage, the eyes overlarge and open in a blank glare. The hands, folded on her stomach, had little claws instead of nails.

On the side of the tomb were the words: SKADE OF WITHYPOOL.

Kullervo looked down on her face. "Hello, Mother. Remember me? I've grown up a lot since I saw you."

Of course, Skade did not reply. Unlike her lover, she had been allowed to pass on after her death and would not return to haunt her son. Kullervo wondered if she would bother to try if she could. Probably not. She hadn't cared about him when she was alive, so why would she care now?

He sighed and moved away to inspect the other tombs. There weren't many.

An odd draught led him to investigate the wall opposite the entrance. He scratched at the dirt and found a hanging sheet of cloth, disguised by a layer of dust and cobwebs.

Underneath it was another entrance.

Kullervo shouldered his way through and found himself in an adjoining chamber. This one was much smaller, and only had three tombs.

He inspected the nearest one. It had a carving of a man—a stocky, strong-looking one who did not have the build of a Northerner at all. His face was square-jawed and heroic, but it looked sad. The hands were wrapped around the hilt of a long sword.

On the side of the tomb was the name.

ERIAN RANNAGONSON OF EAGLEHOLM.

Kullervo hissed to himself in astonishment. Moving quickly now, he went to the next tomb, which had been placed close beside the first. This one had been made for a woman. Her carving made her look young and thin, but she wore a flowing gown, and her hair was decorated with delicately carved flowers. And the name . . .

LADY ELKIN, EYRIE MISTRESS OF MALVERN.

The third tomb also belonged to a woman, but one who looked much stronger than the other. She was plainly clad, but someone had laid flowers at her feet—Kullervo could see the dried remains.

FLELL OF EAGLEHOLM, said the inscription.

Kullervo sat on his haunches and stared at the three tombs. He knew all three of their occupants. He knew who had murdered them. And he could guess who had ordered these tombs to be made and who had brought those flowers.

"He remembered," he said aloud. "He remembered Flell. Somewhere deep down, he remembered that he used to love her."

He stayed where he was and stared at the tombs for some time, trying to take in the meaning of them.

Now he understood whose son he really was.

Senneck returned some days after this, with the Unpartnered who had chosen to go with her. Typically, she went straight to report to Laela and Skandar.

"I have done as you commanded," she said, dipping her head toward Skandar. "We killed every human we found on that island."

"An' Caedmon?" Laela interrupted.

"He was there," said Senneck. "As I said, we killed every human there. The island burned. Nothing escaped alive. I myself killed his mate, who was carrying his pup."

"What about Saeddryn's body?" asked Laela. "Did yeh destroy it?"

"I threw it into the fires and watched it burn," said Senneck. She uncurled her talons and dropped a blackened skull onto the floor. It broke apart with the impact.

Laela sat back with a satisfied expression. "Good. Skandar an' I are pleased. In return, we'll give yeh the bounties for Caedmon an' Saeddryn."

"I am pleased to have done my part for us all," Senneck said haughtily. "Is my human well?"

"Griffin, at the moment," said Laela. She frowned. "He ain't been the same since Warwick. He won't turn human again. Won't speak to anyone either. I'm worried about him."

"Then I will go to him," said Senneck. She bowed her head again to Skandar and left.

It wasn't long, however, before she returned. She came back running, and stumbled to a halt in front of the startled Skandar.

"He is gone!" she exclaimed. "Kullervo has left the Eyrie. Where is he?"

"Not know," said Skandar, irritated by her sudden arrival. "Ugly one is your human; you go look for him. Not Mighty Skandar's problem."

Laela, however, grimaced. "Are yeh sure he's gone?"

"Certain," said Senneck. "His room has not been occupied in days. I found no fresh scent anywhere."

"Damn!" Laela rubbed her forehead. "I ain't seen him in at least four days either. Been too busy t'think much about it, but now . . . gods, he'd better not have gone an' done somethin' stupid."

"I must search the Eyrie," said Senneck. "Someone will know where he has gone."

She darted away.

Her search of the Eyrie towers took some time. She questioned every griffin she came across, and several griffiners as well, especially Kullervo's Southern friends.

Out of them, only Lady Isleen had something useful to offer. "Resling and Lady Della left four days ago," she said. "I think they went with Prince Kullervo, but I couldn't say where."

Senneck relaxed at that. Kullervo would at least have some protection with him. She went back to her own quarters to rest. Rushing around wouldn't help her find out where her human had flown off to.

Kraego was in her nest, dozing, with his head on his paws. He woke up when she entered, and mother and son regarded each other warily. Now that Kraego had chosen his name he wasn't her chick any more, and her mothering instincts toward him had long since disappeared.

"You are in my territory," she said brusquely.

Kraego stood up as if to leave, but there was something overpoweringly self-confident in his stance and the way he looked at her. "You were not here, so it was my territory," he said. "Your human said I could have it until you returned."

"You have seen him?" said Senneck. "Do you know where he is?"

"I do," said Kraego. He yawned and stretched, mostly for effect. "He and his two inferiors have flown to Warwick. He meant to go alone, but they discovered him and insisted that they go with him."

"Why has he gone there?" said Senneck.

"He missed you and hoped that he might meet you there," said Kraego. "But you did not see him?"

"No," said Senneck. "I came here directly and did not stop except to sleep. Did he say when he would come back?"

"He did not," said Kraego. "You should not let him leave his territory without you, Mother."

His tone made her hiss. "You are far too bold for a human-less youngster."

Kraego did not back down. "I am not afraid."

"Be afraid," Senneck advised. "I will not kill you because I am your mother, but others will not spare you because you are a youngster. Now leave my nest, or I will drive you out."

Kraego took the hint. He yawned at her again, and sauntered away.

Once he had gone, Senneck drank from her trough and lay down on her belly to think, ignoring the faint whispering in her mind as Oeka's invisible presence drifted past, as it did every so often these days. If she went flying off frantically after Kullervo, it would make her look weak and panicky, as if she didn't trust her human. Besides, Kullervo had left of his own free will, and with Saeddryn dead, there was no serious danger left for him. He would return to Malvern on his own sooner or later, so Senneck would wait for him calmly, as if she had planned it with him beforehand. Then, when he got back, she would warn him not to do something like this again. He would listen.

* * *

Meanwhile, Kraego was feeling vaguely annoyed. He was still tired and thirsty, and now that his mother had sent him packing, he wanted somewhere else to sleep. It was very difficult for an unpartnered griffin like himself to find a sleeping place in the Eyrie; any unoccupied nest could easily become a trap if its owner returned unexpectedly. As Senneck had reminded him, other than her, any adult who caught him sleeping in its nest could well attack to kill.

Of course, Kraego was small enough to sleep in places other than nests, but he was too stubborn to consider that option for long. He was a griffin, and therefore he should have a nest when he wanted one—and not one in the Hatchery, either. He had grown up surrounded by humans, and the places they lived in made him feel at home.

With that in mind, he started to search the Eyrie, checking the nesting chambers he passed. Some were occupied, and others smelt as if they had owners. He was hoping to find one that was vacant, but unfortunately other unpartnered griffins used the same strategy, and every nest he found had been claimed.

He had worked his way to the top of the Council Tower, when he finally came across an opening he had never investigated before. It looked as if it led to a nest, but it was huge, and built right at the very top—the dominant position in any tower, he knew.

Curious now, Kraego flew to the opening and landed on the ledge provided. The moment his paws touched the ground, he saw the massive talon marks that had scored the stone many times over a long period of time.

Simultaneously, an odour hit his nostrils. It was male, and adult—a sharp, aggressive stench, full of danger.

The nest, however, was empty.

Kraego went in. His eyes, adjusting to the gloom, showed him a nest unlike anything he had ever seen before in his life.

It was huge, with an elegantly arched ceiling. Colourful hides hung on the walls, and shiny stones were scattered underpaw around a golden water trough. Kraego saw—and smelled—the remains of the tenderest and sweetest-smelling carcass he had ever come across. He ripped off a strip of the leftover meat, and it was every bit as delicious as he had expected.

Entranced, he stood by the trough and took in everything, noting the fine grass bedding and the scattered silver feathers and tufts of black fur lying among them. Only one griffin could ever have a nest this magnificent.

"The Mighty Skandar," Kraego rasped to himself.

Oddly enough, the thought only made him bolder. He clambered onto the soft grass and curled up in it, savouring the rich scent of it. No sign of danger. The Queen was busy all day, and Skandar would stay with her.

Lulled by the smell of the grass and the dreams of grandeur filling his head, Kraego fell asleep.

He woke up as something smashed into him, so hard it hurled him into the air. Shrieking in fright, he landed on his side with his wing crumpled beneath him, and before he could even wake up properly, his attacker had pounced on him.

The Mighty Skandar's feathers bristled around his neck, and his eyes were wide open, blazing silver. "You *go!*" he screeched, and raised a massive forepaw over Kraego's head. The talons gleamed dully in the dusk light from outside.

Kraego scrabbled to his paws and darted away, out of his father's reach. He would have flown away, but Skandar moved to follow him and blocked the opening.

Not knowing where to go, Kraego hid behind the water trough. "Do not kill me, Father," he said hastily. "I am only a youngster!"

"My nest!" Skandar bellowed, taking a menacing step toward him. "Not sleep here, only I sleep here!"

"I only came here to speak with you," Kraego lied, amazed by his own calmness. "I have things to ask."

Skandar glared at him. "What speak? What ask?"

Kraego saw he had managed to get his father interested and hurriedly took advantage of it. He bowed his head, and said, "You are the mightiest of griffins. The Mighty Kraal was ancient and famous for his power, but you defeated him and are greater. Every griffin in Cymria must be jealous of you. I want to know how you have become so powerful."

The flattery worked. Skandar sat back and preened. "Am powerful because am very big," he bragged. "Am strong. Have never lost fights. And . . ." He clicked his beak softly and looked down at his huge black talons." . . . and had good human," he admitted. "Chose best human, cleverest human. Human set Skandar free, human save life. Human fight like wild griffin, know how to make other human obey. Mighty Skandar not become Mighty without him."

"I do not believe that," said Kraego. "Your human is gone now, but you have kept your power. I do not think a griffin needs a human to be strong."

"Then you fool!" Skandar rasped at him, all his menace returning. "You humanless griffin, you unpartner. Have no human to bring food and heal wounds and think of clever plans. Can't go to other territory alone, can't live in Eyrie. You weak."

"I am not weak!" said Kraego. Stupidly, he raised his tail in an arrogant gesture, and said, "When I am grown, I will be as large as you, but I will always be more cunning. That is why I will be mightier than you, Father."

It was exactly what nobody should ever say to Skandar. The giant griffin's feathers puffed out again, and a savage hiss began in his throat. "Am . . . not . . . stupid!"

Despite the danger, Kraego enjoyed that moment. He enjoyed the fact that he had found a way to upset his father. Skandar was larger, but Kraego had power over him. "I will go now," he taunted. "But one day I will return. When I am ready, I will come back, and I will challenge you. And I will win."

Skandar snarled at him. "You think you special, but not special. Every chick of Mighty Skandar thinks to challenge, and all lose. You lose, too, one day."

"We will see," said Kraego.

Feeling that he had pushed his luck enough for one day, he backed away through the other entrance and into Laela's bedchamber. Once he was out of sight, he ran off into the Eyrie, hoping that Skandar wouldn't think he was worth chasing.

Back in his nest chamber, Skandar rasped to himself and took a long drink from his trough. The water tasted slightly odd, but not unpleasant, so he swallowed it anyway.

The black-feathered youngster was as clever as his mother, and had invaded Skandar's territory just as she had done. *His* invasion, of course, wasn't welcome at all. Plenty of other griffins had said such boastful things to him before, but none of them had been youngsters. Kraego was far too bold for his own good.

Skandar wondered if he should have just killed him on the spot. He had come close, but his instincts had made him hesitate over killing his own chick. Kraego was a fine example of his father's virility and his ability to father big, strong young.

Let him come back when he thought he was old enough, then. Skandar would be ready. The little fool had no idea of how many younger challengers his father had seen off over the years.

"Am dark griffin," Skandar muttered to himself now. "Never lose." He took another beakful of the odd-tasting water.

Sudden nausea twinged in his stomach. He coughed and shuddered slightly at the sensation, and drank more water to soothe the sensation. The feeling of sickness, however, only grew.

Groaning softly, he curled up in his nest. He must have swallowed another big piece of bone. The feeling shouldn't stay too long, and if it did, he would make his human's youngster fix it for him.

Tiredness and weakness followed the twisting in his stomach. Skandar groaned again, and laid his head on his talons. He needed to sleep . . .

Blackness closed over his eyes.

34

Iron and Rust

Kullervo returned to Malvern more than a week after his sudden departure, but he landed on top of the Council Tower rather than returning to his rooms, and waited there until Laela came.

When she arrived, she took one look at him and ran to his side. "Kullervo! Mighty gods, what happened . . . ?"

Kullervo was still in griffin form. His fur and feathers were bedraggled, his eyes glazed with exhaustion. A long gash down his flank made him drag one foreleg. There was no sign of anybody else with him.

"It's Warwick," he said. "Warwick's fallen."

"What?" said Laela.

Kullervo was swaying slightly where he stood. "Resling and Della are dead, and so are their partners," he said. "The whole city . . . turned on us. Is Senneck here?"

"She's fine," said Laela. "What do yeh mean Warwick's turned on us? What's goin' on?"

"It's Caedmon," said Kullervo, shuddering. "He's alive. He's taken over Warwick. Him and Shar. They—"

"Wait, wait," said Laela. "Start at the beginnin'. What happened?"

Kullervo sat on his haunches and shook his head slowly. "I was with Resling and Della. We went for a walk in the city. There was a riot. People saw us, and they were angry. They threw things and shouted. Then when we started trying to get back to the tower, they attacked. Dozens of them. Even some of the city guard joined in. Della died. We got back to the tower, but then . . . then Caedmon came."

"Just him?" said Laela.

"Him and Shar. They were on the walls, and Shar made a challenge to the tower. The griffins there went to fight her one at a time, and she defeated them. But some of the griffiners in the tower were already on their side. They turned on us. Murdered the governor, and Resling as well, and let Caedmon and Shar in. Your soldiers stood down. The people in the city started attacking them, and . . . I don't know, it was chaos. People dying everywhere. Laela, they hate us." Kullervo looked dully at Laela. "They know what we did to Saeddryn, and they hate us for it."

Rage and horror distorted Laela's face. "They *what*? She was a monster!"

"She was the Night God's chosen," said Kullervo. "The holiest woman in the North. And before that, she was a war hero. Only our father was more respected. And we murdered her. We tortured her. We threw her body in her son's face. And before that . . . we've killed everyone who set them free. Nerth, Iorwerth . . . and Arenadd. Him first."

"I did not kill him!" said Laela. "An' *Saeddryn* killed Iorwerth. Senneck killed Nerth. I never . . ."

"Doesn't matter," said Kullervo. "I realised all that when I wouldn't talk to anyone. Saw what we've done. They already didn't like us. Now we've killed Saeddryn, and we're consorting with Southerners. We've lost, Laela. Lost the North."

"No we ain't," Laela snapped. "We're gonna take the Unpartnered out there an' get Warwick back. Once Caedmon's dead we'll be fine. We're gonna be all right, Kullervo."

Kullervo looked her in the eye. "No we're not," he said. "We're all going to die. And we deserve to."

He turned and limped away.

When Kullervo entered his quarters, he found Senneck there, relaxing in front of the cold fireplace. His heart lightened at the sight of her. Wordlessly, he limped over to her and lay down by her flank.

Senneck relaxed against him. "I am glad to see you again, Kullervo."

Kullervo laid his head down. "I missed you so much."

"And I missed you. Why did you leave here alone? You are wounded. What happened?"

Kullervo told her.

Senneck hissed softly. "Then I was wrong. He did escape."

"You found him, then?" said Kullervo.

"Yes. He was where *Kraeaina kran ae* said he would be, with his mate and a band of other rebels. His mate was carrying his pup, but I killed her."

Kullervo's head came up sharply. "She was pregnant? You killed a pregnant woman?"

"I did not mean to; she threw herself in the way when I tried to kill Caedmon. But I would have killed her anyway. She was a rebel, and if her pup had survived, she would have used it against us." Senneck shook her head. "Caedmon escaped. The Unpartnered killed every human on that island, and I thought that he must have been among them, but he was not. Now he has returned to make war again, and that is good. Out of hiding, we can kill him."

"I don't know if we can, Senneck," said Kullervo. "The people are on his side. If he comes here, they'll rise up just as they did in Warwick."

"It does not matter," said Senneck. "His death will make them lose courage."

"But I don't know if we *can* kill him," said Kullervo. "We've failed every other time. Maybe . . . maybe the Night God is protecting him, somehow . . . "

"Foolery!" Senneck snapped her beak. "There are no gods. And if there were, your Night God did not protect the one who was meant to be her most powerful servant."

"No." Kullervo looked away.

Senneck softened and nibbled gently at his neck feathers. "I am glad to be with you again. Do not be afraid. I will protect you from Caedmon."

"And I'll protect you," said Kullervo. "I'm not leaving Malvern again. I'm tired of travelling. I want to feel like this is my home."

"It is. But Kullervo . . ."

"Yes?"

"It is time you made yourself human again," said Senneck. "You have been a griffin for too long."

"No," Kullervo rasped. "I don't want to be human."

"But you are human," said Senneck. "You wear a griffin's shape, but your nature is not griffin. If you do not change again, you may forget how to."

"I won't," said Kullervo. "I'll change back when I'm ready. Just . . . not now."

Senneck nudged him with her beak. "You are sad. I smell fear and misery on you. Are you afraid to be human?"

"Yes." Kullervo shuddered. "I'm afraid of everything. I'm afraid of what's going to happen."

"And what is going to happen?" asked Senneck.

"I don't know, but . . . I feel . . ." Kullervo's talons curled. "I feel . . . judged. I feel as if we're going to be punished for what we've done. I feel cursed."

"You are only afraid of Caedmon," said Senneck. "Do not be! You have defeated your greatest enemy. You and your sister destroyed what was said to be undestroyable. What do you have to fear from a mere mortal?"

"Nothing, but . . ." Kullervo struggled to find words, and finally gave up.

"Then that is enough," said Senneck. "Stop this now. We have done our duty a hundred times. Now we may rest and eat, and enjoy our rewards. Your Southern friends are doing well and will be glad to see you again. Visit them, and they will make you happy."

"What about Kraego?"

"He is well. Growing larger, and roaming the Eyrie as if he owns it."

That made Kullervo feel better. "He's a good griffin. Sometimes I feel like he's my son."

"You helped to raise him," Senneck admitted. "And I know that he likes you. But I do not think he will stay here forever. He will grow too large and will be a threat to the Mighty Skandar. If he has sense, he will choose a human and leave. In another Eyrie, outside Skandar's territory, he could become a master of his own territory. And he would be safe there."

An ordinary human might have found this incomprehensible,

but Kullervo's griffish instinct was strong enough that it made complete sense to him. "Or he might decide to stay here and challenge Skandar. He's confident enough."

"Foolish enough," Senneck snorted. "But that is his choice. I have done all I can for him, and so have you."

"You think Skandar's too strong for him?"

"Until Kraego reaches maturity, he will be too strong," said Senneck. "And even then, it would be a dangerous battle. But let Kraego choose his own way. Now we must rest and think of what we will do when the rebel Shar brings her human here."

"I won't fight," said Kullervo.

"You must," said Senneck. "If the enemy comes to our nest, you must fight to defend your territory. Every adult male must, and you are a griffiner. A true griffiner fights beside his griffin."

But Kullervo looked away. "I won't fight ever again," he said. "Not even to save my own life."

"Or mine?" Senneck asked sharply. "Or your sister's? Would you stand aside and do nothing if the enemy came after her? Is that what you would do?"

Kullervo jerked away as if she had hit him. "No! I . . . I don't know, but I can't . . . I don't want to hurt anyone."

"In warfare, you must. Only cripples and chicks hide from fighting."

"I know. I . . ." Kullervo stood up abruptly and limped out of the room, almost as if he were trying to escape from something that confused and frightened him but would not leave him alone.

Up at the top of the tower, Arenadd drifted through the familiar chambers that had once been his home and into Skandar's nest. He knew that his old partner was there; his presence and dark power made him feel stronger and more vital. More connected to the world, somehow, as if he could nearly touch it.

Skandar lay curled up in his nest, breathing slowly.

As he had many times before, Arenadd reached out to him in the only way he could. *Skandar. Skandar, it's me.*

The dark griffin's eyes opened, and he looked up blearily at the dark spectre. "You come back," he croaked.

Yes. Skandar, listen. I've been to Warwick. Caedmon's coming. He's coming here. There are griffiners with him, and people are coming, too. He's sent messengers to Skenfrith and Fruitsheart, and they're coming. Griffiners are rushing to join him, and they're coming here. Dozens of them. You have to warn Laela!

Slowly, Skandar raised his head. "Enemy . . . not come," he rasped. "I go . . . go catch them. Take Unpartner. Kill . . ." His head fell back.

Arenadd drifted closer. *Skandar, are you all right?*

"Am strong," said Skandar. But his voice sounded weak, horribly weak. He tried to raise his head again, and once again it fell back.

What was left of Arenadd's emotions turned to fear. *You're sick.*

"Not sick!" Skandar gathered his huge paws beneath him and heaved himself upright. He took several steps forward, but they were shaky steps. His great body swayed precariously from side to side. "Not sick!" he insisted. "I go, go now, fly with . . . with Unpartner. Go kill . . ."

No, Skandar, said Arenadd. *You need to rest. Please, just lie down again . . .*

Skandar ignored him. Moving slowly and unsteadily, he made his way into the audience chamber.

Laela was there, dismissing a tough, scarred Northerner. ". . . go get them organised," she told him as he left. "An' be ready for my orders."

The man nodded curtly and exited just as Skandar made his shambling arrival.

Laela turned to greet him. "There yeh are. I was just about to come see . . . great talons, what's wrong with yeh?"

Skandar sat back on his haunches and regarded her regally. "Am not wrong," he said.

"Good," said Laela. "Listen, Caedmon's taken Warwick. I need yeh t'go out there with the Unpartnered."

"No," said Skandar. He blinked slowly. "Arenadd say Shar's human come here. Come with other griffin, and griffin from Skenfrith and Fruitsheart and other nest. Come to fight *here*. So I go kill them in forest, away from nest."

Laela stared. *"Arenadd says?"*

"Arenadd go see," Skandar said serenely. "See Warwick, see Shar. Come here, tell me. Tell me everything."

"Skandar, Arenadd's dead," said Laela. "He's not here."

"Is here!" said Skandar. "Come here many times, help Mighty Skandar. Warn where *Kraeaina kran ae* is. Show him where you are. Talk to human with wings. Only him and Mighty Skandar hear him."

"But—" Laela began. She stopped, and frowned. "Kullervo . . . ? Is *that* what he . . ." She looked around quickly. "Is Arenadd here now?"

"Is here," said Skandar. "Is *there*." He poked his beak toward a spot of empty air beside Laela. "He say, not bother tell you, you not see him. Mortal not see. Only ones with dark power see. Me, winged human, *Kraeaina kran ae*."

Laela's frown deepened. "Saeddryn kept talkin' to him when we had her locked up."

"Yes, Arenadd there," Skandar said impatiently. "Now here. Say where enemy is. Say must kill before they come here, not break Malvern."

Laela pulled herself together. "Right then," she said. "I got my human army here, an' they'll stay here to defend the city. Meanwhile, you an' the Unpartnered can fly out an' attack the bastards along the way. That oughta take care of it."

"I go," Skandar agreed. "Go now." He stood up and immediately toppled over onto his side.

Laela ran to him with a shout of dismay, but the moment she tried to touch him he lashed out at her with his beak and nearly tore her ear off.

She backed off hastily and watched the dark griffin try to get up. He managed it, but his legs splayed out awkwardly, and when he tried to walk, he stumbled and nearly collapsed again.

Laela's heart shrank into a tiny, withered ball. "Skandar, yeh can't fight," she said. "Not like this."

Immediately, Skandar let out a maddened scream and leapt at her with his beak open wide. It was so sudden and violent that if his back legs hadn't given way midspring, he could well have killed her. *"Can fight!"* he bellowed from the floor. *"Am not weak!"*

Laela thought very quickly. "All right, then," she said as soothingly as she could. "I know yeh can fight. But the Unpartnered are

tired and weak after so much fightin'. They might not be much
good. So why don't we let them stay here for a bit? They can
attack the enemy when they're closer. That way, they won't have
t'go lookin' for them, an' they won't be tired from flyin'.""

The tactic worked. Skandar relaxed. "Wait, then," he said.
"Mighty Skandar need water." He stumbled back to his nest.

Laela, too, relaxed, though not much. Maybe her baby had
picked up on its mother's nervousness, because it kicked restlessly. Laela patted her belly. "There, there," she said. "Don't
yeh worry; Mama's gonna sort this out. Somehow."

She hurried off, slowed down by her aching back, to the council chamber for an emergency meeting. The walk gave her plenty
of time to think. Or, rather, to fume and worry. Pregnancy was
not helping her moods at all. Neither was Caedmon.

Damn him! No matter how many times she thought she had
done away with him, he always managed to come back. Forget
his mother; *he* was the real pain in her side and had been for far
too long.

Not for the first time, Laela wished she hadn't judged her
father for his heavy drinking. Nowadays, even getting drunk
wouldn't have given her much relief. Jumping off the tower or
maybe just running away to live in an Amorani monastery
would have been preferable. Ruling the North was far harder
than she had ever imagined, and she refused to consider doing
what some Eyrie Mistresses did and relegating the harder
duties to others. It was *her* Eyrie, and the decisions were hers to
make, stress be damned.

The hardest part, though, wasn't all the work she had to do, or
the fact that she had almost no time to herself any more. The hardest part was simply knowing, every moment of every day, that
thousands of people depended on her. Everything she did affected
them. Every mistake could cost lives. Punishment made enemies,
and mercy made the enemies she already had bolder. Nothing was
simple any more. And now she had to worry about becoming a
mother as well. How in the world was she going to raise a child on
top of everything she already had to do?

Akhane wasn't much help, either. She loved him dearly, but
her husband had very little interest in politics. He preferred to
spend his time reading and writing, or talking to people and
asking them questions about his interests. Laela hadn't tried to

make him be more of a help. It made her feel better to know that he at least had time to be his own person, and his calm presence always managed to cheer her up.

Arriving at the council chamber brought Laela back to the present. Several of her councillors were waiting for her, but the rest weren't, so she took up her place on the platform at the centre and waited impatiently until the last of them had walked or flown in.

"Right," she said unceremoniously. "Let's get started. You all know why yer here, but there's been some more news . . ."

The council listened as she outlined the situation—including the fact that griffiners from other cities were now probably joining up with Caedmon as he marched on Malvern. That part of Skandar's story had sounded plausible enough that she was prepared to repeat it here, and the council listened with alarm.

"So what it comes down to is this," Laela concluded. "They're comin' here, an' the Unpartnered can't be relied on to intercept them." Naturally, she had left out the fact that Skandar was ill. *Nobody* was going to hear that from her, not even Kullervo. "My thought is that it's best if we just stay here an' wait for them. When the Unpartnered see strange griffins coming to attack, they'll fly out after them right away, without being asked. Griffins always defend their territories. Then, if Caedmon has any troops on the ground, you"—she pointed to her new Master of War—"can lead the army out there an' deal with them. That is if the Unpartnered don't do it first. What d'you all think?"

The councillors glanced at each other. Some of them frowned to themselves thoughtfully.

The Master of War spoke up. "Human armies do poorly under the talons of griffins," he said in his thin Amorani accent. "My men would do better to stay behind these walls and defend them."

"That's true," the Master of Building put in. "If you have a defence, use it. We should man the arrow-launchers, and maybe make some more, in case any enemy griffins come into the city."

"Good point," said Laela. "All right, then. We'll let the griffins fly out, an' hopefully they'll keep the fight away from the city. Either way, the army'll stay here an' keep us protected."

"It is a good plan," the Master of War said politely. "My

commanders and I will discuss it and make it more detailed. Give us one day, and we will present it to you then."

"Done," said Laela. She looked at the Master of Building. "You an' yer apprentice should inspect the walls. Make sure they're in good shape. Anyone else got anythin' to add?"

Several of the other councillors had questions or suggestions, so Laela heard them one by one and helped the council debate some minor details. But she knew the decision was already made, and the discussions here were almost a formality.

The meeting eventually broke up, and Laela went to lunch with her husband, thinking grimly that now was the time to do her least favourite thing: wait.

A renadd, however, was not waiting.
      So far the Night God didn't seem to have realised what he had done. Or if she had, she had been unable to find him. Uncertain of how to go on avoiding her attention, he hadn't stopped moving since Saeddryn's death. He felt safer during the day, and at nighttime he would hide near either Kullervo or Skandar. Maybe the dark power inside the two of them would mask his own.

Now, with plenty of daylight left, he watched over the sleeping Skandar and worried. His old partner was clearly very sick. Arenadd hoped Laela would have the sense to get a healer to him as quickly as possible.

The fear hadn't left him. It had taken hold sometime ago, when he had gone to watch over Caedmon and had seen griffiners flocking to his side. Unless the Unpartnered fought them, they could well overrun the city—human army be damned. Humans alone had never been a match for griffins. And now, with Skandar too sick to even walk, and he himself unable to do anything . . .

Damn you, Arenadd said aloud. He looked skyward, ignoring the Eyrie roof in the way, and screamed out a curse. *Damn you! This is it, isn't it? You do know what I've done, and you can see me. This is your punishment. You're going to make me stay here and watch them all die, knowing there's nothing I can do. Damn you!*

Skandar stirred in his sleep but didn't wake. His eyes, half-open, looked dull and cloudy.

Panic filled Arenadd. But there *had* to be something he could do.

For now, at least, Skandar and Laela were more or less safe. But Kullervo was another matter. The man-griffin was clearly very troubled, and troubled people did stupid things. He certainly hadn't done a very good job of keeping himself safe before now.

With that in mind, Arenadd decided to go and check on him.

He found Kullervo alone in his rooms. He was still in his griffin shape, and his tail was waving restlessly as he padded around.

Once again, inexplicably, being in Kullervo's room made Arenadd feel stronger. And he already knew that it wasn't just his imagination. That feeling had been what allowed him to show himself to Kullervo so clearly and speak to him properly, even if it was only in a dream. Last time he had tried to get through to him, he had appeared as something vague and distorted.

Arenadd hovered near the ceiling and wondered what Kullervo was up to. He looked as if he were thinking hard about something. Briefly, Arenadd considered trying to speak to him again. But he decided against it. Kullervo didn't seem to trust him much, and another ghostly vision would probably just disturb him. Besides, manifesting himself to someone again might attract unwanted attention.

While Arenadd thought this over, Kullervo seemed to make up his mind. He loped over to the fireplace and pulled away a rug with his beak. Underneath it were bare floorboards. Kullervo scratched clumsily at them until his talon caught in a gap, and he managed to hook out a loose board.

Underneath that was a space. Kullervo reached into it with his beak, and pulled out a small leather pouch.

The moment the pouch came into view, Arenadd shuddered. Coldness expanded in him, making his cloudy shape turn darker and denser and take on an almost human shape for a moment.

Kullervo looked as if he were affected, too. He carelessly pushed the rug back into place without bothering to replace the board, and limped off into the nest chamber.

When Kullervo took off from the balcony, Arenadd followed him. Surely he wasn't going to leave the city alone again?

But that was exactly what Kullervo did. Flying a little unsteadily thanks to his wound, he headed determinedly out over the city walls and away, the pouch dangling from his beak. He and Arenadd flew together for a long time, and Arenadd reached out to touch the pouch.

The instant he made contact with it, he reeled away. Groaning, he formed himself into a little black cloud in the air and tried to pull his wits back together.

Kullervo flew on obliviously, and Arenadd watched him go without trying to follow. Whatever was in that pouch stank of power, and now that he had finally touched it Arenadd knew what it was. It was Saeddryn's heart, and her power was still locked inside it. *That* was what had been troubling Kullervo, and no wonder. Mortals would never be able to stand having the damn thing anywhere near them.

Arenadd turned away and let Kullervo go. His son was going to hide the heart somewhere, and nobody, especially not Arenadd, could ever know where. If Arenadd knew, then the Night God would know, too.

Unable to let himself rest, Arenadd headed off in a different direction. It was time to see what Caedmon was doing.

Finding him was easy, and fast, just as it had always been. He was flying as well, with Shar, of course, and a band of griffiners flew behind them. On the ground below was a rag-tag army of humans. The griffiners were guarding them.

Going closer to inspect the foot army, Arenadd felt certain that there were even more of them now than when he had last seen them. Almost none of them looked like trained fighters. There were peasants and commoners, tradesmen and servants. Ordinary people from different places, carrying whatever weapons they had been able to find. But at their core there were others who looked much more dangerous.

Men and women, all wiry and scarred, all of them wearing the unmistakable marks of the collar. They marched in perfect formation, and most of them were carrying curved Amorani swords.

Somehow, Caedmon had persuaded Laela's own freed slave army to join him. Arenadd suspected that he had done it by saying they would all die if they didn't. That was a strategy that usually worked.

Above, the griffiners were far less numerous, but there were plenty of them. All of them had humans, except for one. Weirdly enough, it was flying at the front rather than the inferior position that an unpartnered griffin should take up. Even more weirdly, it had a spotted coat.

Arenadd turned his attention to Caedmon, and his fear only increased.

Caedmon was still and silent on his partner's back. He had trimmed his beard and cut his hair, and now should have looked like a city-dwelling lord again. But even though he was better groomed, the tattoos were still there, looking even more striking now that his skin was clean. He was wearing a big, ragged griffin hide over his clothes, and there was a wooden hunting spear tied to his back. But more importantly, there was the look on his face. It was set and hard with determination, and could have looked impressive because of it, but Arenadd could almost feel the hatred underneath that created it.

He was looking at a man who had lost everything—and now had no reason at all to give up, or to spare anyone who stood in his way.

Arenadd's fear turned to something closer to terror. *He's me,* he said, or thought. *He's turned into me. All he has left is hate, and when he gets to Malvern, he'll . . .*

Memories flooded through him. Blood, fire, and murder.

He remembered his own hands when he had still had them, and had used them to kill. And now, at last, he came to feel what his enemies in Malvern must have felt when they had known that he was coming and guessed what he was planning to do when he got there.

He saw the death of Erian in the Sun Temple, only it wasn't Erian now, it was Kullervo, choking and dying on the floor. He saw the death of Flell, but now it was Laela, Laela collapsing over the child she had died to protect. Dying with a snarling Northerner standing over her with a bloodied sickle in his hand. And the child lying there helplessly, watched by a father who could not protect her.

No! It was as if Arenadd's whole form became that word. *No! Please, gods, no!*

Madness gripped him. He turned and flew away from Caedmon, streaking over the lands of the North like a black comet. Further and further North he went, until the green farmlands ran out, and he passed over the ruins of a dead village and into the mountains. He saw the famous stones of Taranis' Throne, the same stones where he had made his first sacrifice to the Night God.

And overlooking it was a cave. It was set into the mountainside, its entrance mostly hidden by a pile of rocks. Arenadd passed through them with ease. Inside the cave was jagged and freezing cold, too high up to be a home for anything.

It wasn't much of a tomb, but it was all he had.

Arenadd's spectre drifted over a dead branch and the rotting remains of some animal, and floated over the withered corpse that had once been him.

Time had not been kind to the mortal remains of Arenadd Tanisäii. The cold had dried out what was left of the flesh, drawing it tightly over the bones and giving the face a horrible grimace. Arenadd stared at it, scarcely able to believe that it had once been *his* face. It barely looked human any more.

But he could see the deformed bones on the left hand, and the long strands of black hair that had fallen away from the skull as the scalp rotted. He could even see the gap where one of the teeth had been knocked out. His robe had gone, but there were a few shreds of trouser fabric lying around, and the peeling remains of his boots.

Arenadd reached down to touch the leering corpse. *It's me,* he said aloud. *It's still me.*

The empty eye-sockets seemed to stare at him. For a moment, the corpse almost looked as if it were laughing silently at him, asking him why he would want it.

But Arenadd needed it now.

He drifted down into the corpse and let himself spread out to fill it. Body and soul, reunited. They had been ripped apart, but now they were together again, and once he had taken control again, his body would heal and turn back into what it had been before. Arenadd would live again, and then he could go back to Malvern and put a stop to everything. His children *needed* him.

Nothing happened.

Arenadd gathered all his will-power and concentrated, trying to remind himself of what it had been like to be alive. To be able to walk and speak and do everything that mortals took for granted. He tried to remember what pain felt like.

He couldn't. He kept trying, but the more he tried, the more those memories slipped away. He had no connection to his body, none at all. It was an object now. Useless and broken beyond repair.

Arenadd persisted, desperate now, unable to let go of his last hope. Without his body, he had no power, and . . .

Dreadful calmness overtook him. *No power,* he thought. That was it. The power that had kept him connected to his body was gone. The Night God had taken it away from him, and she had never given it back.

Arenadd floated back out of his corpse as realisation dawned on him.

I need power, he said. *Power like . . . the heart! I need— Kullervo!*

He rushed toward the entrance and into the sky, filled with his new plan. If he could make Kullervo give the heart to him, then he could use its power to resurrect his body. He could—

In midair, Arenadd jerked to a stop. He tried to keep going, but he couldn't move. Something had hold of him and would not let go.

He looked toward the horizon and saw the thing he had come to dread. The moon, rising inexorably into the darkening sky. His master had woken.

Arenadd struggled, but nothing could save him now. Realising it, he reached out hopelessly toward where his children were, beyond his help forever.

Then the Night God dragged him away into the void.

35

Defection

Flying made Kullervo's wound ache. He took things slowly, partly because of that, but also because there was no need to hurry. And because of the heart.

He had been feeling miserable and listless for a while now, and at first he had thought it was just his guilt and confusion. But now that he was carrying the heart with him, the feeling intensified. It grew even worse when he stopped that night and slept with the leather pouch tucked in under his wing. In the morning, when he took it in his beak again, the feeling eased slightly, but his fear of the heart only increased.

His wound didn't seem to be healing. He slept too deeply and tired too easily. The mere presence of the heart made him feel as if the life were draining out of his body.

He travelled on alone for the next few days, suffering under the effects of the heart's influence but his exhaustion and his illness only made him more determined to hide it. Hide it, and be rid of it for good.

He had already chosen the place though it took longer to get there than he had expected. It was the best place he could think of. Quiet and remote, and best of all, thanks to his own secret meddling in the library, it wasn't on any of the maps in Malvern. Nobody would ever think of looking here.

Once he had found the place, he landed and wandered around for a while, searching for a good spot. Eventually, he found a hollow in a tree, out of reach to an ordinary human.

Rearing onto his hind legs, he thrust the pouch inside and pushed it as far back as it would go.

He didn't mark the tree, or leave any other signs to show where the spot was. If he ever came back here, even he might not be able to find the tree again. That was how it should be.

Satisfied that the heart was safe, Kullervo walked away through the trees. He was horribly tired, but he didn't stop to rest until he was a long way away from the hiding spot. Once he felt he had gone far enough, he lay down in a handy clearing and slept.

When he woke up, he was amazed by how well rested he felt. He stood up and stretched, and for the first time in weeks felt almost cheerful. His wound hurt less, and at last the future looked less dark.

He took off with an easy leap and flew off back toward Malvern. His heart soared as he did. He wanted to laugh. At last! The heart was gone, and he felt as if he had left his troubles and his guilt with it in that tree.

Of course, Senneck would be furious with him for leaving again, and Laela would probably be upset, too. But at least now he had completed his last mission. *Now* there was no reason left for him to leave Malvern.

At least, not until Caedmon came.

Some of Kullervo's good mood left him when he remembered that. But surely . . . surely Skandar and the Unpartnered would be able to stop him when he attacked Malvern. Most likely they would never even touch the city. One more battle, *then* Kullervo could finally live in peace with the family he had worked so hard for. Surely, he thought almost frantically, surely it would end then.

He sighed. All his life he had wanted to have a real home, to be loved, and to have a family of his own. He had gone North to find those things, but he had never imagined that it would be such a long struggle, or that he would see so much horror. Or that he would have to kill people.

Yet again, images of the dead rose in his mind. Saeddryn, dead and mutilated. Lady Morvudd and those guards he had killed to escape from prison. And he himself had nearly died more than once. Death was never far away in this world—the world he had discovered outside the cage where he had spent most of his childhood.

But he would have to accept that if he was going to survive in it. Senneck was right: If Malvern was attacked, then it was his duty to defend it.

He felt slightly ill at the thought, but as he flew on he promised himself that, if he must fight, he wouldn't kill. He would injure if he had to, but not kill. Never again.

"Where have you been?" Senneck asked. To Kullervo's relief, she didn't look particularly annoyed.

"I'm sorry," he said. "I had to deal with something. It's done now."

His answer didn't please her. She thrust her beak forward and peered suspiciously at him. "What did you have to deal with? Why did you not tell me you were going?"

Kullervo gave up. "I went to hide the heart," he said. "I had to keep it secret in case someone tried to follow me."

Senneck relaxed. "It is hidden, then?"

"Yes. Nobody saw me, and I'll never tell anyone where it is. Not even you."

"That is good," said Senneck. She nibbled affectionately at his neck feathers. "You are not so sad now. I am glad to see it."

"So am I," said Kullervo. He rubbed his face against hers. "I think it was the heart. I didn't realise it was making me feel bad until I got rid of it."

Senneck hissed softly. "It is a vile thing. Perhaps that is why I felt uneasy here as well. That feeling is gone now."

"Yes." Kullervo's yellow eyes were brighter than they had been. "We're safe from it now."

"But not from Shar and her human," Senneck said shortly. "They have arrived. While you were gone."

Kullervo tensed again. "I didn't see anything on my way here."

"They have not come to the city," said Senneck. "The griffins have roosted in a place to the west, within sight but not close enough to attack. I think they are waiting for the humans to arrive."

"Why hasn't Laela attacked them?" asked Kullervo.

"She would have, but they have sent a message," said Senneck. "Shar's human wishes to speak with Laela."

"That's good," said Kullervo. "Did Laela say yes?"

"She did. That was today. They will meet tomorrow, outside the city. You and I must go as well."

"Oh," said Kullervo. "I'd better become human again, then."

"Yes," said Senneck. "Do it now, so that you will be strong again tomorrow. We must both be ready in case there is a fight."

"You're right," Kullervo said sadly. "I wouldn't trust us if I were Caedmon."

"We cannot trust him either," said Senneck. "Go, make the change. I will go and tell the Mighty Skandar that you have returned."

Changing was harder than he expected, perhaps because he had spent too much time as a griffin, or maybe just because he was already tired. In any case, he managed it after a struggle and finished up more or less human, and too worn-out to get up.

He fell asleep on the hearth rug where he had transformed, and only woke very briefly when Senneck returned and lay down beside him, warming him with her flank.

The meeting between Laela and Caedmon took place at the halfway point between Malvern and the rebel griffiner camp. It was out of range of the giant bows on Malvern's walls, too far away for any of Caedmon's followers to attack, and out in an open field so an ambush by anyone would be impossible.

Laela arrived with Skandar. Akhane and Zekh flew on her left side, and Senneck and Kullervo took up the right.

Caedmon was waiting for them when they arrived. Shar sat just behind him, and he had brought only two offsiders—a tough-looking middle-aged woman with her partner, a griffin who looked, if anything, even tougher.

When Laela first saw Caedmon, she could hardly believe he was the same man she had fought in Skenfrith. He was leaner and rougher-looking, and though he was well-groomed and wore an ordinary griffiner's flying outfit, there were tattoos on his face and down his neck. And on top of the outfit he wore a large and slightly ragged griffin hide with the head hanging down behind him like a hood.

A light wooden pole had been stuck into the ground beside him, with a grubby white flag on it to mark the spot.

Laela climbed off Skandar's back and took up a position opposite Caedmon. Kullervo and Akhane went to stand on either side of her like guards, with their partners standing behind them.

Laela didn't waste time with formalities. "What do yeh want?" she asked brusquely.

Caedmon inclined his head toward her. "Who are your friends? I don't think I've seen them before."

"My husband, Prince Akhane of Amoran," said Laela. "An' his partner, Zekh. And this is my brother, Kullervo, an' his partner, Senneck."

"Brother?" Caedmon eyed Kullervo.

"Half brother," Kullervo put in. "My mother was Skade."

Caedmon's forehead wrinkled. "So the stories are true. You really *do* have wings."

Kullervo lifted one. "Yes. Skade was a griffin."

"That's enough," Laela interrupted. "Yeh haven't answered me yet, Caedmon. What do yeh want?"

Caedmon returned his attention to her. "That's simple. I want you to step down."

Laela stared at him. "Yeh wanna run that by me again, cousin?"

"Step down," Caedmon repeated. "Surrender the throne to me."

"Or?" said Laela.

"Or my followers and I will take Malvern by force and kill you and everyone else in the Eyrie." Caedmon sounded quite calm.

"Is that a threat?" said Laela.

"A promise," said Caedmon. "I'm offering you this chance for the sake of Malvern. Enough of my people have already died because of you. A peaceful transfer of power will be better for everyone. You would be allowed to go back to Amoran with your husband, and raise your child in peace."

Laela made an exaggerated show of rubbing her chin thoughtfully. "Hm, lemme think about that." She took her hand away and sneered. "Sod off."

"Is that your answer?" said Caedmon.

"Yeah, that's right," said Laela, ignoring the nervous looks on Kullervo's and Akhane's faces. "Yeh think yeh can come here wearin' a dead griffin an' tell me what t'do? An' make threats like yeh had a chance of actin' on any of 'em? Well, yeh can bugger off. That's my answer."

"I told you, that wasn't a threat," Caedmon said sharply. "I give you my word as a Taranisäii that if you don't accept my offer, I'll tear Malvern apart and kill you—pregnancy or no pregnancy. You didn't spare my child's life, and I won't spare yours."

"You ain't a Taranisäii no more," said Laela. "I cut yeh out of my family tree. You an' yer sister an' yer old hag of a mother. Attack Malvern if yeh want, but trust me: When yeh do, it's gonna be your head on a spike, not mine. Now get lost."

"Is that your final answer?" Caedmon asked steadily.

"Yeah, it is."

"Fine." Caedmon pulled the flagpole out of the ground. "Then we'll do it your way, Shar."

He stepped aside, and Shar came forward. She looked as lean and ragged as her partner, and there were numerous scars on her hindquarters. "Mighty Skandar," she said.

Hearing his name, Skandar pushed Laela aside and went to confront the other griffin. Shar looked puny compared to the dark griffin, but she showed no fear. She stood tall, rearing up slightly on her hind legs so she could look him in the eye. "I challenge you," she said. "I challenge you for your territory. Fight me, Mighty Skandar."

Skandar hissed. "This my territory!"

"And soon it will be mine," said Shar. "Once I have killed you, I will win it."

Skandar aimed a blow at her head. She dodged it and darted away from the meeting spot. Skandar went after her.

Laela watched him go with horror. "Skandar, no! Get back here!" Skandar didn't react to her voice at all. She swore. "*Idiot!*"

Caedmon ripped the flag off its pole. "There's nothing you can do," he said. "They'll fight to the death. Whoever wins will control the Unpartnered. It's out of your hands now, half-breed."

Laela spat at him. "You've just lost. Nobody's ever beaten the Mighty Skandar, an' nobody ever will."

"So they say." Caedmon shrugged. "But they said King Arenadd was unkillable, and you proved them wrong. Now, there was one other thing I wanted to do here . . . oh yes." He hefted the flagpole, and all of a sudden Laela realised that its ends were sharp and barbed. Too late. Caedmon hurled the spear, hard and accurate.

It hit Akhane in the throat. The Amorani gave a gurgling yell of surprise, and fell to his knees.

"You killed the one I loved in front of me," said Caedmon. "Now I've returned the favour. Goodbye."

He retreated hastily with his silent offsider. She helped him onto her partner's back, and the griffin flew away, pursued by a screaming Zekh.

Kullervo and Senneck ran to Laela. She had thrown herself down by Akhane's side and was trying to pull the spear out of his throat. Akhane's eyes had rolled back in his head, and blood had begun to appear around his mouth. He clutched weakly at the spear, but his fingers were clumsy.

Laela wrenched at the spear. Instantly, blood spurted around it.

Kullervo grabbed her arm. "Laela, stop! You'll kill him!"

Laela didn't seem to hear him. She pulled again, and the spear came loose, leaving a ghastly wound behind. Blood poured out of it, staining the ground and Laela's hands.

Akhane's eyes slid closed. His dark skin had already turned pale.

"No," said Laela. "No, no, no . . . !" She took her husband's limp hand in hers, and patted at his face, frantically trying to wake him up. "No—!"

"Laela . . ." Kullervo touched her cautiously on the shoulder. "Laela, he's gone."

Laela jerked slightly at his touch. Then she let go of Akhane and put her arms around her brother. Kullervo held on to her, feeling her sob into his chest. "I'm so sorry," he said.

Nearby, Senneck was backing toward them with her wings half-open. "Kullervo!" she said harshly. "We cannot stay here. Come, quickly."

Kullervo nodded sharply. He stood up, easily lifting Laela into his arms. She clung to him, not seeming to care if they might be in danger.

"Can you carry both of us?" Kullervo asked Senneck.

"No," she said. "Come, now!"

Kullervo hurried back toward Malvern, aware of how

vulnerable they were. Senneck brought up the rear, running with an awkward sideways gait as she kept turning to look back and up. Kullervo heard her hiss in alarm, and broke into a sprint without waiting to see what had startled her.

Every moment he expected to be struck from behind, or to hear Senneck be attacked. Ahead, he could see Malvern's walls getting closer. At the top, guards had loaded the giant bows and were aiming them. Kullervo hoped they knew how to use them.

As the walls came closer, he felt a sudden downdraft. He ducked hastily. Behind him, he half saw Senneck rear up and lash out with her talons.

Up on the wall, one of the bows swivelled on its base. The cord slammed forward.

An instant later, something huge crashed onto the ground off to Kullervo's left. A griffin, screaming in agony, a huge arrow jammed through its ribs.

If any others had tried to chase him, he didn't see them. A gate opened up in the wall, and guards ran out to help. Kullervo let them take charge of Laela and waited by the gate until Senneck had gone through before he ducked in after her.

Safe inside the city, Senneck let him onto her back and flew them back to the Eyrie. There, she and Kullervo both stood silently on the balcony outside their quarters and looked out over the plain beyond Malvern. They could both see the distant shapes of two griffins locked in combat, though from here it was impossible to tell which was which.

"Now our future will be decided by the Mighty Skandar," said Senneck. "As it was before. Without him and the Unpartnered, your father would never have taken this territory."

"I'm sure he'll be all right," Kullervo said uncertainly. "I mean, he's never lost a fight."

"That is true," said Senneck. "But he is older now, and I have heard rumours that he has been very ill."

Kullervo went cold. "But . . . but he's the dark griffin! He can't lose. Everyone knows he's the biggest and most powerful griffin in the world."

"After he killed his father Kraal, he was," Senneck admitted. "We will have to hope that his strength does not fail him today."

"It won't," said Kullervo, not sure who he was trying to convince. "I'm sure it won't. He's going to win."

* * *

Skandar chased Shar over the plain, completely unaware of Laela or anything else that happened that day. He was a predator. More than that, he was a warrior, built by nature to fight. The sight of prey was enough to distract him, but the sight of a rival made everything else disappear around him. And Shar was a rival who had been taunting him for far too long.

Shar, however, didn't seem interested in fighting. The red griffin ran away with great, bounding strides, heading straight toward Malvern. It was the perfect way to provoke Skandar even further. He thundered after her, beak open, growing angrier with every step.

But it wasn't just Shar making him angry. He was already angry, and had been that way for days. Not angry with her, or with anything else around him, but with himself.

His sickness had faded eventually, but it had left its mark. Pain burned inside him, in his stomach and further down, radiating into his limbs. It had been with him ever since his illness, and it would not let him sleep. He had been unable to eat or drink without pain, and walking and flying made it flare up as well. He had never been this unwell for this long before, and it had made him savage.

Closer to the walls of Malvern, Shar turned suddenly and leapt at him. Caught by surprise, Skandar lurched into her attack. Her talons came down on his shoulders, and her beak smashed into his head. She hooked it into the base of his neck, and as he wrenched away from her she twisted her head and tore open a deep wound.

Skandar jerked back toward her, and his own beak caught her in the shoulder. She managed to shy away before he could do any serious damage, leaving him snorting and shaking his head as blood ran down into his ears.

Shar reared onto her hind legs and brought her talons down on him with all her might. But Skandar was quicker than he looked. He sprang forward with a thrust of his back paws and hit her full in the belly. She thudded onto her flank, and he pinned her down, talons ripping into her vulnerable underside.

Shar's back paws came up and kicked him in the face. Her

claws glanced off his beak, but her talons at the front found their mark in the dark griffin's side. They went in deep, and she ripped them downward in one ruthless blow.

Skandar screamed and backed away, blood streaming down his left foreleg. Shar took the opportunity to regain her paws and took the opportunity to strike him hard in the face with her beak.

Skandar screamed again. He backed away, lurching alarmingly to one side. Under his wing, a flap of flesh had come loose and hung down his side, showing a glint of white ribs. But his face was just as bad. Shar's beak had torn it open down the side, and his eye had turned into an open wound.

Shuddering in pain, unable to see properly, Skandar made a sudden leap at her. He took her by surprise, and his talons ripped through her chest.

Shar darted away from him and leapt clumsily into the air. Skandar followed, rolling slightly to one side, and chased her up and over the city.

Now Shar stopped trying to attack. She only flew, looping and diving in the air over Malvern, and let Skandar waste his strength trying to catch her. She was faster and more agile in the sky than he, and even more so now, and he could barely see her. She led him toward the Eyrie and around it, and as they flew, she began to screech out her name to taunt him.

It also brought the Unpartnered out. Griffins started to appear around the Eyrie and in the city, None of them tried to interfere, but many of them took to the air and circled overhead to watch more closely. All of them must know what they were seeing.

Half-blinded, trailing blood from his wounds, Skandar beat his wings harder and harder, trying with all his might to catch up with Shar. She circled around and let him come to her. Her talons opened.

Skandar came at her with his beak wide open. *"Am Mighty Skandar!"* he screeched.

Shar's talons struck him across the face. His beak snapped shut around her left forepaw, and as he fell, he tore one of her toes clean off. It fell out of his beak and tumbled down into the city, and Shar's blood splattered over the dark griffin's black head feathers.

But Shar's blow had done its work. Stunned, dizzy from

blood loss, Skandar started to lose control of his wings. He flew lower, struggling to save himself from falling.

Shar did not give him that luxury. She came after him, despite her bleeding forepaw, and rained blows down on him.

"You are not mighty now!" she screeched at him, again and again, for all the griffins in Malvern to hear. *"You are not mighty! I am mighty! Shar! Shar is mighty!"*

Skandar did not try and fight her any more. He could barely even fly. But he did fly, away from her, away from Malvern. Shar went after him, driving him away with mocking calls and cruel blows, and everywhere in the city, other griffins rose, screeching with her, chasing away what had once been the most powerful griffin of them all.

The Mighty Skandar, now no longer mighty.

He flew away from Malvern, heading northward, one eye blinded, leaving the territory he had ruled for more than twenty glorious years. The territory that belonged to Shar now.

Shar chased him until he was nearly out of sight before she returned to Malvern. She flew over the city in a wide circle and screeched out her message. *"Who is the mightiest griffin?"*

And the Unpartnered screeched back. *"Shar! Shar! Mighty Shar!"*

"Then come with me!" Shar called to them. *"Come to me and my human, and together we will capture this city!"*

The Unpartnered came to her, and when she flew away back to Caedmon's camp, they went, too, abandoning Malvern. But they would be back soon enough.

L aela saw it all from the Eyrie. Kullervo and Senneck stood beside her, and the three of them watched Skandar's defeat in silence. After that, they saw the Unpartnered leave, and all of them knew what it meant.

"We've lost," Kullervo mumbled.

Laela's eyes were red. "Shit." She said it in a flat kind of way, as if nothing could truly upset her any more. Quite possibly, it couldn't.

Kullervo turned to her. "We're done for," he said. "The Unpartnered will destroy the city. It'll be Skenfrith all over again. We've got to do something."

"Like what?" Laela said sharply.

"Leave!" Kullervo urged. "Run away! Or surrender. If we take Caedmon's offer . . ."

"Too late for that," said Laela.

"The Mighty Skandar has lost his territory," said Senneck. "This Shar is stronger than I thought."

"Is that so?" Laela snarled at her and walked off.

Kullervo followed anxiously. "What are we going to do? *What are we going to do?"*

Laela rounded on him. "Just shut up, will yeh? I don't bloody know what we're gonna do, all right? I'm callin' an emergency meetin' of the council."

They hurried down toward the council chamber. But Laela didn't need to call anything. The council was already there, along with plenty of other griffiners.

Laela unceremoniously climbed onto her platform. "Skandar's gone, and the Unpartnered have betrayed us," she said abruptly. "We need t'come up with a plan, an' fast."

"Surrender," a councillor said immediately. "We have no other choice."

Laela opened her mouth to reply, but a sudden commotion made everyone stop.

A griffiner and her partner had pushed their way into the meeting. Ignoring the council, the griffiner went straight to Laela's platform and glared up at her.

"Lady Arwydd," said Laela. "What do yeh want?"

Arwydd's face was full of fury. "I know what to do," she said. She raised her voice and spoke to the whole chamber. "I know *exactly* what to do." She turned to Laela and spat at her feet. "I'm leaving. You're a monster, and Essh and I are leaving to go and join up with our rightful leader."

Rage suffused Laela's own face. "Arrest her!" she roared.

Several councillors moved toward Arwydd. But then the Master of Healing suddenly rushed forward. His griffin shoved them aside, and in a moment the pair of them had joined Arwydd and Essh and were fleeing the chamber.

Chaos erupted around the Queen's platform. The two rebel griffins seized their humans and flew away through the openings in the ceiling before anyone could stop them. But that wasn't all.

Everywhere in the gallery, other griffiners were leaving. As if acting on some plan they had made beforehand, they climbed onto their partners and flew away after Arwydd. More followed them—even some of the newer griffiners, who had come as freed slaves from Amoran.

Worse, half the council went as well. The Master of Law followed the Master of Healing, and the Masters of Building and Trade were quick to follow.

By the time the confusion had died down, only a bare handful of griffiners had remained. Former slaves, Akhane's Amorani friends, and the Southerners Kullervo had brought.

In the silence that followed, Kullervo could only stare in utter shock.

Laela stood there frozen for a moment. Then, utterly expressionless, she strode out of the council chamber without a word.

Kullervo looked at Senneck. "What are we going to do?" he asked weakly.

Senneck looked inexplicably calm, even to him. "Your sister has destroyed herself," she said. "We should not stay here."

36

The Wheel Turns

Caedmon didn't waste any time once the Unpartnered had joined him. By evening, his followers had completely surrounded the city. Griffins went up onto the walls and disabled the giant bows, destroying them through sheer weight of numbers. Once they had done that, they took up station on the walls, festooning every rampart like flocking pigeons. But they didn't enter the city itself.

Caedmon, supported by dozens of loyal griffiners, stood by while Shar screeched a warning at the Eyrie. *"Surrender! Surrender now! This is your last chance! Surrender now or die!"*

Kullervo, remaining loyally by Laela's side, heard it and grimaced in fright. "We've got to do what she says."

Laela scowled. "No."

Kullervo stared at her. *"What?* Are you mad? You know what'll happen if we don't!"

"I don't care," said Laela. "This is my home an' my throne, an' they ain't takin' either one without a fight."

"But people will die!"

"So what?" said Laela. "What do I care? I got no friends here, an' neither have you. It's all about fear an' control. The throne's still mine, an' I'll stay on it until I'm dead."

"But all those people in the city—there are innocent people there who'll die!"

Laela shrugged.

Kullervo's face slackened in disbelief. "How could you be so callous?"

Laela prodded him unpleasantly. "I tell yeh, Kullervo, it's a good thing you're never gonna rule a damn thing. Yer too soft by half. Take it from me, griffin-boy, nobody ever got a throne or kept it without bein' callous. I learned that from our dad. Yeh know why he died in the end? Yeh know why he lost everythin'? It's 'cause he started *carin'*. Havin' a heart doesn't work for a man with no pulse. He was doin' fine until then."

"He saved your life!" said Kullervo. "The Night God wanted him to kill you."

Laela shrugged again. "An' now he's gone. These days I never get nothin' but grief from family."

"*I'm* your family," Kullervo pointed out.

"Yeah, an' yer givin' me grief now. Go away."

"You're mad," said Kullervo.

Laela rubbed her face. "Just go away. I ain't gonna tell yeh again."

Kullervo couldn't think of anything else to say. He left, hating himself for being such a coward.

The moment they were out of earshot, Senneck came to his side. Keeping pace with him, she lowered her head to speak into his ear. "Lady Isleen wishes to speak with you. Come with me now."

Kullervo followed her. "What does Isleen want?"

"She will tell you. Come."

Senneck didn't take him to Isleen's temporary home, as he had expected. Instead, she led him down the tower and across one of the covered walkways and into one of the adjoining towers, where the lowlier griffiners lived. Kullervo didn't know the building very well, but Senneck seemed to know exactly where she was going. She loped unhurriedly along a corridor and into a dining hall.

It was full of people. Every one of the Southerners who were staying in the Eyrie was there, along with three of Akhane's griffiner friends. They were gathered around the table, the humans seated, and the griffins sitting on their haunches to take up less space. Kraego was there, too, sitting by the door.

Isleen stood up when Kullervo came in. "Welcome, Prince Kullervo."

Kullervo stood in the doorway, bewildered. "What's all this about?"

"Come in," said Isleen. "Sit. We need to talk."

Kullervo took the seat she offered him at the head of the table, thinking that maybe she and her friends had come up with a plan to save Malvern. Once he was seated, Senneck pushed the door shut with her beak and sat down in front of it so that it couldn't be opened again.

Everyone there focused attention on Kullervo. He shifted nervously and looked at Isleen. "What is it? What's so important?"

Isleen glanced at her friends and got several encouraging nods. She took her cue, and coughed. "Ahem . . . Prince Kullervo, before I begin I want to give you my assurance that everyone in this room can be trusted. All of us are true believers, and we've taken oaths that none of what's discussed here will be shared with anyone else."

"That's good, but what *are* we discussing?" Kullervo began to get impatient.

"Malvern's future," said Isleen. "And the future of the North."

"You have an idea, then?" said Kullervo.

"We do," said Isleen. She smiled at him. "When I first saw you, I admit that I didn't know what to make of you. You didn't look like a noble, and you were alone except for your very fine partner." She nodded respectfully to Senneck.

"Go on," the brown griffin said impatiently.

"But when I saw your wings, everything fell into place for me," Isleen resumed. "I knew that you had been sent as a sign, a message from Gryphus."

Kullervo's eyes narrowed. "I told you: I'm not holy, and I didn't come from Gryphus, or any god."

"But that doesn't matter," Isleen said smoothly. "Gryphus works in mysterious ways, and I believe that you've been carrying his message all this time without even realising it."

Kullervo sighed. "Stop it. What do you want from me?"

"Fine." Isleen pulled herself up. "Then I'll tell you what's become apparent to all of us here, and to your partner. Your sister has failed. The dark griffin is dead, and she is not a griffiner any more. Very soon, she will have lost her throne to this Caedmon, and the chance to make peace between North and South will be gone."

"I know," said Kullervo. "That's why we have to do something, and fast."

"Exactly," said Isleen. She coughed. "The law says that when an Eyrie Master or Mistress loses his or her partner, he or she must immediately step down. An Eyrie can't be ruled by anyone except a griffiner. Your sister is a Queen, but she still qualifies as an Eyrie Mistress."

"She's still Queen," said Kullervo.

"Possibly." Isleen sniffed. "We in the South have no hereditary rulers, and normally when an Eyrie Mistress steps down, her replacement is chosen by the council, usually from among its members, In this case, however, I assume that your sister's succession is hereditary. And with no children, her only heir is you."

Kullervo choked. "*What?* You want *me* to take over?"

"You're the logical choice," Isleen said blandly. "And your partner tells us that your sister has already decided that if anything happened to her, you would succeed her."

"Nothing *has* happened to her," said Kullervo. "She's fine."

"But unpartnered," said Isleen. "And without a council. She has all but lost her power. With most of the griffiners in the Eyrie gone, we outnumber the rest, and if we put our support behind you, you could seize the throne without any trouble."

"I don't want it," said Kullervo.

"But we do," one of the other Southerners put in. "We want to follow you, sacred messenger."

"I'm *not*—" Kullervo began.

"Listen to me," Isleen said sharply. "Something must be done. Your sister won't listen to reason, and if you stand by and do nothing now, then Malvern will be destroyed, and all of us along with it. Someone has to act decisively, and you're the only one in the right position to do it."

"But how will that help?" said Kullervo. "Caedmon will kill us all no matter who's on the throne."

"Agreed," said Isleen. "But you'll have us. Depose your sister. Once you're crowned, you'll be in a position to negotiate with Caedmon. Make a truce, find some terms that appeal to him. Once the rebels have been neutralised, my friends and I can act. We may be from different Eyries, but we have a common goal. Once we send word back to our home territories, we can bring hundreds of faithful griffiners here. The North will be ours in a week."

Kullervo gaped. "An *invasion*?"

"Support," Isleen corrected. "For you, King Kullervo."

"But . . ." said Kullervo. "But . . . but I . . . and you . . . we can't do this . . . !"

"Isleen is right," Senneck interrupted. "I have been speaking with her and all the others here. We made this plan while you were gone, and we have agreed that the time has come for you to claim the power that should be yours."

Kullervo stood up. "No. I can't betray her. She's my sister."

"She betrayed *you*," Senneck rasped. "Or have you forgotten? Who made you watch the torture of *Kraeaina kran ae*? I know that you have never forgotten it. She calls herself your family and uses your love for her to manipulate you. You have been nothing but her lackey since you came here to Malvern. How many times have you almost died doing her will? She is not family to you, Kullervo. She uses you, and you allow it. And now she has told you that she will allow you and all your friends to die for the sake of her pride. *That* is betrayal."

Kullervo quailed. "She gave me a home. She's the only family I've got."

"No," said Senneck. "*We* are your family. Who has been more loyal to you than me?"

"And us?" said Isleen.

"And me," said Kraego. "You raised me like your own son."

"You led all of us," said one of the Southerners. "You showed us your way, and we came here because we loved you."

"You were like a father to us all," said Isleen. "Now we ask for you to lead us one more time. To save lives, and undo your father's crimes. We Southerners are the only way to save Malvern, and you know it."

"You will not need to hurt your sister," Senneck added. "She has done enough, and now she must rest."

Kullervo frowned. "Well . . ."

"And remember that she has no partner," said Kraego. "My father is gone."

"But Skandar wasn't her partner," Kullervo said quietly. "Oeka is."

Senneck snorted. "Oeka is as good as dead. I saw that she

would destroy herself with her mad quest for power, and I fooled her. Now she is nothing. A broken husk—"

She broke off midsentence. Her eyes squeezed closed, and an ugly gurgling sound came from her throat.

"What—?" Isleen began. But then she, too, stopped speaking. She fell forward onto the table and began to convulse.

Off to the left, one of the Amoranis gave a strangled cry and collapsed. Then, one by one, every single conspirator, human and griffin alike, went the same way. In moments, the room was full of cries of pain. Griffins rasped and threw themselves against the walls, humans clutched at their heads.

Above them all, something huge and horrible rose into the air. Something that looked like a griffin—or the coloured shadow of one. A griffin whose expanded mind had finally been roused out of its madness by the sound of treacherous words in the Eyrie she had once ruled. A voice screeched through every mind, including Kullervo's. *Liars! Traitors! Enemies!*

Only Kullervo was unaffected. "Oeka!" he shouted.

The mental projection grew darker and denser. *I see all. I see your thoughts. Your treacherous, scheming thoughts! You cannot hide from me. I will kill you . . .*

Screams split the air. One young woman, a Southerner, curled up into a ball like a dying insect. Moments later she went limp. Dead.

Panicking, Kullervo ran to Senneck and tried to hold her still. She thrust her head into his arms. Blood was starting to bead around her eyelids. "Kullervo," she gurgled. "You must help . . . only you can reach her now . . . !" Her voice ran out.

Kullervo stood there, frozen in horror, watching as his friends started to die. In his arms, Senneck faltered and twitched as Oeka's power began to destroy her mind. Kraego collapsed at his feet, whimpering in pain.

Kullervo snapped. He let go of Senneck and sprinted out of the room, back to the Council Tower. From there he went down and down, running as he had never run before, spiralling with the endless passageways and onto the ground floor. From there he found the entrance to the crypts, and nearly fell down the steps.

Oeka knew he was coming. She started to try to attack him, thrusting into his mind. Pain lanced through his head, but it wasn't enough to slow him down. His thoughts were clear. Even now, Oeka could not hurt him.

Down in the crypt, Kullervo ran to the middle of the room and threw himself down by Oeka's limp body. The pain in his head grew as he reached out to touch her. Oeka was frantic now. She knew what he was doing. Confusion raged through his mind, his vision wavered, and he started to feel sick.

He could feel his talons growing longer. *No killing,* he thought. *Never kill again!*

But the thought of Senneck was too much. His beloved Senneck was enough to make him do anything.

Fighting off the mass of visions flickering through his mind, Kullervo lifted Oeka's small head in his hand, and effortlessly slashed her throat wide open with his talons. Blood gushed out, and the visions vanished at once, showing him a clear image of the limp body in front of him. He let go of her, unable to tell if she was dead or not. Her body was so close to death already that the signs were nearly impossible to see. And then . . .

Pain blinded Kullervo. All thought was wiped out of his mind by a scream that became the whole world.

Then it stopped.

Kullervo opened his eyes, and found himself lying on the ground. He sat up, blinking away a headache, and tentatively touched Oeka's body. There was no sign of a pulse, and the shallow breathing had stopped. She was dead.

Shakily, Kullervo got up and left the crypt as quickly as he could. The moment he felt strong enough, he started to run again, back to the hall. The pain and the unearthly voice had left his mind, and only one word was left—his own word, repeating every time his feet thudded down. *Senneck!*

He found the hall door ajar, and shoved it aside.

Senneck was lying where he had left her. Her head was resting on her talons, but when he came closer, she raised it and peered unsteadily at him. "Kullervo," she said in a thin rasp.

Nearby, the others were getting up, many of the humans grabbing the table and chairs to support themselves. The air was full of groans and mumbling.

Kullervo knelt by Senneck and took her head in his hands. "Are you all right?"

Senneck coughed. "When . . . you left, she saw where you

were going. She forgot us and followed you. But she could not . . . stop you?"

"No," said Kullervo. "She's dead now."

Senneck breathed in shakily. "I knew . . . that you would save me."

"You're not hurt?"

"No . . . help me." Senneck tried to stand up. Kullervo helped her, and she was able to find her paws. She started to groom herself, mostly out of nerves, and Kullervo felt light with relief. She was fine.

The others had not been so lucky. Two of the human Southerners were dead, and one Amorani, and one of the griffins had also succumbed. But Kraego at least looked well enough. He climbed onto the table to watch what happened next, as if he had already guessed that it would be important.

Kullervo found Isleen and helped her into a chair. "You're right," he said. "Something has to be done, and I'm going to do it."

Isleen rubbed her eyes. "When . . . ?"

"As soon as you're recovered," said Kullervo. "We can wait."

"No, we cannot," said Senneck. "There is no time to waste. We must go now!"

"Fine," said Kullervo. "I'm going to Laela."

Isleen gestured at a pair of powerful-looking griffiners, both fellow Liranweeans. "Go with him," she said.

Kullervo took a moment to flatten his hair and strode out. Senneck went beside him, and the two griffiners followed close behind, with their own partners. The moment they were gone, Isleen looked to her friends. "You all know what to do," she said, sounding just a little shaken.

They did.

Kullervo had never felt so afraid and yet so powerful in his life. He walked unhurriedly through the Eyrie, with Senneck, and for the first time, he felt as if he were, after all, an important person. A Prince. Even a King.

His head still ached, but there was no uncertainty left in him. He felt as if it had all left him at the moment he killed Oeka.

I've been uncertain my whole life, he thought. *Uncertain of where to go, uncertain of who to trust, uncertain of who I was.*

But he knew better now. He had learnt. Senneck had shown him, and his father, and Saeddryn, and even Laela had taught him the same thing she had. Uncertainty was weakness. To act was strength, and he had stood by and done nothing for far too long.

Up at his sister's quarters, he found two guards blocking his way. "The Queen is unwell," one said. "She chooses to be alone."

Kullervo eyed them. They were both scarred former slaves, trained warriors from Amoran. Laela had filled the Eyrie with them and replaced nearly every guard.

"I'm her brother, and I need to see her," Kullervo told them. Then, without waiting for an answer, he walked straight past them. They didn't try to stop him, probably thanks to the glowering Senneck, but they quietly fell in behind the two Southerners.

At Laela's bedroom door, Kullervo took a deep breath and knocked.

She appeared a moment later, looking tired and unwell. But there was nothing but plain hostility in her voice. "What do yeh want?" she snapped.

Kullervo's face became set and hard. "You've lost your partner," he said. "You're not a griffiner any more, Laela."

"What?" said Laela. "Oeka's my damn partner, yeh stupid sod."

"Not any more," Kullervo said quietly.

Laela saw the blood on his hands. She stiffened. "What have you *done*?"

"Oeka is dead," said Kullervo, amazed by how calm he sounded. "So is Skandar. You're not a griffiner, and you're not fit to rule."

"*What?*" said Laela.

Kullervo squared his shoulders. "I've been loyal to you ever since I came here, but now you've gone too far. I can't stand aside and let you kill everyone in Mulvern."

"Yer gonna do what I bloody well tell yeh," said Laela. "An' killing Oeka's just earned you a death sentence. But since yer my brother, I'm gonna give yeh a chance t'get out of Malvern before I have yeh arrested."

Kullervo felt himself trembling. "No," he said. "You're not a griffiner any more, and you can't rule this Eyrie. I'm your heir, and I'm taking your throne."

Laela looked flabbergasted. "*What?* Kullervo—!"

"That is enough," said Senneck. "Do it, Kullervo."

Kullervo nodded and stood aside. "Take her to a cell," he told the two griffiners. "But be gentle with her."

"You son of a bitch!" Laela roared. She started forward—and jerked to a stop. Her hand went to her belly. "Oh gods . . ."

Kullervo forgot himself, and took a step toward her. "Laela, what's wrong?"

"I've got a gods-damned traitor for a brother is what's wrong!" Laela shouted at him, but she quickly fell back again, wincing. "An' the baby's comin' . . . oh gods damn everything, I'm gonna . . ."

"Right," said Kullervo. "Take her to the infirmary and find a midwife. But guard the door."

"Yes, Sire."

The two griffiners took Laela by the elbows, and led her away. In the audience chamber, the guards pointed their spears. Without a word, one of the griffins who had come up with his partner pounced on them.

"Hey—!" Kullervo shouted, but the griffin ignored him. He and his fellow killed the two men in moments, and the two griffins calmly fell back in behind their partners as if nothing had happened.

Kullervo went with the little group to the infirmary and stood by while Laela was helped into a bed and several doctors and midwives were summoned. She went ungraciously, screaming insults and threats, and every one hit Kullervo hard.

But, just as Laela had once stood by in silence and let Saeddryn suffer, nobody helped Laela now. Not even Kullervo, who, once he had locked her and her doctors into the room and pocketed the key, left the two griffiners to stand guard and went away to find Isleen and the rest of his new council.

37

King Kullervo

The crowning of King Kullervo was a hasty affair, attended by the Southerners, Akhane's Amoranis, and the handful of Northerner griffiners who were left. Nobody had been able to find the High Priestess, so the two Amorani priests conducted the ceremony—using the ritual words usually meant for the crowning of an Emperor, since neither of them knew any others that would fit the occasion.

Kullervo and Senneck stood on the Eyrie Master's platform, surrounded by their rag-tag audience—which also included some servants who had been quickly summoned to make the chamber look fuller.

Kullervo stood patiently through the chants and prayers and invocations, all of which were in Amorani and meant nothing to him. His heart pounded sickeningly.

Beside him, Senneck radiated confidence. The truth was that she didn't look much like an Eyrie ruler. Time and its troubles had taken a toll on her. She had grown bony with age, and her coat had faded. Tufts of grey had appeared on her hindquarters, and her shoulders were balding. Scars made some of her fur and feathers sit at awkward angles.

But there was enough pride in her that day for ten griffins, and everyone who saw her knew it.

As for Kullervo, he had done his best—but he would never look handsome or elegant, and he couldn't seem to manage "well-groomed" either. His wiry hair was hopelessly untidy, and his wings, despite being feathered, made him look bizarre and unbalanced. But he became a King that day, and Senneck his ruling partner, and when the senior priest put Laela's stolen crown on his head, the Southerners there cheered with real pride and excitement.

Kullervo couldn't help but feel some pride of his own just then. But it was pride that was tainted by the knowledge of what he had done—and of what he was going to do.

Once the cheering had died down, Lady Isleen spoke up. "Sire," she said. "What is your first command?"

Absolute silence fell.

Kullervo coughed. "The North is mine now," he said. "And so is this Eyrie. Can I count on your loyalty to help me do what's right for my people?"

Everyone there, even the Northerners, cheered their agreement.

"Then here are my orders," said Kullervo. "I want all of you to stay here. None of you are allowed to attack Caedmon or his followers. Not for any reason. If they attack here, then you will run away. Leave Malvern. I mean it!" he roared, when the crowd shouted in protest. "I don't want any fighting here. I want everyone in here to live, and everyone out there as well. Now I'm going to go and speak with Caedmon, and none of you will come with me. Only Senneck can come. And remember: If the Eyrie is attacked, leave Malvern. Go back to your homes."

"But what about our friends at home?" Isleen asked. "Do you want us to send word back now?"

"No," said Kullervo. "None of you will send for help."

Isleen looked utterly dismayed. "But, Sire—"

Kullervo bared his teeth. All of a sudden they didn't look pathetic or comical. They looked horribly jagged and sharp. *"Do as I say!"* His voice came out as a griffin's voice, hissing and vicious. "You made me your ruler, and you'll obey me or leave my Kingdom."

Isleen glanced at the others for support, but they all looked nervous and uncertain, and none of them stepped forward to help her.

Kullervo nodded. "Good. Now I'm going to go and get ready. Stay here in the Eyrie and be on the lookout. When I return, I'll tell you what to do next."

He hurried away, out of the council chamber and back toward his own rooms.

Senneck followed. "What are you doing?" she asked once they were out of earshot. "I do not understand. Without followers from the South, we can never keep control of the North."

"We can't stay here, Senneck," Kullervo replied, without breaking stride. "They'll take months to get here. I need to make a truce with Caedmon first."

"You have a plan?"

"Yes." Kullervo shoved open the door to his room and almost ran to the cupboard. He pulled out the finest set of clothing Laela had given him and pulled it on. It hid his wings quite well.

Once he was dressed, he tucked the crown into his pocket.

Senneck had fetched her harness, and she tossed it to Kullervo. He caught it, put it on her, and climbed onto her back. "I just hope we're not too late," he muttered.

"We will need a white flag," Senneck reminded him.

"Damn!" Kullervo dismounted and rummaged in the cupboard until he came up with a white tunic. "This'll do. Here."

Senneck took the shirt in her beak, and once Kullervo was on her back again she dashed out through her nest and launched herself into the sky.

Outside, the Unpartnered were still on the walls. Others had strayed into the city and were flying over it, but not attacking yet. It seemed Caedmon was still hoping for a reply from Laela.

When the rebels saw Senneck coming, they immediately flew to intercept her. Seeing the white "flag" flapping around her neck, they formed into a guard around her and flew with her, guiding her out of the city and down toward Caedmon's camp.

Senneck landed where they directed her, and they pressed in around her while Kullervo dismounted.

Kullervo hastily picked up the white tunic and held it up. "I am Kullervo," he said loudly, in griffish. "And this is Senneck. We've come to talk with Caedmon and Shai."

One of the griffiners there glared at him. "What do you want?"

"To make a truce," said Kullervo. "I'm unarmed."

"Wait here," said the griffiner. "I'll bring Caedmon. You'd better have a good answer for him, freak."

Kullervo tried to wait beside Senneck while the griffiner ran off, but their captors seemed to have anticipated this. They put themselves in the way, shoving the two apart, and though they didn't attack, four of them surrounded Senneck, flanking her so that she couldn't take off. Two more guarded Kullervo, but less closely. He wasn't a threat.

Soon enough, Caedmon arrived, flying on Shar's back. She landed neatly not far from the two prisoners, and once Caedmon had jumped down, man and griffin approached on foot, side by side.

They made an impressive pair. Caedmon, scarred and grim, kept pace with Shar, who was limping from her wounds but only managed to look more powerful because of them. Maybe it was the mere fact that she had fought the Mighty Skandar and was still able to walk at all.

Kullervo shrugged off his guards and moved toward Caedmon, dropping the tunic at his feet. "Lord Caedmon," he said. "I've come to make you an offer."

"An offer from your Queen?" Caedmon asked, suspiciously.

"No," said Kullervo. "Queen Laela has been deposed. I've had her locked up. The crown is mine now."

Caedmon raised an eyebrow. "Oh? So now Malvern has another half-breed pretender on the throne. Do you think you'll survive any longer than your sister did?"

"I don't," said Kullervo. "And I don't intend to. Listen . . . Caedmon, I don't know if this will mean anything to you, but I have to say it. I'm sorry. I'm sorry for everything I've done. I was weak. Laela is the only family I've got, and I would have done anything she told me to just so I could try to live like I always wanted to. But I did terrible things, and now I know I could never have a real home here."

"And?" said Caedmon, unmoved.

"And I hope that one day you'll forgive me," said Kullervo. "I meant it for the best. Either way, I've come here to offer you something that I hope will make things better for you."

"Surrender?" said Caedmon.

"No," said Kullervo. He reached into his pocket and brought out the crown. "I've come to give you this."

Surrounded by her guards, Senneck screamed. *"No! Kullervo, no! Stop!"*

Kullervo ignored her. He stepped forward, and knelt to

Caedmon, holding up the crown in both hands. "My sister isn't fit to rule, and neither am I. You're the true King, and you're what the North deserves."

Now, at last, Caedmon's cold exterior cracked. He took the crown, with an expression of utter surprise. "Just like that?"

"Yes." Kullervo stood up. "The Southerners I brought here tried to use me so they could take over the North. I can't let them do that. So here's my offer. I'll go back to Malvern and order the surrender. I'll tell all the Southerners to leave—I can't promise that they will, but I'll tell them anyway. In return, I want you to promise me some things."

"And what are they?" asked Caedmon.

"First, promise that you won't hurt any of them," said Kullervo. "Just make them leave—don't kill them. And you must promise not to hurt Laela. Once this is over, I'll take her away with me. We'll go to Amoran or somewhere, and live in exile." He looked at Senneck, who was staring at him in sheer horror and rage. His expression saddened. "And promise not to hurt Senneck, either."

"Agreed," said Caedmon. "The Southerners will be allowed to go home unharmed, and you and your sister, and your partner, will be spared as long as you leave my Kingdom and never return. But I can't promise that the Southerners won't be hurt if they choose to attack us. My followers have to defend themselves."

"That's fine," said Kullervo. "I've warned them not to attack, but if they don't listen, it's their choice. Oh . . . and one other thing."

"Yes?" said Caedmon.

"The Amoranis will want Akhane's body back," said Kullervo. "Bring it to the Eyrie—there are two priests there who can take care of it."

Caedmon nodded. "It will be brought. Is that everything?"

"I think so," said Kullervo. "I should go back now and give the order. Once the gates are open, I'll fly a black flag from the top of the Council Tower. I suggest you come in quickly. Surprise will make the Southerners more likely to run away."

"Understood," said Caedmon. He allowed himself a thin smile. "And thank you."

Kullervo did not smile back. "It's for the good of the North. Please let Senneck go."

Shar hissed commandingly at the griffins surrounding Senneck. She looked ready to attack Kullervo, but she didn't. She allowed him to get onto her back and flew him back to the Eyrie in silence.

She landed at the top of the Council Tower.

"I'm sorry, Senneck," Kullervo said once he had dismounted. "But it had to be done."

Senneck stared at him through dull eyes. "All my life I dreamed of becoming an Eyrie ruler. Today, I made that dream true, and you have taken it away."

"I'm sorry," Kullervo said again. "But there are times when you have to think about what's best for everybody—not just yourself."

Senneck did not blink. "You have betrayed me," she said in a flat voice. "You are no longer my human." She reached up, and tore the harness off her head with her talons. Then she turned her back on Kullervo, walked away to the edge of the tower, and flew off.

Kullervo stood there silently and watched her fly away out of Malvern, dodging Unpartnered along the way. Eventually, she disappeared beyond the horizon, heading east.

Gone.

Feeling more alone than he ever had before, Kullervo went down into the Eyrie. In the audience chamber, the dead guards had been removed. And, incredibly, two more had taken their place, standing on either side of the doorway as if nothing had happened.

"You and you—come with me," Kullervo told them.

They wordlessly came to his side, and their presence made him feel a little stronger.

"Now," said Kullervo. "I want to speak to your commander. Take me to him."

"Yes, Sire." Word must have spread through the Eyrie already.

The two guards took him to a modest room in one of the smaller towers, where a wiry, middle-aged man greeted them. "Yes, my Lord?"

"Spread the word to every guard in this tower," said Kullervo. "I want the Eyrie opened up. Every gate must be unlocked. Lord

Caedmon and his followers are coming in, and when they do, I want your men to stand down."

The commander must have been trained in absolute obedience because he barely even blinked. "It will be done immediately, my Lord."

"Good. Once the order has been given, go up to the top of the Council Tower and hang up a black flag. Make sure it's a big one. A tablecloth will do if you can't find anything else."

"Yes, my Lord." The commander hurried off.

Kullervo moved on, with his guards still flanking him, and went to find Lady Isleen and the other Southerners.

Most of them had returned to their quarters, but he found Isleen still in the council chamber with her partner. Both of them looked uneasy.

"What news?" Isleen demanded instantly. "Have you made a truce?"

"Yes," said Kullervo. "I've handed the throne to Caedmon. He'll be here very soon to take control of the Eyrie, and I suggest you leave before that happens."

Isleen went white. *"What?"*

"Caedmon is coming to take control of the Eyrie," Kullervo said patiently. "I've made him promise not to kill any of you, but you have to leave the North."

"But . . . but our plan—!" said Isleen.

"No, Isleen," said Kullervo. *"Your* plan. You wanted to take the North for yourself and make my father's people your slaves again. I can't let you do that. So I'm asking you to leave."

"We will *not* leave," said Isleen. "The North is ours by right."

Kullervo's shoulders hunched, and he hissed at her like a griffin. "I brought you here because I trusted you. My sister and I wanted to make peace with your people. You've proven that you're not worthy of that trust, and you're not welcome in this Eyrie any more. Leave now, before Caedmon drives you out. This is your last warning."

Isleen looked livid, but her partner spoke up. "The winged one is right. Without numbers, we have no hope of surviving here. The red griffin and her human will kill us. Come, we must prepare to leave. This is beyond us."

Furious, but knowing she was beaten, Isleen started to follow him out. But she looked back at Kullervo before she left. "You've betrayed us, and Gryphus as well."

"I told you," Kullervo growled. "I was never loyal to Gryphus in the first place. Now get out."

Isleen left.

After that, Kullervo painstakingly tracked down all the other Southern griffiners and repeated his warning. Some were angry, all of them were shocked, but none of them were stupid enough to refuse. They all knew it was over.

Kullervo watched them leave, in dribs and drabs. He hoped they would make it home safely and that the Unpartnered would leave them alone.

Once they were gone, the Eyrie felt utterly empty.

Kullervo wandered along its passages at a loose end, feeling like the last man in the world. Everything was gone. He had turned his back on everyone, and they had turned their backs on him. If doing justice felt like this, then justice must be something hollow and painful.

"Lord Kullervo."

Kullervo turned sharply. Then he relaxed. "Vander. I didn't know you were still here."

Vander looked as tired and worn as Kullervo felt. "I have been with Inva. Her childbirth began this morning."

"Oh!" said Kullervo. "Did it go well?"

Vander closed his eyes for a moment. "She is asking to see you."

"I'll come, then," said Kullervo, cheering up slightly. He loved children.

He wondered, guiltily, if Laela's had been born yet. But he couldn't face her just yet.

Vander showed him to the room he shared with Inva. It was in one of the quieter areas of the Eyrie—though now, of course, the whole Eyrie was quiet.

Inva was propped up in bed, and she looked even more exhausted than her husband. There was a bundle in her arms. "Lord Kullervo," she said. Her clear, precise tones had become rough and dry. Her eyes looked red.

Kullervo managed a smile—being careful to hide his teeth. "Hello, Inva! I haven't seen you in a while. How are you?"

She smiled back weakly. "I am tired. I have heard what happened to your sister."

"Yes . . . she hasn't been hurt. But she's in labour. I don't know if her child has come yet."

"Mine has." Inva coughed a dry, painful cough. "I am afraid for my Queen. Lord Caedmon will soon take this Eyrie, and without her partner, she cannot flee."

"No," said Kullervo. "But don't worry. Caedmon's promised to let her go. I'll take her away from here, and we'll find a new home. In Amoran, maybe."

"You have made a treaty?" asked Vander.

"Yes," said Kullervo. "I've handed the throne to Caedmon, and he's promised to let us live."

Inva and her husband exchanged dark looks.

Inva offered up the bundle in her arms. "My child," she said. "It is a daughter."

"May I?" Kullervo took the bundle and looked down at the baby's face. She looked asleep. Her skin was a colour Kullervo had never seen before—a light brown, somewhere between Inva's pale complexion and Vander's dark one. Kullervo smiled. "Aren't you beautiful?" he said to the child. "Your parents must be very proud."

Neither Vander nor Inva smiled.

Kullervo lost his smile. "What's wrong?"

Nobody spoke. Kullervo looked down at the child again. She hadn't moved.

He realised suddenly that the bundle was cold in his arms.

"Oh Inva . . . I'm so sorry."

Inva's expression remained steady. "I want Queen Laela to see my child. Take it to her."

"I will," said Kullervo. "But . . ."

"Many infants do not survive birth," said Vander. "But some are more important than others. Caedmon will not want another rival to the throne."

Realisation dawned on Kullervo. "But he promised . . ."

"Nobles promise many things," said Vander. "But truth does not keep power. Surely you know that now, Lord Kullervo."

Kullervo's heart sank. "You're right. We didn't spare his child, so why would he spare Laela's?"

"Go and see her," Inva urged. "Show her my child. She must see it."

Kullervo nodded sharply. "I'll bring it back here afterward, yes?"

"Yes," said Vander. "Now go, and quickly, before Caedmon comes."

Kullervo left with the cold bundle in his arms. Every moment on his journey to the infirmary, he expected someone to spot him, to realise what was wrong. But nobody did. A few people looked curiously at the bundle, but they only smiled and looked away when they saw the small face peeking out.

At the door to the infirmary, Kullervo found the two griffiner guards still there. They bowed low to him. "Nothing to report, Sire," one said. "Nobody's gone in or out. We're not sure if the birthing is over yet."

"Thank you." Kullervo brought the key out of his pocket. "You two can go now. Go and find the others who are still here—they'll tell you what's going on."

He unlocked the door and went in.

Inside, the doctors and midwives were resting. He could see the mess that Laela's birthing had left—bloodied cloths and basins of water, but whatever the outcome had been, it was plainly over now. Laela was lying in bed, apparently asleep, and there was a crib next to her.

"Is she all right?" Kullervo asked.

"The birth was a difficult one," one of the midwives said. "My lord . . . your sister is very weak."

"And the child?"

"A girl. She's strong enough, my Lord."

"Good. You can go now, all of you. I need to speak with my sister."

They left, looking slightly relieved to be allowed out. Kullervo closed the door behind them.

First he checked on the child. She was sleeping in her crib, and he could easily see the pale brown tone of her skin that matched Inva's child. Half-Amoranis had something in common, it seemed.

Kullervo went to Laela's side. "Laela," he said softly. "Are you awake?"

Her eyes slid open. "Yer a gods-damned bastard, Kullervo," she croaked.

"I haven't done many good things today," Kullervo admitted. "But I have saved the North."

"From what?" said Laela. "From me?"

"No. Lady Isleen and the others wanted to use me to put the North back under Southern rule."

"Oh . . . really?" said Laela. "When did yeh work *that* out?"

"Very quickly," said Kullervo. "Are you saying you knew?"

"I thought they was up to somethin'," said Laela, opening her eyes fully. "An' I'm pretty sure they poisoned Skandar. Poor bastard."

"What? They poisoned . . . ? Why didn't you do something?"

"It was only a suspicion," said Laela. "I always knew they'd try an' use the treaty t'take over. Griffiners are like that, especially in the South. They've had more practice there. But I'm glad yeh didn't fall for it, Kullervo. Ych ain't so stupid as ych look, ch?"

"Not half as stupid as that." Kullervo smiled.

"Yeh got rid of 'em, then?"

"Yes. I've given Caedmon the throne."

Laela jerked. "Yeh did *what*?"

"What else could I do?" said Kullervo. "I couldn't let you rule any more, and I could only rule by letting the Southerners take over. Caedmon's a true Northerner, and a true leader. He can protect our land from people like Isleen."

"Yeah, by makin' war on 'em," said Laela. "What were yeh thinkin'?"

"That there was no other choice," said Kullervo. "And don't worry; he's promised that you and I can leave. We can go and live in Amoran, and we can have peace and quiet and not have to worry about all this ever again."

Laela's mouth twitched in a painful smirk. "I said it before, an' I'll say it again: Yer a stupid sod, Kullervo. Do yeh really think Caedmon's gonna let us live? You maybe, but not me. He's gonna keep me here an' see to it that I get a big public trial, an' then an execution. New rulers gotta do stuff like that, show they mean what they say. Sends a message, like."

"But he promised . . ." Kullervo trailed off as Vander's words returned to him.

"Rulers don't keep promises like that, or they wouldn't be rulers," said Laela. "I never kept promises like that. Anyway, it

doesn't matter much now." Her eyes closed. "I'm all torn up.
Not gonna heal from that; I've lost too much blood. Wish
someone'd told me havin' kids was that hard. Word to the
wise—don't try it yerself."

"I can't," Kullervo said sadly.

"'Course yeh can't, stupid; yer not a woman." Laela shuddered under her covers.

"No, I mean I really can't," said Kullervo. "I'm sterile."

Laela opened her eyes. "Really?"

"Yes." Kullervo shrugged. "It doesn't matter. I've never been
interested in women anyway." He looked toward the crib. "Your
child is the closest I'll ever have to a daughter of my own."

"She ain't gonna live," said Laela. "Like I ain't."

"Maybe." Kullervo showed her the bundle. "I've brought
something to show you."

"What's that?" asked Laela.

"Inva had her child this morning," said Kullervo. "It's a
daughter, too. See?"

Laela peered at the still face of the dead baby. "Poor little
bugger. How's Inva?"

"She seems fine. But she wanted me to show you her child."
Kullervo glanced at the door. "She wants to help you."

Laela's blue eyes brightened slightly. "They could be sisters,
couldn't they?"

"Yes." Kullervo went to the crib and gently lifted out Laela's
child. She stirred but didn't wake. Quickly, Kullervo unwrapped
the dead child and put the blanket around her. He put the dead
child in the crib, covering it up carefully, and took Laela's child
in his arms.

"Lemme see her," said Laela.

Kullervo brought the child over and put it into its mother's
arms.

Laela held her close. "Inva's got a fine child here," she said
with a smile. "She oughta be proud."

"She is," said Kullervo. "But I should take her back now,
before Inva gets worried."

"You do that," said Laela. "An' say thanks for sendin' her
over here." She kissed the child on the forehead. "An' tell her
from me . . ."

"Yes?" said Kullervo.

"If she ain't chosen a name yet," said Laela, "Then tell her I said . . . call her Flell."

"I will," said Kullervo.

Laela cuddled the child one last time and gave her back to him. He took her and made for the door. Before he opened it, he looked back at his sister. "I'm so sorry."

Laela lay back on her pillows. "Get goin', Kullervo. I got things t'do. An' try an' remember one thing . . ."

"What is it?" asked Kullervo.

"Keep yer damn mouth shut," said Laela.

"I'll try." Kullervo closed the door quietly behind him and was gone.

38

The Final Destination

Caedmon and his followers entered the Eyrie shortly after the raising of the black flag. As promised, nobody resisted. The guards stood down, and the few Southerners who were left fled without a struggle. By nightfall, the rebels were ensconced in the towers, many of them simply going back to homes they had abandoned and others claiming new ones. The Unpartnered returned to the Hatchery, disappointed by the lack of fighting, and Caedmon and Shar settled themselves in the royal nest and bedchamber.

That night, they held a feast in the Council Tower's biggest dining hall. It was a rough-and-ready affair, but a joyful one, and Caedmon knew that there would never be another one like it in his lifetime. Nothing could ever replicate that feeling of triumph. The Eyrie was his, the Unpartnered were his, and the North was his. The city governors would stand down, submit to him, or be killed. Nobody could stand in his way; Malvern was his, and all the power that went with it. The Southerners had fled, the Amoranis had stood aside, and Laela was locked up.

There was only one small problem: Nobody had been able to find Kullervo. Nobody admitted to having seen him, and no-one seemed to know where he had gone. But that didn't matter much. He had already agreed to go into exile, and what people *did* know was that his partner had abandoned him. He was no leader and would not be a threat.

That night, after the feast, Caedmon went to visit Laela. He was particularly glad that Kullervo hadn't taken her with him. He needed her alive.

The former Queen was under guard in the infirmary where she had given birth, but a guard wasn't particularly necessary. She was in no condition to run away.

Caedmon stood over her and looked pitilessly down at her drawn face. "So, how are you, cousin?" he asked. "I heard you had your child."

"Yeah," Laela mumbled. "It wasn't much fun."

"Can I ask if it was a boy or a girl? I haven't found out yet."

"A girl, an' yeh got nothin' to fear from her," said Laela.

"Haven't I?" Caedmon went to inspect the crib. When he saw the dead child inside, he couldn't help but feel relieved. "My sympathies."

"Sympathy my arse," Laela spat. "I got none for you, an' you got none for me. Let's not play games. I ain't in the mood, an' I always cheat anyway."

"Agreed," said Caedmon. "Where's your brother?"

"Burnin' in Gryphus' fires, I hope," said Laela.

"He said he would take you with him."

"Do I look like I'm up to goin' anywhere?" said Laela. "He wasn't gonna help me anyway. He's a damn liar an' a traitor."

"Like me?" said Caedmon.

"Yeah, like you."

"It's just as well." Caedmon shrugged. "You have to stand trial for what you've done."

"Not a chance." Laela pulled herself up, and glared at him. "Yeh think yeh got what it takes to be King here? Do yeh? Do yeh really know what it means? What it's like?"

"It's my right," Caedmon said coldly. "And my duty."

"So they say," said Laela. She reached under her pillow and brought out a small object, clasping it between her hands. "Yeh know, once I was an ordinary peasant girl what couldn't read. I never thought nothin' about ruling, or hurtin' anyone. I just wanted a place in the world. Half-breeds don't get them easy. But once they put that crown on my head . . ." She grimaced. "An' my dad—he used to be a boot-maker's son. Didn't know that, did yeh? He never talked about it. Didn't remember it. Then he got that crown, an' then . . . hah." She fixed Caedmon with a chilling blue stare. "What do yeh think's gonna happen to you? Eh, Caedmon? How many people're you gonna kill? Do yeh reckon you'll start drinkin' like my dad did? Or maybe you'll just go mad."

"Be quiet," said Caedmon. "What are you holding?"

Laela uncurled her fingers, and showed him the little stone bottle in her hand. She flicked the cork out with her thumb, and nodded cordially at him. "Have fun findin' out, Sire. As for me, I'm outta here." She gulped down the bottle's contents in one go.

Caedmon leapt forward to try to stop her, but he was far too late. Laela shuddered and groaned as the poison took effect.

Then, smiling horribly at him, she fell back onto her pillows and did not move again. Caedmon knew that her words, and that smile, would stay with him for the rest of his life.

As the poison spread through her, a blessed numbness replaced the pain of Laela's ruined body. She didn't fight it. She was ready to die. Akhane was dead, her throne was lost, and nothing mattered any more but to escape from the slow death she would have faced from her own injuries or the execution Caedmon would have forced her to suffer.

The pain faded along with every other sensation as she sank back into her pillow, and moments later her mind went numb as well. Thought drained away, and her last sensation was one of icy cold and a blackness that spread over her eyes.

The void opened up before her, pulling her away from life. She knew in that moment that it was all over for her. She was dead.

She sank into absolute blackness, ready to enter the afterlife that must lie beyond it, but then it all stopped, as a pair of hands reached out toward her and a voice murmured her name—a deep, calm voice she had never expected to hear again.

"Laela."

Laela stood up on a ground she could not see, and there he was. Standing there in the void, waiting for her. For a moment, she just stared at him, and then a slow, joyful grin spread over her face. "Arenadd!"

Arenadd reached out to her, a little hesitantly. "Laela . . . I've missed you so much."

Laela didn't hesitate at all. She rushed forward and embraced him fiercely. "Arenadd!"

He held her, and even here he felt just the same as she remembered—cold, gaunt, but so strong. "Laela, my Laela."

Laela held him as if she would never let him go. "I thought yeh were gone forever, I thought . . ."

"I can't," Arenadd murmured back. "I can't be gone. I can't move on. She won't let me. Laela, I'm so sorry."

"No." Laela let him go. "I know yeh think yeh used me . . . making me Queen just to spit in the Night God's eye. But I'd have done it anyhow. You taught me how important it all was, an' I wasn't just there to spite her an' Saeddryn, was I? I was protectin' the South, an' I always would've wanted to do that. I oughta be apologisin' to you." She looked away. "I did my best, but it was all too much for an ignorant girl like me."

"No." Arenadd smiled. "You did as well as I would have done. I'm proud of you. Remember that, Laela. No matter what happens, remember that your father loves you and always will."

"I will," Laela promised.

Arenadd began to shudder, and the coldness all about deepened and grew sharper and crueler. "I'm sorry . . . I did everything I could to protect you, but—but here . . ."

But here I rule, and you do not, a voice whispered.

The two of them turned, and she was there, standing over them, tall and terrible.

The Night God's eye looked down on Laela, pitiless and full of hate. *And now, at last, you are mine,* she said, with awful calmness.

Laela knew she should be afraid, but all she felt now was a calmness of her own, deep and strong. She stared back without flinching.

"I ain't scared of you no more, you bony hag," she spat back. "You reckon you're so strong, but you ain't nothing. Arenadd got away from yeh, didn't he? Yeh couldn't even stop me! You sent that Saeddryn to do it for yeh, an' she failed! I threw her straight back at yeh. Eh? Eh? Didn't I? You ain't *nothin'*." And then she did spit, straight at the savage god of death.

The Night God actually laughed—a low, cold laugh. *All mortals come to me,* she said. *I do not need the Shadow That*

Walks to send them. Saeddryn is gone, you say, and yet here you are.

Arenadd came forward, putting himself between Laela and the Night God. "Leave her alone," he said.

The Night God glanced briefly at him. *You shall watch this, Arenadd,* she said. *I command you. Stay beside me and witness it.*

"No!" Arenadd shouted. "No, don't!"

His pleading fell on deaf ears. The Night God made a short gesture that shoved him aside and advanced on Laela, whispering her curse. *Faithless mortal, half-breed scum. She who abandons the gods shall be herself abandoned. Go now . . .*

But Laela did not look at her, but at Arenadd. "Arenadd!" she called over the Night God's relentless voice. "It's all up with me. Promise me . . ."

"Laela!" Arenadd called back, his voice distant, as if there were a great chasm between them. "No!"

Laela grinned the same horrible grin she had given to Caedmon. "You're an evil bastard, Dad," she said. "Use it. Make it all right again. Save . . ."

Go! the Night God snarled. *As all worthless souls do . . . become nothing.*

At her command, Laela's soul began to fade. The last little remnant of her bled away into the void, leaving only her last word. ". . . *us* . . ."

And then she was gone, her body dead and her soul obliterated, and all Arenadd could do was stand there and stare at the blackness where she had been but was no longer. She was gone forever.

"No," he whispered. "No. No, no, no!" He fell to his knees and started to tear at his hair, unable to contain his agony. "No! *Laela!*"

Now you see what you sacrificed yourself for, the Night God said pitilessly. *Nothing.*

Arenadd hurled himself at her. "You—!"

She threw him back without effort. *You monster?* she said. *Now you have not only seen the final result of your betrayal, but you have also seen the consequence of your deeds in the living world. Your daughter has gone to oblivion, along with all those you killed. You saw the terror in their faces as they died, and now you know they had far more than you to fear.*

Arenadd sat where she had thrown him, unable to get up, unable to speak, and only stared at her in utter disbelief.

The Night God smiled. *Now come back and be with me, Arenadd, and feel only gratitude that I hold you here and do not let you join them as you should have done long ago.*

Arenadd obeyed, as he had always obeyed, all his freedom stripped away. But as he returned to her side he turned his head away from her, so she could not see the expression of pure and eternal hatred on his face.

That night, far away in the icy sky, the griffin who had once been the Mighty Skandar flew.

His flight was slow and erratic, leaning to one side. The wounds on his body had congealed, but could not scab over. Blood still dribbled slowly out of the one on his chest, and his ruined eye wept.

Pain had dulled his mind and his senses. He had forgotten everything now but the need every animal felt at least once in its life: the need to leave. To go somewhere quiet and safe, and be alone. For him, there was only one safe place left. Only one place he wanted to be any more.

He made his slow journey North, back to the mountains. Back to the place where he had once lived. He landed on a mountainside, where a pile of rocks stood, and wearily dug his talons into the heap. They tumbled down, and he crawled in through the hole underneath.

Inside the cave, he dragged himself over the floor and finally collapsed beside the body of Arenadd. His only true human, and the only friend he had ever known.

He laid his head down beside the withered corpse, and slept—or fainted.

After that, he didn't get up again. He stayed there, mostly unconscious, through the next day and into another night. All the while, when he was awake, he could feel his body growing cold. His limbs felt stiff and useless, as if they no longer belonged to him. The world had begun to turn grey and fade away from his eye.

He managed to turn his head slightly, to stare at Arenadd's body. Even now, it would not move. Even now, his human would not return to him.

Skandar's beak opened. "Human," he groaned. "Human . . . human come . . . now. Come to Mighty . . . Skandar. Need . . . human."

But there was no reply.

Skandar called on into the night, his voice growing steadily fainter. But the weaker it became, the louder it sounded in the void. It reached into the darkness of death, and it was heard by the one who heard every dying voice.

And the servant who stood beside her heard it, too.

Arenadd turned to the Night God. "Let me go to him," he said. "Please. I'm begging you."

He is nearly dead, said the Night God. *You cannot help him now.*

"He needs me," said Arenadd. "Let me go. Let me be with him."

The Night God sighed. *Very well . . .*

The world opened up to Arenadd one last time, and he slipped through, becoming the dark spirit once again.

He went to Skandar's side, and as he moved, something changed. His form lightened, and colour returned. He pulled his shape together, and the smoky outline of before disappeared. That night, just for a little while, Arenadd Taranisäii had a body again, and a face.

He knelt by Skandar, and reached out to touch his face with spectral hands. *Skandar, I'm here.*

Skandar shuddered ever so slightly. "Human . . ."

"Yes," said Arenadd, and his voice grew stronger—audible to mortal ears. "Our master let me come back to you."

Skandar looked up at him through a glassy silver eye. "Human come. Am . . . glad."

Arenadd smiled. "I'm glad, too, Skandar, and I'm sorry I kept you waiting so long. Can you forgive me?"

"Not forgive," said Skandar. "Only am."

"Yes, Skandar," said Arenadd. "You are, just as you always have been. Haven't you? The Mighty Skandar! The dark griffin!"

"Dark . . . human," said Skandar. "For dark griffin."

"So you always said," said Arenadd. "You were right."

Skandar made the slightest move, as if to try and get up. "Human . . . was . . . best human," he said. "Human . . . always best. Arenadd best."

Tears shone in Arenadd's ghostly eyes. "You're the best griffin there ever was, Skandar," he said. "I know it. But you can rest now. You've earned it."

Barely audibly, Skandar said, "Yes . . . rest. Rest . . . Arenadd." His eye closed.

Arenadd stayed beside the dark griffin's body for a long time, long after it had grown cold and stiff. Nobody would ever find it. It would rest here forever, beside his own. They would be together in death, as they had been in life.

Shortly before dawn, he sensed the Night God appearing behind him. He didn't turn around.

It is time to return to the void, she said.

Arenadd did not look at her. "You can take me to the void again," he said, "But I'll never leave here. I'll be bound to this cave forever."

Yes, said the Night God. *It is your tomb.*

Arenadd kept his eyes on Skandar. "And his."

And his. The Night God's voice was as dispassionate as always.

"What are you going to do to me?" Arenadd asked. "Are you going to put me back into my body and make me feel it rot, like you said you would at the Throne? Or are you going to destroy me? Make me into nothing?" There was only resignation in his own voice.

No, said the Night God. *You are troublesome, but you are too useful to destroy.*

"Hah."

But it is true, said the Night God. *You must be punished for what you have done. But I think I see the way to ensure that you will never disobey me again.*

"Oh, and what's that?" Arenadd asked savagely. "More pain? More suffering? I've had enough of that for three lifetimes. You don't think that's going to make a difference, do you?"

No. Your disobedience confused me at first, but now I understand it. The Night God came to his side, looking down at Skandar. *It is your love that makes you be this way. Your love for your children. Your love for your partner. I allowed you to keep your love because I thought I could make you give it to me. But you only allowed it to lead you astray.*

"I never loved you," said Arenadd. "And I never will."

No, you will not, said the Night God. *You will never love again. When we return to the void, I will take that from you.*

Arenadd finally turned to look at her. "Do you really think that will help you?"

I do. You will be what I make of you, and nothing else. That is the only way to salvation.

Arenadd turned his head away from her. "You're evil," he snarled. "And you made me evil. I hate you."

The Night God laughed softly. *Poor, lost Arenadd. You do not understand. You are so innocent.*

"Innocent? Me?" Arenadd spat.

You know nothing, said the Night God. *You think that I am the tyrant, forcing you to do my will? I am a slave, Arenadd. I have no will of my own. I am nothing more than what my people have made me to be, and whatever they wish, whether kind or selfish, must be what I wish for as well. I have no choice.*

"Yes you do," said Arenadd. "You're so powerful . . ."

My power comes from my people, said the Night God. *And my weakness.* She smiled. *And that is why I cannot and will not destroy you. That is why I will always forgive you, no matter how many times you defy me. My people love and trust you. And so I must love and trust you as well, sweet Arenadd.*

"And what about them?" said Arenadd. "Do you love *them*?"

With all my silent heart, said the Night God. She held out a hand. *Come, we must go before the sun rises.*

"And then what?"

And then we must do what we have always done, said the Night God. *Watch over our people. Together.*

"Will we ever return?"

When they need us, we will be there, said the Night God. *Always.*

Arenadd rose and took her hand. "Yes," he said quietly. "Always."

Kullervo walked through the lands of the North, alone. When he was younger, he had been alone, but now that he had had a family and lost it, he felt more isolated and abandoned than he ever had before. Now that there were people to remember, and to miss . . .

His parents were gone. Laela, too, was gone. He knew she must be dead by now. Skandar was gone. And Senneck was gone. His beloved Senneck had left him.

Travelling alone and on foot was hard, especially since he had to avoid people. He could have changed into a griffin, but he felt too miserable to bother. Before he had stayed a griffin to punish himself; now he was staying human. Besides, the change took energy, and he had lost his.

He didn't even really know where he was going. He supposed he should be heading for the coast, to take a ship to Amoran. So, bit by bit, he started to head in more or less that direction. But some part of him felt as if he weren't going to Amoran, or to Maijan. It didn't feel right. Surely, though, there was nothing left for him in the North.

At night, unable to sleep, he huddled down in whatever hollows or thickets he could find and wondered, yet again, if he had done the right thing. Deep down he knew that there would never be an answer for him. Some questions had no real answers.

But, gradually, as he worked his way east bit by bit, one answer did come to him. It was an answer to a different question, and he thought about it more and more as the days went by. And the more he thought about it, the more right it seemed.

One day, when he stopped at an abandoned griffiner outpost, he saw a pair of griffins in the sky. He hid, and watched them, but when they landed he recognised them, and came out to meet them.

"Lord Kullervo!" Vander climbed off Ymazu's back, and turned to help Inva.

Inva came awkwardly, hampered by the bundle in her arms. "My Lord," she said. "We had hoped to find you."

"And I was hoping to see you, too," said Kullervo. "How did you know I was here?"

"We did not," said Vander. "We are travelling to the coast to take ship for Maijan. We thought that you might go there as well."

"I thought so, too, but now I'm not so sure," said Kullervo. "How's my niece?"

Inva handed the child to him. "Growing well."

Flell gurgled in her uncle's arms.

"I'm glad to see you again," Kullervo told her. "I thought something might happen to you. But you're all right, aren't you?"

"She is," said Inva. "We had planned to take her to Maijan to raise, but you are her family, and my Queen appointed you as her guardian. We will take her if you ask, but we knew that once we were away from Malvern, we should ask you if you wished to raise her yourself."

Kullervo hesitated. He knew he should give the child to Vander and Inva, who could give her a proper home, but . . .

"You should take her," Vander said kindly. "Perhaps Inva and I are too old to be parents. And we are not her family. Do you know a place where you can go with her?"

"I . . ." Kullervo hugged the child to him, and her tiny warmth made him feel stronger inside. "I do," he said, with sudden certainty. "There's a place I can take her. It's secret and safe, and I can give her a good home there."

"Then you will take her?" asked Inva.

"Yes," said Kullervo. "Can you come with me? It's not too far from the coast."

"Agreed," said Inva.

Skarok and Ymazu exchanged glances.

"I have had enough of this," Skarok said lazily. "There has been too much travelling for me, and I am tired of it. Let us do this quickly!"

"If you think that you can fly fast enough to keep pace with me, you may try," Ymazu teased.

The younger griffin huffed at her. "I shall!"

So the little group set out together. Kullervo became a griffin and showed them the way. Over the hills and forests, following the landmarks he had memorised from the maps he had defaced, north, then east, until at last he recognised the forest, which was as close to the village of Gwernyfed as he could go without the others seeing it.

There, Kullervo touched down. "I have to go on alone from here," he said. "This place has to be a secret."

"We understand," said Vander. "We will wait while you transform."

"Thank you." Kullervo went off into the nearby trees by himself and made the change.

Once he had recovered, he took the child from Inva. She and Vander said their farewells to their ward, and to Kullervo as well.

"I'll never forget what you did for me," said Kullervo. "For us. When she's old enough, I'll tell her all about you."

"Will you tell her who she is?" asked Inva.

"Yes," said Kullervo. "Laela and I were both brought up not knowing, and I don't think it was good for us. Nobody should have to live a lie."

"It could be dangerous," said Vander.

"Then we'll deal with that when it comes," said Kullervo. "She can keep it a secret if she wants to. It'll be her choice, not mine."

"Then I hope you have good luck," said Inva. "Farewell."

Kullervo nodded and smiled, and walked away with the child cradled in his powerful arms. His wings hung on his back, bared to the world. The truth, there for all to see.

He walked down through the hills and through the fields, toward the one place he had been truly happy, and the one place he could ever call home.

Gwernyfed.

There were people about among the houses, and they soon spotted him. In moments, a dozen people had come running, all excited shouts.

"It's him! It's Kullervo! He's come back!"

Kullervo laughed aloud. "Hello, everyone! Yes, that's right, I'm back again. I hope you don't mind."

"Of course we don't mind!" One man laughed back. "Come on, come to the square—everyone will want to see you!"

Kullervo let himself be led to the village square, and before long he was surrounded by a chattering crowd. Northerners, Southerners, and some in between.

"Where did the baby come from?" a woman asked.

Kullervo held the child up for them all to see. "This is Flell," he said. "She's my niece. But she's lost both her parents now, and I have to care for her. I thought there's no better place in all of Cymria to raise a child than Gwernyfed. So here I am! But where's Lord Rufus?"

"He died," said one of the Southerners. "Just a few months ago."

Kullervo sighed sadly. "Was it peaceful?"

"He died in his sleep," said a woman. "He had a good long life. But now you've both returned, we're complete again, aren't we?"

"Complete?" said Kullervo. "How?"

"Well, you've come back, haven't you?" said the woman. "Gryphus sent you back here to be our new elder."

"I'm not—" Kullervo began, but then he gave up. "I'd like to live here if you don't mind."

"Of course we don't!" several people said.

"You're welcome here, Kullervo," said the woman. "And we'll be glad to have you here to help us the way Rufus did."

"If you want me to, I will," said Kullervo. "Wait—what do you mean 'both'? You said we've *both* returned?"

"Yes, that's right," said the woman. "It's been an odd week. We never expected to see either of you again, and you both turn up a few days apart! First Senneck, then . . ."

Kullervo leapt to his feet. "Senneck? Senneck's here?"

"Yes, she got here a few days ago . . ."

Kullervo didn't hear anything more. He almost ran through the village, calling Senneck's name.

He didn't need to do it for long. She was there. Real and alive, coming out of a barn to meet him.

Kullervo stood there stupidly, and stared at her. "Senneck . . ."

Senneck stared back. "Is that your sister's pup?"

"Yes. Her name's Flell. Senneck, I . . ."

"Enough." Senneck came closer. "I did not know where to go, and so I came here. It is the only home I have had other than Malvern. It sheltered me when I lost Erian, and when I lost you, I returned."

"You left me," said Kullervo.

"Lost you," said Senneck. She sighed. "I have lived a long life and seen many things. Since I was a youngster at Eagleholm, I have done nothing but chase power wherever I found it. My mother Shoa taught me to be this way when I was in the nest, and I have followed her words ever since. But no matter where I went or what I did, true power evaded me. I was an Eyrie ruler for a day, and now I am nothing again. Unpartnered again. Powerless again."

"You're not unpartnered," said Kullervo. "You still have me."

"I made myself unpartnered by leaving you," said Senneck. "And since then I have thought. All my struggles won me nothing. Nothing but you, and a tiny human nest far from anywhere."

"And what did you decide?" asked Kullervo.

"I have seen that perhaps it will be better for me not to struggle any more," said Senneck. "I have done many things and won many battles. Perhaps it is enough for one life. And you . . . why are you here?"

"I don't have a home any more," said Kullervo. "This is the only place I was ever happy. It's where I met you. Laela's child and I both need somewhere to live, so I've chosen here. I think we can be happy here. And safe."

"My home is wherever you are, Kullervo," said Senneck. "You are my human."

Kullervo smiled a soft, loving smile. "You're right, Senneck. About everything. Since we left here together, we've done so much, but we ended up right back where we started. So we might as well accept it. Besides, the people here want me to be the new elder now that Rufus is gone. Maybe we can be rulers after all."

"Of a sort," said Senneck, but she sounded amused.

"And we'll raise this child," said Kullervo, cradling Flell. "We can be the family to her that I never had. I'll teach her everything I know."

"That will not take long," said Senneck.

Kullervo laughed. "Then once I'm finished, you can teach her everything *you* know, and that'll take a lifetime."

"I shall," said Senneck. "Now, I think your new followers wish to celebrate."

"Then let's go!" said Kullervo. "Come on, Flell, let's go and meet your new friends."

He went off back to the village square, where a fire pit was already being dug, and felt his heart soar. The war was lost, but it didn't matter to him any more. The world was too big for him to change. Let North and South do whatever the two races decided. One day, maybe, a united Cymria would come. And when it did, he hoped he would be there to see it. Or Flell perhaps, or her descendants.

This will be my task, he thought. *My life's work. I will be Flell's guardian. And . . .*

Some of his joy darkened, as he remembered the thing he had hidden outside the village.

And I will guard the heart. I will make sure that its powers are never used again. I swear.

F ar away, in Malvern, a very different sort of celebration took place.

Caedmon was crowned at midnight, not in the Eyrie's council chamber but in the new Moon Temple out in the city. Whatever else Laela had been, she had done a fine job of rebuilding it.

The new High Priestess and her underlings conducted the ceremony, and every griffiner in Malvern came to witness it. Commoners came, too, packed into the Temple and spilling out into the street.

Caedmon and Shar stood together in front of the altar, as young and proud as Arenadd and Skandar had been at their own ascension. Shar held out her forelegs to accept her golden bands of office, and Caedmon accepted the crown. It was a simple thing—a band of silver, set with a single blue stone. Once Arenadd's, and now his. And because he had fought so hard for it, and lost so much, it meant more to him than it could ever have if it had been simply handed to him, as it had with Laela. Nobody, of course, would mention her again except in the worst terms. Caedmon had already ordered her name stricken from the records, and had had her body burned without ceremony and the ashes thrown away. She would never be officially recognised as a Taranisäii, or as a true Queen, and his people would curse her name forever.

When the crown touched Caedmon's head, the Temple erupted in cheering and applause. Griffins screeched Shar's name, and humans shouted Caedmon's.

Caedmon raised a hand, and silence fell.

"Sire," the High Priestess said. "What do ye command?"

Caedmon's black eyes glinted. "The Southerners who came here before came hoping to take our lands for themselves.

They've proven that they can't be trusted, whether full-blooded or only half-."

The crowd hissed hatefully.

"We have rebuilding to do," Caedmon continued. "There will be hard work ahead, traitors to subdue, cities to repair. But with loyalty and dedication, we can do it. After all, we know who we are, and we are united!"

Cheers rose to the roof.

"But," said Caedmon, "here today, before that hard work begins, I have one promise to make. And it's a promise that will be kept. I, King Caedmon Taranisäii I of Tara, hereby swear that one day, maybe in one year, or maybe in ten . . . when the day comes that we're ready, we will declare war on the South."

Excitement rippled through the crowd.

"We will go beyond the Northgate Mountains," Caedmon said. "And we will enter the South. We will smash the Southerners. We will take their cities for ourselves and sell their people into slavery just as they did to us. We will show them what a true Northern army can do, and we will show them—we will show them what happens to our enemies!"

Excitement turned to ugly shouts and roars of approval.

"The Southerners thought they could take us!" Caedmon shouted. "But we will take the South!"

"Caedmon!" the people shouted back. *"King Caedmon! Conqueror of the South!"*

"Death to the Southerners!" others bellowed.

Shar lifted her head high. "We will have their territory for our own!" she screeched. "Griffins, are you with me?"

"Shar!" they screamed back. *"Mighty Shar!"*

But there was one griffin there who did not screech, did not rear up and spread his wings.

Lurking among the legs of the adults, Kraego listened and glared silently up at Shar. Shar, who had killed his father. Shar, who had stolen the glory that should have been his. Shar, who thought she could be mightier than a dark griffin.

Kraego kept his eyes on the red griffin and rasped a curse that no-one heard but himself. "I will return," he said. "I will be back, Shar. You conquered my father, but one day *I* will conquer *you*."

He turned and slunk out of the Temple, unnoticed in all the confusion. Once he was in the open, he took to the air and flew away out of Malvern.

However, he did not head North, but South. In the South, he would be safe. And to him, it was home.

But I will return, he promised himself.

And then let the land tremble . . .

About the Author

K. J. Taylor was born in Australia in 1986 and plans to stay alive for as long as possible. She went to Radford College and achieved a bachelor's degree in communications at the University of Canberra before going on to complete a master's in information studies. She currently hopes to pursue a second career as an archivist.

She published her first work, *The Land of Bad Fantasy*, through Scholastic when she was just eighteen, and went on to publish *The Dark Griffin* in Australia and New Zealand five years later. *The Griffin's Flight* and *The Griffin's War* followed in the same year and were released in America and Canada in 2011.

K. J. Taylor's real first name is Katie, but not many people know what the *J* stands for. She collects movie sound tracks and keeps pet rats and isn't quite as angst-ridden as her books might suggest.

Visit her website at kjtaylor.com.

FROM

K. J. TAYLOR

The Shadow's Heir

THE RISEN SUN
BOOK ONE

Laela Redguard was born with the black hair of the Northern Kingdom and the blue eyes of the Southern people,
forever marking her as a hated half-breed child of both.
While Laela's Northern features allow her to blend into
the crowds of King Arenadd's seat at Malvern, she cannot
avoid falling victim to a pair of common thugs. But when a
stranger saves her life and gives her a place to stay, Laela is
shocked to learn he is Arenadd himself—a man said to be
a murderer who sold his soul to the Night God—the King
without a heart...

**"Clearly, this is a universe that is going to be visited for
some time to come, and with its diverse characters, political machinations, and issues of class, as well as fantastic
griffins, it's one that readers will eagerly return to with
each new book."** —*A Book Obsession*

kjtaylor.com
facebook.com/AceRocBooks
facebook.com/DestinationElsewhere
penguin.com